Queen of the Desert

Marie Laval

Choc Lit

Where heroes are like chocolate – irresistible!

Published 2022 by Choc Lit Limited

Penrose House, Crawley Drive, Camberley, Surrey GU15 2AB, UK

www.choc-lit.com

First published as *The Lion's Embrace* by Accent Press in 2015.
Edited and revised in 2022 by Choc Lit Limited

EPUB: 978-1-78189-049-3
PRINT: 978-1-78189-100-1

For Thomas, Nicolas and Clémence, and for my mother

Acknowledgements

This novel is dedicated to my children who have such touching faith in me and give me so much love and encouragement, and to my mother whose stories about growing up in Algeria were always a source of inspiration. Ever since I was little I have dreamt of going to North Africa and seeing the ksars, the oases of the Sahara and the peaks of the Hoggar mountains for myself. I hope I will one day, but in the meantime I shall use my imagination...

I loved every minute of writing Harriet's and Lucas's story and of researching some of the history, myths and legends of the Tuareg people, as well as their culture and traditions, and finding out about their ancestral queen, Tin Hinan. I have tried to be accurate and I do apologise if I made any mistakes.

Whilst writing *Queen of the Desert* I discovered a fascinating culture and some wonderful musicians who accompanied me in my imaginary journey, among which Bombino, Imzad-Ténéré or again Tinariwen. Music really does bring people and hearts together. Thank you all for making me dream.

Thanks to my talented friends and fellow 'Moonshiners' from Authors on the Edge, even if it hasn't been possible to meet up much these past few months. I really do appreciate your friendship – Helena Fairfax, Kate Field, Melinda Hammond, Helen Pollard, Sophie Claire, Jacqueline Cooper, Mary Jayne Baker and Angela Wren.

Thank you so much to the Choc Lit team too for their support, and to my wonderful editor for her excellent suggestions which helped make the story stronger. My thanks also go to the designers who have once more given me a stunning cover. And of course, thanks to the Choc Lit Tasting Panel, especially: Mel Fairbairn, Elisabeth Hall, Hilary Brown, Fran Stevens, Honor Gilbert, Margaret Marshall, Barbara Wickham, Rachel Masters, Jo Osborne, Haley Eyre, Bee Master, Carol Fletcher, Janice Butler, Lorna Baker and Yvonne Greene. I am so happy that you enjoyed the story and gave me the chance to see it published today.

Chapter One

Algiers, April 1845

'*Fissa, fissa,*' Harriet urged as she followed the boy down the narrow alleyways leading to the harbour. It wasn't dark yet but already a full moon lit the Algiers sky, shimmered on the surface of the sea, and steeped the walls of the old town in its silver light.

Drunken, rowdy sailors and soldiers on leave crowded the streets. Men lurked in shadowy doorways. She had been in too much of a rush getting out of Lord Callaghan's palace to be scared earlier, but anxiety now knotted her stomach and tightened her throat. She gripped the dagger at her side. Coming here on her own might not be such a good idea after all, even if Lucas Saintclair was at the Seventh Star and she desperately needed to talk to him. Even if he was the best guide in the whole of the Barbary States, and the only man who could help her.

At least nobody gave her a second glance. With her indigo blue tunic and trousers and the turban she had bought at the souk, she looked like a Tuareg fighter – albeit a diminutive one.

In front of her, a man relieved himself against a wall and stumbled into a pile of rotten rubbish, his breeches still open. She wrinkled her nose in disgust and stepped over him.

The boy pointed to a blue door above which a crudely painted golden star dangled precariously. Harriet slipped a silver coin in his hand and was about to push the door open when it flew straight back in her face. A short, stocky man ran out into the street. Wheezing loudly, his eyes bulging with fear, he looked as if the devil himself was on his tail.

And it was.

A tall, dark-haired man entirely dressed in black strode out of the tavern and bumped into her.

'*Alkhurūja min ṭarīqī!*' he growled, grabbing her arm to push her out of the way.

She tilted her face up to look at him. If there was something of a pirate in his strong, weather-beaten face covered with dark stubble, it was his eyes that sent a shiver down her spine. They were the coldest eyes she had ever seen; icy blue, and so pale they were almost transparent.

He stared down at her. She held her breath, fearful he had seen through her disguise and would rip her scarf off, but he only shoved her aside before sliding a hand in the pocket of his leather waistcoat, and pulling out a dagger with a curved blade. In long, supple strides he caught up with the other man and toppled him onto the ground.

'Now, Rachid, you snivelling rat,' he said in French as he pressed the tip of his black riding boot onto the other man's throat. 'You have five seconds to tell me where the map is. *Un ... deux ...*' He flipped the dagger like a toy between his fingers.

'Oh, my God,' Harriet breathed out. She glanced around, but nobody was paying the two men the slightest notice. There was no time to think. A man's life was at stake. With a muffled cry she hurled herself at the tall stranger, jumped on his back and hooked her arms around his neck.

He let out a roar of anger and swirled round to shake her off. She wrapped her legs more tightly around his waist.

'*Bon sang! Qu'est-ce que ...*'

He dropped the dagger, twisted his body and managed to grab her waist to slide her to the front so she was now against his chest. Aware she was losing her grip, she lunged forward and sank her teeth into his shoulder.

He growled, held her at arm's length and threw her off. She fell onto the cobbles. The turban softened the impact to the back of her head, but a vicious pain at the bottom of her spine made her cry out. The man swore in French. Although she only caught a few words, she understood he was angry. Very angry. His victim had escaped.

She let out a sigh of relief. She'd done it. She'd saved the man's life. Her joy, however, was short-lived. The Frenchman leaned over, picked her up by the collar of her tunic and lifted her as if she was no heavier than a bundle of cloth. The savage glint in his eyes dried her throat and made her heart hammer against her ribs.

'Please, don't hurt me,' she pleaded, breathless.

His eyes opened wide in shock.

Since when did Tuareg fighters speak fluent English? Come to think of it, since when did they smell of Damascus rose soap?

He peered more closely at the face in front of him and saw two grey eyes bordered with long, dark eyelashes and the tip of a small nose above the dark blue scarf. He recalled the odd sensations when the soft, curvy body had thrust against him earlier. This wasn't a Tuareg fighter at all, it was a … He ripped the headdress off and a mass of thick honey blonde hair tumbled out.

'A woman? I thought as much. Who are you?' he asked in English. 'What the hell did you think you were doing just then?' He shook her a little, not to hurt, but enough to give her a fright.

The woman didn't answer.

'You're not so bold now, are you?' He narrowed his eyes, smiled his meanest smile, and was satisfied to hear her helpless cry. She'd cost him days of patient stake-out. Now, because of her, Rachid was free to sell the map to the highest bidder. And he knew exactly who that would be. 'Maybe you'd like to take another bite?' he snarled, pointing to his shoulder.

She shook her head.

'Actually, maybe I'll be the one to take a bite. You look appetising enough.' He lifted her closer, until his mouth almost touched hers and he felt her warm breath on his skin.

He gazed into her grey eyes and time seemed to stop.

'Please,' she whispered.

'You've some explaining to do, lady.' His voice was hoarse and he felt dizzy, like someone pulled too abruptly out of a dream.

She was shaking like a leaf now. He let her down, keeping a firm hold on her arm. He didn't trust her. She might stand in front of him, small and fragile, but he wouldn't put it past her to run off and disappear into the maze of alleys of the old town.

She wouldn't go anywhere before he had answers.

A curious crowd had gathered around them. The man's fingers were a steel vice around her arm. Surely he wouldn't hurt her in front of so many witnesses?

'Get your hands off her, you scoundrel!' A man's voice called.

Thank God.

'Archie!' she cried, flooded with relief as her oldest, most trusted friend sliced through the crowd towards her.

The man let go of her. She ran to Archie, welcoming the strong, safe arm he wrapped around her. She noticed that he gripped the butt of a pistol under his jacket.

'Are you hurt? Did he hit you?' His face was flushed and his blond moustache quivered with indignation.

'I didn't touch her,' the Frenchman said calmly. 'She's the one who jumped on me like a banshee, bit me and set my man free.'

He clenched his fists.

'You were going to kill him!' Harriet protested.

'What I was doing was none of your goddamned business.' He narrowed his cool blue eyes to stare at her. 'You don't seem the type to work for Rachid. Who are you? What do you want?'

Archie's arm tensed around her as a warning but she ignored him.

'I'm looking for Lucas Saintclair,' she said.

'Whatever for?' The man cocked his head to one side.

'I have a proposal for him.'

A slow grin spread on his lips. 'Then it looks like you found him, darling.'

There was a moment of stunned silence.

'You're Saintclair?' Harriet and Archie exclaimed in unison.

The man nodded, bent down to pick up his dagger and slid it into his pocket. 'What do you want with me? Apart from spoiling a nice evening, that is.'

'Is hounding a poor man to the ground your idea of a nice evening?' Harriet tilted her chin to stare at Saintclair.

'Now I'm sure you don't know Rachid.' His lips curled into a cruel smile. 'No one acquainted with that weasel could possibly harbour any sympathy for him. So I repeat, what is it you want?'

'Monsieur Saintclair, we desperately need your help …'

'Let me deal with this, Harriet,' Archie interrupted, stepping forward.

'My name is Archibald Drake, from the British Museum. I've been looking for you all over town these past few days.'

Saintclair shrugged. 'I've been busy.' He paused. 'The British Museum? Has this anything to do with the English professor captured in the south of the country?'

Harriet nodded. 'He's my father, Professor Oscar Montague. He was abducted by bandits in …'

'Tamanrasset,' Saintclair finished. 'Yes, I know. So you're Montague's daughter?'

His eyes searched her face, travelled down her body and back up again. An uncomfortable heat spread across her cheeks.

'What are you thinking of, Drake, taking your woman to the docks with you?' he asked curtly. 'That disguise wouldn't fool a blind beggar.'

'I'm not his—'

'Harriet is my fiancée,' Archie interrupted, laying a possessive hand on her forearm.

She tightened her lips. It did make sense to pretend they were engaged. She should have suggested it herself.

'And you're right,' Archie continued, 'she shouldn't be here.' He turned to Harriet. 'In fact, I expressly forbade you to leave Lord Callaghan's palace tonight, so what are you doing alone in the docks?'

Two pairs of hard, disapproving male eyes stared at her.

She bit her lower lip, looked down and kicked the cobbles with the tip of her boot.

'A boy came for you,' she muttered. 'He said he knew where to find Monsieur Saintclair. As you weren't there I thought I'd come down here to meet him myself.'

'What a very foolish, very dangerous idea.' Archie sighed. 'But now we're here, is there anywhere we can talk?'

Saintclair gestured towards the Seventh Star.

'In there, but you'll have to make it quick. I've plans for tonight.'

They followed him into the tavern. Inside, the atmosphere was so thick with tobacco smoke, alcohol fumes and the stench of too many bodies pressed together in too small a space that it was hard to breathe. Saintclair found a table and gestured to a serving woman.

'Is rum all right for you?'

Archie nodded. 'Fine.'

Saintclair spoke to the woman in Arabic. She whispered something into his ear that made him smile and walked away, swaying her curvaceous hips. Harriet looked on in dismay. What kind of man was this Lucas Saintclair? Could she ever trust anyone who sweet-talked a tavern girl minutes after attempting to kill a man in the street?

'I'm listening.' Saintclair turned to Archie.

'We need you to take us to Tamanrasset, find the Tuaregs who captured Oscar Montague, and help us rescue him.'

Saintclair let out a short laugh and raked his fingers through his dark hair. 'Is that all? Do you have any idea who these men are – and more importantly, do you have any idea how angry they are?'

Suddenly serious, he looked at Harriet. 'I'm sorry to have to tell you this, miss, but I don't think you've much chance of finding your father alive.' His voice was almost kind now, his eyes softer.

'But we have his ransom. Lord Welsford, the British consul, sent a message to the Tuaregs to let them know we're bringing a large amount of gold in exchange for his safe return. Surely they wouldn't harm my father before we got down there, would they? Not if they want money!' Her throat closed and dread filled her heart. Saintclair's words echoed her worst, unspoken fears.

'These men are criminals.' Archie slammed the palm of his hand onto the table. 'I hope the French catch them and deal with them as they deserve.'

'I must disagree with you here.'

Saintclair reclined on his chair, stretched his long legs in front of him. Any trace of kindness disappeared from his face as he stared hard at Archie.

'Montague desecrated a Tuareg tomb. And not any tomb – Tin Hinan's, the ancient queen of the Tuaregs and the woman they refer to as Mother. Rumour is that he stole precious artefacts, too.'

'How dare you!' Harriet cried out in outrage. 'My father is a respected historian, not a tomb robber. Everything he does is for the museum.'

Archie patted her arm. 'Harriet, dear, calm down. We all know how devoted to historical research your father is.'

He turned to Saintclair. 'How can you defend what these men have done? Montague is being held against his will, his whole team was butchered and left to rot in the sun.'

Harriet felt the blood drain from her face. The room became a blur and started to spin as she struggled to catch her breath. 'They are dead? Archie, you never said …'

'I am very sorry, dear. I didn't want to tell you, but Lord Welsford got the news from the French garrison in Tamanrasset. Every single member of the expedition apart from your father was killed.'

'I thought they were safe,' she whispered. 'Captive, but safe.' She blinked back the tears. 'Joseph? Alfred? Charles?'

Every time she mentioned a name, Archie nodded and sighed. A cry of anguish escaped her lips. Her father's most trusted associates, men he'd worked with for over twenty years, who had stayed at their London house … dead. Murdered in the desert.

The waitress came back with a wooden tray and placed tumblers of rum in front of them. Saintclair patted her bottom. She let out a coarse laugh and blew him a kiss before walking away. Harriet pursed her lips in distaste.

'I see my father's predicament doesn't distract you from more pressing issues,' she remarked, aware of sounding just like prim Aunt Elizabeth.

Saintclair arched his eyebrows but didn't reply. He pulled a cigar out of his waistcoat pocket.

'All you have to do is name your price,' Archie said. 'My employer, Lord Callaghan, is a very generous man. He's paying for the rescue mission and most of the ransom. One thousand gold napoleons.'

'I heard about that, too.' Sainclair leaned over the table to hold the cigar to the flame of a candle. 'You should be more careful, Drake. It's not wise to advertise the fact that you're travelling across the country with so much gold.'

Harriet shrugged. 'We'll be armed and ready.'

Saintclair almost choked on his cigar. 'You're not thinking of going to Tamanrasset?' His eyes were cold as he stared at her.

'Of course I am.'

'Of all the stupid things I ever heard, this has got to be the—'

'Why? Because I'm a woman? I'm as capable as any man, Monsieur Saintclair, and it's my duty to help my father.' She drank some of her rum. The liquid burnt her throat and brought fresh tears to her eyes, but she managed to swallow it without coughing.

Saintclair shook his head. 'Your duty is to stay at home, do your needlework, or whatever it is you women do, and look pretty. If I lead the expedition, there's no way I'm taking you with us. You can't possibly imagine the dangers we'll face, and I'm not talking about the heat and the harshness of the terrain. There's the wildlife – lions, leopards, and Saharan cheetahs, snakes and scorpions, and the most deadly of all – men.'

'I have to agree with you there,' Archie cut in. 'I tried to talk Harriet out of it, but she's very determined and …' He raised his hands in a helpless gesture.

Saintclair raised his eyebrows. 'If she were my woman, she'd do exactly what I told her to do.'

'Let's be thankful I'm not, then.' Harriet crossed her arms on her chest and tilted her chin.

Saintclair leaned forward and she was faced with his icy, crystal clear stare once more.

'I am not taking a woman to the Sahara, and that is final.' He spoke slowly, detaching every syllable as if he was talking to a particularly silly and stubborn child.

He drew on his cigar, blew a few circles of smoke, and smiled. 'And I'm ready to wager a hundred francs no other guide in Algiers will either.'

Harriet clenched her fists and struggled to control the urge to slap the smirk off his face. Now was the time to produce her trump card.

She took a deep breath and asked with her sweetest voice, 'Not even for the map of the location of Khayr ad-Dīn's last ever loot?'

Chapter Two

Saintclair put his tumbler on the table.

'Barbarossa's treasure map? What about it?' He tried to keep his voice casual.

'It's yours once my father and I are back safe and sound in London. *If* and only *if* you take me with you to Tamanrasset, that is.'

'You are telling me that you have the map showing where the spoils of Barbarossa's last raid are hidden?'

She nodded. 'I do indeed, Monsieur Saintclair, have the map of the legendary lost treasure of the Old Chief of the Sea himself.'

He found it hard to breathe.

'How do I know you're not making this up? How do I know the map you have is genuine?'

Her grey eyes looked directly into his, and he felt once again their strange, compelling attraction.

'You have my word of honour as a gentlewoman, monsieur.' She crossed her hands in her lap and sat up straight. 'However, if that's not enough, I happen to have a letter from my father authenticating the map.'

She bent down, took a crumpled sheet of paper out of the leather purse dangling at her belt and slid it across the table.

It took him a few seconds to focus on the spidery handwriting covering the letter and understand what he was reading. Professor Montague wrote that the signature on the map appeared to be Barbarossa's, and that the quality of the parchment and ink, as well as the wording and symbols used, were consistent with a naval document dating from the mid-sixteenth century. The old document bore references to the Turkish corsair's impious alliance with Francis I of France against Charles, Emperor of the Holy Roman Empire, and the trail of destruction he left on the coasts of France and Italy after the siege of Nice and Toulon in the winter of 1543 and 1544. There was also a tally of the loot carried by Barbarossa's fleet – one hundred galleys filled to the brim with gold and previous artefacts, not to forget slaves to be sold at Constantinople. The second part of the letter was more personal and he only skimmed over it.

For a prize like the map – and the treasure it led to – he would promise to take Harriet Montague anywhere she wanted. Hell, he would even promise to take her to Timbuktu!

He grinned. He might promise, but he'd make it very hard for her to keep up.

As he read the letter again, he became aware of the tension between Drake and his fiancée. From the way the Englishman stared open-mouthed at her, it was safe to presume he didn't know anything about the pirate's treasure map.

'Hang on a minute, Harriet.' Drake's voice was a harsh whisper. 'What are you talking about? Your father never wrote to me about the Barbarossa map.'

Harriet Montague frowned. 'Didn't he? How odd ... He found it in Hassan Pasha's library when he was in Algiers shortly before leaving for Tamanrasset, and sent it to me for safekeeping. He didn't trust anyone here with it, and he certainly didn't want it to get lost or damaged during his journey to the Sahara.'

Drake narrowed his eyes. 'Where is it now?'

'Safe,' she replied with a shrewd smile.

Drake grabbed her hand, his blue eyes harsh. 'I asked you where it was.'

'Archie!' Harriet breathed out, struggling to pull her hand free.

Lucas folded the letter and leaned over the table. 'Is there a problem, Drake?'

Immediately, the Englishman's expression changed. His lips stretched into an easy smile and he released the young woman's hand.

'No, everything's fine. I was just a little taken aback by Harriet's news, that's all. It's always a shock for a man to discover that his fiancée has been keeping secrets from him, especially secrets of such importance.' A harsh look lingered in his eyes.

Lucas frowned. His first impression had been wrong. The man wasn't a pushover at all. He was a bully. He wondered how long it would take the young woman to realise that. He hoped for her sake she figured it out before the wedding.

He slid the letter across to her and smiled. 'You didn't get on with your Aunt Elizabeth, did you?'

'What makes you say that?'

'A line at the end of your father's letter, referring to some mischief you played on her.'

'Oh that!' She pulled a face. 'My mother passed away when I was very young, so it's my Aunt Elizabeth who looked after me when my father was away on expeditions. He and she never agreed on what was proper for a young lady to know. She used to read my father's letters before passing them on to me and black out entire sections she deemed inappropriate for my eyes. So he started writing messages in invisible ink … It was great fun and to this day she still doesn't know anything about it.'

She paused. 'So, do you agree to take us to Tamanrasset, Monsieur Saintclair?'

He drank more rum and toyed with his tumbler. 'I would get the map on top of the fee Lord Callaghan is willing to pay?'

'That's right.'

'I'll think about it,' he said at last.

He'd already decided, of course, but he didn't want to appear too keen. His heart beat hard, and his mind was bursting with plans and ideas. He could do so much with the Barbarossa treasure.

There was something else to consider too. He had to travel south anyway, now that Rachid had fled with the map. Professor Montague's rescue mission would be the perfect cover for him and his men. What's more, if he played his cards right, he might even end up with the ransom money as well. The professor was already dead, he was sure of it. This could turn out to be a very profitable trip indeed.

Out of habit, he glanced around the room and frowned as he recognised a couple of unsavoury characters lurking by the door. The men caught him looking and slipped out.

Harriet repressed a grin. Saintclair was hooked. She had won. However, being a male – and an arrogant one at that – he would never admit to being outmanoeuvred by a woman and was playing hard to get. This was a game she could play, too.

'We'll need your answer by tomorrow,' she said, stuffing the letter back into her leather purse, 'so we can find another guide if you're not interested.' She forced another sip of rum down. It tasted less fiery; she must be getting used to it. She drank a little more.

'I hope your employer is aware of the costs involved,' Saintclair said.

Archie nodded. 'Lord Callaghan is a very wealthy man. As the chairman of the museum's board of trustees, he felt it was his duty to arrange for Montague's ransom.'

'There will be men to hire, horses and camels to buy, rights of passages to local dignitaries and tribes to pay. Not to mention buying weapons and ammunitions. And entertainment, of course.'

'What do you mean by entertainment?' Harriet interrupted. 'There won't be time for the theatre, the opera, or the ballet, or anything like that. Why are you laughing?'

Saintclair cleared his throat. 'Not that kind of entertainment, miss. I was thinking of the kind involving playing cards and warm, willing women.'

'There's no need to be crude, Saintclair,' Archie snapped. 'These are things a young lady doesn't need to know.'

'Miss Montague will soon learn about the facts of life and the nature of men if she insists on coming along.'

It sounded like a promise – or a threat. Saintclair darted his clear blue eyes into hers. His lips curled into a smile and she found herself grow hot. She put her hands against her burning cheeks, struggled, and failed, to find something clever to say, which rarely happened. It was because of the rum, of course. It didn't agree with her.

Archie stood up and pulled her to her feet. 'Come on, dear, we will leave Monsieur Saintclair to think about our proposal.'

Saintclair drained his rum. 'I'll walk you back.'

'That won't be necessary,' Archie objected.

The Frenchman stood up, threw the butt of his cigar on the floor and stubbed it out with the heel of his riding boot. 'I insist.'

It was pitch-black as they made their way along the docks. Light-headed from the rum, Harriet held onto Archie's arm. As they turned into a dark alleyway, Saintclair froze and gestured for them to stop. Footsteps echoed behind them. Someone whistled. Immediately, they heard another whistle in front of them, and two shadows stepped out from a doorway.

'Here they are. I knew it,' Saintclair muttered through his teeth.

He pulled his dagger out and pushed Harriet into Archie's arms. 'They're after me. I saw them earlier in the Seventh Star. Take her away, quickly. I'll deal with them.'

Looking over her shoulder, Harriet saw that two men behind them blocked their retreat.

Saintclair pointed to a narrow passage, shrouded in darkness. 'Run through there and you'll end up at the top of the kasbah.'

'What's happening, Archie?' She glanced at Saintclair and Archie in turn, fear tightening around her heart like a fist.

'Come now, dear. Hurry.' Archie pulled her arm and urged her forward.

'We can't leave Saintclair alone against four men – he doesn't stand a chance,' she protested. 'You have your pistol, don't you? You must help him.'

'He'll be all right,' Archie retorted. 'If he isn't, then he isn't as good as I thought. Now, run!'

The passageway led to a narrow street, then a steep staircase. When they reached the top, Harriet put a hand on her heart and tried to catch her breath, but Archie dragged her on.

'Come on, we're almost there.'

They soon found themselves in front of Lord Callaghan's palace and its imposing carved doors. Archie rapped his fingers on the thick wood a few times until a sleepy-eyed servant let them in.

'I'm going to bed,' Archie declared straight away. 'And so should you.'

She turned to him, surprised. 'What about Saintclair? Are you not going back with a couple of men to check that he's all right?'

'Don't worry – I heard he was very skilled with a knife.'

He walked up to her, put his hands on her shoulders and looked down at her. 'I'm still not sure about taking you along to Tamanrasset. Do you really think you're strong enough to ride hundreds of miles with half a dozen ruffians for company? You saw Saintclair – coarse, brutal, ill-mannered. His men won't be much better.'

She smiled. 'You're not a ruffian. You'll look after me, won't you? And you'll take care of Father when we find him.'

'Of course.' He let go of her. 'But what about your Aunt Elizabeth? She only let you come to Algiers because you promised to wait here, in Lord Callaghan's palace.'

'I lied.' She stood on her tiptoes and pecked a kiss on his cheek. 'Don't worry about Aunt Elizabeth. I'll tell her you were against the idea from the start but I didn't listen, as usual. She won't be surprised. You know what she thinks about me.'

The elderly lady often complained that Harriet would end up a sad and lonely spinster. According to her, being able to decipher ancient scrolls, brush dust off potsherds and animal bones, and sketch the ruins of Greek temples would never get her a husband.

It didn't matter a jot to Harriet. She had no intention of getting married. All she wanted was to follow in her father's footsteps and help bring forgotten civilisations back to life.

Archie sighed. 'And there's this business of the map. I still can't believe you never breathed a word about it.'

'I thought you knew. Father always tells you everything.'

'Not this time. Why offer it to Saintclair? Do you have any idea how precious it is, and I'm not even talking about the treasure itself?'

'The greatest treasure in the world is nothing compared to my father's life,' she answered quietly. 'You said yourself that Saintclair was the best. I needed to offer him something unique, something he couldn't refuse.'

'A man like him would have been happy with a few jugs of rum.' He stepped closer, taking her hand. There was a strange glint in his eyes.

'You look so different tonight, so … beautiful.' He lifted her hand to his lips. His moustache brushed her skin in a caress so incongruous she opened her mouth but no sound came out.

'I suppose I shall have to get used to the idea the little girl who used to sit on my knees to listen to bedtime stories is all grown up.' He sounded slightly hoarse all of a sudden.

She withdrew her hand and stepped back, uneasy. 'I've been grown up for a while … And your stories were always far too exciting for bedtime – full of decaying corpses in forgotten tombs, curses written in blood, and old parchments. No wonder I grew up wanting to be like you.'

'You grew up all right, and thank goodness you look nothing like me.' He took a deep breath and turned away. 'You should go to bed now.'

It was with a sense of relief that she bid him good night and climbed the stairs leading to her apartment. For an uncomfortable moment it looked as if Archie wanted to kiss her – a proper kiss, a lover's kiss. The thought made her shudder.

She put her white nightdress on and slipped into the silky sheets of her four poster bed. Sleep, however, eluded her.

Images of a tall, dark-haired man danced in front of her. His eyes were as clear as a dawn sky. His mouth was sensual and strong. She swallowed hard and sat up, holding her hand to her racing heart. What was wrong with her? It must be that awful rum giving her palpitations.

She lay down again and stared at the shadows moving on the ceiling as the moon followed its course in the night sky.

She had never met anyone like Lucas Saintclair. Anyone so arrogant, rude and dangerous. He would have killed that man tonight had she not stopped him. He hadn't even looked scared when the four muggers stepped out of the shadows to attack him in the kasbah. He was a strange man, able to converse in faultless French and English, and speak Arabic like a native. He belonged to another world, a world of wilderness, vast spaces, arid plains, and violence. A world she knew nothing about, but was about to step into.

There were two other things she'd found out tonight about Saintclair. His opinion of women belonged in the Dark Ages. And she'd outwitted him. He would take up her offer.

Smiling to herself, she closed her eyes and this time drifted to sleep.

Early the next morning, Harriet dressed in a long white *gandourah*, covered her head with a veil, and went to the souk with Aicha, one of Lord Callaghan's women servants she'd befriended. The market square offered a good view of the bay. The turquoise sea, criss-crossed by small fishing boats and larger ships, their white sails billowing in the breeze, sparkled under the bright sunshine.

The town climbed up the hill in a semicircle. Tall white minarets darted like arrows into the pure blue sky among the whitewashed walls of houses and palaces nestling in emerald oases of vegetation.

Aicha had proved a godsend. Not only had she taught her a few basic words of Arabic, but she'd found clothes for her to dress up in when exploring some of Algiers' treasures. Fairy-tale palaces with walls covered in colourful mosaics. Secret gardens full of palms, aloes, blossoming almond trees, red and orange cannas and zinnias. And the most poignant and magical of all places – a tiny cemetery hidden in the heart of the kasbah where she liked to sit every day.

The young maid told her about the two princesses who were buried there, their graves shaded by the canopy of an ancient fig tree. They'd died of sorrow when the man they both loved vanished in the Sahara desert. Even if Harriet dismissed the story as fanciful and overly sentimental, the cemetery's peace and cool shade appealed to her.

She breathed in the marine breeze mixed with smells of food frying on a nearby stove; red peppers and onions, fish and lamb in crispy batter. Live poultry clucked in wooden cages, goats bleated and chewed on hay, and donkeys stood placid and laden with baskets overflowing with fresh produce.

She could almost picture her father stopping in front of the same stalls and licking his lips in front of their displays of honey and date pastries, crumbly halva or Turkish delights covered with a dusting of sugar.

She bought a honey pastry and was about to bite into it when an uneasy sensation prickled the back of her neck. She turned round. A tall man dressed like a Tuareg, his face hidden behind his indigo blue veil, stared at her. As he lifted his hand to readjust his turban, the large silver ring he wore on the middle finger of his right hand sparkled in the sunlight. As soon as he saw her looking, he stepped away and melted into the market crowd.

Her throat tightened. She couldn't be sure, but she had the feeling the same man had followed her on previous occasions. She sighed and shook her head. Maybe her imagination was running wild. What reason would anyone have to follow her?

She spotted a jewellery booth held by an old Bedouin. A good-luck charm, that's what she needed for the journey ahead.

'Fatima's hand will protect you,' Aicha explained in hesitant English. She pointed to a gold pendant in the shape of an open hand.

'I'll take it.'

Harriet paid for the necklace and insisted on wearing it immediately. The two women then made their way back to the palace, weighed down with baskets of fruit and vegetables, and the pastries Harriet liked so much.

Lucas Saintclair was standing in the courtyard, waiting for her.

As soon as she saw him, her pulse started racing and she was glad for the white veil hiding her burning cheeks. Her first thought was that he still looked like a pirate in his black clothes and dusty riding boots. Her second thought, that he had come to accept her offer.

His eyes flickered with surprise when she walked up to him and pulled her veil down.

'Miss Montague? I could have passed you in the street and not recognised you.'

'That's the idea, Monsieur Saintclair.' She smoothed her hair away from her face. 'I'm so happy to see you're safe. Who were those horrid men waiting for you?'

Saintclair looked down and held her in his crystal clear gaze. 'Remember Rachid, the man whose life you had the bad idea to save last night? Well, he's far too much of a coward to try and kill me himself, so he hired a few thugs to do the job for him.'

She put her hand in front of her mouth. 'He tried to have you killed?' What had she done? If Rachid's thugs succeeded, she'd be responsible for Saintclair's death – and be without a guide to rescue her father.

He nodded. 'I told you, the man's a weasel. Now at least, you know that in this country things aren't always what they seem.'

They stood close, too close. She felt the heat from his body, breathed in the manly scent of his sandalwood shaving soap mixed with cigar smoke and leather.

He relaxed into a smile and stepped back. 'I came to tell you that I decided to take up your offer, providing you agree to my conditions.'

Harriet lowered her face to hide a smile of triumph. She'd been right, the lure of the Barbarossa map was too strong to resist.

'I'm afraid Archie isn't here. He had some errands in town.'

Lucas saw her smile and felt suddenly very annoyed. This wasn't a game. The rescue mission could cost them their lives. He crossed his arms on his chest and cast Harriet a cold glance. He might want the Barbarossa map, but he also wanted the silly woman to realise what she was embarking on.

'Actually, it's you I wanted to talk to,' he said, shortly.

'Really? What about?'

'Our journey, of course, what else?' She was indeed a silly woman. He didn't have time for silly women, however attractive they were. 'I take it you can sit on a horse without falling off?'

Her eyes flashed in anger. 'My father brought me up to take care of myself, Monsieur Saintclair. I can ride, read maps and find my way out of a forest. And I can shoot all my targets at fifty feet …'

'Well, almost all,' she corrected with an impatient sigh. 'I can light a fire and cook and I can—'

He held his hand up. 'All right, I get it. Your father taught you well.

But you forgot something.'

'And what is that?' She tilted her face towards him.

'You can bite.' He rubbed his shoulder to make his point.

She blushed crimson and twisted her fingers. 'It was a mistake. I'm sorry, I didn't—'

'Never mind,' he interrupted and leaned towards her.

He liked the way the colour on her cheeks deepened, the way her lips parted, showing her pearly white teeth. He recognised the faint rose perfume in her hair, wondered if she smelled that way all over. He came a little closer and forgot what he wanted to say. Annoyed, he took a deep breath and hardened his gaze. He should know better than to be distracted by a pretty woman.

'There're a few things we need to get straight if you insist on coming along.' He paused. 'There will be no tantrums if you don't have time to do your hair or there's no water for a bath. No hysterics because you've broken a nail or found a cockroach or a snake in your bed. No tears because I shot a cute-looking gazelle for supper and I ask you to skin it and cut it up. Is that clear?'

She tilted her chin again, her cheeks bright red with anger, and stomped her foot on the marble floor. 'Oh yes, it's all perfectly clear, Monsieur Saintclair. I'm aware of the dangers we will face. I'm not some vain, silly girl just out of the nursery.'

Then why did his hard, frosty stare make her feel like one? Why did her heart beat madly when he was close? Why did he manage to make her lose her temper?

He arched his brows and his lips twitched. 'I said no tantrums.'

She clenched her fists, repressing a scream of frustration. 'I'm not having a tantrum. I never have tantrums. I am a responsible, resourceful scholar and archaeologist.'

'Never mind being good with books and long words, what you'll need to be is damned tough out there,' he continued, impervious. 'There's something else. Should you decide to give up part way through the journey, you'll still owe me the Barbarossa map. Do we agree on that?'

'Hmm … Yes. I think so …' She hesitated. Something didn't sound quite right, but there was no time to mull it over.

Saintclair pulled several pieces of paper out of his pocket and handed them over. 'Good. These are my estimates for supplies and the like. Please give them to your fiancé. We're leaving on Wednesday at dawn.'

'So soon? How long before we reach Tamanrasset?'

'I give you my word we'll be there at the end of May.'

In just a few weeks she'd be reunited with her father. Resolutely, she pushed any doubt aside. She didn't want to think about the things which could go wrong on route, or about what they would find once there, in the ancient tribal grounds of the Tuaregs.

She turned to Lucas Saintclair and offered her hand. 'Thank you. You don't know what this means to me.'

He seemed surprised but took her hand. It looked very pale and very small in his. His fingers closed tightly around hers, so strong they could crush them without effort if he chose to. The thought made her shiver.

'I hope you'll have something to thank me for, Miss Montague, but I very much doubt it.'

Chapter Three

'Look at the orange blossom, Archie. Don't the white flowers look pretty? And what wonderful scent …'

Harriet pulled on the reins until her horse slowed to a gentle trot. She breathed in the heady fragrance of the orange grove. In front of her the Atlas mountain range stood, rugged tips shrouded in a pale pink and blue haze as the afternoon drew to a close.

'Blida is over there,' Saintclair announced. He turned round to her and pointed to a town nestled against the mountain slopes in the distance.

After uttering orders in Arabic, he spurred his black thoroughbred forward on the sandy track, followed by the six men he'd hired to escort them to Tamanrasset. Two of them were Tuareg warriors who kept their faces hidden behind blue scarves at all times, only showing their eyes, as tradition demanded.

Some said Tuareg men were afraid of demons snatching their souls; others, more pragmatic, maintained that by hiding their faces Tuaregs could raid and steal without fear of being identified.

The other members of the expedition were native tribesmen, lean and wiry, dark-eyed and fierce-looking. Saintclair said he'd travelled with his men across the country many times before and trusted them with his life. He seemed particularly close to a tall man called Ahmoud who followed him like a shadow.

Harriet watched them disappear in a cloud of dust. 'Why are they in such a rush?'

Archie shrugged. 'I don't know, but we'd better follow them.'

They spurred their horses into a gallop.

They had to wait at the town gates while a French sentinel scrutinised their travel documents. Saintclair exchanged greetings with the soldiers while his companions remained silent and stared ahead, their eyes hard and giving nothing away.

'Blida was pacified only recently,' Archie explained in a low voice. 'The mountains still harbour hostile tribes who regularly attack the French.'

At last the soldiers gave them their papers back and allowed access.

They rode along the main street and dismounted in front of a tavern with whitewashed walls. After unbuckling their saddlebags, they handed over the horses to a couple of stable boys. Saintclair pushed the door of the tavern open. Heady scents of spicy vegetable and mutton stew, of coffee and warm bread, welcomed them. A man came over, a wide grin on his face, wiped his hands on a towel hanging from his belt and launched into a litany in Arabic punctuated with slaps on his round belly. Saintclair laughed good-heartedly, clapped the innkeeper on the back and gestured towards a couple of tables.

'Let's sit over there,' he said. Turning to the innkeeper, he asked in French for some wine for himself and Archie, tea for Harriet, and coffee for the men. 'We'll have some of your soup too. Hurry, we don't have long.'

'Hurry, hurry, that's all you ever say when you come here,' the man grumbled as he walked towards the kitchen.

'What was he talking about earlier?' Archie enquired.

Saintclair smiled. 'Woman trouble, what else? Poor Slimane has been henpecked by his wife for the best part of twenty years. I always wondered how a good man like Slimane could tolerate such a harpy.'

'Maybe he loves her,' Harriet ventured.

'Love? What's that?' Sainclair shrugged. Darting his blue gaze straight at Harriet, he added in a low voice, 'Isn't it just a fancy word for lust?'

Her heart skipped a beat and she looked away, annoyed to feel she was blushing.

'Are we stopping here tonight?' Archie asked. 'This looks like a nice, comfortable place and it'll be dark soon.'

'No, we're going up to the mountains, and into the Chiffa gorges.'

'I don't think Harriet can cope with hiking up a mountain at dusk,' Archie objected. 'She didn't sleep at all last night. The camp was terribly uncomfortable.'

Saintclair looked at Harriet and arched his brows. 'What a shame … Was the ground too hard for you?'

'No, of course it wasn't,' she lied. 'It was perfectly fine. I slept like a log.' In truth, it had been horrid, with the ground too cold and rocky for her to get comfortable, even with three blankets under her.

Saintclair smiled as if he could read her thoughts. 'Can you carry on tonight, or would you rather stop here? The last thing I want is for you to fall off your horse and roll down the mountain slope.'

It took all her strength to straighten up in her chair. 'I said I wasn't tired.'

'There you have it, Drake. Your fiancée wants to carry on.'

From the amused glint in his eyes, she realised she'd played right into his hands. She pulled off her kid gloves and put them on the table.

'And yet she doesn't look well,' Archie remarked. 'I'm sure she could do with sleeping in a proper bed.'

'I wish you'd stop talking about me as if I wasn't here,' Harriet blurted out. Her fingers were shaking so much she hid them in her lap under the table. She would never admit she was exhausted.

'I was only trying to help, dear,' Archie muttered.

The innkeeper came back with a pot of steaming soup which he placed on the table. He was followed by a woman carrying bowls and cutlery, and a loaf of bread.

'Enjoy, my friends.' He turned to Sainctlair and winked. 'Then you can tell me what you're planning to do about lovely Djamila. The poor girl has been sighing ever since you left. She even stopped singing, claiming she lost her voice when you broke her heart.'

'I'll pay her a visit later. I'm sure to make her sing again.' Saintclair dipped his spoon into the thick, fragrant soup.

How crude, how vain he was! Harriet repressed a sneer. The man was really full of himself … Then she remembered the eyes full of longing of the serving girl at the Seventh Star, her own racing pulse when he held her hand in his at Lord Callaghan's palace, and the unnerving way her heart tightened every time he looked at her.

'Are you all right, dear? You look a little flushed,' Archie remarked, full of concern. 'I don't think you should eat the soup. You won't like it, it's very spicy.'

'Drake's right, it's rather fiery. I'll ask Slimane to bring you something else.' Saintclair gestured to the innkeeper.

Harriet picked up her spoon. 'There's no need. If you can eat it, so can I.'

She ate one spoonful, spat it out, and started coughing violently.

'Tea, please,' she whispered when able to talk.

Archie filled a glass of sweet mint tea and held it out for her.

'There, there, dear, this will help. I did tell you it was spicy. You should have listened.'

Her fingers tightened around the small, hot glass. She gulped the tea down, tears running down her face, her mouth on fire. She was painfully aware of Saintclair's mocking grin.

In the end, she had to be content with a piece of bread and some cheese for supper.

They rode into the mountains at dusk and climbed a rocky slope as the shadows of the night closed in. They dismounted halfway up and carried on by foot, leading their horses on a narrow path. To the left was a steep ravine covered with a carpet of fragrant bushes and small, twisted trees. To the right stood rugged and fast disappearing summits. As the trail got steeper, Harriet focused all her efforts on putting one foot in front of the other without stumbling. She could hardly see Archie's tall silhouette at the front now.

'How are you holding on?' Saintclair appeared noiselessly beside her.

She gritted her teeth. 'Fine.'

'We're in the Chiffa gorges now – that's Mouzaïa territory.'

'Mouzaïa?'

'A tribe under the allegiance of the bey of Constantine, one of the last rebel chiefs.'

'What about Abdelkader? I read all about him in the papers. He has managed to hold the French back, hasn't he?'

Saintclair cast a surprised glance in her direction, as if he hadn't expected her to know anything about the emir who had for the past ten years headed the resistance against the French colonial army and tried to rally the beys to his cause.

'That's right, but he's in hiding now.'

A sharp, opalescent crescent of moon and hundreds of stars lit the evening sky even if it was still pale towards the west where the last of the daylight lingered. Harriet's breath steamed in front of her. She shivered, draping her wool *burnous* more closely around her, the hooded cape made of camel wool hardly enough to keep her warm. Her legs felt like lead. She lost her footing a couple of times and slipped on loose rocks. Saintclair held her elbow to steady her but she shook him off.

'I said I was fine.'

It was becoming hard to see. The tip of her boot caught on a rock. Off-balance, she tripped and would have stumbled into the ravine had Saintclair not wrapped his arm around her waist to hold her back. For a brief moment she was against him, close enough to feel the hard line of his thighs, hips and stomach against her body, his heat seeping through her layers of clothing.

He looked down, his arm a band of steel around her. 'Watch your step.'

She swallowed hard, nodded. Her heart thundered in her chest. Fear and relief coursed through her veins, together with something else she didn't recognise – a hot, uncomfortable sensation at the centre of her body that was almost a pain.

Saintclair let her go and looked up to the mountain slope. 'Here they are.'

A man's voice called from the darkness, and soon a dozen men appeared on the path in front of them. Dressed in black, with long curvy daggers hanging from their sides and their eyes reflecting the moonlight, they looked more like mountain demons than men of flesh and blood.

Saintclair spoke to them and turned to Archie and Harriet. 'They'll escort us to the *caravansérai.*' He gestured towards the ravine. 'It's down by the torrent. Will you be all right?'

Although her body screamed with aches and pains and the skin of her feet rubbed in her boots, Harriet forced a smile. 'Of course.'

They reached a one-storey house half an hour later. In the golden light of a lantern hanging from the front porch, an old man sat on a rickety old chair, sucking on a long pipe. As soon as he saw them he stood up, muttered something and disappeared inside.

'Old Chehani is bringing hot water to the washroom,' Saintclair explained. 'Don't expect too much. It's only a shelter for shepherds and travellers.'

'I still don't understand why we didn't stop at Blida.' Archie took his hat off and wiped his forehead with his handkerchief.

'Too risky,' Saintclair replied. 'Word travels fast. People know we're carrying a large amount of gold. Blida is full of men who wouldn't hesitate to slit our throats for the ransom money. We're much safer here. The Mouzaïas will keep guard for us. Trust them, they won't let anybody through.'

'How can we trust them? They're rebels, bloodthirsty thugs who massacred a whole French garrison less than two years ago,' Archie protested.

'Some might consider the French to be the bloodthirsty thugs and the Mouzaïas to do nothing more than protect their land and their people.'

Archie snorted. 'I see where your loyalties lie, Saintclair.'

'Loyalties? What loyalties?' Saintclair shrugged. 'The only loyalty I have is to myself and to whoever's paying my fee – for now, that would be you. And the only thing I care about is spending my money on a jug of good wine and a beautiful woman.'

He walked away, leading the horses to the stables.

Archie sneered. 'At least we know what kind of man he is,' he said before striding into the house.

Harriet let out a long breath to smooth out the odd pang of disappointment caused by Saintclair's answer. How could a man live like that – ruthless, without honour, indifferent to others and preoccupied only by his own pleasure?

She followed Archie inside. The first room was a large common room with scattered chairs and tables and a fire burning low in a fireplace. She wrinkled her nose at the sickly smell of burnt fat that lingered in the room. The bedrooms were located on either side of a long corridor. Instead of doors, there were only curtains for privacy.

'Where are you, Archie?'

'In here.'

She pulled the grey curtain aside and walked into a tiny room with a couple of straw pallets on either side. It was more than sparse – it wasn't much better than a hovel.

'I told you it would be hard, my dear,' he said when he caught her staring with dismay at the room. 'It isn't too late to turn back, you know. Saintclair told me only this morning that he'll spare two of his men to ride back to Algiers with you.'

'Did he, now?'

'In fact, he has a bet going with his men that you'll turn back before we reach Boghar at the end of the week. For once, I happen to agree with him. I'm really not happy about you being here, Harriet.'

He stepped towards her, taking her hands in his. 'This isn't like our archaeological digs in Greece or Italy. There are tribes fighting for their land, bandits planning to ambush us along the way to steal our gold. Further south there'll be the Sahara, the Tuaregs—'

'I'm staying and Saintclair had better get used to the idea.' She pulled her hands away, turning to one of the straw beds. 'Would you mind if I shared your room tonight?'

He opened his eyes wide and she added quickly, 'I would feel better if you were close by. After all, you told Saintclair we're … you know … engaged, and we did share the tent last night.'

'Of course, dear,' he said. 'It's a good idea, for your own protection.'

There was colour on his cheeks now. He cleared his throat and gestured to the beds. 'Pick your side and get ready. I'll wait until you're settled for the night.'

She unpacked a wash cloth and a bar of soap and proceeded to the washroom at the end of the corridor. There she splashed water on her face and performed a quick toilette. Back in the room, she slipped into her nightgown and untied her hair. She brushed it until it fell, shiny and silky on her shoulders. Wrapping herself in the musty woollen blanket, she got into bed, turned towards the wall and closed her eyes. She was fast asleep within seconds and didn't even hear Archie come in.

She didn't know what woke her late in the night. Was it Archie's snores, the gushing torrent nearby, or the snorting and stomping of horses under her window?

She sat up, filled with panic and her heart beating fast and loud. For a few seconds she couldn't remember where she was. As her eyes got accustomed to the darkness, she made out Archie's body stretched out on the bed opposite, their bags and boots scattered on the beaten earth floor.

There were people out there, talking with hushed voices. What if, contrary to what Saintclair had claimed, the Mouzaïas had decided to rob their gold? Or if a gang of raiders had followed them from Blida?

She must find Saintclair and warn him of the danger. She sprang out of bed, pulled the curtain, and walked into the corridor. A couple of oil lamps hanging from the low ceiling gave out a weak light. All the curtains were drawn. She hesitated. Which room was Saintclair's?

There was a noise near the front door. A tall figure stood in the doorway, outlined by the cold moonlight. She froze and held her breath. The man moved, fast and silent towards her, his hand to his side. The glint of a blade shone in the silver moon rays.

'Miss Montague? What are you doing out of your room?' Saintclair grabbed her arm.

'I could ask you the same question.' She tried to shake him off but he held her too tightly.

'I don't want you wandering at night, especially dressed like that.'

He looked down to her bare feet and his eyes travelled slowly upward. She was cruelly aware that only the thin linen nightgown stood between him and her naked body.

A violent heat burned her face. He extended his hand towards her pendant.

'Fatima's hand …' His fingers brushed against her good luck charm. She felt their warmth against her skin. 'That's sweet, but I think we'll need more than that to keep us alive, darling.'

'Don't call me darling, and let go of me,' she snapped.

'What are you doing up?' He dropped his hand to his side.

'I came to warn you. I heard men's voices outside.'

He smiled. 'Why didn't you wake Drake? You're in the same room.'

'I don't know,' she answered, confused. The thought of waking Archie had never occurred to her.

'There's nothing to worry about. I was outside with a few friends.'

'In the middle of the night? What were you doing?'

'That's none of your business, darling,' he said with a mocking smile, emphasising the last word. 'Now run along back to bed like a good girl, and next time you venture out of your room, make sure you're dressed properly. You don't want to give my men – or me – any ideas.'

He turned round and went back outside. She waited a few seconds before following him. When she got to the door, he was already climbing up the ravine trail along with a dozen other men all dressed in black.

Where were they going?

She tiptoed back to her room, lay down on the straw mattress, and pulled the blankets over her head.

Of course.

How could she have forgotten what Slimane, the innkeeper, had said earlier? Saintclair was on his way to meet a woman – probably Djamila, who was pining for him in Blida. Didn't he say he only cared about drinking wine and having a beautiful woman by his side?

Chapter Four

A piece of flat bread, half a dozen candied figs and a cup of bitter tea may not have been Harriet's ordinary choice of breakfast, but that morning in the pink and blue dawn rising over the Chiffa gorges, it tasted like heaven. She gulped down her hot drink, licked the sugar off her fingers and bit hungrily into the bread. Outside, Saintclair barked orders as he supervised the saddling of the horses and the loading of bags and supplies. It was his voice, brusque and bad-tempered, that had woke her up half an hour before. At first she had tried to ignore him and pulled the scratchy blanket over her head. Her body ached so much that even the prickly straw mattress was more agreeable than the prospect of spending a day in the saddle or scrambling up and down a mountain track. Then, groaning with pain, she'd had to get up and get ready.

Saintclair sounded positively rugged this morning, not at all like a man who'd spent the night in his lover's arms. But had he? Perhaps the lovely Djamila hadn't welcomed his return with the enthusiasm he'd expected and he hadn't been able to make her sing? It would almost be funny if it wasn't so infuriating. How could he be irresponsible enough to abandon them in the mountains to chase after a woman?

She went outside, looked up towards the peaks and snuggled into the burnous she wore over her layers of clothing – trousers tucked in riding boots, two cotton chemises under a thick blue tunic, all of which should have been more than adequate to keep her warm. Holding her sketch pad and a couple of pencils, she wandered away from the caravanserai. She had decided to keep a record of their journey, and now was her only chance to draw the gorges.

Archie stood apart, cradling a cup of tea, a morose expression on his face. He'd been short with her earlier when she asked about the arrangements for the day ahead.

'I'm as much in the dark as you regarding Saintclair's plans,' he'd replied, sitting on his bed and pulling his boots on.

Better let him sulk on his own for now. The problem, she decided as she made her way to the torrent, was that Archie was used to being in charge. Here, he had to comply with Saintclair's orders and rely on their guide's experience and knowledge of the terrain, and he didn't like it.

Shivering with cold despite her thick clothing, she walked across dew-covered grass, wild thyme and coriander before choosing a boulder near the water to sit on and start sketching.

'We're leaving soon.' Saintclair's abrupt voice behind her made her jump. She had been so completely absorbed in her drawing that she hadn't noticed time passing.

She closed the cover of her drawing book. 'Fine. I'm ready.' She stood up to face him.

He looked just as rough as he sounded. His eyes were weary and slightly bloodshot as if he'd not slept. He rubbed his bristly cheeks and raked his fingers in his dark hair. 'Come on then.'

He turned round and strode back to the caravanserai without waiting, leaving Harriett to hurry after him with her sketchbook under her arm. Men and horses were lining up on the path, ready to depart, but one of the Tuareg men appeared to be injured and had a thick bandage wrapped around his hand. 'What's wrong with him?' she asked.

'A card game which got a little rowdy last night in Blida, that's all. Gambling, wine and women … Always a recipe for a fight.'

Gesturing towards the injured man, he added with a shrug. 'Hakim will be all right in a couple of days, don't worry.'

Harriet looked at him, wide-eyed. He'd just confirmed her suspicions. 'You're telling me not to worry when you sneak out at night to play cards, drink liquor and chase after women instead of safekeeping the ransom money and working out a plan to get my father out of the Tuaregs' clutches?'

Blood rushed to her face. Filled with an anger she couldn't control, she stepped forward and jabbed a finger into his chest. 'Why should I worry indeed, when my life is in the hands of a second-rate Casanova and his band of merry men? What if you were injured, or killed, in a tavern brawl? What would we do then?'

She was about to poke his chest again when he caught her wrist.

'Don't do that, miss, I find it irritating.' He bent down. 'Let's get one thing straight. You may have a claim on my days, but you have none on my nights.' He lowered his voice, cocking his head. 'Unless, of course, you're jealous of the dancing girls I sleep with and you're offering to share my bed.'

'How dare you talk to me like that? You are nothing but a … a …' She almost choked with righteous outrage.

Still holding her wrist in his iron grip, he pulled her a little closer until she felt the heat, the hardness of his body.

'If my presence is so odious to you, you can always return to Algiers.'

The absolute ice blue of his eyes struck her like a physical blow but she held her ground. 'I am going all the way to Tamanrasset, Saintclair, whether you like it or not.'

He released her wrist. 'Then take care of your horse instead of drawing pretty flowers.' He pointed to her sketch pad before turning round and marching towards his men.

She stomped her foot and let out a cry of frustration, but what she really wanted to do was pick up a stone and throw it at his back. Never had anyone made her so angry before. She had every right to scold Saintclair for failing in his duty, for leaving them during the night to go gallivanting. Yet somehow he'd managed to make fun of her.

'Harriet! Hurry up!' Archie called.

They walked all morning to a pass from where they could see all the way to the Mediterranean sea to the north and to the Alfa plains to the south, which Archie said were known for mirages.

'Travellers have reported seeing fortresses with golden walls, mountains or oases which aren't on any map, even strange animals no one's ever seen before.'

They were enjoying a rest and a frugal lunch before walking down the other side of the mountain.

'I'd like to see a mirage.' Harriet broke a piece of flat bread almost as hard as the sole of her boots into tiny pieces to make it more palatable. Archie gave her a gourd filled with fresh water.

'You seemed rather upset with Saintclair this morning. What were you arguing about?'

'Nothing. He was just being his usual charming self.' She was reluctant to tell him about the guide's nocturnal escapade and add to Archie's worries. He'd so much to think about already.

'I know, dear.' He leaned towards her to take the gourd. 'You have to remember that he isn't like us. He was probably brought up in a hovel in one of those Saharan garrison towns. I bet his father was a soldier, his mother a *cantinière*, or worse ...'

Ahmoud approached them. 'Are you ready? We have to leave now if we want to be in Médéa by sunset.' It was the first time he'd spoken directly to Harriet.

‘Is that where we’re spending the night?’

Ahmoud gestured towards Saintclair. ‘He decides.’

Archie’s mouth hardened. ‘I don’t see why our stopover is such a closely guarded secret.’

‘Maybe it’s because of the ransom gold,’ she ventured. ‘Saintclair wants to keep marauders guessing about our whereabouts.’

They started down the mountain, on a track so narrow they had to pull their horses behind them. The track overlooked vertiginous precipices covered with prickly bushes and small, twisted pine trees. By mid-afternoon, Harriet’s legs were weak and shaky. She almost wept with relief when Saintclair gave the signal to stop on the bank of a small lake that mirrored the bright blue, cloudless sky above. Goats roamed under the watchful eye of a shepherd who played soulful tunes on a flute.

She sat on the soft grass, stretched her legs in front of her and took out her sketch pad and pencil to draw. After a while, she untied her turban and closed her eyes to enjoy the warm caress of the sun on her face and listen to the shepherd’s tune, timeless and poignant, that hovered around her, carried by the breeze.

He watched her as she squeezed her eyes shut against the sun and sat so still it looked as though she was asleep. He’d been watching her since they left Algiers. Damn the woman. She was holding up much better than he expected. He’d banked on her turning into a hysterical female, complaining of the heat during the day, the cold at night, and demanding hot baths, feather beds and decent food. She’d done none of that. She followed without complaining, ate what she was given – almost. Slimane’s spicy soup had been a touch too much for her, he recalled with a smile.

She was intriguing, unconventional … and courageous. Not many young women would follow their lover halfway across the world without a care for their reputation, and brave both danger and discomfort as she did.

She was also a distraction he could well do without. Her hair shone in the sun, the colour of ripe wheat, and her eyes were fascinating. For as long as he could remember he’d dreamed of the changeable skies of the Devonshire coast where his mother had grown up, and where she’d met brave and indomitable French cuirassier Hugo Saintclair – his father. Although now settled at Bou Saada where his father had bought land, she still talked from time to time about the wild and beautiful part of England she was from; about the rain, the storms and the drizzle that tasted of salt and was brought by the sea fog.

Harriet Montague's grey eyes were the colour of a storm cloud. They were cool and soothing, like a promise of rain.

The sound of the shepherd's flute drew him back to reality. He shook his head, annoyed. He couldn't let himself be distracted by a woman's eyes, even if they were as captivating as Harriet Montague's. It was time to up his game, change his angle. The woman must go back to Algiers, for her own sake. They'd stop at Safir's tavern tonight, where a particularly beautiful dancer owed him a favour or two. After last night, his men could do with a rest. It had been too close a call in Blida.

He walked to her, crouched at her side and picked up her sketch pad. Flicking through the pages, he saw portraits of the young shepherd and Old Chehani, drawings of the gorges and torrent. There were pages after pages of detailed sketches of Algiers houses, old carved doors and mosaics, and even what appeared to be a small cemetery. He smiled, pleasantly surprised. The young woman had talent.

'You'll soon run out of pages at this rate,' he remarked.

She jumped and opened her eyes. How could a man of his stature be so light on his feet?

'I wish you'd stop doing that.' She straightened up, extended her hand to take her pad from him and held it against her chest.

'Doing what?'

'Sneaking up on me.'

He lifted the corner of his mouth in something which could pass as a smile. 'I'm a scout. Sneaking up on people is what I do.'

Unsettled by his presence, she pulled her knees up to her chin and wrapped her arms around them. She pointed her chin towards the shepherd boy. 'He is so young to be wandering the mountain alone. Where does he sleep at night?'

'Here and there, under the stars, in a makeshift hut or in a cave. People are poor around here.'

'And yet, he plays his music and roams free …'

Saintclair's face hardened. He picked up a stick and toyed with it. 'He won't be free for much longer if the French have their way.'

'Aren't they going to improve life here for people, bring civilisation?'

He snorted, snapping the twig in two. 'Civilisation? What is civilisation and who's to decide what country needs to be civilised? Didn't you see great palaces and artwork dating back hundreds of years when you were in Algiers? What about the well-tended farmland and orchards we travelled through yesterday? They've been there for a long time. Isn't that civilisation enough?'

He spread his arms as if to encompass the mountains, the lake. Then he narrowed his eyes and pointed to the shepherd. 'And what about him and his way of life? Who's to decide he isn't civilised?'

He picked up another twig to dig into the dusty ground.

She could feel the anger inside him, raw, burning. So he did care, despite what he'd said earlier … Cautiously, she shifted the conversation onto more neutral ground.

'Are we heading to Médéa?'

He nodded. 'Médéa tonight. Berrouaghia tomorrow. Then we'll follow the ancient nomadic route to the south, maybe even hook up with a caravan.' He smiled. 'There's safety in numbers.'

'And then where? Djelfa and Laghouat?'

He arched his eyebrows. She felt pleased to see he was impressed.

'So it's true, you can read maps.' He carried on. 'You'll like Médéa. I know a hotel where you'll have all the comfort you women can't do without.'

'Meaning?' She narrowed her eyes.

'A hot bath, soft towels, a dressing table with a mirror to do your hair – those kinds of things.'

She realised she was clenching her fists and forced herself to relax her fingers. 'I don't need a hot bath or soft towels, Monsieur Saintclair. If I wanted a wash, I could easily take my clothes off, jump into this lake and stand naked in the sunshine to dry.'

The words died on her lips when she saw the sudden heat in his eyes.

He cleared his throat. 'Please, don't let me stop you.'

Her cheeks warm, she looked away. 'That was a figure of speech, of course.'

He got up, held out his hand to help her up. 'We've a long way to go. Enjoy what's on offer when you can. The thing is … I don't know how to say this without sounding rude, but we could all do with a good, long soak in a bath, even you.'

His nostrils flared as if catching the whiff of an unpleasant smell.

'You're saying that I smell bad? Really, you are the most …' The words stuck in her throat.

Her eyes ablaze with fury, she left him standing there and marched off to the lakeside where she started kicking stones into the water as hard as she could. It didn't calm her down one bit. It was Saintclair's head, not stones, she wanted to kick.

'Harriet, what on earth are you doing?' Archie put a hand on her shoulder, bending down to look at her face. 'I've never seen you so angry.'

Harriet breathed in, out, in again. 'Saintclair just told me that we're stopping in a hotel tonight, for my benefit, apparently. According to him, I smell like a goat and need a good long soak in the bath.'

Archie burst out laughing. 'Is that what he said? What a boor! Well, I for one, welcome the news. I could do with a bath and a nice soft bed.' He took her hand, lifted it to his lips. 'I hope you aren't taking his remarks too seriously, my dear.'

She sighed and linked arms with him to walk back to the horses.

'Wait a minute. I forgot something.' She dug her fingers into her leather purse and extracted a couple of coins, then ran to the shepherd and left the money in front of him.

The boy stopped playing and smiled. '*Saha,*' he said. *Thank you.*

She smiled and ran back to Archie.

'What did you do that for?' he asked, an angry frown creasing his forehead. 'Now we'll have the whole tribe running after us.'

'I don't mind giving them a bit of money. They probably need it more than us.'

He shook his head. 'You are too soft-hearted for your own good, my dear.'

They walked in the dust and heat for several hours, leaving the rocky mountain path at the end of the afternoon to enter a deep cedar forest. It was dark and cool, and eerily silent apart from the sounds of the horses' hooves. There was no birdsong, no rustling of leaves in the breeze. When they came out, Harriet squinted against the bright sunshine.

Suddenly there were shouts and cheers at the front of the line.

‘What’s happening?’
Archie craned his neck to look ahead and relaxed into a smile.
‘Médéa. Get ready for your bath, dear.’

Chapter Five

Safir's wasn't a hotel. It wasn't even an inn. It was a dark, smelly backstreet tavern with a dozen rooms on the first floor and a stable block next to it.

Harriet had been given her own room at the bottom end of the corridor. However basic it was, it had a real bed, clean sheets, and a couple of reasonably soft blankets – and a door she could lock. She sat on the bed, took her turban off, and untied her hair. Maybe Saintclair was right, she thought, loosening her hair and combing it with her fingers. Maybe she should enjoy what little comfort she could tonight. She would probably sleep better than the past couple of nights.

She searched through her bag for fresh undergarments and the large bar of Damascus rose-scented soap and lotion she'd brought from Algiers – her only concession to female vanity – grabbed a bath sheet and made her way to the washroom.

A dozen buckets of warm water had been brought up. She poured them all into the small, chipped enamel bath, stripped out of her dirty clothes and slipped into the water with a sigh of delight. Was it only three days since her last bath?

She lathered every inch of her body with soap, scrubbed her skin with a sponge and washed her hair. And when she got out, she massaged a generous amount of lotion onto her skin. Tonight, Lucas Saintclair would find that she smelled heavenly.

She pouted, and closed the lid of the rose lotion pot with a sharp click. What did she care what Saintclair thought? He was a brute, rude enough to tell her she needed a bath! Then again, what else could she expect from a man who associated with gamblers and tavern girls, and who coursed this wild country for a living?

Now, Archie was totally different. He was a gentleman. Her father was very fond of Archie – so fond Harriet knew he considered him to be the son he never had, and the man who would succeed him one day in his position at the museum.

She started buttoning her chemise, but stopped, uneasy.

How odd that her father had sent her, and not Archie, the Barbarossa map. How strange that he hadn't even written to him about his discovery. The map was a major find. In itself a valuable historical document, it could also lead to the legendary pirate's hoard. She shook her head. Her father *must* have written to Archie, but the letter had got lost between Algiers and London.

Loud banging on the door made her jump and cry out in shock.

'Miss Montague, what are you doing in there? Get out now or I'll join you in the bath. I'm sick of waiting,' Saintclair's grumpy voice called.

'Just a moment, Monsieur Saintclair,' she replied, striving to remain calm despite the rising panic the thought of Saintclair breaking down the door and finding her in her drawers and chemise awakened inside her.

Her heart racing, she put on trousers and a shirt, but in her hurry left the shirt hanging out and only partly buttoned. She was still barefoot when she opened the door.

'About time,' he grumbled. He was leaning against the wall, arms crossed on his chest, leaving hardly any room for her to walk past. 'I hope you left me some hot water.'

Her hand flew to her mouth. 'Oh, no, I'm sorry. I thought it was all for me. I poured it all in. And now it's …'

Her cheeks burning with embarrassment, she gestured towards the bath with its standing water topped with a frothy layer of rose-scented soap flakes.

'Never mind, it'll have to do,' he said. 'By the way, Drake doesn't want you to come downstairs. He's going to arrange for a tray to be brought up to your room.'

'I beg your pardon?' She lifted her head to stare into his eyes. 'Why should I stay in my room?'

'There's going to be some … hum … entertainment for gentlemen later.'

'I see.' She pursed her lips. So there'd be women, dancing girls, prostitutes even. 'Thank you for your concern, but I'll stay downstairs with Archie. Now if you'll excuse me …'

She squeezed past him and started down the corridor.

He moved fast. Suddenly his hand was on her shoulder, spinning her around, pinning her against the wall.

'What do you think you're doing?' Her voice had turned to ice, but inside she was shaking. Her back to the wall, there was nowhere for her to go.

He took her chin between his thumb and forefinger to tilt her face upward and glare at her. 'You must stay in your room tonight. Things are going to become a little hot downstairs. You won't like it.'

'And how would you know what I like or not?' she blurted out.

He sighed. 'Do you really have to be so contrary?'

She didn't answer, mesmerised by the look in his eyes.

His finger stroked the outline of her cheek in a caress that made her shiver. 'Hmm … You smell nice tonight, Miss Montague.' His voice was low and deep.

His finger followed the line of her throat, down to the hollow where her pulse beat frantically, a little further still, where her Fatima pendant sparkled against her skin just above the groove between her breasts. She couldn't move. His finger slowly traced the outline of the pendant, creating ripples of shivers on her skin. He was close, too close, and he came closer still. As he leaned down she breathed in his scent – heat, leather, horse, and the faintest trace of sandalwood.

Finally coming back to her senses, she balled her fists against his chest and pushed him away. 'Go to hell Saintclair, and be damned!'

He made a tutting sound and crossed his arms on his chest, a wide grin on his face. 'Where did a nice young lady pick up that kind of language?'

He turned and walked to the washroom, whistling a cheerful tune.

She let out a strangled cry before running to her room and slamming the door behind her. Then there was only the thunder of her heartbeat and the roar of blood pulsing through her veins as a riot of conflicting emotions raged inside her. Shock, defiance, shame, confusion. She could still feel Saintclair's body close to her, breathe in his scent. She bit her lips hard and walked to the washstand. Her hands shook when she cupped water to wash her face.

She mustn't tell Archie what had just happened. He might fire Saintclair on the spot, which would leave them stranded here without a guide or an escort. Or he might send her straight back to Algiers … Either way it was a risk she didn't want to take. She dried her hair with the towel, combed and plaited it.

When ready, she took a deep breath and opened her door.

Downstairs, the tavern was heaving. She pushed her way through the crowd, looked for Archie, and saw he'd secured a table close to the dance floor.

'Harriet! What are you doing down here?' He stood up. 'Saintclair was supposed to tell you to stay in your room. I knew I couldn't trust him.'

'He did tell me, but I wanted to come down. I'm hungry.'

'I'll have some food sent up to your room. This just isn't a place for you.' He was distracted by something over her shoulder.

Turning round, Harriet saw a young woman dancing to the sounds of lute, tambourine and flute. She was barefoot and wore sheer purple pantaloons with a gold and purple top which left her midriff exposed. Every time she moved, the bangles around her wrists and ankles jingled. Her hips rolled and undulated in fluid movements. When she lifted her bare arms above her head, a smile appeared on her painted red lips which seemed directly targeted at Archie.

'I won't stay long,' Harriet promised.

Archie shrugged. 'Oh well, please yourself.' He pulled out a chair for her, sat down again, but his eyes wandered back to the woman.

'What are the plans for tomorrow?' Harriet asked.

When he didn't reply, she slapped the back of his hand.

'What?' His eyes focused on her. 'Tomorrow? I think we're heading for Berrouaghia, but'—he gestured towards Ahmoud and the others—'as usual, neither Saintclair nor his men are particularly forthcoming with information.'

He muttered something about getting a fresh pitcher of wine and walked to the counter as two young boys brought a pile of wooden platters and large dishes of meat and vegetable stew over to their table.

Saintclair walked in, hair damp, face freshly shaven, and he'd changed into a white shirt. He ruffled the boys' hair, exchanged a few words in Arabic with them, and gave each a coin before sitting down next to her.

She focused on her breathing even though her face was hot and her whole body prickled, as if covered in goose pimples.

To hide her confusion, she spooned a generous helping of stew onto her wooden platter and started eating. Safir's might only be a backstreet tavern but the food it served was delicious. The lamb melted in the mouth, the semolina was light and fluffy, and the vegetables well done and tasty.

It took only minutes for her to finish the platter. She sponged the sauce with a piece of bread, reclined on her seat and licked her lips. This was the best meal she'd eaten for weeks. If it wasn't for the insistent, high-pitched music, she might fall asleep right here and now. It was probably time to go to her room and make the most of the bed.

Her good mood vanished when she saw Saintclair staring at her.

'It looks like you enjoyed that.'

'Yes, it was very nice.' She straightened on her chair.

The dancer in purple had been replaced by another, older, but just as agile.

'Did you see where Archie went?' She glanced at the empty space and at the untouched plate next to her. 'He said he was going for a pitcher of wine ages ago. He didn't even have anything to eat.'

'I'm sure food is the last thing on his mind right now.'

Why was he smiling that way? 'Why do you say that?'

He shrugged, sipping some wine. 'I don't want to make things difficult between you two. After all, he is your fiancé.'

She narrowed her eyes. 'I don't understand. Where is he?'

He didn't answer straight away. 'I saw him go upstairs with one of the dancers. It seemed to me that he was enjoying her conversation rather a lot.' He grinned.

'Archie can't speak Arabic.'

Then she understood. She put a hand in front of her mouth and gasped. 'Surely you're not implying that he … he …'

It was impossible. Archie was a gentleman. He wouldn't take a tavern dancer, a prostitute, to his room. That was what men like Saintclair did.

Saintclair stared over her shoulder and his smile froze. His fingers gripped his tumbler of wine so tightly the knuckles became white.

Surprised at the change in his expression, Harriet turned round. Behind her stood an officer in a French uniform.

'Mortemer,' Saintclair said between clenched teeth.

'Saintclair.' The man bowed stiffly. 'What a surprise to see you here. I should fire my informers. According to their latest reports, you're still in the mountains.'

'I didn't know I was under surveillance.'

'You're not, of course.' The man's smile stretched his thin lips. 'I'm sorry to intrude upon you in this way, Mademoiselle.'

He took off his hat, uncovering dark brown hair, the same colour as his neat beard and moustache, and bowed stiffly once again.

'Lieutenant Guy de Mortemer, French colonial army, at your service.'

He had strange eyes, she thought, repressing a shiver of revulsion. They were very dark. There was no light, no life in them. 'Lieutenant.'

She wasn't tired any longer, but curious. Something was going on between Saintclair and the lieutenant, and she wanted to know what it was.

'What do you want, Mortemer? I take it you're not here for the girls.' Saintclair reclined on his chair, stretching his legs in front of him. He drank some wine, his eyes never leaving the French officer for one second.

Mortemer smiled again. 'I want information.'

'About what?' Saintclair pulled his knife out of his pocket, pricked his thumb at the tip of the blade, as if to test its sharpness.

'Mind if I sit down?'

Saintclair gestured to an empty chair.

'There was an attack on the ammunition depot in Blida last night,' Mortemer started. 'It was the Mouzaïas.'

'Who says?'

'It bears their hallmark. Night job. Quick, efficient … deadly.'

Saintclair shrugged. 'It could be anybody with a grudge against the French. Was there much damage?'

'Five dead, all of them ours. The whole depot was destroyed. It will take weeks, months even, to restock.' Mortemer's face was grim.

'I suppose that's what happens when you bite off more than you can chew, stretch your resources over too wide a distance, and understaff your outposts. The weakest points give, eventually.'

'They didn't give, Saintclair,' Mortemer said coldly. 'The Blida depot was deliberately targeted.'

He paused and smoothed the tip of his moustache. 'You were in Blida yesterday, weren't you? Did you happen to see, or hear, anything?'

Saintclair looked at him and smiled apologetically. 'Nothing. But then again, I was rather busy with a very pretty, very demanding dancing girl.'

Mortemer held his gaze. 'As it happens, a mutual acquaintance recently sold me a map of Abdelkader's weapons and ammunitions' caches. The man in question told me you tried to get the map from him in Algiers. Now, I wonder why you'd do that.'

Harriet held her breath. He must be talking about the man she'd saved from Saintclair's clutches in Algiers. Rachid.

Saintclair took a cigar from his pocket. He lit it in the flame of a candle in the centre of the table, sucked on it a few times then relaxed in his seat.

'Rachid sold you the map? I hope you didn't pay a lot for it. It's a fake. That's why I wanted to destroy it. I didn't want the French army to be sent on a wild goose chase.'

Mortemer arched his eyebrows. 'That was very noble of you. Still, I think I'll hang on to it a while longer. Interestingly, one of the caches is very close to Bou Saada.' He paused, as if he wanted to study Saintclair's reaction, but the scout's face had disappeared behind a cloud of cigar smoke.

'How are your family these days? Your delightful mother? And your even more delightful sister?'

'Last I heard from them, they were fine. Why?' There was a steely edge to Saintclair's voice now.

'I hope to pay them my respects. I'm heading to Bou Saada in a few days to make sure there's no mishap with the new outpost we're establishing there, and to check out that rebel cache.'

'Keep away from my mother, Mortemer,' Saintclair said between his teeth. 'You're not welcome in her house.'

Mortemer let out a joyless laugh. 'It's not for you to say, my friend.' He leaned closer. 'And between you and me, I don't think you're welcome there either.'

He rose, and bowed in front of Harriet. 'Mademoiselle, I'm sure we'll meet again.' She felt sucked into the dark pits of his eyes.

'By the way,' he told Saintclair. 'I'm sending my trackers into the mountains at first light. We'll torch the Mouzaïa village and get rid of them once and for all.'

He turned around and walked out.

Saintclair cursed under his breath and poured himself a black coffee.

'Torch the village?' Harriet remembered the young shepherd they'd met in the mountains. Was he in danger? Was his family?

'Scorched earth. That's what the French army have been doing for the past ten years. Burn villages, grain stores, fields.' Saintclair's eyes were hard, his jaw set.

'But what about the people who live there?'

He looked at her, a nasty glint in his eyes. 'If they're not killed in the raid, they die of famine or they have to leave. That way, the French get the land for nothing.'

'Where do they go?'

Saintclair shrugged, threw his cigar on the floor, and stubbed it out with his boot. 'Who cares, as long as they're gone?'

He got up, signalling to Ahmoud. The two men talked with hushed voices for a while then Ahmoud slipped out with a couple of his men.

'Get back to your room now,' Saintclair said. 'I have things to do. I'll see you in the morning.'

This time, exhausted and longing for her bed, Harriet did as he said. She went upstairs, unlocked her room. Her hand on the door knob, she hesitated.

Something was bothering her, a nasty, niggling thought.

Her cheeks hot with shame, she tiptoed up to Archie's room and stuck her ear to the door. It was silly to give any credence to Saintclair's malicious gossip. Archie was too much of a gentleman to ever consider taking a tavern woman to his bed.

The sounds from behind the door told another story. The throaty chuckles, the low moans, the regular creaking of the bed … Even someone as inexperienced as Harriet understood what those noises meant.

She stifled a gasp, walked back to her room and shut her door. Her head ached, her heart throbbed, and she was overcome by a wave of nausea. She rushed to the basin on the washstand.

When it was over, she wiped her mouth with a cloth and sat on the bed.

Would she be able to face Archie tomorrow? And what about Saintclair and the others? They would make fun of her. They probably already did …

Chapter Six

They were three men short when they set off the following morning. Saintclair explained that Ahmoud and two of his companions were running errands and would catch up with them later.

Archie eyed the scout with suspicion. 'Where did he send his men to and why, I wonder?'

Harriet didn't answer but gave her horse a kick to set it on its way.

'Is everything all right, dear?' Archie leaned towards her and touched her forearm. 'You are awfully quiet.'

She glanced at him. Her sense of betrayal was so acute she even wondered if she'd ever known him at all. Yet he looked like he always did – the same familiar, closely shaven face, neat blond moustache. The same trusted blue eyes.

Ignoring the puzzled look on his face, she spurred her horse on and found herself riding next to Saintclair at the front. He turned to her, lifting his eyebrows. She didn't really want his company but the street suddenly narrowed and she'd no choice except ride beside him.

Médéa was a small town with a market square at its centre and arched buildings along its main street. A few Roman ruins were dotted around – columns and half-derelict walls, some still covered with faded, chipped mosaics. She knew of the vast ancient Roman towns further north – Tipasa, Djemila, and especially Timgad – that her father and his team helped excavate two years before. Here in Médéa, there wasn't much left.

What she noticed, however, was the large French army presence. Soldiers and cavalry officers of the colonial army, wearing red trousers, light blue coats, and matching kepi seemed to have taken over the town.

'Why are there so many of them?'

'Because of Abdelkader,' Saintclair answered.

'I thought he was no longer a threat since he lost most of his men two years ago.'

'He's still the emir, the leader of the rebellion. He won't give up that easily.'

They rode past several one-storey buildings guarded by French sentinels. It must be where that man, Lieutenant Mortemer, was based. She repressed a shiver, recalling the Lieutenant's cold, dark eyes.

'Do you think the Lieutenant carried out his threat about the

Mouzaïas?'

'Mortemer always carries out his threats.'

'You know him, don't you? Did you work for him as a scout?' she asked, curious.

He stared ahead. 'I made that mistake, once.'

'Your mother and sister live in Bou Saada. That's an oasis town in the south, isn't it? Do you get to see them often?'

He turned his head sharply. 'What business is it of yours?'

She shrugged. 'It's none of my business, of course. You seemed a little worried when Lieutenant Mortemer mentioned them yesterday.'

'I'm worried about anything and anyone Mortemer mentions. The man's a snake, a dangerous, deadly snake. Even more so now he finally has what he's been after all these months. Thanks to you.'

'You mean the map of Abdelkader's weapons caches?' she asked in a weak voice.

He nodded. 'That's right. The map I almost had in my possession, until your untimely intervention.'

The bite in his voice made her blush. He'd never let her forget her mistake.

'How was I to know you weren't some dangerous thug?' she asked, defensively. 'Anyway, you told Mortemer the map was a fake, so why did you want it so badly?'

'This is none of your concern, Miss Montague. This isn't your country, your people, or your fight. In a few months' time, when you're back sipping tea in your cosy London house, all of this will be no more than a bad memory for you.'

He picked up speed and left her behind to breathe in the cloud of dust kicked by his horse.

What fight, what people was he talking about – the French, or the tribes, the native people from this country? He seemed to care an awful lot for a man who claimed no loyalty to anyone but himself.

They rode through a surprisingly green and lush landscape, through lemon and orange groves and well tended farmland. Shrouded in blue mist, the mountains looked mysterious and unreachable, like a land of dreams. They reached a high plateau and climbed further still, overtaking wagons and carts full of supplies, people on foot carrying baskets tied to their backs with ropes and scarves.

Once in a while they met small detachments of French soldiers or cavalry. Each time, Saintclair saluted the officer in charge and exchanged a few words. Although her French wasn't fluent, Harriet understood he was asking if the road ahead was clear or if any rebels had been sighted that day.

By late morning, they reached the mountain pass overlooking Berrouaghia.

'What is that?' She pointed to a large, fenced estate lying apart from the town.

'The French penitentiary,' Saintclair said, 'the largest in the north of the country.' He pulled on the reins. 'We'll stop here for now.'

Harriet dismounted and tied her horse to the lowest branch of an olive tree.

'I think we should push ahead.' Archie approached Saintclair, a frown on his face. 'We're wasting time.' He took his hat off, mopped the sweat off his forehead, and put his hat back on.

Unhurried, Saintclair finished untying his saddlebag, pulled out a parcel with flat bread, strips of dried meat and a packet of candied dates he handed to Harriet.

'By the way, I forgot to give those to you the other day,' he said. 'They're from Slimane, the innkeeper at Blida. He said you needed sweetening.'

She gasped. 'Well, really …'

Ignoring her, Saintclair turned to Archie. 'The horses need a rest, Drake. Don't worry, we'll be in Berrouaghia soon enough.'

He went to speak to his men, sitting in the shade of a grove of pine trees.

'I bet he's waiting for Ahmoud and the other two,' Archie grumbled as he retrieved some food from his bag. 'What got into you earlier, riding away from me in that way? You should always stay with me. Don't forget we told the others that I'm your fiancé.'

She faced him, eyes sharp with temper. 'Really? So what were you doing last night with that girl?'

She left him standing there, his mouth gaping open. Flushed, and embarrassed already by her outburst, she went to sit on her own. She was behaving like a jealous woman.

Archie had been part of her small family circle for almost as long as she could remember. She admired and respected his work. Her father often commented on his scientific approach and his vast historical knowledge. Even Lord Callaghan, the haughty and notoriously hard to please Chairman of the Board of Trustees, had recently given him the responsibility of cataloguing the museum's Oriental stock. His new position kept Archie busy, and his visits had been less frequent before her father left for Algiers.

Archie was also her oldest ally against Aunt Elizabeth. He always flew to her defence when his father's older sister criticised her lack of interest in fashion or society gossip, or despaired at her passion for study. 'So what if Harriet is different? Intelligent, cultured women are so much more interesting than boring, brainless dolls,' he would say.

What a hypocrite! Harriet snorted aloud, kicking a stone with the tip of her boot. He certainly hadn't found the dancer boring last night.

She took a deep, calming breath. Why did she feel so betrayed? She shouldn't be outraged or disappointed to find Archie was like any other man – easily led astray by a beautiful woman. It wasn't as if she was in love with him. She shook her head, impatiently. The very thought of it was ludicrous.

She had no idea what being in love felt like. She didn't *ever* want to be in love. She wanted to devote herself to research and the study of ancient history. That was what her father had educated her for. He'd taught her to be calm, rational and level-headed. She could only imagine his disappointment at her shouting at Archie like one of those emotional, hysterical women he so despised.

High up in the cloudless sky, a hawk let out a piercing cry that reverberated around the rocky face of the mountains and seemed to go on forever.

'Mind if I join you?' Saintclair's shadow stretched across the rocky ground.

He didn't wait for her answer but sat on a boulder and started chewing on his bread and dried meat.

She sighed with impatience. Couldn't the man leave her alone?

'Tell me about your father.' He passed his gourd of fresh water over. 'I need to know what kind of man he is and how you think he's coping.'

At once, and much to her disgust, Harriet's eyes filled with tears. Here she was, being emotional again. She drank a long sip of water, and waited until she was sure her voice wouldn't quiver.

'My father is a tough man, Monsieur Saintclair. He's spent much of his life digging up ancient sites in Greece and Italy, and more recently in

Timgad. A few years ago he travelled to the Tripoli territories, where he discovered the Garamantes' civilisation.'

'What made him set up this expedition to the Sahara?' Saintclair took another bite of meat.

'Last year, he came across incredible sketches of rock paintings made by travellers to the region and he became obsessed with proving that the Sahara hadn't always been the desert it is now, but had once been a thriving part of the Garamantes' lost kingdom. He also wanted to see for himself the Hoggar Mountains and the fabulous treasures hidden there.'

Her voice became dreamy. She shared her father's passion about the Hoggar rock art.

'For hundreds of years, the Garamantes controlled the salt, gold, and slave caravans linking sub-Saharan regions to the Mediterranean ports,' she carried on. 'They traded with Rome and Egypt, and with the great African kingdoms from Libya and Tunisia to Morocco.'

'What treasure was he after?'

'One of the drawings featured what appeared to be gems – the emeralds mined by the Garamantes' slaves which Herodotus wrote about. My father believed he might find inscriptions referring to the location of the mines.'

The mention of the Garamantes' emeralds made his heart beat faster.

'So it was all about the Garamantes' mines … And you're telling me your father isn't a treasure hunter.' He carried on before she could protest. 'I've seen some rock paintings in the Hoggar, and further east towards the Tripoli territories too.'

'Have you really? Did you see drawings of giraffes and elephants? Of hunters and chariots?'

He smiled, amused by the enthusiasm in her voice and the wonder in her eyes. 'Indeed. There are rhinoceroses, ostriches, crocodiles and lions, as well as men and women, hunters and horse-drawn chariots.'

'What about the writing? Can you read the writing?'

Saintclair closed his eyes a moment, trying to remember how the Tuaregs described their language. 'I wish I could, but I'm afraid the lines, crosses, dots and circles that form the alphabet don't make any sense to me. The nomads of the desert say their writing represents their way of life. The lines are the legs of men, camels and gazelles travelling across the desert. The crosses are the cardinal points. The dots represent the stars and constellations leading them safely to their destination. A circle, of course, always stands for the sun.'

He opened his eyes to find her staring at him in disbelief.

'It's very poetic,' she said with a faint smile. 'I do hope my father had time to study the inscriptions before he went to Tamanrasset. He spent most of his life deciphering the ancient Garamantes' writing. As far as I know, he's the only scholar who can read it.'

'The Tuaregs would have left him in peace if he'd stayed in the Hoggar. Why on earth did he decide to go to Tamanrasset and desecrate Tin Hinan's tomb?'

'He never wanted to desecrate anything!' She pushed the top of the gourd down and handed it back to him. 'Only ignorant people would confuse the documented study of an ancient monument with—'

'Don't expect the nomads of the desert to share your enlightened view of tomb raiding, Miss Montague,' he interrupted sharply. 'Whatever you choose to call it, it shows a lack of respect for people and their customs. Your father's actions have cost many lives.'

She must have known he was right because she bowed her head. He was being a little unfair. She wasn't responsible for her father's actions after all.

'He would never have knowingly put his men in danger. They were his colleagues, his friends.' She choked on the last words, and wiped her eyes roughly with the back of her hand.

'There's something I don't understand. The location of Tin Hinan's tomb has been a well-guarded secret for centuries,' Saintclair resumed speaking. 'Even I, who spent years with the Tuaregs in the far south, was never told of its location. All I know is that it's in an oasis near Tamanrasset. So how did your father find it?'

She shook her head. 'I don't know.'

They were silent for a while. There was something else he wanted to ask.

'What do you know about the Barbarossa treasure?'

If she was surprised by his sudden question, she didn't show it. She frowned in concentration.

'I tried to gather information about it when I received the map but couldn't find very much. All I know is that Khayr ad Dīn – that was Barbarossa's real name – looted and pillaged the coasts of France and

Italy two years before his death. When he finally decided to return to Istanbul, he set sail with over one hundred galleys filled with loot and captives for the Pasha's harems. Only fifty actually arrived. He claimed the others sank in a storm. Several of his men, however, revealed he'd buried a large part of the loot in a secret location because he didn't want to surrender it to his master, the Great Pasha of Constantinople. Nobody knew where to look for it, nobody knew if it was even true …'

She paused and smiled. 'Until my father found the map in Algiers.'

'And he didn't tell anyone but you about it?'

She shook her head. 'I don't think so. Not even Archie.'

He arched his eyebrows. 'That's strange, don't you think? It looks like your father was planning to keep Barbarossa's treasure for himself.'

'No! Of course not!' She stood up, indignant. 'My father is an honest man. 'Everything he does is for the British Museum.'

'If you say so … I know from experience that greed does strange things to men, even the most upright, law-abiding citizens.'

'Not all men have mercenary motives, you know,' she retorted. 'Some, like my father and Archie, devote their whole life to research and the advancement of knowledge.'

'Their whole life? Really?' He pulled a face. He couldn't understand why he was suddenly so annoyed at Harriet Montague's seemingly boundless admiration for her fiancé. He rolled the sleeves of his white shirt to his elbows.

'What will you do with Barbarossa's treasure when you find it?' she asked, her grey eyes serious.

'I haven't thought about it yet,' he lied. 'I'll travel around, I suppose, enjoy myself.'

'You could do a lot of good with it. Build schools, orphanages, housing and hospitals.'

He let out a short laugh and shook his head. 'I think you're mistaking me for somebody else entirely, Miss Montague. I'm no philanthropist.'

Her lip took a scornful downward curve, her eyes becoming cool. He didn't like it, but in the end, what did it matter? Let her believe what she wanted.

'I see … I would like a few moments to myself, if you don't mind.' She pulled her sketch pad and pencil from her bag, sitting down to sketch the scenery.

He stared at the line of the horizon, at the rugged mountain summits, the hawks gliding in the skies like spirits, casting their shadow on the plains below. His glance slid to Harriet, drawing with application, a view of the mountains and the valley. She was pale today. The purple shadows under her eyes a sure sign she hadn't slept well. She was jumpy, emotional, and angry. He turned away, a satisfied smile on his lips. His plan had worked.

What he should do now was aggravate the rift between the lovers, find another woman or two for Drake to enjoy. He should be as obnoxious as he could towards her, unsettle her, and push her all the way back to Algiers.

Absent-mindedly, he lifted a hand to the shoulder which still bore the faintest trace of her teeth. The woman knew how to put up a fight, he'd grant her that. Other memories assailed him. The feel of her body against his, of her breasts pressed against his back and her legs encircling his waist when she'd attacked him down in the Algiers docks.

He loosened the collar of his shirt, feeling a rush of heat in his blood.

Drake was a fool. What did he need a dancing girl for when he had a woman like Harriet Montague to warm his bed?

They would be in Boggar in a couple of days. By then, if he played his cards right, Harriet Montague would be so confused about him and so mad at her fiancé that she'd beg to be sent back to Algiers. No way would he risk her life, and the life of others, by taking her any further.

He clenched his jaw. There were other reasons why he didn't want her to come to Tamanrasset. Her father was most probably dead by now and he wanted to spare her the ordeal of facing his killers. He knew all too well how that felt.

He pulled his hat down to shelter his eyes from the fierce sunshine and stood up to give the signal to pack up. Ahmoud and the others would join them shortly. Other dangers awaited in Berrouaghia.

Chapter Seven

They didn't reach Berrouaghia. The mountain road was so busy, with soldiers on foot and on horses, carts, and wagons carrying ammunitions and supplies that it took all afternoon to ride down into the valley. The sun was setting, blood red, behind the darkened peaks of the Atlas mountain range, and the muezzin was calling the faithful to prayer when they rode through the gates of Sour Djouab, a fortified village lying at the entrance of the valley.

Saintclair led them into a maze of alleyways which reminded Harriet of the Algiers kasbah. They might be safe enough for now, but it would definitely not be a good idea to venture there alone after nightfall. They left their horses in a small stable and carried their saddlebags with them to the nearby inn where an old woman dressed in a long white robe sat in the doorway. She led them into a shabby front room with stained, yellow walls and a dirty floor. Saintclair pointed at Harriet and told the woman something in Arabic which made her laugh whole-heartedly as she handed him a bunch of keys.

'Do we have to stay in this fleapit?' Archie pursed his lips as he looked around.

'I stay with people I trust not to slit our throat while we're sleeping,' Saintclair said. He grinned and added, 'You'll change your mind about this place later on when the dancers arrive.'

'I really don't know what you mean …' Archie muttered, but the glint in his eyes didn't escape Harriet's attention.

She breathed in sharply. Surely he wasn't planning on taking another girl to his room tonight?

'The best room is for you, Miss Montague,' Saintclair declared. He handed her a large brass key with a red tassel tied to it. 'It's your lucky night. They usually keep it for important dignitaries.'

'Important dignitaries? In this place?' Now it was her turn to look around the inn with doubt.

'It's also the furthest from the stairs. You won't be disturbed by comings and goings.'

Her fingers gripped the key more tightly as understanding dawned. What he meant of course was that the men, Archie included, would be able to take women up to their rooms and she'd be none the wiser.

'Very well.'

She marched up the staircase, her bag on her shoulder, with as much dignity as she could muster. This journey was turning into a farce, with Saintclair and Archie obviously more concerned with sampling the delights of local dancing girls than rescuing her father from the Tuaregs. She stomped now, her nerves so raw she didn't know if she wanted to laugh or cry.

A few minutes later, she was doing both at the same time. The key Saintclair had given her was stuck in the lock of the bedroom door and despite her best efforts it wasn't shifting. No way was she going back downstairs to ask for help. Saintclair and the others would only make fun of her. She gave the door a kick and burst into tears.

'Let me help.'

He was behind her. As usual, she hadn't heard him approach.

She spun around, almost bumping into his chest. 'I can't seem t-to … t-turn the … key.' She bowed her head, embarrassed to be caught sobbing over such a trivial matter.

'There's no need to cry.' His voice was surprisingly gentle, his eyes warm, almost kind, and for once he didn't look like he wanted to make fun of her. He wriggled the key in the lock a few times until finally it turned. The door creaked open.

He took her bag and carried it into the room.

She wiped her tears with the back of her hands, sniffled a few times, and followed him in. If this was the room reserved for dignitaries, she didn't want to see what the ordinary ones looked like.

The large bed was partly hidden by a gold-coloured curtain that clashed with the gaudy red counterpane and cushions. The walls were covered with a red and yellow paint so garish it hurt her eyes. On one side of the bed was a full-length mirror and on the opposite wall hang the painting of a woman. A very nude woman, in a very unusual position.

'It *is* colourful,' she said quickly, looking away from the painting, conscious her cheeks were probably as red as the bed covers.

She knew what this place was now. It wasn't an inn. Why wasn't she surprised? 'You've brought us to a brothel, haven't you?'

Saintclair arched his eyebrows as if shocked. 'Miss Montague, I can assure you that—' But his lips twitched and there was a glint in his eyes.

'Never mind. Thank you for helping me with the door. That will be all,' she said, not caring if she sounded like a queen dismissing a servant. 'By the way, what did you tell that old woman when we arrived?'

He shrugged. 'I made something up to ensure you'd have the best room. It's not important what.'

She narrowed her eyes. 'What did you tell her?'

'You don't really want to know.'

'Yes, I do,' she insisted. 'I want to know why she looked at me with a silly grin on her face.'

'You won't like it,' he objected.

'I insist, Monsieur Saintclair.'

He sighed. 'I told her I abducted you from your father and was planning to ravish you later tonight. That's why I wanted the largest, softest bed.'

'What?' She almost shrieked.

'I did warn you.' He walked towards the door. 'Someone will bring you hot water and food in a short while. I strongly advise you stay in here and lock your door. Wandering out wouldn't be a good idea.'

He looked at the key in the palm of his hand. 'Actually, now that I think about it, it might be wiser if I keep the key, just in case you get it stuck in the door again, of course.'

'You wouldn't dare!' She started towards him, but wasn't fast enough.

He was out of the room and she heard the key turn.

'Saintclair! Open this door right now!' She slammed her fists on the door, hearing his footsteps down the corridor. She banged on the door a few more times, but it was useless.

She walked to the bed and pulled back the covers, her lips pursed in distaste. At least the sheets were clean, but she'd have to block any thought of what went on in that bed before she'd be able to sleep tonight. She examined her surroundings in more detail. Her eyes skimmed over the painting, then came back to it. This time it wasn't the woman's nude body that brought a hot flush to her cheeks and dried her throat. It was her eyes – dark, full of surrender, desire and anticipation. She shuddered, feeling a strange heat creep inside her. She crossed her arms on her chest and made herself look away.

She caught sight of her reflection in the mirror on the other side of the bed. Her lips parted and she breathed faster. Would she ever look at a man with the same feverish abandon? She swallowed hard and walked around the bedroom. Concealed behind a red curtain was a door she hadn't noticed before. It led to a tiny bathroom, an unexpected luxury in this place. She walked back into the room and stood at the latticed window. The room overlooked a small courtyard where a couple of ragged palm trees stood in the grey-blue light of dusk.

The sound of a key in the lock made her turn round. Saintclair was back. She'd have a word or two to say to him. He had no right keeping her locked up in this room.

But it wasn't Saintclair who walked in. It was the old woman and a young girl. The girl carried two large buckets of water into the washroom. She kept her eyes averted and never looked once at Harriet. The old woman put a tray of food on the rickety dressing table and busied herself with lighting an oil lamp.

When she'd finished, she smiled her toothless smile and walked back to the door.

'Wait!' Harriet cried out. 'Give me the key.' She pointed to the door and made the gesture of turning a key in the lock.

The woman shook her head and spoke very fast. There was a glint of panic in her eyes. She must be following Saintclair's orders and feared he'd be angry if she surrendered the key. The last thing Harriet wanted was for an old woman to be scared because of her.

She shrugged, defeated. 'It doesn't matter,' she whispered, watching the door close again and hearing the key turn in the lock.

Lucas toyed with the key the old woman had given him before slipping it inside the pocket of his waistcoat. At least he needn't worry about Harriet Montague for now. She couldn't get into any trouble tonight. She'd be safely tucked in that big, soft bed, probably cursing him all the way to the devil and back. Or crying. His eyes grew sombre. He hadn't liked seeing her cry before. It had tugged at him, made him feel guilty, uncomfortable. And yet, he should be satisfied. Despite the brave face she put on, she was weakening. He only had to push a little harder for her to decide to give up this ridiculous idea of travelling the desert.

He sat at the table set aside for him and his men in the darkest corner of the room, away from all the dancing and the gambling. They'd finished eating and were sipping strong, black coffee. He lit a cigar, tasted the smoke, blew it out and looked at Drake. The Englishman was the only one drinking wine. He emptied the pitcher into his tumbler, gulped it down, oblivious to the men's tense looks, their hushed voices. Lucas leaned back in his chair, confident the laudanum he'd slipped into the wine earlier would soon take effect.

Drake slouched on the table. 'Damn this place,' he muttered. 'Where are the pretty dancers you promised me, Saintclair?'

He craned his neck to catch a glimpse of the dance floor where a woman moved and swirled to the wild tunes of tambourines, zurnas and flutes. 'This one is way past her prime.'

'What do you care when your lovely fiancée is all alone in that big bed, Drake?' Lucas asked. Not that he'd any intention of relinquishing the key to her bedroom to anyone, even her fiancé. His fingers tapped impatiently on the table.

Archie hiccupped. 'Back off, S-Saintclair! You've no business f-finding Harriet lovely. She's mine. All mine.' He threw a black glance to Lucas. 'And I tell you what. Yeah, she's pretty, and clever, and wild too … Exactly what a man wants between the sheets.' He chuckled and smacked his lips.

'You're a lucky man, Drake.' Lucas tightened his hold on the cigar, so much it snapped in two. He cursed. That was a waste of a good cigar. It was none of his business if Drake and Harriet Montague slept together. Why then did he feel like punching the man?

Anyway, why was Drake still awake? He had a remarkable resistance to drugs. The dose he'd slipped into his wine would have been enough to put an ox to sleep.

'She's wild and hot … and sh-she's all m-ine,' Drake repeated, slurring his words now. He burst out laughing then he muttered something unintelligible, dropped his goblet of wine and collapsed on the table.

At last! Lucas signalled to two of his men to take him away. He didn't even open his eyes when they lifted him up and carried him upstairs to his room. He would be dead to the world until the following morning. To be on the safe side, he asked the men to lock him in his room too.

Drake and Harriet's relationship was odd, certainly. Lucas frowned. The Englishman didn't behave like a besotted fiancé. There was something callous about the way he'd just spoken of her. Maybe he saw Harriet as a way to further his position at the British Museum. As for her … He narrowed his eyes. She seemed upset enough when she found out that Drake had bedded a dancing girl. One thing was certain. She wasn't afraid of braving social conventions and following him across Europe and North Africa openly, as his mistress. She must be very much in love with him.

Ahmoud walked in. He looked around, and nodded. Everything was in place. Lucas forgot all about Harriet and focused on the task ahead. He gestured to his men. They all got up but for one who would stay at the inn. They wore dark clothing and grim, purposeful expressions on their faces as they slipped out of the tavern and dissolved into the shadows.

Chapter Eight

'The French took over the fort Abdelkader built when he controlled the area.' Saintclair gestured towards the cluster of buildings surrounded by a wall and fortification.

In front of them, the steppes stretched as far as the eye could see. They were the reason this region had been, and still was, of vital importance both to the rebels and to the French who sought to control the country.

'Boghar overlooks the caravan trails used by the nomads from the Sahara when they come to the North of the country,' Saintclair explained.

'What are those mountains over there?' Harriet pointed to the faint outline of a mountain range in the far distance.

'The Djebel Amour.'

'What a beautiful, romantic name.' Harriet smiled.

'There's nothing romantic about it,' he answered. 'It's just the name of the main tribe who live in the area.'

Her smile vanished, wiped by the sharpness of his tone. She stared at the landscape stretching in front of her. It wasn't only the scenery that was breathtaking, with groves of pine, junipers and thujas trees, waterfalls and streams meandering between the rocks. The light was different here too. The sky was higher, bigger.

There seemed to be a lot going on around the French fort, with troops on foot and horses moving carts, cannons and weapons.

'Looks like the French are getting ready for an attack,' Archie remarked.

He rubbed his pale, unshaven face, pulled his hat down over his bloodshot eyes. He'd hardly talked all day and even seemed half-asleep at times, about to fall off his horse. And he reeked of cheap wine. What had got into him? He didn't behave like the Archie she knew any more. Only a week before, she'd never have believed he drank so much or took tavern girls to his bed.

'I guess we'll soon find out,' Saintclair said.

A small detachment of French cavalry was riding their way. Saintclair raised his hand, both in salute to the French chasseurs and to signal his men to stop. The French rode up to them, a hostile look on their faces. As soon as they halted, they put their hands on the sabres or rifles tucked in a harness on their sides. The officer in charge asked Saintclair for travelling documents in a tense voice.

'Nobody's allowed in the fort today,' he said after checking the papers and handing them back.

'Has something happened?' Saintclair folded the documents and put them back in the leather pouch that hung across his body.

'There was a jailbreak at the penitentiary last night,' the French officer answered. 'El-Berkani and three of his lieutenants escaped. There's no trace of them.'

Saintclair raised his eyebrows. 'They'll be far away by now.'

The man tightened his lips, the resolve on his face plain. 'We'll get them. Lieutenant Mortemer has just arrived with his best trackers. If anyone can catch El-Berkani, they can.' He bowed his head slightly, touched the brim of his kepi and turned around, followed by the rest of the chasseurs.

'Who is El-Berkani?' Archie asked as they set off again.

'One of Abdelkader's most trusted men,' Saintclair replied. 'He was taken two years ago, along with the emir's army.'

'Blast! Things are getting more dangerous by the day!' Archie pushed his hat back on his forehead and leaned over to Harriet. 'That's it, dear. Saintclair was right all along. This isn't the place for you. I'm sending you back to Algiers, and that's final.'

Cold rage rose inside her, choking her. 'Really? So you agree with Saintclair now … That must be why you've embraced his ways regarding drinking and women. Well, I know what your game is, *dear,*' she replied, striving hard to keep calm. 'You can drink yourself into a stupor and sleep with dancing girls every night if you want, but you won't get rid of me so easily. I told you before, I am going all the way to Tamanrasset, whether you and Saintclair like it or not.'

She gave her horse a sharp kick and trotted off, but not before she heard Saintclair laugh.

'I see the candied dates did nothing to sweeten your fiancée's temper, Drake. She's as bitter as a dozen lemons.'

That did it. She gripped the reins hard and spurred the horse. What right had he to make fun of her?

Her horse picked up speed, then broke into a full gallop and veered off the road to race over the steppe. It jumped over streams and prickly bushes. The sound of its hooves hammering the ground resonated like thunder, as fast and loud as her heartbeat. The horse's gallop made the blood rush in her veins. She had never ridden so fast, so freely before, and for a moment it was exhilarating.

Then her *cheche* got caught in a branch, her hair fell down onto her shoulders. She tried pulling on the reins, but the horse, drunk on speed and the scents of water and vegetation, didn't respond. Fear tightened around her chest. She couldn't control her horse any longer, all she could do was hang onto the reins. Hopefully, it would soon exhaust itself and slow down. She only prayed the beast wouldn't stumble and injure itself on the rocks or the prickly bushes before then.

She caught movement from the corner of her eye. A black horse was gaining ground. When he was next to her, the rider leaned over, seized her reins and pulled. They rode side by side for what felt like long minutes. Then the horses slowed down and came to a stop.

'What are you trying to do? Kill your horse?'

Saintclair's eyes flashed with fury. He dropped the reins, gripped the collar of her tunic and twisted her to one side, almost lifting her off the saddle to pull her closer. So close their legs touched. So close she saw the yellow specks inside the pale blue iris of his eyes and felt his warm breath on her face.

'I don't care if you break your neck, but I care about that horse getting injured because of a foolish, inexperienced rider. If you ever try anything like that again, I'll strap you onto a mule and send you back to Algiers, and nothing you say will make a blind bit of difference. Is that clear?'

Her throat was too tight to answer.

He shook her a little. 'Is that clear?'

'Yes,' she whispered.

He didn't release his grip. Instead, he yanked her to him and kissed her. It wasn't a gentle kiss. It was savage, an echo of the look in his eyes moments before. His mouth moved over hers, prised her lips open, took possession. And her heart stopped.

Their horses stomped, shifted, prompting her out of her daze. She pulled away and slapped his face. With a growl, he pulled back, still holding her. His eyes searched, kept her under their spell, before finally releasing her.

Without a word, he turned his horse and started back towards the others.

She remained frozen on the spot. Her legs, her hands wouldn't respond. Her lips throbbed. She licked them and tasted him. Her heart leapt in her chest. It beat so hard it hurt.

Saintclair stopped and turned round. 'What are you waiting for?'

She swallowed hard, applied a gentle pressure on the horse's sides with her knees. Her hands shook, her legs felt weak. The horse was so tired from its race across the steppe it obeyed her prompting, however slight. She forced herself to look at Saintclair when she came close to him, willing her eyes to convey nothing but the contempt she felt for him. No way would she let him see that she was trembling.

He didn't have time for this.

He narrowed his eyes, watching her ride up to him, sitting straight in the saddle, her head high, her eyes defiant and full of scorn. He spurred his horse as soon as she caught up with him, impatient and as much annoyed with himself for kissing her as he'd been with her for riding away in a temper and almost getting herself killed.

He shouldn't have kissed her. It was the wrong place, the wrong time. He just hadn't been able to resist.

After returning to the tavern the night before, he'd toyed with the key to her room for several tantalising minutes, imagining what it would feel like to wake her with long, lingering kisses. His lips would first touch the palm of her hand, then the tender skin of her wrist, next trail slowly up to her collarbone and along the side of her throat, before finally ravishing her mouth. She might be reluctant at first. She might even scream at him to leave her alone, but something told him she wouldn't fight him for long. She was attracted to him. It was plain from the way she looked at him, from the way her breathing became faster and her face flushed the most delightful pink every time he came close to her. The woman puzzled him. She acted like an innocent, yet according to Drake, she was no timid virgin.

The fact Harriet Montague belonged to another man didn't bother Lucas at all, just the opposite. Experienced women were easier to deal with. Bedding a virgin brought far too many complications. Of course, once she slept with him she'd have to return to Algiers. Lucas would make sure of it, if necessary by using a little blackmail.

Last night, however, he decided against going up to Harriet Montague's room. Instead he ordered a pitcher of wine to kill the fire that images of her in that big red bed ignited inside him. And put the key back into his pocket.

He gave his horse a kick and cursed himself again.

Kissing her had been a bad idea. It had done nothing to cool his heated blood and was foolhardy. What if Drake had seen them? He needed this mission. Too many people depended on him. The problem was, he hadn't been thinking. His brain stopped working the second he stared into her grey eyes.

And now he'd tasted her, he wanted more.

It was market day at Ksar el boukhari, the largest fortified village of the area. The market was in full swing when they arrived. A riot of colours, sounds, and smells, it covered the whole of the central square. There were stalls selling rugs, baskets, camel-wool burnous and leatherwork, as well as fresh produce, poultry and goats.

'Miss Montague's horse needs seeing to, it's limping,' Saintclair decreed as they rode off the square into a quiet street. He told Archie and the men to find a stabling block and have a wander around while they found a blacksmith.

'Do I really need to come with you?' she started, anxious not to be alone with him. 'I'd rather take a look at the market—'

'It's your horse, your responsibility.' The look in his eyes silenced any further protest.

They dismounted and led their horses through narrow alleys up to a workshop at the edge of the village. The man working the forge was a giant, and the scariest looking man Harriet had ever seen. His upper body was covered with a thick leather apron, his forearms with leather plates. He held huge iron tongs in his gloved hands. Standing in front of the fire, his black hair tied back and his face smeared with soot, he reminded Harriet of a demon from hell.

Saintclair walked up to him, touched his shoulder. The blacksmith dropped his tongs, grabbed Saintclair's hand, and enfolded him into his arms in a warm greeting. The two men talked for a short while then Saintclair pointed to Harriet's horse. The big man gave her a sunny smile before walking to the horse and delicately lifting its hind leg in his enormous hands. He shook his head.

'It needs reshoeing,' Saintclair told her a moment later. 'Akhtar can do it later, but it means we have to stay here tonight. I was planning to push further south.'

He tied her horse to a post outside the forge and turned to her. 'Your little tantrum is costing us time we don't have. It might have been worse, I suppose. It might have cost us a good horse.'

He was right, of course. It was lucky the horse wasn't seriously injured. She followed him back to the market square. She would have liked to touch the fine woollen cloaks, feel the rugs woven with rich earthy colours, try on an intricate leather belt or a finely chiselled silver necklace. Her mouth watered in front of baskets of plump figs, candied apricots, trays of halva and pastries scented with honey and orange blossom, but Saintclair strode out in front, slicing through the market crowd, and she dared not stop.

An uneasy feeling crept along her back as she ran to keep up with him. Someone was watching her. She spun round and bumped into a man wearing Tuareg clothing. A headdress covered his face, but when she glanced up she saw that his eyes were blue! As he lifted his hand to shelter his eyes from the sun, his silver ring caught the light and she gasped. She'd seen such a ring before, she was sure of it, but where?

The man mumbled an apology in Arabic and walked away.

'Wait!' she called. 'Who are you?'

He didn't hear her. Was she imagining things or had he been following her?

She felt an insistent tugging at her side and looked down. A small boy was pulling at her tunic. He held a basket filled with candied fruit and almonds. His eyes were huge, his face streaked with dirt. A fez hat perched on his matted hair.

Harriet crouched down to his height. 'How much?' she asked in Arabic, pointing to the basket.

'*Kamsa*,' the boy said, showing five fingers.

'Five dinars,' she repeated in English, pulling coins out of her purse.

The boy's face lit up with a smile. He dipped into the basket and chose some fruit for her. Suddenly the square erupted with the thunder of horses galloping through in clouds of dust, of people screaming and shouting. Harriet stood up and instinctively pulled the boy against her. There must have been over fifty French soldiers riding at speed through the market, trampling on people, stalls and animals. They overturned urns, jars and baskets, and used their leather whips to disperse what was left of the crowd.

The boy pressed his shaking body against hers. She had to get him to safety before they got crushed. She grabbed his basket, held his hand tight, and pulled him behind her. They ran through the chaos, ducked under overturned market booths, jumped over the fragments of broken oil jars. All the time she managed to avoid the soldiers' whips and the hooves of their massive horses. Still holding the boy's hand and his small basket, she ran to the safety of a side street and found an empty doorway where they could hide.

Why were French soldiers destroying the market? Why the indiscriminate killing? There'd been children, women and old men in the square. Images of corpses lying on the ground among the wreckage filled her eyes. She could still hear the screams as people tried to escape, blood running down their faces.

She closed her eyes and clung to the boy. They remained hidden a long time, until the streets became quiet, until everyone had fled. The market square now offered a scene of utter carnage and devastation. The boy took hold of her hand and pulled her along in the direction of the blacksmith. They walked fast, careful to keep their heads down so as not to attract the attention of the soldiers keeping watch on every street corner. He pointed to a small adobe house with a flat roof covered with palm branches at the end of the street. Letting go of Harriet's hand, he grabbed his basket and started running.

Then everything happened too fast.

'*Arrête*!' A soldier shouted from behind.

Harriet turned, opened her eyes in disbelief as she watched the man lift his rifle onto his shoulder and aim at the boy.

She shouted in alarm but the boy carried on running.

The noise of the shot cracked like thunder. Hit in the back, the little boy collapsed onto the ground, only a few feet from his house.

'No! Oh, my God, no!'

Harriet ran so fast her heart hammered in her chest. She knelt next to the boy's lifeless body and turned him over gently. His eyes were already glazed. Blood stained the front of his *djellabah*. She gathered him close, rocked his small body against her. In the dust next to his overturned basket lay a few candied almonds and his tiny fez hat.

'Why? Why?' she repeated, tears streaming down her face.

Alerted by the noise, people opened their doors and ventured out. When they saw the boy lying in the street, women started crying. A man came out of the adobe house. He stared at the boy in disbelief before carefully lifting him in his arms. Soon he was surrounded by people who wailed and cried.

More French soldiers arrived. They fired shots in the air to disperse the crowd.

'Harriet!'

She knelt in the dust, numb, unable to move. She heard Archie's voice in the distance, but it was Saintclair who got to her first and pulled her up.

'What happened?' he asked, holding her against him.

'He was only a boy, he didn't do anything wrong,' she sobbed, pressing her face against his chest.

He pulled her turban off to stroke her hair, put his hand on the nape of her neck to hold her still and close. She heard the steady beat of his heart against her cheek, felt his warmth surrounding her. If only she could stay like this, safe and surrounded by his strength, and forget the horror of the boy's death.

'Harriet, are you all right?' Archie was now next to her.

'Here, Drake. You'd better take care of her.' Saintclair pulled away slowly and stood back.

'Poor dear.' Archie put his arm around her shoulders, kissed the top of her head. 'Let's get you away from here.'

Harriet nodded, wiped her cheeks with her sleeve and stiffened. The soldier who had shot the boy was here, right in front of her. Before either Archie or Saintclair could hold her back, she marched up to him.

'Why did you shoot that little boy?' she asked in her hesitant French.

The man shrugged then spat on the ground. 'He should've stopped like I told him to. For all I knew, he was going to warn the rebels.'

'He was a child!'

She wanted to make him understand what he'd done.

'The rebels use children and women. You can't trust anyone in this bloody country.' The soldier looked at her with suspicion. 'Anyway, what's it to you?'

A strong hand took hold of her elbow, pulling her away.

'Come with me.' Saintclair guided her out of the crowd.

'He was the man who shot the boy. We must see that he's punished!' she protested, trying to shake him off.

He stopped and looked down at her. 'If you want to get shot too, you're going about it the right way,' he said in a low voice. 'There's nothing you can do for the boy now.'

She managed to pull away. This time, she was angry. A life had been lost, for no reason. A little boy's life. And no one cared. 'You didn't see his father's eyes when he took him in his arms. You didn't hear the women cry.' Her voice broke, tears spilling down her cheeks all over again. 'How can you be so cold, so heartless? You obviously have no idea what it's like to lose someone you love.'

He spun her around until she faced him and held her arms so tight it hurt.

A storm darkened his pale blue eyes.

'Obviously.'

He released her and walked away.

Chapter Nine

The streets were empty. The French soldiers had decreed a curfew and the ksar was mourning its dead. In the small inn at the edge of the village where they were staying, nobody was in the mood for talking, playing cards or listening to music. Harriet retreated to her tiny, airless bedroom immediately after the evening meal. She pulled off her boots, slipped out of her trousers and tunic, and crawled into bed. She was so tired it should have taken only minutes to fall asleep, but she kept seeing the boy's eyes – his huge, lifeless eyes – and the red stain on his clothing.

One life lost, and why? Because a French soldier made a mistake. Or rather, because he didn't care whether firing his rifle was a mistake or not. The boy's life hadn't mattered to him. How frightening it was to realise not everybody believed human life was precious and sacred. What about the Tuaregs who held her father prisoner? Did they care about his life at all, or was he valuable only because of the ransom? Would they kill him if they didn't get the money soon? Tamanrasset was still a long way away.

It was after midnight and she was wide awake. She remembered the terrace at the back of the tavern. It was bound to be deserted at this time of night, and fresh air was exactly what she needed. She jumped out of bed, pulled her boots and her tunic on. As an afterthought, she wrapped her belt around her waist and slid her dagger in the scabbard. Downstairs, the tavern was dark and empty. She pushed the back door and found her way out into the courtyard and the terrace.

The light of the moon and stars shimmered on the city walls and made huge, ghostly shadows on the steppe below. Spellbound, Harriet walked to the edge of the garden and leaned on the wall, holding her breath, afraid that any sound, any movement would make the magic disappear.

'Beautiful, isn't it?'

She let out a cry and spun round. Saintclair leaned against the wall, completely still, steeped in shadows. It was no wonder she hadn't seen him.

'It's the most magical night I've ever seen,' she agreed.

'Wait until we are in Bou Saada. Over there, every night is enchanted.'

She looked up, surprised. 'Why are we going to Bou Saada? It's out of our way.'

'After what happened here today, I want to check on my people. It won't delay us too much, I promise,' he answered. 'Anyway, what are you doing out here all on your own? It's not safe.'

Never had she agreed with him more than now, as she watched him move out of the shadows towards her. Like a feline gauging its prey, he walked in silent, supple strides, his eyes never leaving hers for a second.

'It was too hot. I couldn't sleep. I think I'll go back to my room now.' But her legs felt like lead and she didn't move.

Now he was in front of her, and it was too late.

He put his hands on the parapet, caging her in. She retreated until the wall dug into her back. Although he wasn't touching her, his heat radiated onto her body. The moonlight cast shadows on his face and lit his eyes with a metallic silver glow. Her breath caught in her throat as he bent down, slowly, inexorably, his eyes still holding hers in a silent challenge. Blood raced through her veins, her pulse beat hard. He was going to kiss her. She should move, right now. Instead she tilted her head up towards him.

His mouth was warm, smelled of coffee and cigar smoke. His lips brushed hers, teased them open. It was nothing like the deep, savage kiss he'd given her before. It was slow and confident. It was the kiss of a man who had all the time in the world and knew he was going to get more. Much more.

At last, she struggled to free herself. 'No, Saintclair, I don't want you to …'

'Don't you want me to do this?'

His hands leisurely slid up and down her arms, from her wrists to her shoulders, awakening ripples of sensations all over her body.

'And this?'

His lips claimed hers again. This time they were more demanding. He slid his hands behind her, clasped them around her waist and pulled her tightly against him. The buckle of his belt, the buttons of his leather waistcoat and the hard heat of his body imprinted on her.

She wanted this, his lips on hers, his hands on her skin. The shocking realisation made her gasp. His body moulded hers. His chest was broad and unyielding. She should move away now, she should … His hands stroked her hips in slow circles and she stopped thinking. She closed her eyes and slid into the darkness, the softness of his kiss.

He bent her waist backward, ran his lips along her throat and into the opening of her tunic, down to the spot where her pulse beat wildly. The rough stubble on his cheeks scraped her skin, light and insistent, adding to the myriad of sensations overwhelming her. Letting out a soft groan, he lifted her up and held her in his arms to kiss her mouth again. Every inch of her was aware of him and longing for his touch. She lifted a tentative hand to his shoulder. Her hips arched towards his. She never imagined kissing a man could feel like this, never knew that it could set her body ablaze and make her lose control.

'Shall we go up to my room or shall we get comfortable out here?'

It was like a slap in the face.

She let out a cry, pressed the palms of her hands to his chest to push him away. He didn't budge an inch.

'Let go of me at once or—'

'What will you do this time? Hit me, bite me again?' His voice was low and deep, his smile mocking. 'Listen, darling, I don't believe in wasting opportunities to have a good time.'

'Don't call me darling. You are mistaking me for one of your cheap dancing girls.' She wriggled against him.

He threw his head back and let out a soft laugh. 'There's nothing cheap about them, and from where I'm standing you're not that different. At least they don't make a fuss and pretend they're not enjoying themselves.'

She bit her lower lip and thanked the darkness for hiding the violent blush she felt spreading like wildfire all over her face and throat. She'd enjoyed his kiss a little too much and he knew it.

When he bent down to kiss her again, she tried to break free, but his arms were like bands of steel around her. He wasn't leaving her any choice. She slid her hand to her waist and pulled her dagger out. In a flash she brought it up and held the sharp tip to his chest.

'A knife? I think I prefer those sharp teeth of yours.' He stepped back, a smirk on his face. 'Come on, give it to me. You're going to hurt yourself.'

'Move back right now. If you don't, I will …'

'Kill me? I don't think so.'

He caught her wrist and shook the dagger out. It fell to the ground with a metallic sound.

'Can we start again where we left off? I'm getting a little impatient.' Still holding her wrist, he pulled her to him and clasped his other hand firmly on her hip to pull her against his heat.

She said the first thing that came to her mind. 'Archie will be very angry when he finds out.'

'Then we won't tell him. What he doesn't know can't hurt him.' He sighed. 'It's not as if he's playing fair with you, is it?'

There was nothing she could say to that.

He put a finger on her mouth before she could talk and traced the outline of her lips. And when she turned away, he buried his face in her neck. His mouth lingered, nipped at her skin between her earlobe and her shoulder. She stiffened, clenched her fists. She didn't want to respond. She didn't want to feel weak and warm and shivery all at once. Her fingers went up to his shoulders, clinging for support.

He tugged at the collar of her tunic to loosen it, pulled her chemise down, and his mouth was on the swelling of her breasts. She threw her head back and he whispered something against her skin, his breath warm and fast. Then his hands closed onto the softness of her hips and dug in.

If only she could lose herself in the whirlwind and stop thinking, just exist and feel. If only she could shut out the nagging voice whispering from a corner of her mind that if she had the slightest crumb of dignity she'd stop him now.

Saintclair was right. She was no better than a tavern girl. No, she was worse … she didn't do this for subsistence or money. She was actually enjoying it.

Gathering the last of her self-control, she stiffened in his arms.

'Listen to me, please, Saintclair. I told you before. I don't want this.'

He pulled away, his gaze heavy, his eyes dark.

'I didn't think you were the type to force a woman,' she added.

This time he let go of her and stepped back.

Her words hurt, like a stab to the heart.

Of course he wouldn't force a woman, not ever.

How beautiful she looked, drenched in moonlight, her lips swollen from his kisses, her eyes, at the same time wild and inviting, her hair threads of silver on her shoulders. Her body was soft and pliable, his for the taking. Her chest heaved, pale and white in the moonlight. The golden pendant rested in the groove between her breasts. His fingers ached to follow the tempting line, pull her chemise down all the way this time. He wanted to touch her, taste her. He swallowed hard, balling his fists at his sides.

What was he thinking? His desire for the woman was taking over, hot and throbbing. It was one thing to tease her and make her uncomfortable so that continuing the journey with both her fiancé and him would be impossible. Give her no option but to return to Algiers. It was another altogether to ignore her protests, her pleas for him to stop. He hadn't even backed down when she drew her dagger and pointed it at his chest.

Damn, she was right. He'd been about to force himself on her and take her there and then. He lowered his head, disgusted.

'Go back to your room.'

She breathed in and darted across the terrace as if she was afraid he'd change his mind and go after her.

'Miss Montague,' he called just before she pushed the door. She turned around, eyes wide, lips parted.

'For what it's worth, I'm sorry. It won't happen again.' Without waiting for her reply, he leaned over the parapet and stared at the moonlit plains below.

She didn't want to see him or talk to him, she didn't want to be anywhere near him, but she couldn't hide in her bedroom all day. She jumped out of bed as soon as the muezzin call to prayer hovered in the stillness of dawn. Splashing cold water on her face had done little to cool her eyes, red and swollen with tears and lack of sleep. She got dressed, plaited her hair and packed her bag. She even started a few sketches in a bid to forget about her moonlit encounter with Saintclair but couldn't concentrate long enough to complete a single one. Nothing could make her forget the searing sensations he awakened. Nothing could alleviate her shame or her guilt.

Feeling trapped, miserable and angry, she paced the room, studied every crack in the whitewashed wall, every detail of the mosaics on the floor.

What gave her the right to judge Archie when a few kisses from Lucas Saintclair turned her into this weak, pathetic creature? She didn't even like the man. He was arrogant, selfish, and ruthless. So why did she respond to his touch and his kisses? She couldn't even blame him for taking advantage of her. She'd been willing, pliable, like wet clay in his hands.

But however much she loathed him, and herself, she must go down for breakfast. She wrapped an indigo scarf around her head the way Aicha had shown her. She needed to conceal her face this morning. No doubt the mere sight of Saintclair, the sound of his voice even, would be enough to set her cheeks on fire.

The tavern was empty. Neither Saintclair nor Archie were anywhere to be seen.

Weak with relief, she sat alone at a table and pulled her veil aside. A servant brought her tea, a bowl of yoghurt sprinkled with raisins, and a piece of warm bread. Where were the men? For a few seconds, she had the crazy idea Saintclair had convinced them all to leave without her. Then she remembered her horse at the blacksmith. He must have gone to fetch it. She would meet him there. The sooner she faced him, the better. She rushed her breakfast, put her veil back on and wandered into the streets.

The town bore the scars of the French raid the day before. The market still lay in tatters on the main square. Soldiers patrolled the streets, adding to the atmosphere of fear and desolation.

The forge was closed. A tall, dark-haired man in blue and red uniform walked out of the house next to it. Lieutenant Mortemer. What was he doing there?

'Lieutenant!' she called, walking towards him.

She heard French soldiers shout a warning. They lifted their rifles towards her. She froze and slowly uncovered her face, remembering just in time the market boy.

Mortemer raised his eyebrows, gestured for the soldiers to lower their weapons and walked to her. '*Morbleu,* woman, you could have got yourself killed!' He bowed stiffly in front of her. 'What is Saintclair thinking of, letting you out of his sight in this place after what happened yesterday?'

'Monsieur Saintclair isn't my keeper, Lieutenant,' she replied. 'What happened to the blacksmith? I have come to collect my horse – it needed reshoeing.'

Mortemer arched his eyebrows. 'Is that so?' He slapped his gloves in the palm of his hand.

'The blacksmith is a friend of Saintclair's,' she explained.

'We closed the forge and cleared the house,' Mortemer answered. 'We had a tip that the blacksmith was one of Abdelkader's men and that he helped El-Berkani escape from prison.'

'A tip? Who from?' Her throat felt too constricted to talk. She remembered the good-natured giant who talked to Saintclair the day before and beamed his sunny smile at her.

Mortemer's lips stretched into a thin smile. 'It was anonymous, of course. Nobody in their right mind would ever give us their name. They know full well the rebels would make sure they didn't live to see the sunset otherwise.'

'You said you cleared out the house …?'

He nodded. 'The stupid man wouldn't tell us where El-Berkani was hiding.' He shrugged.

'And?'

He turned his dark, soulless eyes to her. 'You really don't need to know the rest, mademoiselle. Let's say that El-Berkani, his associates, or anyone else for that matter, won't use his forge any more.'

She let out a cry. 'You mean he's dead?'

'Whoever sides with Abdelkader's rebels knows and accepts the risks.' He looked down at her. 'Whoever they are. Natives, French or English.'

It felt like a personal warning. Harriet swallowed hard, feeling sick.

The lieutenant looked up and his face stiffened. Saintclair was coming towards them, leading her horse by the reins.

'Saintclair, I found mademoiselle wandering in the street. You should be more careful with your clients. She almost got herself shot.'

'Mademoiselle Montague has the annoying habit of doing the opposite of what she's told. You were told to wait for me at the inn.' Saintclair stared hard at Harriet.

'Isn't it odd how trouble seems to follow you, Saintclair?' Mortemer asked. 'First Blida and the ammunition depot, then the jail break at Berrouaghia. And now this very forge where you take mademoiselle's horse happens to be a rebel hideout. I should assign a couple of men to keep an eye on you, just in case …'

'Please feel free, but I doubt they could keep up.' A smile curled the side of Saintclair's mouth.

'By the way, I thought you would be interested to know we missed the Mouzaïas the other day,' Mortemer said. 'When my men got to their village, it was empty.'

Saintclair shrugged. 'Probably moved on to their summer pastures higher up in the mountains.'

'Hmm … It was rather good timing, don't you think?'

He narrowed his eyes and looked at the French scout with suspicion. 'And another coincidence,' he added, 'all the rebel hideouts on Rachid's map we visited so far have been empty – cleared out.'

Saintclair patted Harriet's horse and stroked its chestnut mane. He turned to Mortemer.

'Didn't I tell you it was a fake? You should have listened to me.'

Mortemer ignored him. He took hold of Harriet's hand. 'I look forward to meeting you again, mademoiselle.' He lifted her hand to his lips. 'Until then, please be careful. As you can see, the country isn't safe.'

'I will, Lieutenant.' She resisted the urge to snatch her hand away, but couldn't repress an involuntary shudder when his lips brushed her skin, and heaved a sigh of relief when he walked away.

'Now you've finished being nice to the lieutenant,' Saintclair scorned once they were alone, 'tell me what exactly happened.'

She took a step towards him. 'I'm so sorry. Your friend, the blacksmith … they killed him. They said he was a rebel. There's so much death … death everywhere.'

Blood drained from her face, black butterflies fluttered closer and closer until they filled the very air around her and she couldn't breathe any more, and she collapsed.

Chapter Ten

They rode hard and fast under the blazing sun all day, stopping only a couple of times to rest the horses and eat. Early in the evening, Saintclair gave the signal to set up camp on the sheltered bank of an *oued*, a shallow river meandering between low, rocky hills and thickets of trees and prickly bushes. Shadows lengthened on the ground and the sky took that peculiar transparent blue shade announcing the end of a hot day as the sun threw its last golden rays on the tawny steppe.

'The colour of lion.' Ahmoud, close to her, gazed intently at the steppe. 'Sahara.'

She glanced at him, surprised. Ahmoud rarely talked to her. He usually stared straight through her as if she was invisible.

'Is that what *Sahara* means?'

Ahmoud nodded.

'You mean there are lions around here?' She held her breath and looked around. The thought was both scary and thrilling.

He gestured towards the south. 'This is lion country, all the way to Bou Saada. They have lairs in the caves.'

Harriet narrowed her eyes to scrutinise the landscape.

Ahmoud pointed to a clump of trees to the east, to the rocky face of a hill to the west. 'Caves, there and there … the steppe is full of them, you just need to know where to look.

'They're more dangerous at this time of year. The females are protecting their young. You must never leave the camp alone.'

While they were talking, Saintclair's men were starting a fire and pitching tents in a circle on the riverbank. The horses were unsaddled and left to roam free in the thin, rough pasture close to the river.

Saintclair walked past, a rifle in hand. He said something in Arabic to Ahmoud but didn't even glance at her. In fact, he hadn't taken any notice of her since that morning when, despite her protests, he'd carried her back to the inn after she fainted in the street. It was as if she'd imagined their encounter on the terrace the night before, his kisses, and the heat of his caresses.

She watched him climb effortlessly up the rocky hill face and disappear when he reached the top.

'He's going to kill something for us to eat tonight. Fresh meat, no lions,' Ahmoud said, a rare smile on his lips.

'Does he hunt lions?'

Ahmoud shook his head. 'Not any more. Our fathers were great lion hunters. Lucas' father was called '*Ahar*' – mountain lion – by our people. He passed the name on to his son.'

'*Ahar*,' she repeated, dreamily.

'I need to set up camp,' he said before leaving her.

Thoughtful, she turned to watch as the last of the daylight became engulfed in shadows.

'Wild country, isn't it?' Archie said next to her. 'I don't want to alarm you, my dear, but I've been told there are lions and leopards around. However, both Saintclair and Ahmoud are seasoned lion hunters, so we should be reasonably safe.'

He smiled, sliding his arm around her shoulders. She forgot her recent doubts about him, nestled in his arms and rested her head against his shoulder, glad for his reassuring presence. He was really the only man she could trust, the only one whose friendship and strength she could rely on. In the grand scheme of things, his escapade with a dancing girl – or two – was nothing more than a slight disappointment she must forget.

Shots echoed in the hills. A flock of birds took off from nearby trees, swirled in a dark ribbon in the sky before settling on the plain again.

'It must be Saintclair shooting our supper,' Archie commented.

'How much do you know about him and his family?' she asked, lowering her voice to a whisper.

'Not much. Only that he's the best guide money can buy.' He paused. 'The most arrogant too,' he muttered between his teeth.

'You don't think he's in any way involved with the rebels, do you?'

Archie dropped his arm, turning to face her, deadly serious. 'What makes you say that, dear? Did you hear, or see, anything?'

She shook her head, regretting her words already. There was nothing to back her suspicions, just a vague feeling born out of Saintclair's obvious dislike of the French army and Lieutenant Mortemer's insinuations.

Two more shots echoed on the hillside, and a short while later Saintclair walked back into camp, a dead gazelle slung over a shoulder and a brace of hares in his hand.

'Forget about it, I'm just being silly,' she said. 'The man is far too selfish to be concerned with any cause but his own. He has no loyalties to anyone but himself, and all he cares about is his own pleasures – gambling, drinking and chasing after women – he said so himself.'

And getting his hands on Barbarossa's treasure, of course, she added silently. He probably had plans to spend the gold in the country's most seedy taverns with a whole troop of dancing girls.

'Now I remember, he did say a few things against the French army,' Archie remarked.

Harriet stood on her tiptoes and pecked a kiss on his cheek. 'Don't think about it.' She hesitated. 'I know the two of you don't get on. I find him hard to understand too, but we must try for my father's sake.'

There'd been a heated exchange between Archie and the Frenchman that morning when Saintclair found Archie had gone for a walk in the ksar on his own. He called Archie a fool. Archie retorted that he wasn't answerable to anyone. 'As long as I head this expedition,' Saintclair had said, his eyes cold and his tone cutting, 'you are under my care and you *will* do as I say.'

Something else Archie obviously resented was the fact that Saintclair took full responsibility for the ransom money. He kept it with him, either during the day or when they made camp or slept in taverns and inns. 'I'm the one who should have the ransom gold since I'm the one Lord Callaghan chose for the mission,' Archie complained time and time again.

As night fell, Saintclair's men gathered the horses and led them to a hastily cordoned-off enclosure near the camp. The sky was pricked with thousands of stars. A half-moon threw its shiny, opalescent light on the world around. Shivering with cold, Harriet nestled closer to Archie. Together they stood for a long time listening to the sounds of the night – the calling of birds and the rumbling of rocks disturbed by nocturnal animals hiding or hunting, the crackling of the fire behind them.

Was her father looking at the same sky wherever he was, a long, long way away, in the Sahara?

'What do you think we'll find when we reach Tamanrasset? My father …' Her breath caught in her throat.

'Your father is a strong, healthy man, dear.' Archie stroked her shoulders. 'Don't forget he's worked in the most inhospitable places. He'll be fine.'

'I hope you're right. Why do you think he went to Tin Hinan's tomb? Why did he not stay in the Hoggar to study the rock paintings as planned?'

'Your father was always a little … eccentric. Who knew what he hoped to find there?' Archie answered coldly. 'You'll have the chance to ask him yourself soon. In the meantime, something smells good around here and I'm famished.'

It was true that a heavenly smell of grilled meat seasoned with fresh herbs drifted from the campfire. Everybody sat down, tore off strips of meat, and stuffed them into pieces of flat bread. Ahmoud poured sweet tea into tumblers.

After the meal, two men stood up to take first watch. Ahmoud took out his dagger and started sharpening the end of a long stick. Saintclair pulled a cigar from his waistcoat, lit it with a firebrand and reclined against his saddlebag, his legs stretched in front of him. Shadows from the fire danced on his face, flames reflecting in his eyes.

'Why don't you tell us about these lion hunts you and your father took part in?' Archie broke the silence.

Ahmoud stopped carving the wood and glanced up at Saintclair.

There was a minute of silence.

'Why would you like to hear about that?' Saintclair asked at last.

'It isn't often one encounters lion hunters.' Archie sounded a little envious.

There was another silence. Harriet held her breath, aware of a sudden tension around the campfire, and wondered why Saintclair appeared so reluctant to talk about a lion hunt.

'Tell them about your first hunt – our first hunt,' Ahmoud suggested. His lips stretched in a gentle, encouraging smile.

Saintclair let out a sigh. 'Very well … We were both boys of fourteen,' he started, staring into the flames. 'After days of incessant pestering, we were finally allowed to accompany our fathers to the hunt.' He glanced up at his friend.

'I will never forget the exhilaration I felt when we left Bou Saada that day. It was before dawn, so early there were still stars in the sky and the sun wasn't even visible above the horizon. We were a party of ten, armed with spears, sabres and rifles, although we didn't intend to use those to kill the lions, and we rode into the hills where there were reports of a pride of lions raiding herds.'

'Why not use rifles?' Harriet asked.

‘Rifles are the coward’s weapon. Lions deserve the spear or the knife,’ Saintclair answered matter-of-factly.

Ahmoud and the other men nodded in approval.

‘By the time we got to the hills, the sun was rising. We knew the lions would be resting after a night of hunting. We left our horses on a sheltered riverbank and started climbing up a rocky hillside. The scouts, dispatched ahead, pointed to the entrance of a cave – the lions’ lair. The plan was to attract the lions out in the open and spear them. We climbed as silently as we could to a ledge above the cave.’

He turned to Ahmoud. ‘And then we made noise, enough noise to wake all the *djinouns* and mountain spirits for miles around. We banged rocks together, shouted and screamed. Finally, the male came out. He roared in fury, followed closely by his lioness.’ Saintclair closed his eyes.

‘We speared the lion but the lioness bounded onto the ledge where we stood and sprang on my father.’ He smiled. ‘I was never so frightened in my life. I jumped on her and used my own knife to cut her throat. Underneath, my father didn’t move. He was covered in blood. The lioness had swept across his chest with her paw. In utter panic, I pushed her body aside and just when I thought he was dead, he opened his eyes and laughed. ‘From this day, my son,’ he said, ‘you’re coming to every hunt.’ And I did.’

‘The lioness’ hide still hangs in your house, you know,’ Ahmoud said with sadness in his brown eyes. ‘People in Bou Saada called you *Ahar* ever since—like your father.’

‘I bet they call me a lot of other names too,’ Saintclair retorted, his voice bitter. He threw a couple of sticks into the fire.

Archie let out a whistle. ‘Impressive. Not many men, let alone boys of fourteen, can claim having killed a lion with a knife. I can sleep soundly now.’ He yawned, pecked a kiss on Harriet’s cheek. ‘Don’t be too long, dear.’

He got up, gathered his bag and crawled into one of the tents pitched nearby. She too yawned, but didn’t move. Her eyes were drawn to the hypnotic dance of the flames, her senses soothed by the hissing, crackling and sizzling of the fire. Ahmoud was absorbed once again in scraping and sharpening his spear. The other men smoked or lay down, arms behind their head, eyes lost in the starry sky.

She wrapped herself more closely into her burnous.

Saintclair threw the butt of his cigar into the fire.

'I'm planning to ride flat out to Bou Saada tomorrow,' he said. 'You should get some rest. I don't want to waste time because you can't keep up.'

Stung by his condescending tone, she straightened her spine. 'If you don't want to waste time, then we shouldn't go to Bou Saada in the first place,' she said. 'We hired you to take us to Tamanrasset, not to pay your family a visit. You know very well the danger my father is in. A few days could make all the difference.'

'Unfortunately, I don't think a few days will matter much to your father at this point.' There was weariness in his voice. 'And I told you I was worried about Mortemer and wanted to check on my mother and sister.'

She tilted her chin to look at him, defiant. 'What about your father? Can he not look after them?'

Ahmoud stopped working and looked at her, then at his friend. Saintclair got up.

'I'm getting some sleep and I suggest you do the same,' he said. But instead of going into a tent, he walked away from the camp and disappeared into the night.

Ahmoud shook his head slowly and sighed. 'You shouldn't have said that, miss,' he said.

'Said what? That this unplanned trip to Bou Saada was a waste of precious time?'

He shook his head. 'No. About his father.'

'Why?'

'He was murdered, along with my own father and almost a hundred villagers from In Shba five years ago. Saintclair never, ever talks about it.'

'Oh …' Harriet put her hand in front of her mouth, looking in the direction Saintclair had gone. 'I'm sorry, I had no idea. Who killed them all? Bandits?'

'The French.'

'You mean, the French army?'

Ahmoud nodded. 'I suppose I might as well tell you. You will hear about it when we get to Bou Saada anyway.'

He took a deep breath. 'It was five years ago last September. After fierce fighting in the Bou Saada province the French were tipped off that

Abdelkader's men were hiding in the hills and that the local population was helping them out. So they burnt down villages and fields, killed dozens and dozens of people. Those who managed to escape took refuge in a cave. As soon as he got word of what was happening, my father rode out. Saintclair's father decided to go with him, hoping that together they could help with negotiations between the rebels, the villagers, and the French. When they arrived in the hills, they made straight for the cave where the villagers were hiding instead of letting the French know they'd arrived. The soldiers found the hiding place, built huge bonfires in the entrance to the cave and set them alight.'

'Bonfires, whatever for?'

Ahmoud stopped his work. 'To smoke people out so that they could shoot them. The soldiers fuelled the fires throughout the night and had fun shooting at the children, men and women who stumbled out, gasping for air. My father and Saintclair's were among the first to be shot when they came out to talk to the soldiers.'

He concentrated on his carving for a while. 'The following morning, the fires had died down. When they got into the caves, the soldiers found only dead bodies – women, children, old men and peasants, but no rebels.'

'That's barbaric! The officer in charge should be disgraced, court-martialled. Who was he?' Harriet's voice rose in shock and indignation.

Ahmoud sighed. 'It was Lieutenant Mortemer.'

She gasped.

Now she understood the open hostility between the two men, and the reason for Saintclair's visit to Bou Saada.

'But surely you and Saintclair complained to the authorities? Your father, Saintclair's father, all those innocent people killed. Mortemer must be made accountable for his actions.'

Ahmoud spat on the ground. 'It was the French governor himself, Maréchal Bugeaud, who pioneered this way of dealing with rebels. He won't discipline his men for doing what he has done before.'

'But I'm sure there'd be a public outcry if people knew about this and—'

'There's more,' Ahmoud interrupted, his face grim. 'Lucas believes he's as much to blame for what happened as Mortemer.'

She stared at him. 'Why would he think that?'

'He was the one who led Mortemer to the cave.'

Chapter Eleven

Harriet sat still, trying to comprehend what Ahmoud had just said.

'Lucas had been away for some time, scouting in the south, and mapping out new roads. Mortemer tricked him. He found him one night in a tavern and told him it was the rebels who'd ransacked and burned the villages. It happens sometimes, when Abdelkader wants to force people to side with him and fight the French.'

'The emir hurts his own people?'

Ahmoud shrugged. 'This is a cruel war, miss, with men determined to win on both sides. Anyway, Lucas knew the area so well it wasn't hard for him to point out the cave to Mortemer before riding back to Bou Saada. He only heard about the fires and the shootings the following day.'

Harriet pressed her hand hard against her heart, her throat too tight to speak. What did he do then?

As if he understood the silent question in her eyes, Ahmoud answered. 'He left, disappeared. Nobody knew where he was. When I eventually found him, he'd explored the far south and stayed with a Tuareg tribe for a while. He never went back to Bou Saada. Not once in five years – not even for his father's funeral.'

She smiled tentatively. 'You forgave him for your father's death.'

Ahmoud's face was solemn. 'What happened wasn't his fault. He wasn't to know who was in the cave and what Mortemer was planning. He believed the rebels would be arrested.'

He stood up, bowed his head to bid her goodnight. 'I'm taking second watch, so I'm going to rest now. You can't stay out here, mademoiselle, you should go to your tent.'

He was right, of course, yet she was reluctant to leave the comfort, the warmth and light of the campfire. Shivering, she walked to the tent she shared with Archie. Even though it was safer that way, she felt awkward about it. She lifted the flap, listened a minute to Archie's regular breathing, and satisfied that he was fast asleep, crawled to her side to pull her blankets down. It was pitch black. Praying that there was no bug, snake or scorpion lurking around, she sat on her makeshift bed, pulled her boots and *cheche* off, and wrapped herself in the blankets.

Ahmoud's story preyed on her mind … and heart. Something had shifted, mellowed inside her concerning Lucas Saintclair. It wasn't pity, but a feeling that went far deeper. It was sorrow and compassion. How could a man live with such a burden, knowing that somehow he'd been instrumental to his father's death – and the death of innocent children, men and women?

What must he be feeling tonight? He must be wondering how his mother and sister would react when they saw him. Did they hold him responsible, did they hate him? Surely they couldn't hate him as much as he hated himself.

She closed her eyes and drifted into sleep. She dreamt of a lion – standing, majestic, on top of a crag, peering into the distant steppes. His eyes were the same pale, crystal clear blue as Lucas Saintclair's eyes.

It was just before dawn. The light was grey and blue, but already birds sang and men talked in hushed voices outside, probably busy getting the campfire ready for the morning meal. She stretched, raked her fingers in her hair and pulled a face. The last couple of days' riding in the heat had taken their toll. She was filthy.

Maybe she could take advantage of the river? Spurred by the prospect of bathing in cool, fresh water, she pulled the blankets down and rummaged in her bag to find clean clothing and her bar of soap.

'Is it time to get up?' Archie peered at her over the covers.

'Not yet,' she whispered.

'Good.' He closed his eyes and rolled over to the other side.

Walking past the fire over which water boiled in a tin pot, ready for tea and coffee, she breathed in the enticing fragrance of bread warming on hot, flat stones. She followed the riverbank upstream for ten minutes or so, until she found what she was looking for. The perfect spot. She smiled triumphantly.

It was a narrow valley where the river curved into a bend, secluded by thick bushes and reeds. After a quick glance around to make sure she was alone, she stripped and walked naked into the water. It was so cold it took her breath away. She gritted her teeth, clutched her bar of soap and walked into the river until the water reached her hips. Getting rid of the grime and sweat of the past few days was worth the torture …

Holding her breath, she dipped into the water before standing and lathering soap over her body and her hair.

The light was changing. A transparent gold dust touched the hillside, the top of the trees. The sunrise streaked the sky with red, orange and pink hues, reflecting into the river. She was alone in the world, in a bubble hovering between sky and water.

Then she heard the growling. Stones tumbled down the hillside seconds before a male lion jumped onto the river bank, sleek and agile. It approached the river and started drinking. It hadn't seen her. Yet.

Her heart thumping with terror, she ducked under the water very slowly, careful not to make any ripples on the surface. How long would she have to hold her breath? How long did it take a lion to quench its thirst after a night spent hunting? What if it saw her and came after her? Did lions, like cats, hate water? Her lungs started to burn, she felt close to choking. When she couldn't hold on any longer, she popped her head above the water and took a long, long breath.

The lion had gone.

'You are one lucky woman,' a voice called from the bank.

Still breathless, she spun round. Saintclair crouched near the water, a knife in one hand, a pistol in the other.

'How l-long have you b-been here?' she stuttered, her teeth chattering from cold and shock.

'Long enough.'

Had he watched her undress and get into the water? Actually, she'd rather not know. She moved her legs and arms, numb and stiff with cold.

'Is it safe? Has the lion gone?' She looked towards the hillside.

'You're safe. From the lion, that is.' He narrowed his eyes. 'I, on the other hand, might just want to throttle you for disregarding my orders. I knew taking you with us was a mistake. I knew you were stubborn. I didn't realise just how reckless you were. You could have been mauled to death just then.'

'I handled the lion perfectly well on my own.' She tilted her chin. Her heart had almost stopped with fright, but there was no reason to tell him that.

He stood up, put his pistol in the holster on his hip, slid the knife in his boot, and walked towards the edge of the water. His face was so tense, his eyes so steely, that she recoiled. He was going to walk into the river, pull her out and …

'Damn it, woman, you were told not to leave the camp alone. You were warned about lions roaming this area. There are all sorts of dangers here – wild animals, snakes, scorpions.' He looked up towards the hillside. 'Raiders.'

She swallowed hard, following his gaze towards the top of the hills.

He shook his head. 'If that lion hadn't been so old and half-blind, you wouldn't be talking to me now.'

'It seemed pretty sprightly to me,' she muttered.

He snorted. 'Get out. You're freezing and your lips are blue,' There wasn't a trace of sympathy in his voice.

She shivered. 'Only if you turn round.'

'It's a bit late to play the prude,' he muttered, but obliged and faced the other way.

So he had seen her naked. Well, he wouldn't see her now. She crossed her arms over her chest and walked to the shore. Throwing a nervous glance in his direction she stepped out of the water whilst he remained immobile with his back to her, as if he'd been turned into rock.

She gathered her clothes as fast as she could, stumbling on pebbles in her haste, and chose a large bush behind which to get dressed. Her fingers were too cold, too stiff to fasten her tunic's tiny buttons. She'd leave it open for now. She put her boots on and ventured out of the bushes. Saintclair took one look at her and snarled.

'You can't go back to camp half dressed.'

She pulled her tunic across her chest to cover up, and shifted uncomfortably on her feet. 'I can't do the buttons up.' She showed him her hands still red raw with cold.

He tightened his lips but didn't answer.

The sun now peeped above the rugged hilltop, a huge orange ball setting the sky on fire. Dazzled, Harriet caught her breath.

'This is … magnificent. We don't have sunrises like this in England.'

He gazed at her face, at her eyes filled with wonder.

'No but you have rain and summer storms.'

He stepped closer and looked down into her eyes. 'I always wanted to stand outside in a thunderstorm.' Her eyes were a rain cloud right now, cool and soothing.

She smiled. 'You might get hit by lightning.'

'Maybe, but what a beautiful way to die.' His breathing was a little faster, his gaze heavier.

She parted her lips but didn't answer. The colour of her cheeks deepened. In the opening of her tunic, the gold pendant gleamed against her milky white skin. His fingers itched to toy with it and bring it to his lips, still hot and fragrant from her body. He could breathe her scent, the Damascus rose soap she'd lathered all over her round breasts, her smooth stomach, and into her hair. He hadn't meant to watch, but once she'd stepped out of her clothes he simply hadn't been able to take his eyes off her, hungry for her, throbbing with the need to enfold her into his arms, pin her under his weight and take her.

If he didn't move now, that's exactly what he'd do.

He took a deep breath, clenched his fists, and stepped back.

There was something she wanted to say to him before they went back to the others.

'Ahmoud told me last night, about your father,' she started, hesitant. 'I understand now why you have to go to Bou Saada, and I'm sorry if I offended you.'

The savage glint in his eyes stopped her, making her gasp.

'I am not discussing my family with you, or anyone else,' he snapped. And without waiting for her, he started in the direction of camp.

He never turned once to check if she was following him and she had to run to keep up. She'd no idea he would react this way. She wanted to apologise for being insensitive, but it seemed she'd made things worse.

When they reached the camp, breakfast was over. There was only one piece of bread left and hardly enough coffee for two.

Saintclair sat down near the fire, broke the warm bread into two and handed her the bigger piece.

She shook her head. 'No, keep it. It was my fault we missed breakfast.' Her throat was too tight to eat anything.

'Harriet, there you are!' Archie came out of the tent. He grabbed her elbows, leaned down towards her, an angry look in his eyes. 'Where on earth did you disappear to?'

He looked at her, then Saintclair, and frowned. 'What happened? Are you all right?'

She shrugged. 'Of course. I went to the river for a swim and had a surprise encounter with a lion. I'll start packing my things now.'

'A lion?' Archie gasped.

'Yes, what about it? It was old, half-blind, and not in the least interested in eating me. Ask Monsieur Saintclair.'

She freed herself from his grasp and walked into the tent. It didn't take long to run a comb through her wet hair, plait it, and arrange her turban. Then she rolled her blankets, gathered her things into her saddlebag, and went out to saddle her horse. A tap on her shoulder made her jump.

'Be careful!' Saintclair grumbled when she swung round. 'I almost spilled the last of the coffee.'

He held out a tin cup of warm coffee and the piece of bread she'd rejected earlier. 'You must have something to eat. We won't be stopping for a long time.'

He shoved the bread and coffee in her hands and walked away.

Half an hour later, they were on their way to Bou Saada. As promised, Saintclair led a relentless pace across the steppes. To the inexperienced eye, the landscape was bleak, parched and empty, with only tufts of coarse bushes sprouting between rocks and the occasional grooves and rocky outcrops on the flat landscape. But there were hidden valleys with fresh streams running through, acacia and pistachio trees, and pastures where Saintclair took them at regular intervals to feed and rest the horses.

'Damn country,' Archie complained during their midday stop.

He took his hat off and wiped his forehead with a handkerchief. The sun was beating hard on them now. It would be even hotter later in the afternoon.

'It all looks the same to me,' he carried on. 'Rocks, coarse grass, a few bushes, more rocks. How does Saintclair find these valleys? I could ride past this place a hundred times and never even guess it was there.' A note of admiration grudgingly pierced his voice.

Harriet cupped water in her hands and splashed her face, enjoying the cool droplets trickling on her throat and into her tunic.

'That's why he's a guide.' She stole a glance towards Saintclair.

If Saintclair was anxious about returning to Bou Saada after his five-year self-imposed exile, he didn't show it. He was talking to Hakim, the man who got hurt in the tavern brawl in Blida. Like all Tuaregs, Hakim's face was veiled at all times. He seemed to have recovered from his injuries, even if his hand still bore traces of a burn.

'I don't understand this detour to Bou Saada. We're wasting time,' Archie said. He put his hat back on, and screwed the top of his gourd shut. 'I asked the men about it, but no one's talking. They're all too loyal to discuss Saintclair's plans, even though I'm the one paying for his services.'

'Saintclair wants to visit his mother and sister,' she said. 'Lieutenant Mortemer is heading for Bou Saada and Saintclair is worried.' She decided not to say any more. It was, after all, not her story to tell.

'Why should he be worried about Mortemer? Unless you were right and he's on the rebels' side.' He frowned.

She didn't answer.

Too soon it was time to leave the fresh, secluded valley and follow the dusty track across the steppes once again. The sun beat hard now. Sweat ran along Harriet's face, her neck, to trickle down her back. Its white glare hurt her eyes. The hazy landscape wavered in the heat. She closed her eyes, slowing her horse down.

She needed to drink and pour some water on her face, or she'd collapse. Yet asking Saintclair to stop was out of the question.

When she opened her eyes again, a vision of heaven stood in front of her. There was a lake, vast and clear and as blue as the sky.

'Water, over there!' She pointed to the far distance and licked her lips in anticipation. When they reached it, she'd jump down from her horse and run into the lake fully clothed. She could almost feel the glorious sensations of the cool, fresh water on her body.

Saintclair reined his horse in to bring it parallel to hers. 'There's nothing there, it's the heat playing a trick on you. A mirage,' he said, riding alongside her.

She peered in the distance again. The blue lake was still there. 'But I can see it, so clearly.' She bit her lip to stop it from quivering. A mirage, it was nothing more than a mirage. Tears stung her eyes.

He frowned and gave her an odd look. 'You're about to pass out. You're going to ride with me for a while.'

It took all her strength to straighten in the saddle. 'No, I'm all right,' she said, blinking away the tears.

'Then we'll stop for a rest.' He gave his horse a heel kick to spur it on and led them to a thicket of acacia trees.

She saw more mirages that afternoon during the ride to Bou Saada – more lakes, as well as the towers of a fortified village in the distance.

It was night when they reached Saintclair's home town. "The City of Happiness", as it was known, was one of the largest oases in this part of the country. They rode through plantations of palm, olive and fig trees, of orange and lemon groves and jujube and pistachio trees. Silver moonlight bathed the plantation in a ghostly, silver light. After the dryness of the steppes, the air was moist and fresh, thick with the heady scent of vegetation.

Ahmoud left their group and rode ahead.

'Where is he going?' Archie asked.

'Warning the guards we're on our way, and then home to his family,' Saintclair answered. 'He hasn't seen them for a while.'

He took off his hat, hooked it on his saddle and raked his dark hair with his fingers before taking hold of the reins again. He sounded calm and composed but in the bright clear silver moonlight, Harriet saw how tightly he gripped his reins.

There was a tugging at her heart. It must be so hard for him to face his mother, her anger and accusations maybe.

The gates of the ksar stood open for them. The guards waved and saluted Saintclair as he rode past. The streets were empty. The hooves of their horses echoed in the dusty alleyways as they meandered towards a central square and climbed up a small hill to a large house with whitewashed walls partly covered with mosaics and dark purple bougainvillea.

Saintclair dismounted and walked to an imposing carved door lit by two large oil lamps.

She was surprised when he turned round to look at her, as if seeking reassurance.

Their eyes locked. Her lips stretched into a smile and she nodded.

The door suddenly opened on a small, slender woman wearing a simple blue dress. Her thick, curly blonde hair was twisted into a loose bun on the nape of her neck. She stood in the doorway for a moment, her eyes wide open.

'So it's true,' she said in English. 'You are back.'

She stepped forward, lifted a hand to Saintclair's cheek in a caress.

'Oh, my son, what took you so long?'

Chapter Twelve

He was home.

After five years spent running across deserts, steppes, and mountains. After losing himself inside the deepest canyons, the seediest taverns, the most potent wines, and the most beautiful women, he'd come home to Bou Saada.

His mother hadn't changed at all. She was as kind and forgiving as he remembered. As he enfolded her in his arms, he breathed in the subtle orange blossom scent of her hair – the one he remembered from his childhood.

'I missed you so much, my love,' she whispered.

He pulled out of her embrace, his heart breaking. 'How can you say that? How can you pretend I did nothing wrong?' he said in a low, almost growling voice. 'Mother, I was the one who …'

He'd committed the worst crime a son could commit. He had sent Mortemer to the cave where his father sheltered, along with dozens of innocent people. He caused the death of the man his mother loved more than anyone on earth. Why didn't she hate him for it? Why did she hold him so tightly in her arms?

She caressed his cheek in the way she used to when he was a child, and smiled sadly. 'You didn't know your father was there, Lucas. You didn't know what Lieutenant Mortemer planned to do. All these years I thought I'd lost you, like I lost your father.' Her voice broke. 'All these years I wanted to tell you how much I love you, how much I hurt for you.'

He squeezed his eyes shut a moment. 'Why don't you listen? You didn't lose him, I killed him. I killed all those people who were hiding in the cave. I don't deserve you to hurt for me. I deserve you to hate me.'

He was angry, as angry as five years before when he learned what Mortemer had done – what *he* had done. Nobody should love him, least of all his mother, who'd lost so much because of him. Hell, he hated himself, and would hate himself until the day he died.

'I'm so happy you're here,' she said as if she hadn't heard a word of what he said. She looked over his shoulder. 'Who are your travelling companions? You must tell them to come in.'

As he turned round, he met Harriet Montague's gentle smile again. For some strange reason it warmed him, soothed him and gave him strength for what was to come. There was someone else he had to face, someone who might not be as forgiving as his mother.

He took a long, deep breath to steady himself. 'They're clients – English people I'm taking to Tamanrasset.' He gestured for Harriet and Drake to dismount so he could introduce them.

'This is Harriet Montague and Archibald Drake.' For some reason he was reluctant to mention they were engaged. 'Miss Montague's father is being held to ransom by a Tuareg tribe.'

Pointing to the rest of the party, he added, 'And these are my men who will escort us all the way there.'

While her mother welcomed her guests and asked Harriet about her father, he walked ahead into the house he'd left five years before. Nothing had changed. The large courtyard with elegant arches on three sides, the fountain that whispered its pure, crystalline song in the night, the palm trees which provided much-needed shade during the day, and the abundance of flowers – zinnias, bignones, and geraniums, splashes of colour in the sunlight, bathed in shadows for now.

'Lucas!' A shriek pierced the night.

He braced himself.

A young woman ran into the courtyard, threw herself against him like a sandstorm djinn.

'And who can this be?' He held her at arms' length.

'Don't you dare say you don't remember me!'

His sister, Rose – *Ourida,* or little Rose in Arabic, as their father used to call her – stamped her foot on the tiled courtyard. He swallowed hard. She'd grown into a beauty. With her mass of curly blonde hair, her dark blue eyes and rosebud lips, she was just like their mother. She even smelled of the same orange blossom cologne. How old was she now – nineteen, twenty?

'Let me look at you,' he said. 'You've become so pretty.'

'Well, you haven't!' she retorted. 'And you stink of horse.' She hugged him again.

Yes, he was home. As he looked around the courtyard and entered the house, he couldn't help listening for another voice – a deep, warm voice he would never hear again.

They were shown into a large room decorated with colourful rugs and furniture made of dark wood with intricate mother of pearl inlays.

Gilded mirrors and watercolours hung on the whitewashed walls. On one of the walls, a tawny lioness' hide hung sideways. Harriet stared in awe at the beast's glassy eyes, at the growl frozen on its open mouth, the sharp protruding yellow teeth.

'That would be the lioness he told us about last night,' Archie remarked.

Servants brought trays of drinks, hot spicy tea, coffee, and cool sherbets, dishes of mutton and semolina, plates of candied dates, apricots and figs. It was a banquet fit for a prince in a fairy-tale palace.

Archie and the men ate with appetite, but Harriet was too tired to try anything other than an orange sherbet and a few candied fruit. She stole a curious glance towards the head of the table where Saintclair sat with his mother and sister. The contrast between his serious, almost sombre, look and their ecstatic smiles was striking. The women talked and laughed whereas he remained mostly silent and toyed with his food or his glass of wine.

'Not quite what I expected, this house,' Archie said, looking around the room. 'Saintclair's family is far wealthier than we thought.'

He gave her a knowing smile. 'Like me, you had him down as a lowly-born ruffian, an adventurer, didn't you?'

'That's the impression he gives of himself, most of the time—'

A cry from Saintclair's sister interrupted her.

'That man isn't setting one foot in Bou Saada. I forbid it!' The girl's face was livid.

'Calm down, Rose.' Saintclair squeezed his sister's hand. 'We can't deny him access to the town. He said he is here to set up some French outpost.'

'That's right, the soldiers took over the old fort to the south of the oasis,' his mother concurred. She twisted a handkerchief in her hands. 'Is there really nothing you can do to stop him from coming here, Lucas?'

'I think it's wiser not to oppose Mortemer just now. There's been a lot of unrest in the north of the country and—'

'If you're too much of a coward to stop him, then *I*'ll order our guards to throw boiling oil onto them,' Rose started. 'I'll shoot him myself from the town walls and I don't care if the French take me to prison for it. That man killed my father.'

'Rose, this isn't the time or the place,' Saintclair's mother pleaded, her voice shaking.

'I will slip a *naja* in his bed, a scorpion in his boot. I will poison his food with *falazlez* leaves and he'll die a raving lunatic …' The girl's eyes flashed with fury and she turned to her brother. 'At least, I'll do something. I won't run away and hide like you did.'

Saintclair stood up so abruptly his chair fell back behind him and crashed on the tiled floor, and he walked out, a stormy look on his face.

'That was unfair, Rose,' Saintclair's mother said before turning to Archie and Harriet.

'I apologise for this unpleasant scene, Miss Montague, Mr Drake.'

She ordered her daughter to come with her. The girl bowed her head and followed her mother out without protest.

'By God, what was all that about?' Archie asked. Without waiting for an answer, he helped himself to some more wine and a large piece of halva sprinkled with raisins and almonds.

The sweet smell of the pudding made Harriet heave. 'I need some fresh air,' she whispered, rubbing her forehead.

'Do you want me to come with you, dear?'

'No, it's just a headache, I'll be fine. Finish your meal.'

She retraced her steps along the corridor to the courtyard and followed a path to the gardens at the back of the house. Tonight like every night, the moon and the stars were so bright she didn't need any oil lamp or lantern to guide her. She found a parapet overlooking the oasis at the far end of the garden and sat down.

Saintclair had been right when he said nights were magical here. The view of the hundreds of palm trees bathed in silvery moonlight was worthy of a fairy tale.

And yet anxiety tightened her chest, knotted her stomach. Would Lieutenant Mortemer be the evil genie who wreaked chaos and destruction on this enchanting oasis?

Chapter Thirteen

'You can find anything and everything in the medina,' Rose stated, waving at the leather belts and scabbards, the finely chiselled silver jewellery and colourful woven rugs. 'Even a wife or a husband, if you stand in the market square long enough!' Her deep blue eyes sparkled and dimples appeared in her round cheeks as she smiled.

Saintclair's sister had nominated herself her guide for the day and was taking her role very much to heart. Determined to show Harriet the old town with its bazaar, workshops, food stalls and market, she walked fast and talked incessantly. She was in a much better mood than the night before.

'I used to say Lucas would have to stand on the market square for weeks before a woman picked him for a husband, and then only a crazy old crone would have him.'

Harriet laughed wholeheartedly. Rose had been regaling her with tales of her brother's youthful exploits, and there'd been many. Her good humour was contagious.

'He was always creating havoc with his climbing contests in the palm tree plantation, his camel races on the steppes or his spear-throwing tournaments. He even ran away on a mule once, only to get stuck in the salt marshes. My father had to send a search party for him. He said he wanted to see Algiers! And I don't even count the times he escaped our father's vigilance to hunt lions on his own or with Ahmoud.'

She smiled again, but this time her eyes were dreamy.

'Anyway, it seems I was wrong. My brother never had to stand in the marketplace to find himself a woman,' she finished with a shrug. 'There were always far too many girls chasing after him, although I never understood what they ever saw in him.'

She led the way through the narrow streets, pointing out the many stalls where a particularly fine roll of cloth, a colourful woven rug or silver pendants caught her attention.

'These would look pretty on you.' She held out a pair of earrings. 'My dress does suit you, by the way. It's far prettier than your tunic and breeches.' Rose had lent Harriet a pale blue silk dress while her clothes were being laundered.

'I think he likes you, you know,' Rose declared all of a sudden.

'Who?'

Rose shrugged. 'Lucas, of course.'

'No, he doesn't,' Harriet protested. 'He says I'm obstinate, annoying and stupid, and he's always trying to find excuses to send me back to Algiers.'

'Exactly. He likes you. He wouldn't waste his breath talking to you otherwise.' Rose lifted her chin. 'Come on, let's see if we can find the Ouled Nail dancers. I bet you've never seen the likes of them.'

She leaned over to Harriet and lowered her voice. 'Mother doesn't want me watching them. She says they are awfully indecent, but I'll let you in on my secret.' Playfully, she lifted a strand of Harriet's hair to whisper into her ear. 'I can dance just like them, and I've been told I'm rather good.'

There were no dancers on the square that day, but Rose assured Harriet they'd probably be performing in the town taverns in the evening.

'Don't look back. I think you have an admirer,' she whispered in Harriet's ear as they stood looking at a display of leather belts. 'He's been following us all morning.'

'Really? What's he like?'

'Tall, but I can't see if he's handsome or not because he's wearing a *cheche*.' She pouted.

'Maybe it's you he's following. You're very pretty, you know.'

Rose blushed. 'No, he's definitely watching you.' She frowned. 'That's strange. I could swear he has blue eyes.'

Harriet gasped. Could it be the same man she'd seen before? She turned around but the man had gone.

'Now look what you've done, you frightened him away,' Rose said. 'He must be very shy.'

Rose linked arms with her and they made their way back to the house for lunch, walking under the palm branches placed on the houses' flat roofs and across the alleyways to provide shade. Harriet kept glancing over her shoulder. She had an uneasy feeling about the man Rose said was following them.

The house was empty. The men had gone to buy fresh horses for the journey to the south and Saintclair had planned a tour of the estate with his mother.

After lunch, Harriet took her sketch pad and sat alone outside since

Rose had some studying to do.

The garden was ablaze with red and orange flowers, and shaded by large palm trees, almond and pistachio trees fluffy with pink and white blooms. It overlooked the oasis, which stood like an island of fresh green against the dramatic backdrop of bare, arid hills. She'd found it beautiful in the moonlight. It was just as breathtaking in the daytime.

She drew a few sketches of the plantation and the garden, enjoying the caress of the scented breeze on her skin, before reclining on the wicker seat and closing her eyes. Lulled by the rustling of palms in the breeze, the sound of the water trickling in the fountain and the rhythmical, woody noise of the cicadas, she didn't even realise she was falling asleep.

It was late afternoon when she woke. The sky was pale blue, the light a dusty, transparent gold. Saintclair sat on the parapet close to her, still as a statue, his arms crossed on his chest, his expression unreadable.

Startled, she put a hand to her heart, straightening in her chair. 'I didn't know you were here.'

Smoothing her hair away from her face, she got up and came to stand next to him.

He unfolded his arms. 'Sorry, I didn't mean to frighten you.'

'I can't get used to your habit of sneaking up on people.'

'One day you'll thank me for it.' He looked down at her. 'You look different with a dress on.'

She felt she was blushing, but he'd already turned away.

He pointed at the steppes where a long convoy of cavaliers and carts stretched among clouds of dust. 'Mortemer is here. He'll probably pay us a visit tonight. He knows we're at Bou Saada.'

'How can he know?'

'He has spies, of course. Hakim said he saw a group of riders on the salt plains yesterday. The route I chose was well off the beaten track, so they had to be following us.'

Could the man who she thought was watching over her be one of Mortemer's spies?

'What about Rose?' she asked. 'I heard what she said last night …'

He glanced at her, frowning. 'Rose will be kept well away from him, and from any food or drink he may be served. Not that I'd mind if she poisoned him.' His lips stretched into a joyless smile. 'Maybe I too should steer clear of her. She made no secret about her feelings towards me.'

The sadness in his voice touched her heart. She put her hand on his forearm. The need to comfort him, to erase all traces of sorrow from his eyes was so overwhelming it took her breath away.

'You're wrong. Rose adores you. She told me stories about you this morning.'

He lifted his eyebrows, but his expression was guarded. 'What kind of stories?'

'Some mishaps you got into when you were young. It was all very entertaining.' She forced a smile. 'Your sister's a lovely girl.'

He caught her hand in his and lifted it to his mouth. 'She isn't the only one.'

Her smile froze, her heart thundered.

His lips brushed the palm of her hand, her wrist. The feel of his mouth, of the harsh stubble on his cheeks against her delicate skin, sent tingles all over her body. He looked deep into her eyes as if he was daring her to withdraw her hand.

She swallowed hard, her throat dry and tight. She didn't want to pull away. She craved his mouth on hers and his arms around her, like the other night. Desire rushed through her veins like a fever. She started trembling.

He let her hand drop. 'I have to go.'

She cleared her throat, tried to focus. 'Of course …'

Before turning away, he pointed to her sketch pad and added, 'You really do have a talent. Make sure you keep enough paper for the Hoggar, the lost oases of the Sahara, and the Tuaregs … you must draw the Tuaregs.'

'I will,' she whispered, watching his tall, black-clad silhouette disappear down the path.

Right now, he was the only man she wanted to draw. Sitting on the parapet, the pad in her lap, frowning with intense concentration, she traced the harsh lines of his face – from his crystal blue eyes to the line of his mouth – as if she could engrave it in her heart forever.

'You're not welcome here, Lieutenant.' Lucas kept his hand firmly on his mother's shoulder for support. He could feel her body shake even if her stony expression gave nothing away of the turmoil she suffered inside.

'I won't impose upon you very long.' Mortemer bowed deeply, holding his hat in his gloved hands as if he were at a reception at the governor's palace in Algiers. 'I came to assure you of the protection of the French army in these difficult times, Madame,' he started. 'There has been much unrest in the country lately. Abdelkader was sighted not very far from here last week, and one of his men escaped from a nearby penitentiary. However, I can promise you that Bou Saada is safe. I've decided to leave a permanent garrison of seventy men in the fort, together with an ammunition depot large enough to sustain repeated attacks by rebels and five pieces of artillery.'

'Artillery? Surely that's unnecessary. We've never had any reason to fear Abdelkader or his men here, Lieutenant,' Lucas' mother retorted. 'Bou Saada is a peaceful town.'

'It's also a crossroads for nomads, travellers, and, unfortunately, rebels,' Mortemer objected. 'The performance and versatility of our light shell cannons have been proven on many battlefields.'

'Bou Saada isn't a battlefield!' she protested.

'Will the cannon be kept on the walls or in the fort?' Lucas interrupted. He removed his hand from his mother's shoulder and dug a cigar out of his pocket.

'We'll keep them in the barracks which are going to be extended and fortified. Until then, they're under armed guard in an outbuilding.'

'Hmm ...' Lucas lit his cigar, blew the smoke out slowly. 'Isn't it a little risky? What if Abdelkader got hold of them?'

Mortemer narrowed his eyes. 'There's no chance of that. I'll make sure of it.'

He turned to Lucas and added, 'When are you leaving with your English clients?'

'Tomorrow at dawn.'

'I'll see you again, then. I'm travelling to Tamanrasset too.' He bowed curtly. 'Good evening, Madame.'

As Saintclair's mother didn't answer, he put his hat on and walked out.

Lucas crushed his cigar into an obsidian bowl.

'Damn!' He raked his fingers through his dark hair. 'I'm sorry, Mother. I have to meet a few people. I'll be late back. Don't wait for me tonight.'

'What about your guests? Harriet Montague is such a nice young lady. I was hoping you'd show her the oasis by moonlight. I'm sure she'd find it fascinating.'

'Miss Montague has been nothing but a pain in the backside from the moment I met her,' Lucas answered, surprised by the twinge he felt in his chest at the mention of her name. She'd got to him today, again. It had taken all his willpower to walk away from her in the garden. What he needed was a woman, any woman, to get her out of his mind. He was in danger of becoming dangerously obsessed.

'I hoped she'd give up after a few days, but she's tenacious. Like a tick on an old dog.'

His mother gasped. 'Lucas! That's not the way to speak about a courageous young lady who is putting up with a perilous and most uncomfortable journey and is probably terribly worried about her father. You never used to be so callous, or inconsiderate.'

He gave a harsh laugh. 'I guess that's what I am now, Mother, callous and inconsiderate, and a few other things as well. In fact …'

He hesitated. Now was the time to tell her what exactly happened the night before his father was killed. She would at last know the truth about him.

'There is something else I should have told you before,' he started, his throat tight, 'something regarding Father's death which—'

'No, Lucas!' She stood up. 'I will not hear another word about it. Never!'

She walked up to him and looked at him, her eyes full of tears. 'It's taken me a long time to learn to live without your father, to start enjoying the sun on my skin again, the scent of the flowers in the garden, and the sight of the mountains in the distance.' Her voice became stronger. 'Your sister has healed too. And now you've come back and I can finally tell you how much I love you, how much I missed you. I won't let you stir the past again and destroy what little peace and happiness we have managed to find.'

She stood on her tiptoes and kissed his cheek. 'Please, Lucas, let it be, and accept that I have forgiven you.'

He let out a long breath. She shouldn't have forgiven him. He would never forgive himself. He would, however, respect his mother's wishes.

'Don't worry about Harriet Montague,' he said. 'I'll ask Drake to take her out tonight. As for Mortemer, I'm going to deal with him once and for all.'

He left before she could ask him what he meant.

Chapter Fourteen

Harriet leaned closer to Archie and gripped his arm. After the eerie silence of the moonlit oasis, walking into the bright and crowded tavern was a shock to the senses.

'I think I should take you back.' Archie glanced around the room. He looked worried. 'This really isn't a place for you.'

'I told you I wanted to see these dancing girls,' she answered, feeling a little guilty that her request should make Archie so ill at ease.

She'd insisted that he take her to see the Ouled Nail dancers tonight. Anywhere was better than going back to the Saintclair house where Lucas must be spending the evening with his mother and sister.

No man ever made her feel the way he did. It wasn't only the hundreds of sensations he could spark inside her with just one look of his clear blue eyes. It was the burning ache she felt deep inside her heart whenever he was close, whenever she thought about him. She didn't like that wretched, churning pain. She didn't understand it. Absent-mindedly, she rubbed her hand on her heart as if she could make it all go away.

Archie pushed his way through the crowd, craned his neck, and frowned in concentration.

'Are you looking for someone?'

He shrugged. 'No, of course not.'

She frowned. She was almost sure he'd just signalled to a tall man standing near the counter. There was something vaguely familiar about him. Before she could take a better look at him, he turned away and Archie pushed her forward.

'I heard people talk about these Ouled Nail dancing girls and I don't believe it's something ladies should watch. You must promise not to be shocked by what you see tonight.'

'You know I'm not easily shocked,' she said. 'I'm here purely as an observer of local customs.'

Her words were drowned in the clamour which announced the women's arrival. A circle was cleared at the centre of the tavern. Voices hushed. In the silence, a flute started a thin, whiny tune. Tambourines and a goat-skin drum followed, beating a slow rhythm that echoed the hammering of her heart.

Two women appeared from behind a screen, faces uncovered, eyes darkened with kohl. They wore heavy gold and silver jewellery on their headdress, and their large earrings, necklaces, bangles, anklets jingled and clunked as their fluid limbs undulated like snakes. Their waists bent and twisted, their hips rolled and heaved provocatively and followed the music's increasing tempo.

One of the women unfastened her top and shrugged it off. It slipped onto the ground, revealing a sheer white blouse that didn't leave much to the imagination. The other dancer circled around her for a while, then she pulled her hand and they danced their way back behind the screen. The audience started clapping and stamping their feet. The noise was deafening.

'What are they doing? Is it finished already?' Harriet shouted above the noise.

Archie was very red. He bent down towards her. 'Ah, I think that … well, this next bit really isn't …' he stammered. 'I'd better stand in front of you so you can't see.'

'Can't see what?'

'Oh dear.' Archie's face turned the colour of beetroot. He shoved her behind him so as to block her view, but not before she caught a glimpse of naked bodies.

She put her hand to her mouth. Rose hadn't mentioned anything about the women dancing naked.

The music changed tempo, became slow and lascivious. Stuck between Archie and the wall, Harriet looked around and saw a secluded alcove at the back. Her heart skipped a beat. Saintclair was there, together with Ahmoud, Hakim and Musa, and other men she'd never seen before. In front of them were pitchers of wine, tall coffee pots and cups, and a map.

They weren't watching the girls but talking, huddled over the map. Why was Saintclair spending the last evening of his visit to Bou Saada with these men instead of his family?

The music stopped. There was clapping, cheering and whistling as the dancers left the makeshift dance floor.

Archie turned round and pointed to Saintclair. 'Look who's here. Let's go over.' He grabbed her elbow before she could protest and they cut through the crowd.

The men looked up and stared at them in stunned silence.

'Good evening,' Archie said. 'I'm glad to see you. I was getting a little uneasy here on my own with Harriet.' He pulled an apologetic grimace. 'She was so determined to come here. There was nothing I could say to change her mind.'

He pulled Harriet over. 'Now, dear, you stay here and I'll get us something to drink.' And he disappeared into the crowd.

Saintclair stood, towering over her, and gave her a frosty glare. 'He seemed in a great hurry to get rid of you.'

'He went to the counter, that's all,' Harriet answered, but she too had noticed Archie's haste.

'Have you two lost your minds?' Saintclair said between clenched teeth. 'Has Drake no idea what kind of place this is?'

She stared blankly into his eyes. 'I'm the one who insisted on coming here. Archie is kind. He likes to make me happy.'

'Putting you in unnecessary danger isn't being kind, it's being bloody stupid,' he retorted. 'Does he think he can protect you on his own?'

'I'm in no danger, and Archie is great at fighting,' she said, defiant.

Saintclair shrugged and sat next to her. 'You mean like that time in the kasbah?' He gestured towards a chair and she sat down.

Her face burnt now, but not from the heat. She didn't want to be reminded about that night and how promptly Archie abandoned Saintclair to fend for himself.

'You don't even have your dagger, not that it would do much good.' Saintclair shook his head. She was still wearing the silk dress Rose had lent her and had left her dagger behind. 'Anyway, what did you want to come here for?'

She pointed towards the dancing area. 'I wanted to see the Ouled Nails for myself, find out what all the fuss was about,' she muttered, slightly embarrassed. 'I really had no idea they were so …'

'Skilled? Imaginative? Entertaining?' Saintclair smiled.

'Hmm, yes …' She avoided his eye and pointed to the map. 'Are you planning the route for the rest of your journey?'

He nodded. 'That's right.'

'Can I take a look?'

'No. It's all sorted now.'

He swiftly folded the map and put it in his pocket. He leaned over to speak to Ahmoud. They exchanged a few, knowing looks and the men got up and left.

'We have an early start tomorrow.' Saintclair lifted his wine glass to his lips.

A shadow passed across his eyes and she briefly wondered if he was telling the truth.

'What is taking Drake so long?' he asked. He put his glass down, drumming his fingers on the table.

'Do you think something happened to him?'

He shrugged and got up. 'Stay here, I'll be right back.'

In a couple of long strides, he pushed his way into the crowd.

Suddenly there was shouting, the sounds of tables and chairs being overturned and crashing on the ground, and women screaming. A few seconds later, men were fighting everywhere. Harriet jumped to her feet, looking around in panic. Neither Saintclair nor Archie were anywhere to be seen. There was nothing else to do but stand against the alcove wall and pray that nobody would notice her.

A couple of men wrestled their way in her direction. One of them threw his opponent onto the table, squeezed his hands around his throat until the man's face was bright red and his eyes bulged out of their sockets. Harriet grabbed the nearest thing at hand, which happened to be a pitcher of wine, and brought it down onto his back as hard as she could. Furious, he spun round, a snarl on his face, fury shining in his eyes. She recoiled in fear against the wall.

The man shouted something and stepped forward, a sinister grin twisting his lips. She held her breath, searched for the dagger on her side and remembered she didn't have it. The man lifted his hands to take hold of her when Saintclair appeared behind him, grabbed his shoulder to spin him around, and knocked him out with a blow to the nose.

'Come now.'

He took her hand and pulled her along with so much strength her feet barely touched the ground. 'Drake's injured, he's outside.'

He pushed and shoved and they made it through the tavern door. Archie was slumped against the tavern door, barely conscious.

'Archie!' Harriet rushed to kneel down next to him. A purple bump marked his forehead; his left eye was swollen and closed. She turned to Saintclair.

'What happened?'

He shrugged. 'No idea. I found him on the floor and dragged him out.' He bent down and slipped his hands under Archie's armpits to lift him.

'Help me,' he said, once Archie was upright. 'Put your arm around his waist to support him. Luckily, the house isn't far.'

Nevertheless, it took half an hour to reach it, by which time Harriet was exhausted, hot, and sweaty. She sighed with relief when they entered the dark and silent house, thankful for the late hour. At least she wouldn't have to explain to Madame Saintclair that they'd been caught in a brawl in a seedy tavern. She helped Saintclair take Archie to his bedroom and together they laid him on the bed.

'Shall we call a doctor?' she asked, hesitant.

'Let's get him comfortable first. Don't just stand there. Help me take some of his clothes off.'

Harriet drew in her breath. Of course, he probably believed they were lovers since they'd shared a tent on a few occasions, as well as a room in the shelter in the mountains.

Saintclair pulled Archie's boots off while Harriet unfastened his jacket and shirt. Her fingers shook slightly as she slipped his jacket off his shoulders then loosened his shirt out of his breeches. She let out a little cough.

He looked up, inquisitive. He must have thought she was upset because the harsh lines of his face softened.

'Don't worry. I'm sure he'll be fine. Now, can I let you do the rest while I get some water and ointment for his head? I'll be as quick as I can.'

'The rest?'

'You know …' He gestured towards Archie's breeches.

Harriet opened her eyes wide. 'Oh no, I couldn't possibly … He'll have to stay like that for now.'

On the bed, Archie moaned and coughed, then cursed as he tried to sit up.

Harriet hastened to his side and took his hand. 'Don't try and move. You've had a nasty blow to the head.'

'I'll be back in a minute,' Saintclair said and he slipped out of the room.

'What happened to you?' Harriet asked.

He lifted a hand to his swollen eye, touched his forehead and pulled a face. 'Don't know.' He winced in pain. 'Last thing I remember was standing at the counter getting us some rum. Then it all went black.' He sighed. 'Help me sit up.'

Saintclair came back with an enamel bowl filled with water, some cloth and a pot of liniment he placed on the bedside table. 'How're you feeling?' he asked gruffly.

'I'll live,' Archie answered.

'Do you think you'll be up to travelling tomorrow?'

Archie nodded. 'Sure, I'll be fine.'

'I'll bring you something to drink.'

Once he'd left, Harriet dipped the cloth into the water. 'I'll clean that up for you.' She sat on the bed next to him.

She dabbed his swollen eye, then the bump on his forehead with cool water. The sleeve of her dress and her breasts brushed against his chest as she leaned over him. Neither of them talked. In the silence of the night she was aware of his breathing becoming faster, of his eyes growing dark and heavy when he looked at her.

She opened the jar of liniment and took a sniff of it. 'I don't know what this is but it sure smells bad,' she joked, desperate to diffuse the tension she could feel thickening around them now.

'Harriet,' he said in a low voice.

'Hmm? What?' She started spreading the paste onto Archie's forehead.

He grabbed her wrist.

'I want to kiss you.'

She dropped the jar on the bed and stared at him in horror. He took her other hand.

'Dammit, we're supposed to be engaged, aren't we?' He struggled to pull her close as she tried to get up.

'But it's not true, we're just pretending,' she protested as panic rose inside her. 'We're just friends.'

'It's driving me insane to feel you touch me like that. Kiss me.'

It was a nightmare, surely, and she'd wake up any minute now. The man holding her wrists, pulling her towards him, couldn't be the Archie she knew and trusted since she was a child, the man she considered a member of her family.

'No, Archie, let go of me. What's got into you? I don't want to.'

He pressed her against her chest, his mouth found hers and devoured, hungrily.

She choked. It took all her strength to pull away. 'I told you I don't

…'

With a grunt, he wrapped his arms around her waist and wrestled her onto the bed. 'Stop being such a prude. I'll warm you up, you'll see.'

She let out a desperate sob. 'No, Archie!'

'You heard the woman. Let her go.' A voice spoke, cold and steely.

Archie froze.

Saintclair stood in the doorway. 'Much as I dislike beating up a wounded man, I'd have no scruple giving you another black eye to even out your face.'

He put a tray of drinks on a table and stepped into the room.

'I'll damn well do as I please with my fiancée. Mind your own business,' Archie said, between clenched teeth. Nevertheless, he released Harriet from his grip. Quick as a gazelle, she jumped off the bed and out of his reach.

'Are you all right?' Saintclair asked her, his eyes never leaving Archie.

'Yes … It's a misunderstanding, really, nothing to worry about. He had a bump to his head.' Her voice shook with repressed sobs.

'Of course she's all right,' Archie said, sitting up, indignant. 'I didn't do anything wrong.'

'Shut up and get some sleep, I'll see you in the morning,' Saintclair ordered. He took Harriet's elbow and led her out. 'Come with me. I'll take you to your room.'

He closed the door behind them and, without talking, led Harriet through silent, dark corridors. The tears she'd been holding back now streamed down her face. She rubbed her cheeks with the back of her hands.

'Silly of me to get so upset,' she mumbled, waving her hand dismissively. 'He's suffering from shock, that's all. Archie would never hurt me.'

'Well, he looked rather determined from where I stood,' Saintclair said as they reached her room. 'Get into your room and lock your door.'

She gave him a weak smile. 'Yes. Thank you.'

He stayed in the corridor until he heard the key turn in the lock. What was he to think of the evening's events? No matter how hard he tried, he couldn't make out Drake as a man. It was obvious he was a knowledgeable, ambitious and highly respected scholar, with connections to very wealthy men back in England, like Lord Callaghan who was paying for Professor Montague's ransom.

Yet he sensed that the man had a secret, darker side. A few things didn't quite add up about him, not to mention his behaviour with Harriet tonight. Why did he force himself upon her if they were lovers already? And why should she be so upset about it? Her distress had been real enough. Just for that the man deserved to get beaten, hard. It was only the thought of upsetting Harriet any further that held him back.

He punched the wall to relieve the tension inside him. This was no time to get distracted by Harriet Montague. He had things to do tonight. Losing focus was a very bad idea.

Chapter Fifteen

Three days later ...

'Get down and stay down!' Saintclair pushed her roughly behind a large rock and squatted next to her.

'Who are they?'

'Raiders. They must have been following us ever since we left Bou Saada. Strange I never spotted them.' He let out an impatient sigh. 'Do you have your dagger?'

She nodded and pulled it out of the scabbard.

'You may need to use it tonight.' He eyed her with concern. 'If it comes to that, will you be able to?'

She swallowed hard. The dagger slipped in her sweaty hand. Her fingers curled more tightly around the hilt.

'Yes, of course,' she answered with more assurance than she felt.

She glanced nervously at the surrounding shadows. Where were their attackers now?

Saintclair gestured silently towards Ahmoud who crouched, still as a statue about fifty feet away at the bottom of the hill.

'Don't move from this spot. You're safe here. We'll come back for you,' he promised.

He pulled his knife out of his boot, slid it between his teeth and started crawling across the rocky ground towards his friend. Soon they were both no more than moving shadows. She said a silent prayer for them, for all of them, as dark clouds obscured the moon and the hillside was finally plunged into total darkness.

Only a few minutes before, she was preparing food for the evening meal while the men led the horses to graze. Archie had left, alone, to fetch water from a nearby river. It was Musa who raised the alarm. Saintclair wasted no time before strapping the three ransom bags around his body and taking her to safety.

'Musa said there are half a dozen men hiding in the bushes. They must be waiting for full cover of darkness to attack the camp,' he'd explained, pulling Harriet up the hill.

Halfway up, he found a hole big enough to hide the bags. He then pulled her further up.

She now peered so hard into the night her eyes hurt. All her senses seemed sharpened. Night birds called from treetops. Branches rustled in the light wind. Then she heard muffled cries and the thud of bodies falling to the ground in the distance. Her heart hammered in her chest, so loud everybody could probably hear it for miles around. Her fingers tightened around the hilt of the knife. Her legs hurt from squatting but she dared not move.

A light breeze pushed the clouds and the pale moon appeared in the sky. The sound of footsteps behind her made her turn around. The silhouette of a man stood out against the sky. He lunged towards her before she could move and he pushed her back on the ground so hard it knocked the breath out of her. He straddled her, fastening his hands around her neck. His efforts to strangle her were hampered by her *cheche* so he pulled the headdress off. That was the distraction she needed. Bringing the dagger up, she plunged it into his stomach.

He groaned as she pushed the knife in, then slumped on top of her. She let out a cry and pulled the knife out with a sickening slurping sound. The man rolled off her, and she jumped to her feet.

She didn't wait to check if he was dead but ran downhill as fast as she could. Her feet slipped on loose stones. She fell roughly on her backside, and bit back a yelp of pain. Her dagger flew from her hand. There was no time to look for it, so she scrambled to her feet again and carried on running until she reached the bottom of the hill.

What now? Should she run towards the river or the camp? As she stood, indecisive, a man's hand flew across her face to gag her, and a strong arm encircled her chest. Her heart stopped, her throat closed … They'd caught her. She wasn't however going to die without putting up a fight. She kicked the man's shin as hard as she could with the heel of her boot and heard a satisfying grunt of pain.

The man tightened his hold, squeezing the air from her lungs.

'I thought I told you to stay up there.'

She closed her eyes and let out a sigh of relief. Saintclair took his hand off her mouth, turned her round so that she faced him, but he didn't let go of her.

'You also said I was safe,' she whispered back.

'Why didn't you stay put?'

'There was a man … I stabbed him.' She started shaking. 'It was horrible. I'll never forget it.'

'Yes, you will. You did what you had to.'

He bent down and lifted her chin between his thumb and forefinger. There was just enough moonlight now for her to see the clear irises of his eyes and the line of his mouth.

'I think we managed to scare our attackers away,' he said. 'Come.'

He took her hand and led her across the riverbank towards the camp. A scene of utter devastation awaited them. The tents flapped in the breeze, ripped open, their contents strewn around. Among empty bags, parcels of food, and torn blankets were the bodies of five men. Harriet didn't stop to examine them too closely. From their clothing she could see they didn't belong to their party.

They found Ahmoud sitting on the ground, wrapping a strip of cloth around his hand. Archie crouched next to him.

'Harriet! Thank God you're safe,' Archie exclaimed on seeing her.

At one time, she would have rushed into his arms for comfort and reassurance. Not any more. Something was irreversibly broken between them since he'd attacked her – was it friendship, trust, or a deeper feeling she might have once had for him? She didn't know, but she found herself looking at him and wondering where the man she knew had gone.

Saintclair knelt down next to Ahmoud, to speak to him and make sure he wasn't badly injured. 'Where are Musa, Hakim and the others?' he asked.

'They're chasing after the few raiders still alive.' Ahmoud waved at the dead bodies. His lips curled into a smile. 'You did well there, my friend. You got them one by one. They never saw you come. They were far too busy ransacking the camp.'

'They were after the ransom money, of course,' Saintclair said, grimly. 'I can't understand how they managed to find us. I only decided about our route at the last minute.'

'Did they get the money?' Archie asked.

'No, I had time to hide it. We'd better tidy the camp now, get rid of these'—he pointed towards the bodies—'and prepare something to eat. Everybody will be hungry and tired.'

It took over an hour to put the camp back to order. Two of the tents were too badly ripped to be fixed, but the others were roughly stitched back together. Ahmoud and Saintclair disposed of the dead bodies while Archie helped Harriet tidy up before she took care of the meal. By the time Musa, Hakim and the other men came back, she'd a pot of water to boil above the fire, pieces of bread lay on hot stones and she'd mixed strips of meat with semolina, chickpeas and raisins.

Harriet's cheeks glowed from the heat of the fire as she stirred the couscous, breathing enticing aromas of vegetables and spices. She thought of Aunt Elizabeth, who always complained about her lack of domestic skills. Her elderly relative would be pleased with her tonight. Tidying the camp and rustling something to eat for everybody in such a short time was no mean feat.

Harriet shook her head. Actually, Aunt Elizabeth wouldn't be pleased at all. Not only had she killed a man to defend her own life, but she camped out most nights in the wilderness, exposed to terrible perils and in the company of wild, dangerous men. She wore men's clothing, hadn't combed her hair or taken a bath in three days, and probably looked like … No, it was best not to think about what she looked like.

'That smells good,' Saintclair remarked, coming up behind her. Her heart skipped a beat and she dropped the spoon into the cauldron.

There was something else Aunt Elizabeth wouldn't approve of, she pondered as she tried to retrieve the spoon without burning her fingers. Something Harriet couldn't hide from any longer. She added more raisins and stirred the couscous. Hoping that focusing on practical things would help block out the unwelcome, confusing, painful, yet exhilarating sensations the man standing close by aroused. It didn't. To be honest, he didn't even have to be near for her to feel that way. The sound of his voice, the mere thought of him, were enough for her heart to beat faster, for her skin to become hot and shivery.

She let out an impatient sigh and turned her attention to making tea. She was behaving like a naïve, infatuated girl. With her very limited experience of men, it was only natural that she'd be impressed by Lucas Saintclair. After all, he was handsome, brave, and unlike any man she'd encountered before. His was a life of danger and adventure in a wild, fascinating country. She spent every single day and most nights in his company.

There was also the fact that he'd kissed and touched her like no man had before.

The memory of the moonlit terrace at Ksar el boukhari made her hands shake as she added yet more tea leaves to the boiling water. She took a deep breath. She might be attracted to him but she neither liked nor respected him. Saintclair wasn't chivalrous. He was ruthless and callous, a mercenary without any morals. He only agreed to help rescue her father because she offered him access to one of the greatest treasures of all times.

She wasn't in love with him.

She shook her head. Of course, she wasn't in love with him. What a silly thought! Love was warm, strong, tranquil and reassuring. It didn't cause deep churning pain, unbearable ache or constant torment. Did it?

'If you add any more tea to that pot of water, we won't have enough for the rest of the journey, Miss Montague,' Saintclair remarked as he sat down and leaned against a large rock. He stretched his legs in front of him and closed his eyes, so still for a moment she thought he'd fallen asleep.

'I'll show you something tomorrow morning,' he said, his eyes still closed. 'I think you'll like it.'

'What is it?'

He opened his eyes and smiled. 'It's a surprise.'

The evening was spent talking about the raiders' failed attack and devising a new route to Laghouat, their next stop. Saintclair believed the bandits would rally more men and try again.

'Something puzzles me,' he added. 'At first I thought they'd followed us here, but now I'm not so sure. I would have seen them trailing after us … No, the only explanation is that they knew we'd come this way and were lying in wait. What I can't understand is how they found out about our route. This isn't the easiest or the fastest way to the Sahara.' He shook his head.

'They were Tuaregs, weren't they?' Archie asked, finishing his second helping of couscous. 'They're known to track travellers, and raid villages and caravans.'

Lucas set his cup of mint tea on his knee and looked straight at him. 'They weren't Tuaregs. If they had been, we'd be dead by now.'

He drank his tea and stood up. 'I'm taking first watch with Hakim. The rest of you should get some sleep. Watch changes every four hours.'

Once the food and pots had been cleared and tidied away, Harriet spread a thick blanket on the ground and wrapped herself into her burnous.

The men rolled themselves inside the coats and blankets. Archie chose to sleep inside a tent. Soon the camp was quiet, and the only sounds troubling the night were the men's snores, the crackling of the fire and the occasional night bird.

Harriet couldn't get comfortable. The ground was hard and cold, so cold she kept shivering, unable to fall asleep. She was still wide awake hours later when Saintclair and Hakim came back from their watch.

'What are you doing out here?' Saintclair asked, standing next to her.

'Trying to sleep,' she mumbled.

'Why don't you go in a tent?' He grabbed his saddlebag and unfolded his blanket.

'I want to keep an eye on things.'

He let out a laugh and crouched down next to her. 'I see you don't trust us to keep watch.'

'You can laugh all you want, but the more of us who are alert, the better our chances of staying alive.'

'You're damned right, Miss Montague. You look cold,' he said, suddenly serious. 'Move over.'

Ignoring her startled expression, he pushed her to one side so that they could both fit on the same blanket, then lay down against her and wrapped his own cover over both of them.

'What are you doing, Saintclair? This isn't appropriate,' she protested, trying to pull away from him.

'Do you want to be warm?' He looked her over and raised an eyebrow. 'There's no better way than this, believe me. Don't worry. I won't try to take advantage of you. I'm far too tired.'

Silently, she lay down again.

'Now, turn around. That's it.' He wrapped his arm around her waist and snuggled against her back.

Oh God, how was she supposed to sleep now? She lay still, hardly able to breathe. His hand was so hot on her stomach it burned, and his arm pinned her safely in place. She felt the warmth of his chest, of his legs encasing her.

He coughed. 'I feel like I'm holding a wooden plank. Could you relax a little?'

'It's just that ...'

'Go to sleep, Harriet,' he whispered.

It was the first time he'd used her name. It made her feel warm and mellow inside.

Within seconds, his breathing was deep, slow and regular. His arm slackened but still held her in place. She drew air in slowly, deliciously conscious of his warmth enveloping her, his body cradling her. Feeling a little bolder now he was asleep, she touched his hand, traced the outline of his fingers. He stirred and murmured something against her and she froze. What if he should wake up now? She would die of shame.

Better do as he said and try to fall asleep. She closed her eyes and imitated the regular pattern of his breathing, and surprisingly she drifted to sleep.

He'd been awake since the last star disappeared in the dawn sky. It was a habit of his, never to sleep past dawn. The light was changing from dark blue to grey. To the east, pale yellow and pink hues added touches of warmth to the sky. He should get up, start the fire and go down to the river to fetch some water for the tea. Instead, he buried his face in Harriet's neck and breathed in her scent – the rose soap she liked so much and her own delicious, female scent.

This was sheer torture. All he wanted to do was explore her body, slide his hands down the soft curves of her hips then slowly glide upward to her breasts. Even though she wore far too many layers of clothing for his liking, the feel of her body nestling snugly against his thighs and his chest stirred a savage, almost uncontrollable urge inside him.

He pushed her hair aside and kissed her neck. She murmured something. Unable to resist any longer, he caressed her stomach in light, slow circles. He heard her moan softly. His fingers itched to explore further. He already imagined the feel of her breasts in his hands, the tightening buds of her nipples under his thumbs. She stirred in her sleep. Her hips moved against him. He drew a sharp breath as fire coursed through his veins and pressure built. His hands reached up, eager to hold, caress. And take. Overwhelmed by the need to have her naked under him, to lose himself inside her, he pulled her closer and trailed his mouth along the tender skin of her neck.

He used the last of his self-control to make himself stop. He wouldn't force himself on her. The scornful words she'd said not so long before echoed in his mind. He wasn't about to forget them.

He wanted her, that much was true, but if he ever made love to her, she would be awake, wide awake, and she would want him as much as he wanted her. He would look into her misty grey eyes and watch them become stormy and dark with passion. And then she'd beg him to take her.

He pulled away slowly, made sure she was well covered and got up. A swim in the river, that's what he needed. The cold, freezing water was sure to tame the fire inside him. As he walked away from camp, he waved at Musa and Ahmoud who'd taken last watch. The raiders, whoever they were, hadn't come back. They were safe. For now.

Chapter Sixteen

It was cold and she was alone.

She shivered and opened her eyes to a transparent dawn. She hadn't heard Lucas leave. Heaving a sigh, partly relief and partly regret, she sat up and lifted a hand to softly stroke her neck. She'd just had the most delicious, shameful dream in which he'd kissed her just there, again and again. He kissed her as if he really wanted her, and she'd whispered his name. Lucas … She withdrew her hand. Enough. It was only a dream.

She got up and rubbed her hands along her arms. Her breath steamed in front of her. The difference of temperature between night and day never ceased to amaze her. How could it be so hot during the day and so cold at night? The heat would soar from the moment the sun appeared beyond the line of the horizon until the steppes became a hazy, burning hell, after noon. It was May and they hadn't even reached the Sahara yet … She would never admit it to anyone but the journey was proving far harder than she'd anticipated. It wasn't only the heat and the relentless pace dictated by Lucas that she found gruelling. There was the promiscuity, the lack of privacy. Her clothes were filthy, her hair stiff and matted.

She closed her eyes and felt a sudden yearning for the study in her London house. She could almost breathe in the mixed scents of leather, paper and wax furniture polish, feel the grain of her armchair under her fingertips and hear the soft ticking of the clock on the mantelpiece. She pictured herself opening the patio door onto the terrace and walking out into the spring rain. It was so vivid she licked her lips as if to taste the cool drizzle.

She shook her head, opened her eyes, and sighed as she looked at the camp. This was no time to daydream. She'd better get ready while the men were still asleep and wrapped up in their blankets. It was the perfect time to go down to the river. She took a liquorice stick out of her bag and started chewing on it to clean her teeth and freshen her breath. Then she extracted a clean pair of drawers and a chemise and grabbed hold of her bar of soap.

'Where do you think you're going?'

Lucas was in front of her. With his damp hair curling at the tips, his white shirt open on his chest and the dark stubble on his cheeks, he reminded her more than ever of a pirate – a strange pirate, of course, stranded in the desert, and a long way away from the sea.

She stared at the droplets of water that glistened on his chest, at the hard plane of his stomach, and swallowed hard.

'I'm going for a swim.' She gestured towards the river.

'Oh no, you're not.' He crossed his arms on his chest.

'Why not? What are the chances of my meeting with a lion again?' she asked, defiant.

'I wasn't thinking about lions, more about raiders. The men who attacked us may still be lurking around.'

'I think I proved last night that I could defend myself.' Her voice quivered as she relived her terror of the man jumping on her and trying to strangle her, of pulling her dagger out and plunging it into his stomach.

'Hmm … You did well, that much is true.' Lucas started fastening his shirt.

'Is the man I killed still up there?'

'He must be. I didn't move him. I had enough with the other five.'

'Then we must bury him. No man deserves to be left in the open to rot or be eaten by predators.'

He narrowed his eyes. 'Some do.'

'If you're not prepared to show any Christian compassion, then I'll go up there and deal with him myself,' she replied, although she had no idea how she'd be able to bury a dead man on her own. She wasn't even sure she'd have the nerve to look at him, let alone touch him.

He shrugged. 'All right, I suppose I'd better come with you. I did say I had something to show you. It's up there, in a cave.'

Her eyes lit up. 'Rock paintings?'

He nodded.

'Wait a minute. I'll take my drawing things!'

She dug into her bag for her sketch pad, her pencils and a box of pastels, and stuffed the bar of soap, the drawers, the chemise, her comb and the liquorice stick in the large pockets of her burnous. Lucas looked at her. His lips twitched with repressed laughter.

'Anything else you want to shove into your pockets?' he asked. 'Maybe you could take the tea pot with you. I'm sure we'll be thirsty later.'

She threw him a black glance. He grabbed a shovel then led the way up the hillside. She slowed down when they approached the spot where she'd stabbed the raider.

Lucas glanced at her. 'Sit down here, I'll deal with him.'

'I was the one who killed him. I should help.'

He put his hands on her shoulders and forced her down. 'I said I would do it. Sit.'

This time she didn't protest. He walked up to the corpse and knelt beside it.

She heard him mutter to himself in French. She might not understand the words, but his tone left little doubt in her mind that he was cursing.

'That's strange,' he said at last. 'I didn't think the raiders were Tuaregs, but this one isn't even a native.'

She jumped to her feet and rushed to his side. 'Let me see!'

'Look at his hair.' He pulled the man's turban off to reveal a head of dark blond hair. He turned the man's head towards him. The open, glazed eyes were blue.

Kneeling down next to the body, he patted the man's black tunic, the pockets of his trousers and shook his head. 'There's nothing, no papers, no letters, nothing we could identify him with.'

He slid a ring off the dead man's finger and showed it to Harriet. 'Only that ring.'

She held it in front of her. It was a large signet ring made of jade featuring a snarling silver wolf. She had seen such a ring before, but where? She closed her eyes, chasing after an elusive memory. Images flashed in her mind. A castle with square towers. A terrace overlooking a park that sloped down towards a lake. Stormy clouds in an evening sky. She was standing on the terrace, looking in through a window at a group of men arguing in a dimly lit parlour. Her father was there, holding a glass of brandy. Something glittered on his finger as he lifted his glass to his lips. He was shouting. She had never seen him so angry before and it frightened her almost as much as the nightmarish ring on his finger – a green ring with a snarling silver wolf. She'd sat on the cold stone flags and curled up into a ball, too terrified to move.

Her mind went blank. That's all she could remember. Maybe it had been a dream … Maybe she shouldn't say anything to Lucas until she could remember more.

Her hand shook as she handed the ring back to Lucas. 'What can this mean? Do you think he was English or French? But why would he want to attack us?'

Lucas toyed with the ring. 'For your father's ransom gold, of course. The others were Arabs, I know. I buried them myself with Ahmoud. But who was *he*?' He gestured towards the dead man. He raked his hand through his hair, deep in thought. 'The ring is peculiar enough. It might be the emblem for a regiment, or a secret organisation,' he ventured.

She nodded. 'You're probably right. Archie might recognise it.'

And if her memories were real, and not a figment of her imagination, he would surely remember that her father had worn one similar.

'We'll see if he does.' Lucas put the ring in his pocket.

A detail bothered her. A tall European man dressed as a Tuareg had followed her before, she was sure of it. In Algiers, Ksar el boukhari and Bou Saada. Could he and the dead man lying here on the hillside be the same?

Lucas stood up. 'I'll show you the rock paintings now. You can start drawing while I deal with him.'

He took her further up the hill and pushed a boulder obstructing the mouth of a cave. 'Now you must promise me you won't go wandering anywhere. There should be enough to keep you happy in here.'

Harriet stepped into the cave. Lucas pushed a few more rocks and daylight flooded in, revealing dozens of drawings on the surface of the cave.

'Lucas, this is wonderful!' Immediately, heat burned her cheeks and she walked to the other end of the cave to hide her embarrassment. Was she mad? She called him by his first name! Fortunately, he didn't seem to have noticed. She started walking around and soon nothing mattered but the paintings. Antelopes, lions, elephants and buffalos; hunters with spears and arrows, women nursing children. This place was a treasure trove.

'Look!' she pointed to the walls of the cave. 'They used paint – black, red and white pigments.' She turned a beaming smile to Lucas. 'Thank you, thank you so much for bringing me here.'

'If it keeps you quiet for a while, then it's worth it,' he said gruffly. 'Have fun. I'll be back shortly.'

She wasn't listening any longer. She didn't even see him leave. This was the most wonderful collection of primitive art she had ever hoped to see. How old were these drawings? How long ago had men wandered this land and made a record of the world around them, of their day-to-day struggle to survive? She took hold of her sketch pad, her pencil and colours, and lost track of time.

She would copy every single drawing. She didn't feel hunger or thirst. When her hair fell in front of her eyes, she pushed it away absent-mindedly, not caring if she smudged charcoal crayon on her forehead and cheeks. The sun rose and a fiery pink and orange light bathed the interior of the cave. It became hot, so hot she took her tunic off and carried on drawing in her chemise. Irritatingly, one of the straps kept falling off her shoulder. After a while she didn't even bother to pull it back up.

She covered a dozen pages of drawings and sketches, looked around, and sighed in frustration. She would never have time to copy everything. A shadow fell across the mouth of the cave. Lucas leaned against the wall, arms crossed on his chest, head cocked to one side.

He'd been watching her for a while. Enraptured in her work, she hadn't noticed him.

'So? What do you make of this place?'

Startled, she jumped before smiling at him. 'You said you knew other places like this?'

He nodded. 'I do, but we don't have time to look at them now.'

She stood up. 'We must, if only for a few hours. Do you realise what we have here? It's a treasure. Proof of the existence of art in primitive times.'

Pointing to the painting of a lion devouring an antelope, she added, 'Look at the detail. The expression of the lion, fierce and savage, whereas the antelope has already given up the struggle for survival.'

He walked towards her. His eyes were on her, not on the paintings. 'You have dirt on your face,' he said, his voice hoarse.

He lifted his hand to her face to rub a smear of charcoal on her forehead. Her skin felt like silk. Slowly he traced the outline of her face, her cheeks, her jawline and her throat. He put his hand on her bare shoulder. It was warm and smooth. He stroked her collarbone, marvelled to feel it so delicate under his fingers.

'We can't stay here, Harriet. I want to be in Laghouat tonight.' He pulled the strap of her chemise up, but didn't withdraw his hand.

His heart thundered. His blood pulsed hard. The throbbing ache in his body was almost unbearable. She looked so fresh and innocent, yet he knew she wasn't since she was Drake's mistress. Her eyes were dark and heavy, her mouth slightly open, as if waiting for his kiss. No woman should be allowed to look at a man like that. The sunlight warmed her milky white skin. Her thin chemise outlined the curves of her breasts and the darker tips of her nipples. He licked his lips, imagined how they would taste. He felt their tight buds under his tongue already …

As if she sensed the hard, hot desire inside him, she parted her lips even more and let out a shaky breath. It was almost his undoing.

In a desperate attempt to regain control, he dropped his hand and narrowed his eyes to a slit. 'Get dressed and take your things,' he ordered before turning around and walking out.

Disappointment churned inside her. She stomped the rocky ground and let out a cry of frustration. He really was a hateful man! She wanted him to kiss her, so desperately – and he'd walked away!

Then she felt almost sick with shame. Not only was she behaving like a wanton woman, but she was being illogical and unreasonable too. Only a few days before at Ksar el boukhari she pushed him away, accused him of forcing himself on her. He promised then that it wouldn't happen again. How could she now resent him for keeping his word?

She needed to get hold of herself, learn to rein in this maddening infatuation she felt for him. Her father's life depended on her being her usual cool, level-headed self. She should never forget about him. Nothing, and no one else mattered.

She rearranged her clothing as quickly as she could, gathered her things and followed Saintclair out.

He was already a long way down the hill and she had to run to catch up with him. He didn't speak or look at her once. His jaw was set, his fingers clenched so tight around the handle of the shovel his knuckles were white. She wondered if he'd buried the man or simply pushed his body down a hole and covered it with stones.

Back at the camp, the men had left some bread and tea near the fire for them. Lucas grabbed a tin cup and walked off towards the horse enclosure without a word to anyone. Harriet put her drawing pad on the ground to pour some mint tea.

'Where have you been?' Archie sprung up next to her.

'Oh Archie, I wish you could have seen it!' She picked up the sketch book and showed him the pages with the rock art paintings. 'Saintclair took me to a cave covered with paintings. It was wonderful.'

'Why didn't you come to get me?' He frowned as he looked at the drawings.

She felt a pang of guilt. It hadn't even crossed her mind, not for one second.

'Never mind.' He sighed. 'What have we here? Well, well, you have kept busy. These are drawings of Bou Saada, the market, the oasis.'

He stood up and thumbed through more pages.

'Give me back the book, Archie.'

He laughed and held it out of her reach. 'Come on, Harriet. What's the big deal? You always show me your drawings.'

'Archie, please, give it back.' Tears of frustration stung her eyes. She would die of shame if he came across some of the sketches she'd made recently.

'You can't keep any secrets from your fiancé, my dear.' Archie was still laughing but there was a slightly sinister glint in his eyes now, as if he dared her to deny they were engaged in front of everybody.

She jumped up and extended her hand to grab the book, but he held it higher. 'I wonder what you're so flustered about.'

He stopped and froze, as if changed into stone, and stared at a point beyond Harriet.

She spun round.

Behind her, Lucas held the green ring up to the sunshine as if to examine it more thoroughly. Archie dropped Harriet's sketchbook to the dusty ground and marched up to him.

'Where did you find that?' he asked, holding out his hand.

Lucas carried on studying the ring as if he hadn't heard him. 'Damn ugly, isn't it?' he said at last. 'I gather it's made of silver and imperial jade. What do you think, Drake? You're the expert.'

Harriet picked up her book and held it against her chest. Curious, she looked at Lucas. What was he playing at? Why not tell Archie straight away where they found the ring?

Archie's hand appeared to shake when he lifted the ring to study it. 'I don't think it's very old, but you're right, it is imperial jade. The rarest.' He sounded a little breathless.

'Have you ever come across one like it?'

Archie shook his head slowly. 'No, never. Where did you find it?'

Lucas stared at him a moment. 'It was on one of the bodies. The man was European.'

Archie became visibly paler. 'I don't understand.'

'Neither do I, but I intend to.' Lucas shrugged and put the ring in his pocket.

Chapter Seventeen

A bath, at last! The sunken tub, filled to the brim with warm water and laced with fragrant jasmine essence, was a vision of heaven after days of riding in the scorching, dusty heat. The problem was the two women servants showing no intention of leaving her alone. Harriet let out a resigned sigh. Now wasn't the time to be prudish. She took her boots off, shed her filthy clothes and stepped down into the bath tub. The sensations of the water on her skin were so delicious she couldn't repress a purr of contentment. She reclined against the smooth alabaster tub and closed her eyes. How wonderful to be stopping the night in the palace of Lucas' friend Nordine and enjoying a little comfort and luxury, and how easily she could fall asleep now if it wasn't for the women's incessant chatter.

She didn't understand a word of what they were saying but knew they were talking about her. Since her arrival earlier that evening, they'd stared at her with unbridled curiosity, as if she was a strange, slightly inferior, species of female. They pursed their lips, shook their head; their eyes filled with pity as they pointed to her clothes, her dirt-streaked skin and her matted tresses.

Now they hovered around her and started scrubbing her back, rubbing jasmine oil into her skin and washing her hair. Harriet wasn't used to being tended to like this. She tried to protest at first, but faced with the cheerful determination on the women's faces, soon gave up. After a few minutes she even enjoyed being pampered. Once the water cooled down, the women helped her out of the bath and wrapped her up in a large, soft cloth.

'I can do that myself.' She tried to move away from their busy hands, but they carried on regardless.

Harriet was given a red pantaloon and then a red and gold tunic which she slipped over her head. The fabric rippled against her bare skin, soft and silky. She pushed her feet into dainty red slippers, and she was ready. At last the two women stood back and nodded, grinning widely.

She followed them along the corridors of the palace to the dining room where Lucas and his friend studied a map spread out on the table. They seemed far too preoccupied to notice them walk in.

'It's a very tight rope you're walking,' Nordine was saying.

'Mortemer will be merciless if he ever catches you. You've made a fool of him far too often these past few years … Do you think he suspects anything?'

Lucas shrugged. 'He might. We were followed on our way to Bou Saada, and then again on our way here.' He paused. 'It doesn't matter. You know I don't care what happens to me.'

Nordine shook his head, a wistful smile on his lips. 'You might lose something very precious, my friend. Your life, for example.'

Lucas let out a harsh laugh. 'So be it. Nothing matters more than making Mortemer pay for what he's done, you know that.'

Harriet felt a tugging to her heart. How bitter he sounded. He might want to punish Mortemer, but he wanted to punish himself even more.

Nordine sighed. 'Don't let this thing with Mortemer cloud your judgment. You are courting danger a little too much these days. Having said that, it was an achievement to capture the five cannon! Where are they now?'

'We hid them in a canyon to the East of Bou Saada.' Lucas pointed a finger to the map. 'I sent word to El-Berkani. He should be able to collect them any day now.'

'They will be much safer in our hands than those of the French. Good work, my friend.' Nordine slapped his back.

What were they talking about? Wasn't El-Berkani the rebel who'd escaped recently from the French penitentiary?

She stepped closer, eager to hear more, but Nordine noticed her and his two women servants. He caught his breath then relaxed into a smile.

'Here they are, my lovelies.' Looking at Harriet, he added with a velvet voice, 'I knew there was a swan hiding somewhere under those ugly clothes.'

Lucas glanced up absent-mindedly from the map. His eyes grew a little wider and he stared at her as if he was seeing her for the first time. She waited for him to say something. Her heart beat faster, harder, but he turned away and proceeded to fold the map.

'I have bad news, I'm afraid,' Nordine remarked. 'Your fiancé won't be joining us tonight. He isn't feeling very well.'

'Archie is ill? Maybe I should go to him.' Harriet started to turn away.

Nordine shook his head. 'Leave him for now. If he's suffering from sunstroke, the best thing he can do is sleep, and I don't think he'll sleep a wink if he sees how ravishing you look tonight.'

He took her hand and led her to the table. 'Lucas told me you were very brave during the attack last night. You should be proud of yourself.'

'I'm not proud I killed a man,' she said, her throat tight.

'You had no choice,' Lucas interrupted. 'It was him or you.'

Nordine clapped his hands and servants brought porcelain plates, glittering crystal glasses and silver cutlery. It could have been a dinner party in an elegant London townhouse were it not for the fragrant dishes of lamb, date and apricot couscous, and spicy vegetables being served.

'I know you appreciate good wine.' Nordine filled Lucas' glass, then hers.

She drank a little wine to ease the tightness in her throat while listening to Nordine talk about his recent travels to Algiers and Constantine. He asked about her father and his work. He was particularly interested in his fascination for the lost Garamantes civilisation.

'Of course I've heard about the emerald mines, who hasn't?' he said. 'So many tried to find them, so many died, lost in the Sahara desert or the Hoggar. They could be anywhere between Ethiopia to Libya. My grandfather claimed the ancients left maps and instructions inside a cave in the Hoggar. Of course, only someone familiar with the old writing would be able to read them.'

Lucas set his glass on the table. 'That's it,' he whispered.

Both Harriet and Nordine looked at him.

'Didn't you say your father was one of the very few scholars who could read the old writing?'

Harriet nodded. 'It took him years to find a way of translating it, using Tifinagh – the alphabet the Tuaregs have used for centuries and which they inherited from the Garamantes – and tablets he discovered in Libya that were written both in Greek, Latin and in the old language.'

'What if he found something referring to Tin Hinan's tomb when he was studying the rock paintings? What if he believed the tomb held the secret of the emerald mines?'

Harriet looked at him. What he said made sense. 'What do you know about Tin Hinan? You said she was a holy woman.'

Lucas nodded and reclined on his chair. 'That's right. According to Tuareg traditions, she travelled from the east with her woman servant at the time of the Emperor Constantine. She settled in an oasis near Tamanrasset where she united all the Tuareg tribes under her rule. That's why they still call her Mother.'

'All Imenokalen – supreme Tuareg chiefs – are said to descend from her bloodline. Thanks to her, women have always occupied a special place in Tuareg society. They are the musicians and the poets, the keepers of oral traditions.' He smiled. 'Men call them "the little queens". They hold games and contests in their honour. It's the women who own the family tent and can even boot their husband out if they so choose. This is part of Tin Hinan's legacy.'

'You said she lived during the reign of Constantine – that would be the fourth century AD.' Harriet frowned in concentration. 'The Garamantes would have been at the peak of their power then, their kingdom stretching from Libya all the way across the Sahara. They would have come in contact with the Tuaregs.'

'If these Garamantes were that important, why have they left almost no traces, cities, or monuments of their civilisation?' Lucas objected.

'There must be some, but they probably lie untouched, buried in the desert sands,' Harriet argued. 'Herodotus wrote about the Garamantes' vast kingdom. He praised their skills for channelling water from underground lakes into oases and changing the desert into fertile lands. He also referred to the speed of the four-horse chariots they used for hunting. Later writers, like Pliny the Elder, mentioned that throughout the centuries they were either fighting against the Romans or trading with them. Rome's appetite for slaves, gold and precious stones, as well as for lions and leopards for the gladiator games, was insatiable. Anything they wanted, the Garamantes could supply. They even traced chariot roads across the Sahara and beyond to make trading faster.'

'How did they manage to keep the location of their mines a secret for so long?' Nordine asked. He clapped his hands and a servant brought in a tray with honey and date pastries – Harriet's favourites. She took one and bit into it.

'It's hard to believe, that's true,' Lucas mused as he drank a sip of wine. 'Maybe there was some disaster. The mines collapsed and people were afraid to go near them. Now, at last, maybe someone deciphered a map painted or carved in the Hoggar mountains, and they followed the trail to Tin Hinan's tomb.'

Lucas turned to Harriet. 'Someone like your father ... But whatever he hoped to find in there, he should have known better. He put his men in mortal danger.'

She put down her pastry. Her throat was tight as tears filled her eyes. 'He wasn't to know that the Tuaregs would kill them all.' She stared at Lucas, bracing herself to ask the question she'd been burning to ask for days.

'You believe he's dead too, don't you?'

'Yes.' He nodded. His eyes were clear and sharp, without the trace of a doubt.

The blood drained from her face and she put a hand against her heart.

'Lucas, you should know better than to upset Miss Harriet,' Nordine scolded. 'I'll ask my women to take her outside for some fresh air. She looks awfully pale.' He gestured to a servant.

Harriet shook her head and pushed her chair away from the table. 'It won't be necessary. I can find my own way.'

But as she started to stand up, the room spun round. It felt as if the ground collapsed from under her and she was dropping down a deep, dark place.

'You need to lie down.' Lucas scooped her up in his arms before she fell, and started to the door.

'It's nothing, I'm quite capable of walking,' she protested, wriggling in his arms.

'Don't move and hold onto me.'

'No, really, I don't …'

This time the glint of steel in his eyes silenced her. Obediently, she wrapped her arms around his neck.

He knew the house well, she noticed, as he marched down the maze of corridors and stairs leading to her room without hesitation.

'Here we are.' He kicked the door open and walked across the tiled floor. An oil lamp burned on a low table and bathed the room in a golden glow. The patio doors were open onto the garden where cicadas sang their cadenced song. Lucas put her down on the bed but didn't release her.

'I'm sorry,' he said, staring into her eyes.

Overcome by dizziness, she didn't answer. This time, however, it had nothing to do with what he'd said about her father and everything to do with the feel of his arms, strong and warm around her, with his mouth just a few inches away from hers, and with the flame of the oil lamp reflecting in his eyes.

'It was tactless of me to speak about your father like I did.'

'Why do you still want to go to Tamanrasset if you're so sure my father is …' She just couldn't say the word and heaved a sigh.

'What I believe doesn't matter. I gave you my word in Algiers.' He paused. 'And I want the Barbarossa map.'

Of course, the treasure map. That's what he really wanted. How could she forget?

'Anyway, I shouldn't have been so blunt.'

'It's quite all right. I asked you and you spoke your mind,' she whispered. 'My father taught me to always speak the truth.'

She realised that her hands were still clasped behind his neck. She unfastened her fingers and slid them down to his shoulders, leaving them there.

There was a moment of silence.

'You mean, you always speak the truth?' he asked at last, his lips curling into a smile.

'Yes, I do,' she answered. There was that small lie about Archie and her being engaged … 'Most of the time,' she corrected.

'So these grey eyes of yours never lie.' He sounded thoughtful.

He sat next to her. His hand glided slowly over the red silk tunic … her waist … the side of her breast.

She stiffened, holding her breath.

'If I ask if you want me to kiss you, you will tell me the truth?' he asked, lowering his voice.

'Well, I …'

'Do you want me to kiss you, Harriet?'

'Oh.' Mesmerised by the desire burning in his eyes, she was unable to move or speak.

He leaned closer. 'Is that a yes or a no?'

All she could hear was her thundering heartbeat. 'Yes.' She breathed out at last.

He covered her mouth with his. It was just like before, an explosion of sensations inside and out that rendered her weak and warm and helpless. With a low groan, he pulled her up against him, his hands moved in a slow caress along her back, tangled into her hair, leaving a burning trail from her hips to the nape of her neck. The silk robe and pantaloons were so light she might as well have been naked under his touch.

A warm breeze blew across the room through the garden doors. It rustled the palms outside and carried almond tree blossoms inside the room. Lucas pushed her down against the mattress, kissed her throat, nibbled at her collarbone. When he murmured something against her skin, his breath was hotter than the desert wind. His mouth claimed hers for another deep, long kiss, and his hands brushed her breasts through the silk, gentle and insistent in turn, making her tight and achy inside. She let out a breathless moan. She was pure, raw feeling.

He started unbuttoning her top then looked up. 'Harriet?' he whispered.

She bit her lower lip and closed her eyes. She wanted him to carry on, more than anything else in the world. Was that so shameful?

'Harriet,' he called again, his voice deeper.

'Yes,' she said. 'Yes.'

He smiled and kissed her slowly as he unfastened her top and his mouth was on the soft swell of her breasts. She opened her eyes, shocked as much by his caress as by her response to it – a hot, liquid pull in her stomach. She looked down at his dark hair, at the warm glow of the light upon it. His lips lingered, the stubble on his face scraped her skin. She tangled her fingers in his hair, arching her hips against him.

He pinned her against the bed, impatient now, and his kisses became hard. She was spiralling down a dark, burning hot pit. Clutching at his shoulders like a woman lost in a storm, she responded to his caresses with mindless whispers and sighs. His fingers trailed over the silk pantaloons and he tugged at them to pull them down … And she came back to her senses. She stiffened in his arms, unable to fight the overwhelming, icy cold panic taking over.

'No.' She managed a strangled cry, hiding her face in her hands.

He drew back, held her at arm's length, exposed, dishevelled, on the bed.

'What do you mean … no?'

She looked up, tried to focus on the unforgiving lines of his face, the even more unforgiving flash of anger in his eyes.

'I mean, I'm not ready for this.'

She should tell him she was afraid, that she'd never been with a man before, but the words choked in her throat.

She pulled the sides of her tunic over her chest and hips in a shaky and clumsy attempt to cover herself.

He leaned down towards her and her eyes opened wide with terror. What if he didn't listen? Did what he pleased.

'Please don't hurt me,' she sobbed, fear almost choking her.

He pulled her to him like a rag doll. 'I have no intention of hurting you, but I'll tell you this.' His voice was a harsh whisper. 'Don't ever again start something with me you're not prepared to finish, because next time I swear I'll finish it, whether you're ready or not.'

He let her go so abruptly she fell back against the pillow. After a last, dark and scorching look at her, he walked out. She bit her fist, hard, and then harder, until it hurt more than the pain inside.

He walked into the garden, craving the shadows, the darkness, and solitude.

Letting out a sharp breath, he clenched his fists into balls and gave the scaly trunk of a palm tree a few quick, hard punches. He scraped his knuckles and didn't feel any better. He couldn't believe Harriet pushed him away. She'd made him feel like a damned fool – a fool with fire in his blood. It had never happened to him before. Maybe that was why he was so angry right now. He'd always had it easy when it came to women. Then again, he'd never met a woman like Harriet Montague.

He didn't understand her at all. He'd seen her eyes heavy with desire, heard her fast, shallow breathing, and felt the feverish grip of her fingers on his shoulders. She wanted him as much as he wanted her. She hadn't been pretending.

He allowed himself a cynical smile.

Of course, she had.

She'd played him and he'd fallen for it. Her soft grey eyes did lie after all. He felt himself grow hot again just remembering the feel of her mouth under his, and her smooth skin under his hands. He hadn't meant what he said about finishing what they'd started should there be a next time. He had spoken in anger and frustration, that was all, but it was … *hell*!

No wonder Harriet drove Drake crazy. He balled his fists again. The thought of the Englishman touching, kissing, making love to her was something he'd managed to keep out of his mind until now. Now it was almost too much to bear.

He gave the palm tree one last, pointless punch before walking into the shadows. There was only one thing to do if he had any hope of snatching a few hours sleep tonight, and that was to pay a visit to one of Laghouat's infamous taverns. Good wine and his friends' company would help him forget about Harriet Montague and the tumult she roused inside him.

He froze and held his breath as he heard a scraping sound behind the garden wall. All senses alert, he slid noiselessly behind a bush and pulled his knife out. A dark figure appeared at the top of the wall, outlined by silvery moonlight. The man jumped down and, on landing, let out a muffled curse in English. Lucas frowned. If there was a time a man let down his guard it was when he was hurt … and when he made love.

The man straightened up and limped along the path. Moonlight outlined his profile in silver as he walked past him. Drake! He said he was too ill to join them tonight. What was the man up to? Where did he go, alone and in secret?

Chapter Eighteen

'Here are the choices,' Lucas said. 'We can follow the caravan route to the Berriane oasis and Ghardaïa or …' He lifted his glass of pomegranate juice and drank it in one long gulp.

'Or what?' Archie asked, helping himself to a cup of black coffee. 'Isn't it time you made up your mind? We were supposed to leave today.'

'We'll leave when I say so.'

Lucas slammed the empty glass on the table. He looked pale and tired this morning, with dark stubble shadowing his cheeks. His temper was just as mean as his looks. He'd just ranted at Nordine for letting him sleep too late and at Hakim for failing to take two of the horses to the blacksmith. Now it was Archie's turn to take the brunt of his bad mood.

'What about the other route?' Harriet asked.

By the harsh stare he gave her, it wasn't hard to guess she was the cause of his temper – as well as a few bottles of strong liquor which had probably given him a sore head. She quickly lowered her eyes to the map and clutched her fingers in her lap to stop them from shaking.

She would have preferred to avoid him altogether and hide in her room, but he sent a servant to say he demanded her immediate presence. Now she had to listen to him, talk to him, and pretend nothing happened between them the night before.

'We could cut through the reg towards In Salah. It would save us over a week, but …' Lucas hesitated, sighed and raked his fingers in his hair.

'So why don't we?' Archie cut in. He leaned over the table to study the map.

It was a map Saintclair had drawn in infinite detail over his years of scouting the country. Ksars, hamlets, trails and roads were marked in ink, as well as mountains, landmarks, wells, and rivers, oases, gorges and canyons. And desert, of course. There were different types of desert, he'd explained. The *reg* was made out of rocks and sand whilst "*grands ergs*" were vast areas of sand dunes extending to the east towards the Tripoli territories and to the west towards Morocco. Both could be deadly.

'It may be faster but we'll be on our own for over a week until we reach In Salah,' Lucas started again. 'There are only a few hamlets on the way. It'll be tough, much tougher than what we've experienced so far. Should anyone get injured or be taken ill, there's no help at hand.'

He turned to Harriet, arching his eyebrows, as if expecting her to object.

'It's fine with me, if that's what you want to do.' She tilted her chin, but once again she couldn't meet his stare and looked away, conscious of the hot flush on her cheeks.

'So it's settled, we're going for the fast route,' Archie said. 'Is that the track we will follow the first few days? To that hamlet there, and then the canyons, and finally …' He traced a line with his finger, repeating the names of different places as if to commit them to memory. 'When do you think we'll reach these gorges here?'

'At the end of the fourth day, if all goes well,' Lucas answered, after a moment's hesitation. He folded the map. 'Today we'll stock up on food and necessities, buy a couple of fresh horses, and three or four camels too. We leave tomorrow at dawn.'

There was much to do for the rest of the day. Harriet and Archie purchased supplies from the medina, while Lucas and Ahmoud went to buy the camels they needed to cross the reg. They were stronger, more resistant than horses, and would be used to carry goods and equipment.

By late afternoon, Harriet and Archie had come back to the palace, but neither of them was in a talkative mood so Archie retired to his room on finishing their evening meal.

'I'll have an early night. Make sure you get a good night's sleep too,' he said. 'It's going to be tough.'

She went to her room but there was nothing left for her to do. Her bags were packed. Her travel clothes were clean and ready for the following morning. After a day or two in the saddle, they'd no doubt be caked with dirt, sand and sweat. She wandered into the garden. It wasn't yet dark, but already stars studded the clear evening sky.

As she reached the outer wall, she stumbled upon a shiny pebble on the path. She bent down to pick it up. It wasn't a pebble but a brass tobacco case. She would recognise it anywhere. Her father gave it to Archie for Christmas a couple of years ago.

She made her way back into the house and knocked on Archie's door. There was no answer. He was probably asleep already. She shrugged and put the case in her pocket. She would give it to him in the morning. Sounds of rapid footfall echoed behind her. Someone tugged at her sleeve.

'Min fadlik,' a woman servant said, her eyes pleading. *Please.* In her hand was a letter.

'*Waech*?' What did she want?

Harriet took the letter, read the elegant handwriting on the front. It was for Lucas and marked urgent. A red wax stamp sealed the back of the letter.

The servant pulled her arm, urged her along to the front of the house where a cavalier waited next to a magnificent grey horse. His face lit up when he saw Harriet and he bowed deeply. She remembered him. He came from Bou Saada.

She showed him the letter. 'Is this from Madame Saintclair?'

He nodded. 'For Lucas. Bad things happen in Bou Saada.'

'Is Madame Saintclair in any danger? Or Rose?'

The man shook his head. 'No, but French army do bad things.' He pointed to the letter in her hand. 'Madame says it's urgent.'

'I will give the letter to Lucas right away,' Harriet promised.

'Thank you.' He smiled tightly before putting his foot in the stirrup and mounting the horse.

'Wait! Why don't you come with me? You can tell him yourself what's going on—'

'No time. I must go back.' He turned the horse and disappeared down the dark alleyway.

It was one thing to promise the messenger she'd give Lucas the letter immediately, but another to find him. She turned to the woman servant.

'*Win Saintclair? Win Nordine*?' she asked. Where were they? They couldn't be still buying camels or supplies for the journey at this time.

The woman answered very fast. Harriet shook her head and pulled a face to show she didn't understand. The servant signalled for her to pull her shawl over her head and to follow her. She led her to a small tavern tucked away in a back alley. It was noisy, packed full of men playing cards or checkers, and women laughing and dancing to a discordant racket of flutes and tambourines. Nordine's servant pointed to the far end of the room and turned away before Harriet could hold her back. She let out a sigh and made her way through the boisterous crowd, careful to keep her head down.

Nordine, Ahmoud, Musa, and Hakim and the other men from their party, were playing cards at the back of the tavern. And at the head of the table, one arm casually looped around the shoulders of a scantily dressed, black-haired beauty who sat on his lap, was Lucas.

Harriet clenched her fists so hard her nails dug into the palm of her hands.

Only last night he'd held her in his arms, trailed his lips on her bare skin, and kissed her as if she was the only woman in the world who mattered. And now he was holding someone else. None of it meant a thing to him. How right she'd been to push him away before she lost herself completely. She had done the right thing. Why then did her heart feel like it was breaking and her eyes fill with tears?

She took a deep breath and almost gagged on the reek of tobacco smoke, sweaty bodies and alcohol fumes. Unfastening her veil, she stepped forward.

Nordine saw her first. His eyes opened wide, his jaw dropped. The others followed his gaze and stopped talking. There was a scraping of chairs against the wooden floor as they jumped to their feet in a respectful greeting. The only man who didn't move was Lucas. He raised his eyebrows and his lips curled into a cruel smile.

'Well, well, look who's gracing us with her presence.' He lifted his pitcher of wine in a mock salute. 'I'd have thought this place far too common for a fine lady like you, Miss Montague.'

He whispered something into the woman's ear. She pouted and stood up, a look of regret in her kohl-lined eyes.

'I'm only here because …' Harriet stammered.

Lucas got up and took hold of her arm. 'No matter how many times I tell you not to venture outside on your own, you still do exactly as you please,' he growled. 'Since you're here, the least you can do is sit with us.'

She swallowed hard and did as she was told. The men sat down and resumed their card playing. Nordine and Ahmoud exchanged a few glances but kept well away from her and Lucas. She searched the pocket of her dress for the letter and held it out.

'This just came for you. A man from Bou Saada brought it. He said it was urgent.' Lucas became pale. He took the letter, broke the seal and unfolded it.

'Where is he now?' he asked, as he started reading.

'He left, he didn't want to stay.' She looked at him, shocked by the worry and anger on his face.

Finally he lifted his eyes from the paper. 'Bastard,' he whispered.

'What's the matter?' she asked as worry gnawed at her now. 'Are your mother and sister hurt?'

'No, they're fine for now, but Mortemer has been up to his usual tricks.' He rested an elbow on the table and rubbed his forehead.

'Can you tell me what happened?' she asked.

He slid the letter over to her. 'Read for yourself.'

Harriet skimmed through Madame Saintclair's letter. In retaliation for the attack on the *fort* and the theft of the five army cannon a few nights before, Lieutenant Mortemer had decided to make an example. He'd rounded up thirty local men, thrown them in jail, and threatened to keep them there without food or water until the culprits were found, however long it took. Meanwhile, French soldiers were rampaging through Bou Saada and nobody, least of all Mortemer, seemed to care about the abuse they perpetrated.

Madame Saintclair entreated her son not to come back for now.

"Be very careful," she wrote. "Mortemer is convinced you had something to do with the whole business. He almost had your sister arrested for throwing a chamber pot on his head from her window. Thankfully, I managed to persuade him that putting her in jail would be a sign of weakness, not a show of strength."

Harriet put the letter down, thoughtful. Lucas and Nordine had talked about capturing the French cannon only the night before; Lucas said they were hidden in some canyon or other until the rebels could come and get them. She'd been right. He was with the rebels. Nordine must be too, but what about the others?

She looked at Ahmoud, Musa and Hakim, and it dawned on her that they must all be rebels. Bits of conversation came back to her. Mortemer had talked about an attack on the ammunition depot in Blida the night Hakim's hand was burned. Lucas said there was a fight in a tavern, but what if he was injured while blowing up the depot? Then there was the jailbreak at Berrouaghia and the escape of Abdelkader's man the very night they were in the vicinity of the penitentiary. She remembered other details too. Ahmoud had probably warned the Mouzaïa that Mortemer's men were on their way to burn their village, which was why it was deserted when the French soldiers arrived. Mortemer also said the rebel caches indicated on Rachid's map were empty. Lucas and his men must be the ones destroying them before the French could get at them … It all made sense now. And it made her angry. Lucas had used her. He'd had a hidden agenda all along.

He spoke in Arabic to Nordine and Ahmoud and pointed to his mother's letter. The men listened, sombre and silent. He then turned to Harriet.

'You're coming with me,' he said. 'I'm in no mood to stay here any longer.'

She had no choice but to follow him. He stormed ahead through the narrow streets before coming to the town's main square, lit by torches burning in tall metal spikes.

'Saintclair! I must speak to you. I know you're one of them,' she said, breathless, when she finally managed to catch up with him.

He slowed his pace, looking down at her. 'One of whom?'

'Abdelkader's rebels,' she answered in a low voice.

He came to a stop, spun around and put his hands on her shoulders. 'And why should you think that?'

His hands burned her through the fine layers of silk, almost as much as his eyes on her face. She cleared her throat.

'I hear things and—'

'Then don't listen,' he said, sharply.

He started walking again.

'I have the right to know what you intend to do,' she insisted, almost running alongside him. 'You could get caught, injured, killed even, and that would leave us without a guide and unable to reach Tamanrasset in time to rescue my father.'

She bit her lip.

'Your concern for my welfare is touching,' he replied, arching his eyebrows. 'I gave you my word we would be in Tamanrasset by the end of May and we will.' He paused. 'You shouldn't meddle in men's business,' he added.

'Men's business?' She gasped. 'I rode through mountains, steppes and desert like the rest of you. I slept rough on blankets out in the cold.' She blushed at the recollection of the night she'd curled up, safe and warm in his arms. She took a deep breath and carried on.

'I killed a bandit who tried to strangle me … and you're telling me not to meddle in your affairs because I'm a woman?' Her voice had risen to a high pitch.

Lucas stared down, a mocking smile on his lips. 'Calm down, darling, you're getting hysterical.'

She put her fists on her hips and stomped her foot. 'I am not hysterical! I don't get hysterical! And don't call me darling. You're the one being unreasonable and dishonest.' She drew in a long breath and looked at him.

'Dishonest?'

Damn. She was beautiful, with her flushed cheeks, her eyes glinting with fury. Her shawl had dropped down and her hair shone like a halo around her face in the torchlight. She had a point. He was being unfair. She'd shown as much courage and determination as any of them. More so, because she was a woman, by nature weaker and more delicate. He wanted to touch her, trail his finger along her cheek, her neck, rub his thumb over her lips. What the hell was wrong with him?

She opened her eyes wider.

'I know all about your double life,' she answered. 'You steal cannon, you blow up French ammunition depots, and you help rebels escape from jail.'

'What are you talking about?' He growled and grabbed hold of her arm. How did the woman know about that?

'I told you. I hear things,' she answered, not looking the least flustered. 'Let go of me.'

He did.

'Will you give the cannon back to Mortemer?'

He shook his head. 'No.'

'What about those poor prisoners?'

'Ahmoud is taking care of it.'

'What is he going to do?'

He took a deep breath. 'That's none of your concern. Despite what you seem to believe, some things are just too dangerous for women to get involved in. Let's go now.'

As she showed no intention of moving, he took her elbow to hurry her along and something fell from her pocket. He bent down to pick it up and frowned.

'Well, well, I didn't know you were a snuff addict, Miss Montague.' He handed the tobacco case to her.

'That is Archie's. And talking about Archie, he would never come up with such a pathetic argument. *He* doesn't think women are inferior to men.'

'I never said women were inferior,' he replied, darting his eyes into hers. 'In many ways, women are far superior to men, especially when it comes to shrewdness and artifice.' She had the good grace to blush.

'Archie always values my opinion.'

Now she was being annoying.

'I suppose he was valuing your opinion the other night when he tried to rape you?'

She shook her head. 'That was a mistake, an aberration which I'm quite sure was caused by the blow to his head. Archie is a gentleman and a respected scholar, not a thug who spends his time drinking in taverns and fondling dancing girls like …'

She bit her lip.

'Like me?' he asked.

'Yes, exactly like you.' She pulled her arm free and ran ahead, clutching the tobacco case.

He strode alongside her. 'The higher the pedestal, the harder the fall,' he muttered between his teeth.

'What did you say?'

He shrugged. 'Nothing.'

His foul mood had returned and he pounded on the door to Nordine's house.

'Do you have to bang on that door so loudly?' she asked while they waited for a servant to let them in. 'You'll wake everybody, everybody except Archie maybe. He could sleep in a battlefield. He didn't even hear me when I knocked on his door earlier to give him the snuff box back.'

'Is that so?' He narrowed his eyes.

'Yes. It was lucky I found the case near the garden wall tonight or it might have been lost forever.'

Was Drake really asleep or had he gone on another secret rendezvous? Something was definitely not right, and by God he'd find out right now what the man was up to.

'Let's give your fiancé his snuff box back, shall we?' he asked as soon as they walked into the house. He grabbed her arm again and pulled her along.

'I'm sure he won't mind being woken if you kiss him nicely. Like you kissed me last night. I know I enjoyed it.'

She pretended she hadn't heard him. 'We can give him the box back tomorrow morning,' she protested.

He tried Archie's door. It was locked. Without a second of hesitation, he kicked it and the door crashed open.

'Saintclair, this is crazy, why are you doing this?' she whispered as they walked across the dark room.

Lucas froze. Archie was sitting up, holding his pistol aimed at him. He was fully dressed.

'Saintclair? What the bloody hell are you doing here? Harriet? Is there anything wrong?' He lowered his weapon slowly.

'You have good reflexes for a man supposed to be fast asleep,' Lucas remarked, crossing his arms on his chest.

Archie narrowed his eyes. 'What is your point?'

'Are you in the habit of getting into bed fully dressed?' Lucas pointed to Archie's clothes.

Archie patted his shirt and jacket and smiled. 'It'll save me time tomorrow morning.'

'I'm sorry, Archie.' Harriet walked up to him. 'I don't know what Monsieur Saintclair was trying to achieve by breaking your door down and waking you up like that. It certainly wasn't my idea.'

Archie shrugged. 'It's quite all right, my dear.' He yawned and ruffled his blond hair. 'I really am tired and would like to go back to sleep now.'

'Of course,' she said. 'Oh, by the way, here's your tobacco case.' She handed it to him. 'I found it while walking around the gardens tonight.'

Archie toyed with the case before slipping it into his pocket. 'Hmm … thank you.' He turned to Lucas and arched his eyebrows. 'You know the way out, don't you, Saintclair?'

Lucas balled his fists at his side and barely resisted the urge to wipe the smirk off his face.

Chapter Nineteen

Lucas dismounted and walked to Harriet's horse.

'Let me help you down,' he said, grabbing the reins.

The young woman didn't answer. She leaned forward on the saddle, her chest resting against her mount's neck and her face almost buried in its black mane. Coming closer, he saw that her eyes were closed. He put his hands around her waist and pulled her gently towards him so that she fell into his arms. She was still fast asleep, her head resting against his shoulder, as he carried her to the camp.

'What's wrong with her?' Drake asked behind him.

'She's exhausted,' Lucas replied. He gave an order for one of the men to spread out a blanket on the ground before laying her down gently. He pulled her *cheche* down on her face so that she could breathe more freely.

'Take the horses to the copse of trees over there. There's a shallow pool which hasn't dried up yet,' he instructed.

The Englishman muttered under his breath, but he did as he was told. After another day of hard riding, both men and animals were in dire need of rest. Lucas stood up and stretched, turning towards the west where the sky glowed with fiery red and orange hues. It wouldn't last long. As soon as the sun dipped behind the line of the horizon, night would fall like a black curtain on the reg.

He lifted his hat to wipe his forehead with the sleeve of his shirt before pulling it down on his eyes again. They were in Tuareg country now. He should start wearing a *cheche* and tunic for better protection against the sun. His lips were parched, his mouth and throat so dry they burned every time he breathed. These were discomforts he was accustomed to, but they would be torture for Harriet. He stole a glance towards her.

He'd seen grown men cry and half lose their minds because of the fierceness of the sun, the bleakness of the landscape, and the agony of going without water. Not to mention the constant threat of attack by the ghosts of the desert – the Tuareg raiders you didn't see until they were upon you – and the sand storms which drowned everything and everyone in their path. Yet in three days the woman hadn't uttered a word of complaint. Once again, she was surprising him.

He narrowed his eyes to stare at the desolate plains around until he found what he was looking for; a pile of rocks in the distance. Then, like every evening, he grabbed hold of the ransom bags and strode away from the camp. When he returned, empty-handed, Hakim and Musa had made a fire, prepared the tea and a frugal supper.

Lucas unsaddled his horse and checked it all over for cuts and signs of injury, then carried his saddle back to camp and sat next to Harriet. He shook her shoulder to wake her up.

'Time to eat.'

'Leave me alone,' she muttered. 'I'm not hungry.'

'You need to eat or you won't have the strength to carry on,' he insisted. 'Sit up.'

'No.' She rolled onto her side, her face away from him.

He leaned over her shoulder. 'I know it's hard for you, *darling*.' He insisted on the last word, waiting for her protest. She hated it when he called her that. Tonight she didn't even react.

He trailed a finger along her arm up to her shoulder, lifted her hair and tickled her neck, revelling in the sensations her soft skin aroused inside him. The last few days had done nothing to dampen his desire for her. He might still be reeling from the way she taunted him at Nordine's house but, if anything, he wanted her even more. He wanted her so much that it wasn't any longer a question of *if* he would have her, but *when*.

'Wake up, Harriet.'

She let out a long sigh and turned to him. Her eyes were unfocused, glazed with exhaustion. Her body was limp against his and he was overwhelmed with the urge to hold her in his arms and kiss her over and over until he breathed his strength into her. He would do none of that, of course. Not here, not now. But he would damn well make sure she ate. He helped her sit up, propped her back against his saddle, and proceeded to cut thin strips of meat to feed her with.

'Eat.'

She did.

After the meat, he gave her candied dates and poured a tumbler of mint tea he held out for her to drink. And then at last he let her sleep and covered her with a blanket.

'You're quite the mama hen, aren't you?' Drake sneered.

Lucas shrugged. 'It'll only delay us if Harriet is too weak to ride tomorrow.' He poked the fire with a stick and watched the sparks fly into the night. 'She's holding up remarkably well, far better than I ever imagined.'

'I suppose so. Do you still think we'll reach the gorges tomorrow night, as planned?' Drake asked.

Lucas looked at him. The Englishman had asked that same question ever since leaving Laghouat. 'Yes.'

Drake nodded. 'Good. By the way, you never said why you sent Ahmoud back to Bou Saada,' he remarked.

'There have been developments there. He was worried about his family,' Lucas answered, his tone curt. As far as he was concerned, the less Drake knew the better.

The Englishman wrapped his burnous around him and lay down. As soon as he started snoring, Lucas stood up and gestured to Hakim and Musa. They had things to discuss.

He walked up to the cairn on top of the sun-baked, rocky mound. Kneeling down beside it, he examined the position and alignment of the stones and sighed. So he'd been right, but this was no cause for celebration.

He ran down the small hill and lifted himself back onto the saddle.

'What were you doing up there?' Harriet called, directing her soothing, misty grey eyes towards him. 'That's the third cairn you stopped at today.'

'I was checking messages Tuareg scouts left for me.' He frowned when he saw her hand shake as she adjusted the dark blue scarf that protected her face against the fierceness of the sun. He pulled out a water gourd from his saddlebag.

'Here, drink some water. You'll be no good to us if you faint,' he added when she started to protest.

'What do you mean you were checking a message? How can a pile of stones mean anything?' Archie grumbled as they set off at a slow trot across the rocky plains. 'And where the bloody hell are Hakim and Musa?'

'I told you. They're riding ahead of us, watching out for caravans or tribes travelling across the reg,' Lucas lied.

'It's a code, isn't it? The stones, I mean.' Harriet's voice was muffled by the scarf.

He nodded. 'You could say that. This is one of the ways Tuareg scouts pass on information to travellers.'

'So what was the message on the cairn?' Harriet asked.

'Nothing much,' Lucas lied again. 'If we carry on south to southeast, we'll reach the Arak gorges in roughly three hours.'

They rode across a flat, dreary landscape scattered with sparse, coarse bushes and isolated trees. Dozens of camel and horse bones, and probably a good few human ones too, bleached white by the sun, littered the ground. They reached the Arak gorges – the gorges of evil spirits, as the locals called them – just as the sun darted its golden, oblique rays over the land.

'Why aren't we camping in the gorges?' Drake asked. 'Surely we'd be more sheltered?'

'We'd also be crushed to death by morning,' Lucas declared.

'Why?' Harriet looked up at the steep rock faces rising in front of them.

He didn't miss her grimace of pain as she dismounted, or the way she rubbed her forehead as if to soothe a throbbing headache. She removed her headdress and gave her hair a light shake which sent it tumbling down her back. He ignored the sudden urge he had to run his fingers through it and concentrated on unsaddling his horse.

'The difference in temperature between day and night causes rocks to explode and fall down the gorges. Locals believe the gorges to be haunted by *djinouns* who throw stones on travellers to scare them away.'

'Then I'll leave them to their tricks and camp out here.' Harriet turned towards the gorges. 'I can understand why people are afraid of this place. It looks sinister.'

'You'll have the chance to see for yourself in a moment,' Lucas told her. 'We have to go in to fetch some water. There's a well a quarter of the way through.'

'I'll come with you instead,' Archie suggested. 'Harriet can rest here. She hardly looks able to stand on her feet, let alone carry gourds of water.'

It may be true, but Lucas had his reasons for wanting her with him right now.

'I'll do it, Archie. I did promise I'd work as hard as the rest of you,' she protested.

'If you'd rather carry water gourds like a mule than rest, my dear, I won't insist.' Drake snorted and walked away.

Lucas turned to hide a smile. He was enjoying seeing the increasing strain on Harriet and Drake's relationship. They hardly shared a conversation these days, let alone a blanket or a tent.

'You might want to take your soap,' he told her.

Her face lit up. 'You mean I can have a wash? In there?'

'That's right.' He helped her gather the gourds before strapping the random bags around his body. He also took a small bag with food.

'Watch out,' he added as they progressed through the eerily quiet canyon, 'these cactuses can be lethal.'

He pointed to fierce looking plants covered with long, sharp needles that lined the bottom of the canyon, then to a few giant cacti. 'These, however, are very useful. They prevent wounds from getting infected.'

'What are they called?' She looked in disbelief at the spiky leaves.

'Aloes.'

The deeper they walked into the gorge, the quieter it got. Soon their footsteps were the only sounds.

Lucas' eyes skimmed the surface of the cliff. There'd been a rock slide since the last time he stopped here, and he couldn't see the entrance to the cave. He walked along the side of the cliff, inserted his hands into crevasses, pulled at loose stones, and found it at last.

'This way.' He led her into a narrow passage. 'The lake is in the second chamber of this cave.'

'A lake, inside the mountain? How wonderful.' Her voice echoed and bounced off the walls.

They reached the second chamber where a large fissure in the roof of the cave let in rays of light that fell like magic dust onto a pool of emerald water surrounded by a beach of fine white sand.

'I've never seen anything so beautiful,' she whispered.

He turned and smiled. No matter how many times he'd come here, the presence of a spring water pool hidden inside a mountain in the middle of the desert never ceased to amaze him. Harriet ran onto the small beach and knelt at the edge of the water. She gathered some sand in her hand and let it trickle through her fingers. Then she looked up and gave him a beaming smile. An odd, warm feeling spread in his chest.

'Thank you.'

'I won't be long,' he grunted.

He walked to the far end of the cave and followed a narrow passage until he reached the third, and last, chamber. It was smaller and darker than the other ones. He located a gap in the rock face and stuffed the bags into it, then pushed a large stone in front.

When he came back, Harriet had filled the gourds and lined them against the cave wall. She pulled the bar of soap out of her pocket.

'You can have a swim once I've spoken to you,' he said, putting his hands on her shoulders.

Surprised, she tilted her head to stare into his eyes. 'What is it?'

'You're not coming back to the camp with me tonight. You're staying here until I come and get you,' he declared. 'I brought you some food and …'

She stiffened under his touch. 'You want me to stay here on my own? Why?'

'The camp is going to be attacked during the night.'

She let out a frightened cry. 'How do you know?'

'That was the message at the last cairn. A gang of riders were spotted in the area yesterday. Hakim and Musa are trying to find them to slow them down, but we must get ready in case they fail. From what I gathered, they're not far behind us – about four to five hours.'

'How will the raiders know we're here?'

That was something he wasn't prepared to tell her yet. He needed proof first.

'What about you and Archie, and the others?' she carried on.

'We're going to set a trap, that's why I don't want you under our feet.'

'But I can help! I can hide and shoot at them or throw stones. I can—'

He released his grip on her shoulders. 'No, Harriet. You're staying here. I won't discuss this.' He gestured to the bag of food. 'You have enough food for—'

Without warning, she bolted towards the entrance of the cave and disappeared in the narrow passage. He cursed loudly. Damn woman. She was running back to the camp. He caught her as she neared the mouth of the cave, grabbed her arm and swung her towards him.

'Let go of me, Saintclair!' she shrieked as he dragged her back to the cave. 'I won't stand in your way, I promise.'

'The answer's no, and if you don't give me your word of honour you'll stay put, I'll have no other choice than to tie you up. Can't you see this is the safest place?'

He stood facing her, his back to the lake. The light from the crevasse in the roof of the cave became pure liquid gold as it touched her hair, her skin, and her eyes. The sight of her lips parting, her chest heaving as she breathed in and out distracted him for a second and she caught him off guard again. Stepping forward, she pushed him hard into the water. He lost his footing, fell backward, and landed in the shallow water on the edge of the lake, banging his head on a rock.

'Saintclair … Lucas, can you hear me? Please wake up.'

His eyes were closed. He lay in the shallow pool, so still she couldn't even tell if he was breathing or not. Panic made her heart race as she knelt down beside him. She slipped her hand behind his head to lift him out of the water and let out a cry of anguish when she saw the bloodied rock underneath.

She had killed him. She had killed the man she loved. It was as if the whole world became suddenly dark and empty and filled with pain and desolation. Her breath caught in her throat, her whole body started shaking, and tears spilled out onto her cheeks.

'What have I done?' she sobbed, gently kissing his lips over and over again.

Two hands gripped her upper arms and pushed her back.

Lucas had opened his eyes and was staring at her.

'Good grief, woman,' he groaned.

'You're alive! Thank God. I didn't kill you after all.' She smiled through her tears.

He let go of her to touch the back of his head and stared at his fingers. They were smeared with blood.

'Of course I'm alive, but that's no thanks to you,' he grumbled.

'Let me look at your head,' she said, overcome with guilt. 'I'll see what I can do.'

'You've done more than enough.' He glared at her, furious, then winced in pain and let out another curse.

She stood up. 'I'm sorry, I truly am,' she whispered, offering her hand to help him up. 'I didn't mean to hurt you.'

He grabbed hold of her hand, but instead of releasing her as soon as he was up he pulled her against him, holding her hand to his chest. His arms wrapped around her waist so tightly she could hardly breathe, let alone move. His body pressed against her, his clothes were soaked through, but he didn't seem to care. Soon the front of her tunic was wet too, as were her breeches. Droplets of water dripped from his hair onto her face, her hair, and shoulders. Breathing hard, he stared into her eyes for what felt like long minutes. His heart thundered under the palm of her hand. It was the most wonderful of sensations. Then he bent down slowly and kissed her eyes, her tear-stricken cheeks, and finally her mouth.

She let out a whimper when his lips touched hers, but she didn't fight him. It felt right. It felt more than right, it was wonderful. This was where she wanted to be, in his arms. Her hands slid up to his shoulders, then clasped behind his neck. She was consumed with one emotion only. Love. Lucas had set her heart, her senses, her whole being ablaze. She loved him, and her love was stronger, wilder, and altogether more dangerous than she could have ever imagined.

'Lucas,' she breathed and she moved against him, tilting her head back so that he could carry on kissing her mouth, her face, her throat.

She trembled, soft and pliable in his arms. She was his. Desire roared and spread through him like a bushfire, heating up his blood, destroying any conscious thought, urging him to touch and take. He pulled back and looked into her eyes. They were wide open, dreamy. A smile lingered on her lips. He let go of her and started taking his waistcoat off. She stared at him as he tucked his shirt out of his breeches and quickly discarded it, and then kicked his boots off.

'What are you doing?' she asked at last, her voice a little shaky, when he started unfastening his breeches.

'What does it look like?' He grinned. 'We might as well enjoy the pool. We won't come across another fresh water lake before In Salah. Grab your soap and get rid of your clothes. Hurry, we don't have long before I have to return to camp.'

'I couldn't possibly bathe with you,' she stammered, her cheeks glowing red.

There she was again, playing the prude when she'd been all but melting in his arms a few seconds before. 'I have seen quite a lot of you in Laghouat already,' he remarked, impatient. He divested himself of his breeches and almost laughed out loud when he found her gaping at him, at all of him, her eyes open wide in alarm as if she'd never seen a man before.

'Are you coming?'

She didn't answer. He shrugged and dived into the pool. He stayed under the water until his blood had cooled down. The woman drove him crazy. Why did she look so innocent when she was – or had been – Drake's mistress? Why was she bent on tormenting him when it was plain she desired him as much as he desired her? Or had he become so useless at gauging a woman's response?

He stood up in the pool.

'Throw me the soap. Or better still, bring it in.'

Her heartbeat was wild, her breathing fast and shallow. The water might reach up to his waist, but it was so clear there wasn't much of him left to her imagination. She had never seen a naked man before, save for statues of Greek gods at the museum. They didn't do men justice. In the flesh, men were completely different, much bigger and imposing than a marble statue, and infinitely more unsettling. Her cheeks burning, she threw the soap to him.

He lathered his body and hair then dived into the pool before standing up and walking towards her. His skin was golden and shiny with droplets, his hair dark, his eyes clearer than the water. He looked straight at her and her heart started to race. Her throat became so dry and tight she could neither swallow nor breathe. At that moment she knew she'd be his.

'What are you waiting for?' he asked.

He wanted her, now, could she not see?

'There's something I must tell you,' she said, her voice so low he could hardly hear.

'What now?' He sighed, impatient, and walked out of the pool.

He was even more annoyed when she turned her back to him. 'Harriet, can't you see you're driving me crazy?' he burst out. He stood behind her and wrapped his arms around her waist and started nuzzling her neck.

'Archie and I were never … are not …' she stuttered.

'Damn, do you think I want to hear about the man now?' he growled against her soft skin.

'It's important.'

'No, it's not,' he said. So what if she felt guilty about betraying her fiancé? He didn't. All he cared about was her and him and now.

'But you don't understand, you see …'

'I want you, Harriet and I think you want me, and nothing you say will change that.'

At last she stopped talking. Heaving a sigh, she leaned against him. His blood started pumping, pulsing, roaring. His hands stroked her stomach, travelled to her breasts, caressed and teased through the wet fabric of her tunic. She lifted her arms and placed her hands behind his neck while he explored and roamed over her, getting wilder with the need to possess her.

With a groan, he unfastened and opened her tunic and tore at the chemise underneath. He wanted her soft, silky skin and her curves under his hands and his mouth. His breath rasped in his throat as he enclosed the soft weight of her breasts in the palm of his hands, rubbed their tips with his thumbs. He was drunk on the smell of her, on the feel of her heart thumping under his touch. Feverish now, he undid her breeches and pulled them down just enough to lay his hand against her heat. She arched and let out a soft moan as his fingers moved and stroked, and when she started crying out he spun her round and stifled her cries with his mouth.

He wanted more. And he wanted it now. His control was slipping away. Yet he held back. At the back of his mind was a warning he didn't understand. He had to be cautious, he mustn't frighten her.

'Come with me.'

He helped her shed the rest of her clothes, kissing and stroking her all the time until she stood naked in his arms. With her eyes now dark and heavy with desire, her lips swollen from his kisses, she was the most beautiful woman he had ever seen.

He grabbed the bar of soap and took her hand and together they walked into the gloriously cool pool, until she was waist deep.

He positioned her in front of him with her back to him and cupped some water in his hand to wash over her shoulders, along her arms, then started sliding the bar of soap on her breasts, her stomach. She leaned back against him again, her legs slightly parted. Working up a thick lather over her body, he circled the bar of soap slowly around her nipples, felt them tighten and peak under his fingers. She gasped and moaned. He washed some water over her, marvelling at her slender waist, her smooth skin and deliciously curvy hips. And then he couldn't wait any more. He turned her around so that she faced him, scooped her in his arms, and walked out of the pool carrying her.

Laying her on the soft white sand, he covered her body with his before kissing her – a long, deep kiss that left him dizzy and gasping. She whispered something against his mouth, something about love and being gentle, but he was in a red haze by then and all he could hear was the thunder of his heart, the roar of his blood. At last, she was going to be his. Rough with need, he parted her legs, slid his hands under her to lift her towards him, and thrust deep inside.

Chapter Twenty

'You have never been with a man,' he said, his voice a harsh whisper.

She stared at him, her eyes full of tears, and nodded.

'Hell, why didn't you say so?' he growled.

He was still inside her. He lifted himself onto his elbows to take his weight off her. What now?

Her lips moved, saying something he wasn't sure he heard correctly.

'Don't stop. I don't want you to stop,' she repeated, louder, before clasping her hands behind his neck and burying her face against his chest.

'Are you sure?'

'Yes,' came her muffled answer. She kissed his chest, then the base of his neck, trailing hot kisses on his skin which set his senses on fire again. Tilting her face towards him, she parted her lips and he kissed her, long and deep. Reaching down to stroke her, he started moving inside her, slowly at first so as not to hurt her. Her head rolled from one side to the other, her hands slid down his back. And when he couldn't hold on any more, he lost himself inside her.

'You tried to tell me and I didn't let you,' he said, flatly, when he caught his breath.

Had he known, had he even suspected the truth, he wouldn't have been so brutal. Hell, he would have held back altogether; he wasn't in the habit of bedding virgins. He'd thought her fair game. It never once occurred to him that Drake lied when he claimed Harriet was his mistress. Her hesitations, her blushes, her reticence, it all made sense now, but he'd been blind to anything but his need to have her.

She clasped her hands around his shoulders and buried her face against his chest once more. It was so unbearably sweet his heart felt like it was bursting – with guilt and remorse, no doubt. He forgot about Drake, about the world outside the cave. Nothing mattered but the woman in his arms and the overpowering need to soothe and comfort her. He moved so that she lay on top of him. Her cheek felt damp against his chest.

'I'm sorry I hurt you,' he said, kissing the top of her head.

She sighed. 'You didn't hurt me … well, maybe at first,' she answered softly.

He knew he had. He hadn't spared her. She'd cried out, clawed at his back when he thrust inside her, and by the time he realised she'd never been touched before, it was too late. And now she was crying. He felt like a brute. He kissed her hair.

'Let me see you.' He tilted her head towards him.

She lifted her face and smiled, which made him feel even worse. It must be guilt tightening his throat until he could hardly breathe, guilt making him kiss her lips lightly and holding her tight. He was about to say he'd be more attentive, more considerate, the next time but he held back the words. What next time? There wouldn't be a next time. If Harriet had been a distraction before, she was more than that now. She was a complication. He cursed himself again. He would deal with that later. For now the woman in his arms was hurting by his fault.

'I am sorry,' he said once more.

'I'm not,' she whispered, trailing her finger along his chest.

Her feather-light touch made him draw breath. She slid her hand up to his shoulder and stroked the side of his neck and snuggled closer to him. Her slender body fitted his perfectly. Her breasts were soft and full against his chest, her skin silky. He stroked her back, followed the curve of her waist, of her hips. His caresses became more precise, urgent. She moved up slowly on top of him. This time it was she who kissed him, a long, deep kiss that left him gasping for more. With a feverish groan, he enfolded her into his arms. Hell, he wanted her again. It wasn't a good idea. It was too soon to make love to her again. She would be sore, and he had things to organise at the camp.

He made himself stop.

'I must go back,' he said, his voice harsher than he intended.

'Yes.'

She immediately rolled off him and stood up, taking great care, it seemed, to keep her eyes averted. He almost drew her back to him, hesitated, and wondered what he could say. His mind was blank. Better leave her alone for now.

He watched her walk into the pool, his throat dry and his chest tight. God, she was beautiful – a mermaid with her long, wet hair clinging like seaweed to her shoulders, to her back. And just then he felt absurdly pleased that Drake lied. That she wasn't any man's lover … but his.

With a sigh, he got up and dressed.

The light in the cave had taken on a silvery blue hue that announced dusk. It would be dark soon. His clothes were still soaking wet. Hers looked damp too.

'Remember,' he said, towering over her once they were ready. 'You are to stay here until I come and get you—' Gunshots erupted outside and echoed in the stillness of the gorges. Lucas froze.

'I don't understand … They weren't supposed to be here before tonight.'

'Let me come with you.' She clutched at his arm.

'No! You're staying here.' He pulled his gun out and ran down the cave passage.

Hiding in here was out of the question. If they were being attacked again, she would help, whether Lucas wanted it or not. She gripped her dagger and went after him. More shots resonated. Then there was silence. Careful not to step on any poisoned cacti and her heart pounding with fear, she ran back towards the camp.

The tents were burning. The pots for the soup had been overturned, their contents spilled on the sandy ground. The travel bags were ripped open and their contents strewn around. But what was more terrifying than the destruction of the camp was the absolute stillness, the silence. She glanced around to make sure the attackers had gone before leaving the safety of the gorge and venturing out in the open. Then she saw the bodies and cried out in shock.

Lucas' men lay on the dusty ground, their eyes wide open in the gathering dusk, a dark red stain on their chest. She kneeled down next to every one of them, but she didn't need to touch them to know they were beyond help. The attackers had taken them by surprise. The men didn't have time to defend themselves. She sprang to her feet, frantic. There was no sign of Lucas or Archie. The horses and the camels were gone. What was she to do now?

Water, she must get some water. She returned into the canyon to get the gourds, and back at the camp, pulled what was left of the smouldering tents out of the flames. Her hands shaking with panic, her eyes filled with tears, she picked up the pots, clothes and bags in a futile attempt at clearing the mess.

Night was falling fast and it was getting cold. She found a burnous lying in the dirt and wrapped herself in it to stand next to the dying fire. She had to keep it going through the night. Not only would it help Lucas or Archie find her, it would also keep wild animals at bay. Lions or leopards might be attracted by the scent of the men's blood. She looked through the remains of the camp for a knife larger than hers then walked to a thicket of acacia trees to cut up some wood. By the time she carried a big pile of kindling back to the camp, the night had thrown its dark velvet cloak onto the desert. She poked the fire and sat down, brutally aware of the dead men's bodies behind her. She would try and bury them in the morning. Then what?

She let out an anguished sob when the enormity of her predicament finally hit her. She was alone in the reg, with no horse or camel and no idea of how to reach In Salah. Archie and Lucas were probably dead too. She would never see them again. She drew her legs in, wrapped her arms around her knees, and cried until there were no more tears left.

She would wait here, she resolved, wiping her eyes. At least there was a supply of water nearby and she could salvage some food from their supplies to last a few days until someone came.

But what if no one came?

The hours passed agonisingly slowly. Alone with her dark thoughts and her terrors, she fed the fire to stave off shadows. She made some tea, nibbled on a few dates. The darkness around her was alive with sounds of furtive pattering and scratching, with growling and yelping. She got used to them eventually. She even got used to the rumbling of rocks falling down from the top of the canyon. A sad smile stretched her lips. Here were the *djinouns* Lucas had told them about.

Lucas … She could still smell him on her skin, feel him inside her. There was a burning, tingling pain deep within her, but if her body ached, her heart ached even more. She'd wanted him with a frightening intensity. She still did, despite the words he hadn't said, the look of confusion and disappointment on his face that hurt far more than his hard, passionate caresses. She let out a shaky breath. He didn't want her – that much was obvious. She might be inexperienced with men, but she knew he meant their lovemaking in the cave as a pleasant interlude, an interlude he immediately and bitterly regretted. She stared at the night around and took a deep breath. It didn't matter that he didn't love her, as long as he was safe and came back to her.

After staring into the fire for hours, her eyelids grew heavy, her weary body slumped down, and her fingers released their grip around the dagger.

Her heart thumping hard woke her up with a start. She straightened up, rubbed her eyes. The fire had died down to a few red hot embers and the shadows had come closer, much closer.

It wasn't her heart that made the ground shake. It was a horse's gallop which reverberated around and inside her. Grabbing her dagger, she stood up, all senses alert. She'd hide until she knew who was riding towards the camp. The only place close enough was the thicket of acacia trees.

There was no time to lose. She ran, stumbled, and fell. A sharp pain stabbed her knee, but she picked herself up and ran again until she reached the trees. She lifted herself up, climbed into the branches, praying they'd hold her weight.

She sat straddling the thickest branch and waited for the cavalier to approach. Her fingers gripped the dagger so tightly they hurt. The gallop slowed to a trot, stopped, but the horse was still too far from the camp to be seen. She heard a soft neighing, the stomping of hooves, then nothing. Her eyes narrowed to a slit as she peered into the darkness. A twig cracked behind her, then two hands grabbed hold of her and pulled her down. She didn't even have time to scream.

'Thank heavens you're safe!' a man's voice said.

Chapter Twenty-One

'By the time I arrived at the camp, they'd already gone. They took the horses and the camels. One horse got loose, so I was able to ride after them. I almost caught up but they shot at me and I had to take shelter. Then they rode on and this time I couldn't keep up so I turned round,' Lucas said as they walked back to camp. 'I didn't want to leave you out here too long.'

He turned to her and put his hand lightly on her forearm. 'They have Drake.'

She gasped. 'They've taken him hostage?'

He shrugged. 'Maybe.'

She didn't understand. 'What else would the bandits take him for? Do you think they'll hurt him?'

She swallowed hard. Her affection for Archie may have dampened these past few weeks, but she still cared for him.

'I don't know. I can't think why they'd take him, unless they plan to exchange him for your father's ransom.' He arched his eyebrows. 'Who will you choose if that happens? Your father or your fiancé?'

'Archie isn't my fiancé.' She spoke without thinking.

'What?' His grip on her arm tightened like a vice.

She looked up at him, hesitated, and bit her lower lip. 'He made it up when we first met you. He thought it would protect me from … you know … unwanted male attention.'

He let out a long sigh. She thought he looked relieved.

'You're hurting me.'

He released her at once.

'Archie may not be my fiancé, but he's still very dear to me,' she added.

'What would you do if you had to choose?' he asked again.

She pressed her hand against her heart. 'I hope I never have to make the choice, but if I did, I would have to choose my father.'

He threw several sticks into the fire and poked at it until flames rose into the night again. Then he put some water to boil, to make tea, and sat down. Only then did she see the blood on the sleeve of his shirt.

'You're injured.'

'It's only a scratch. I'll deal with it later.'

From the amount of blood on his shirt, and the way he winced every time he moved, she gathered it was more than a scratch.

She threw tea leaves into the simmering water and poured some out for him.

'Do you think they'll be back?' She handed him the cup.

'They didn't get the ransom. So yes, I figure they'll try again, maybe even tonight. In any case, we have a long way to go and, now that there's only the two of us, they have an advantage.' He paused. 'Not for long, though.'

'What do you plan to do?'

'There's a Tuareg caravan in the area. We'll hook up with them tomorrow and go south.' He drank his tea and set his cup on the ground.

'How do you know they're here? We haven't seen anyone for days.'

He gave her a quick smile. 'Hakim and Musa left coded messages.'

'The cairns?'

He nodded.

'It looks as if your men were caught off guard and they didn't see their attackers.' She pointed towards the back of the camp where the two bodies lay.

He stared at the fire and frowned. 'Yes, and that's very strange. They were good scouts, exceptional fighters. I don't understand how they were killed, but I intend to find out, and then I'll get even.'

Even though he spoke quietly, his voice was hard. He meant it. 'There's something else I'll get even for,' he added. 'They took our horses and our camels, which in the reg equates to condemning us to death.'

They didn't speak for a while. With Lucas at her side, the sounds of the desert weren't so frightening. A wave of tiredness washed over her, her body relaxed, and her eyes closed. She longed to sleep, yet there was something she had to do first. She got up to search through her things, retrieved one of her chemises which she tore into strips.

'I need to see to your arm now,' she said when she was back at Lucas' side.

He looked up. A smile curled the corners of his lips. 'Maybe you could tend to the bump at the back of my head too since you were the one responsible for it.'

His eyes lingered on her face. She felt a hot blush spread over her cheeks and she turned away, suddenly shy and awkward. He peeled his shirt off. He couldn't hide a grimace of pain when his blood-drenched sleeve stuck to his wound and he had to pull on it.

'You were lucky,' she said, examining his biceps. The bullet had skimmed his arm and left a deep gash.

Her hand shook as she dipped the cloth into the boiled water and dabbed it on his arm. He let out a hiss when she started cleaning the wound, and clenched his fist in his lap. She tried to keep her mind on the task at hand. It was hard to forget that a few hours before she was naked under him, that his hands caressed and ravaged her in turn, and his body possessed hers with a burning passion, but without care or tenderness.

'That's it.' She wrapped a strip of cloth around his arm and stepped back without looking at him.

'Thank you. Now get some sleep while I take a look around.' He stood up bare-chested and walked into the shadows, his pistol in one hand.

She nodded, sat down, and wrapped herself in her burnous. The bag she slipped under her head for a pillow was hard and bumpy, and even curled into a ball, she still shivered with cold.

'Here, take this.' He handed her a blanket which she laid on the ground, and another she spread on top of her.

'Sleep,' he ordered, sitting next to her. She fell asleep and dreamt that he was stroking her hair and pulling her against him to keep her warm.

He had managed to find a fresh shirt in the mess of torn clothes, ripped bags, spilled and smashed supplies that the raiders had made of the camp.

Something wasn't right. His men were experienced trackers. They should have heard or seen their attackers. Who were the raiders and why did they take Drake with them? He thought about all the apparently benign incidents of the past few weeks, but couldn't decide if his suspicions were founded or if his judgement was being clouded by personal feelings. His arm throbbed with pain, but he kept Harriet close.

She felt warm, curled up against him. How frightened she must have felt when she found herself alone in the ruined camp, when she realised she might be alone for good.

She was something else he had to think about. He might have been her first man, but he sure didn't want to be responsible for her. He squared his jaw. He would take her to Tamanrasset, since he'd given her his word, and then back to Algiers where he would personally see she boarded a ship for England. No, he resolved, hardening his stare, there was no room in his life for a woman. There would never be.

Yet his fingers still stroked her hair. He relaxed into a smile. Actually, he did have one responsibility towards her – besides taking her to Tamanrasset. Call it male pride or vanity, but he would show her how pleasurable lovemaking could be.

It was midday and brutally hot when they set off from the Arak gorges. It had taken Lucas all morning to bury his men and select the equipment and supplies he wanted to salvage from the ruined camp. Harriet had a short argument with him about some of the items she insisted on taking – her drawing book and materials, changes of clothes, a few toiletries. In the end, he'd given up and let her decide.

They returned into the gorges to cut a couple of aloe cactus leaves and extract a thick green liquid she then dabbed onto his wounded arm before applying a fresh dressing.

Lucas decided to strap the ransom bags and most of the water and some equipment onto the horse while they walked and carried lighter supplies.

'From my estimations, the nearest Tuareg caravan is half a day away. We should meet them by evening.' Were it not for his eyes, as clear and blue as the sky, he would look like a Tuareg himself. He'd discarded his hat and waistcoat for an indigo blue headdress and slipped a short blue and white tunic over the fresh shirt he'd retrieved from his bag.

'What if they don't want to help us? What if—'

'Don't worry about them. They will help us in exchange for a few gold coins. I'll have to dip into the ransom since the raiders took the bag where I kept our travel money.'

'Where do you think they are?' She glanced around, uneasy. 'If they chose to attack us now, we would be easy targets.'

'You don't have much faith in me, I see.' His lips stretched into a tight smile. 'I still have my rifle and a pistol.' But there was worry in his eyes as he scanned their surroundings.

So they walked. The sun beat onto them, cruel, relentless. Heat rose from the ground, a clear, hazy mist which distorted the landscape. When they set off Harriet thought about Archie and prayed he was safe, but soon all she could think about was water, shade and rest.

A strange landscape appeared in the distance, so strange she thought she was seeing another mirage, but they were only rock formations that the wind and the sand had eroded and moulded into weird, nightmarish shapes. Tents were pitched around them. Two dozen blue tents at least. Then she saw white mehari camels and the tall silhouette of a man outlined against the sunset. He resembled a spectre, still and gaunt, his face covered with a *cheche* and his long tunic floating around him.

Lucas walked over to salute him. The man listened, nodded, and made a wide, sweeping gesture towards the camp before saying a few words.

'He says we are welcome. For now we must pay our respects to their chief. Do everything I do. Don't talk or show your face right now. I need to explain who we are first.'

They followed the man to a large tent pitched at the centre of the camp. A man and two elderly women sat on a rug at the entrance, drinking tea under a canopy. According to Tuareg tradition, the man was veiled but not the women. Harriet held her breath, apprehensive. If the chief refused to help, they'd certainly die in the desert before reaching In Salah.

Lucas bowed once and started talking in Tamasheq, the Tuareg language she heard Hakim and Musa use before. The Tuaregs nodded, looking at her.

'Take your scarf off,' Lucas ordered then.

If the man didn't even blink when she revealed her face, the women smiled and started talking and laughing. The chief gestured for Lucas and her to sit down. Tea was poured, plates of food brought, together with pieces of flat bread still warm from the fire.

'*Saha*', she said, using the Arab word for thanks for want of knowing any Tamasheq.

'That's "Tanemmert" in Tamasheq,' Lucas whispered to her.

She would ask him to teach her more words, she resolved, as she repeated her appreciation. The hot, sweet tea was the best she'd ever had. She bit into the warm bread. It was delicious, if a little tough. Lucas talked in a low voice with the man. He turned to her.

'They will take us up to In Salah and let us have a tent.' He glanced at her, seriously. 'To share.'

‘I can sleep outside, near the fire,’ Harriet objected.

‘That would be disrespectful when they offer you hospitality,’ he interrupted, his voice harsh. ‘I said you were my woman. I’m sure you can put up with me for a few nights.’ He got up. ‘I’ll see to the horse. The women will look after you.’

As if on cue, the two women got up and gestured to her to follow. They took her around the camp, which consisted of two dozen tents with three or four people in each, mostly men. Near the camp was a narrow gorge with trees and rough grass where a full herd of camels grazed, watched over by a couple of men. There must have been over fifty animals in total, tall and gracious with their long, slender necks.

Further along the gorge was a well. Even though it was hardly more than a muddy pond, and a far cry from the hidden lake of the Arak gorges, it was impossible to resist after a long day in the desert’s unforgiving heat. Harriet only hesitated a moment before undressing to her chemise and walking into the water. After her bath, the women led her back to camp and showed her into one of the smaller tents where rugs and a couple of blankets were piled inside and where Lucas had already stored their bags.

During the following hour, as dusk fell onto the desert, she helped the women gather wood to make a fire at the entrance of her tent, returned to the well to get some water for tea, and cooked a basic meal with what was left of their supplies. Similar fires burned in front of every tent as the Tuaregs settled in small groups for the evening.

Lucas untied his belt and threw it in the sand before sitting down.

‘Don’t you want to keep hold of that?’ Harriet stared at the pistol on the ground in alarm, then at the other tents around them. ‘What if they decide to kill us for the gold?’

He shook his head. ‘We are their guests now. If anything, they will die to protect us. It’s a question of honour.’

He turned to her and held out his tin cup. ‘*Nek fouda, aouid ala, Tamat,*’ he said.

‘I’m thirsty, give me some tea, woman,’ he translated, a twinkle in his eye.

She held back a sharp response and crossed her arms on her chest.

‘I thought women were little queens in Tuareg tribes who can boot the man out of the tent if dissatisfied with him?’

He pulled a face. ‘I should have known it was a mistake to tell you that. So, are you going to let me die a thirsty and hungry man?'

She couldn't help smiling.

'Of course not.' She poured some tea and served a generous helping of stew into a bowl for him.

'You said you wanted to learn the language.' He stretched his legs out. 'Let's make a start.'

He proceeded to teach her some basic Tamasheq while they ate their evening meal.

'Is someone playing music?' Harriet asked as a plaintive melody suddenly echoed in the silence.

Lucas nodded. 'The women are playing the imzad – a single-string instrument made with a calebash and covered with animal skin.'

'It's beautiful.' Harriet sighed as the long, monochord lament rose in the night and tugged at her heart.

As they finished eating a man came over and said a few words to Lucas in his language. Lucas turned to her, a startled expression on his face. 'He wants to speak to you about your father.'

Chapter Twenty-Two

The chief gestured for Harriet and Lucas to sit down and started talking.

His face grave, Lucas listened and asked a few questions. Harriet looked at each man in turn. What news did the chief have? Good or bad? With the veil covering his face, there was no way of gauging his expression. At last, Lucas turned to her, a faint smile on his lips.

'Your father was alive and well three weeks ago. The chief heard it from some Tuaregs he met at the fair in Djelfa.'

'Where is he? Who are these men holding him and—'

Lucas lifted a hand to silence her. 'He is being held in Abalessa by the keepers of Tin Hinan's tomb.'

The chief nodded. 'Abalessa,' he repeated, his voice muffled by his veil.

'The keepers?'

'Ever since the great queen died, Tuareg braves have been in charge of the safekeeping of her tomb,' Lucas explained.

She snorted. 'How can you call them braves when they butchered the members of my father's expedition and are now holding a defenceless man against his will?'

'Remember where you are, Harriet,' he said, a quiet warning in his voice. 'Now, there's something very interesting about these *braves'*—he emphasised the word—'holding your father … The chief claims they didn't kill anyone. Just the opposite, in fact. He says they saved your father's life.'

'That's not what the British Consul told Archie.'

Lucas thanked the chief and stood up before pulling her to her feet. 'Let's talk about this somewhere else.'

He released her hand as they walked through the silent camp towards their tent. She knew there were men standing guard – the caravan was bringing expensive goods back from Djelfa and there was always the risk of a raid by bandits – but she couldn't help peering uneasily into the shadows. A few guards wouldn't stand a chance against those men after her father's ransom. And what if Lucas was wrong about the Tuaregs being honour-bound to protect them? What if they claimed the gold for themselves instead?

The fire in front of their small tent was almost out. Lucas grabbed a stick to poke at the red embers. Sparks flew into the night. He added more wood, poked again. When flames rose and crackled, he sat down and stared at the fire, lost in his thoughts.

He looked up at last. 'Sit down.'

He waited for her to settle next to him on the rug.

'The rumour is that your father's expedition was attacked by a gang of mercenaries led by European men – whether French or English, the chief didn't know.'

'It doesn't make sense! The British Consul said Tuaregs attacked my father. The French garrison in Tamanrasset sent a report. Why would they lie about it?'

Lucas shook his head. 'I don't know. One possibility is that the French found it easier to blame the Tuaregs for the massacre than investigate the incident properly.'

'So the French army lied to the British Consul.'

'I said it was one possibility.'

'What else could it be? You couldn't possibly imply that Lord Welsford would lie to Archie.'

Lucas remained silent. 'Did you meet Lord Welsford when in Algiers?'

'No, Archie said it would be too upsetting for me to attend the meetings.'

'Hmm … so you only have Drake's word for what was said at the consulate.'

She drew in a sharp intake of breath. 'What exactly are you implying?'

'Who gave you the news about your father?'

'Lord Callaghan.'

She closed her eyes, remembering the cold, grey January afternoon she'd received her father's employer at their London house. Lord Callaghan had taken his wet coat and hat off, smoothed his thick silver grey hair and begged her to sit down before breaking the awful news of her father's abduction.

'He was very sorry that my father's life should be at risk while he was on a mission for the museum and promised to do everything in his power to help. It was his idea to take a ransom to the Tuaregs in exchange for my father's life.'

'Where did the money for the ransom come from?'

'Lord Callaghan.'

‘Why was Archie entrusted with the rescue mission?’

‘Lord Callaghan said he was the best man for the job. He has field experience and everybody knows how close he is to my father.’

‘You always say they are close, and yet your father didn’t write to him about the Barbarossa map.’ Lucas threw a sidelong glance towards her.

She linked her fingers in her lap, tightly. ‘He must have written to Archie. I can’t think why he’d keep such an important discovery from him. His letter must have got lost between Algiers and London.’

‘If I remember correctly, in his letter authenticating the map, your father wrote not to tell anyone about it and instructed you to keep it safe in a secret place until his return. That’s hardly a man who plans to reveal his discovery to his employer or colleagues, is it?’

‘Don’t start that again! My father wasn’t planning to keep any treasure for himself.’

Lucas frowned. There had been something else in Oscar Montague’s letter, something he was trying to remember, but couldn’t quite recall.

‘You said your father and Archie had grown apart these past few months.’

‘Archie was so busy with his new post he didn’t have time to visit us,’ she answered, hesitant.

That wasn’t completely true. There had been an incident between the two men a week before her father left for Algiers.

‘Actually, they argued before my father departed for Algiers, quite violently. I don’t know what about, but it upset my father. And he isn’t a man easily upset.’ Quite the opposite in fact. Her father prided himself on his cool, even disposition.

‘And then there are the raiders who knew exactly how to find us despite my roundabout routes,’ he said to himself. ‘And the mysterious man with the snarling silver wolf ring.’

She cleared her throat. ‘About that ring …’ She rubbed her forehead with her fingers, willing the memories to be sharper, the images in her mind clearer. ‘I’ve seen such a ring before, when very young. I don’t remember where, just that it was a big house in the country. I was outside on the terrace and I looked through the window into a study or a library …’

She shook her head. ‘There were men there, about a dozen, in evening dress, but I don’t recall their faces. The only man I remember clearly wore the same ring.'

'Why didn't you say anything about it before?' He leaned over and grabbed her shoulders.

She bent her head and swallowed hard. 'I'm sorry. I needed time to think about it, to be sure.'

'Who was the man?' His fingers dug into her.

Her eyes filled with tears. 'My father,' she whispered. She took a deep breath and repeated. 'My father wore the ring.'

Lucas let go of her and swore between his teeth in French. 'Then Drake was lying about that too.'

'Why do you say that?'

'He said he'd never seen the ring. If he was as close to your father as you said, he must have seen him and others around him wear similar ones. The question is why did he lie about it?'

'He must have his reasons. Archie is a good, trustworthy man.'

The fury in his eyes hit her like a blow to the chest. 'Damn it! Why are you so blind where Drake's concerned? What hold does the man have on you?' he growled. 'All you ever see is the wonderful Archibald Drake, all you ever do is praise him or make excuses for him.'

He pulled her closer. Her breath caught in her throat.

'Well, I've got news for you, Harriet. The man is a liar and a bully, a cheat and a drunk. And the sooner you get that into your brain, the better.'

What on earth had possessed him? Where did this blinding rage come from? Anyone would think he was jealous. Drake was the man he should be taking his anger out on, not the woman he held trembling in front of him, her eyes open wide in shock.

Hell, he'd just called Drake a bully but he was no better.

Anger still simmered inside him, mingled with shame now, but words of apology didn't make it past his lips. Instead, he squared his jaw and narrowed his eyes.

'Get inside and go to sleep. The caravan is leaving at dawn.'

He wanted to be alone, calm down, and think things over.

She didn't move.

'You'll be safe. I will stay out here,' he said, his tone softer.

She lifted her eyes towards him; her cool, trusting, misty grey eyes. His throat tightened, his heart started pounding.

‘Please don’t leave me alone,’ she whispered. She put her hand against his chest. ‘Everything is so confused. Nothing makes sense any longer. The only thing I know is that I’m happy you’re here. You are brave and honourable and I believe in you.’ She paused, lowered her eyes briefly, and took a deep breath.

Her words swirled in his mind, in his heart. He blocked them off.

‘Once again, I think you’re mistaking me for someone else,’ he sniggered. ‘I’m not one of the clever scholars or aristocratic patrons of the arts you’re used to. I sell my services for a fee, which I guess makes me no better than the mercenaries who attacked your father or the ones trying to steal his ransom money. All I care about is myself and having enough money for the next card game, the next flask of wine and the next woman.’

She mustn’t have heard him because her hand pressed a little harder against his heart, arousing sensations and feelings he didn’t want.

She shook her head. ‘That’s not true. You’re not as crude as you make out, you have feelings and—’

He snorted, hardening his voice. ‘Feelings? Shall I tell you about my feelings for you?’

He took her hand, pulled it away from him. He had to put an end to this nonsense, be straight with her, get her to see him as he really was. He leaned down towards her and held her gaze. ‘Yes, I want you, I admit it, but there’s nothing sweet or good or loving about it. I need to have you. I need my hands on your skin and your body under mine. And I don’t care if I hurt you like I did yesterday in the cave, as long as I take my pleasure,’ he lied.

He pulled back and grinned. ‘There, that’s the kind of man I am. Now get inside and leave me alone.’

She considered him in silence then smiled again. She closed the short distance between them, pressed her face against his chest and wrapped her arms around his waist.

‘I don’t care what you say. I love you,’ she whispered against his heart. ‘I told you. You didn’t hurt me yesterday.’

Guilt and need, anger and something that felt like joy churned and wrestled inside him. He closed his eyes for a second, drew in breath, and gave up the fight. He brought his arms around her. Holding her felt right, so right. What did it matter if the woman was confused and delusional, if she believed she loved him? He should take whatever was on offer. He usually did. There would be time enough to make her see sense. Later.

His hands brushed her back, slowly, from her hips to the nape of her neck. She murmured something and moulded herself closer to him. He tugged at her hair to angle her face up towards him and leant down to kiss her mouth. If nothing else, he had a promise to keep.

She hadn't planned to tell him about her feelings. She loved him. She trusted him with her life. She admired him, even if she didn't always understand him. He didn't love her, she knew that, but right now being in his arms was enough. It was where she belonged, where she fitted. She would show him what love was.

His lips trailed along her jawline to her earlobe, then down her throat, and back up again. Millions of shivers broke on the surface of her skin. She raised her hands to grip his shoulders. Her head started spinning. Her heart raced a wild gallop.

'We should go inside,' he said, hoarse against her ear. 'We don't want to make a spectacle of ourselves.'

She almost objected that there was nobody to watch them, but remembered the men standing guard somewhere in the shadows.

He took her hand and led her inside the tent. The only light was the fire still burning outside. Thick wool rugs covered the ground, a mattress had been pulled in the centre together with a few blankets, and all their bags piled up to one side.

'Will you lie with me, Harriet?' he asked gently as he cradled her face in the palms of his hands. 'Will you let me make up for yesterday?'

She stared into his eyes. There was no harshness in them now.

'Yes,' she breathed out. 'Yes, I will.'

Chapter Twenty-Three

'Ask him for a story about Tin Hinan,' Harriet whispered.

Like every evening, they sat under a dark velvet sky studded with stars in front of the chief's tent. Tonight was their last night with the caravan before reaching In Salah.

Lucas said a few words to the chief, who searched his leather bag and produced a smooth green stone shaped like an egg. Each stone in the storytelling bag was unique, and prompted a different story by the chief. Tonight was no exception.

'Tin Hinan,' he announced.

Harriet gasped. 'It looks like …'

'An emerald,' Lucas finished, his eyes shining. He stared at the sparkly green pebble the chief held in his hand as he started talking in his low, chanting voice.

'Tin Hinan came from the Western lands beyond the great desert,' Lucas translated. 'She followed the stars and the ancient roads to Abalessa, the blessed.'

The chief talked about the queen's exploits and how she created the Tuareg kingdom, her daughters, Tinert the antelope, Tahenkot the gazelle, and Tamerouelt the hare, each founding their own tribe. Then he paused and stroked the green stone.

'Tin Hinan married a great warrior from the east who gave her the magic mountains where the green stones were found.'

Excited, Harriet squeezed Lucas' hand. 'It has to be the Garamantes' mines!'

Lucas carried on translating the chief's story.

'Since the day she died, every Tuareg who travels to Abalessa lays a rock on her tomb. One day it will reach the sky,' Lucas finished.

'Where are the magic mountains?'

Lucas translated the question. The chief shook his head. 'The earth shook, the mountains collapsed and disappeared into the ground. It was a long, long time ago.'

One of the women musicians picked up her imzad and started drawing soulful sounds while a man played the drum and several others sang and clapped their hands.

Her heart heavy, Harriet locked her fingers together and blinked the tears away. How she would miss the Tuareg caravan – setting off at sunrise in the transparent, purple dawn, camping out in sheltered gorges and lost valleys, and listening to Lucas' voice as he translated the chief's stories in the evenings. Most of all, she would miss the passion, the heat of Lucas' arms every night. They had become as essential as air, water and fire.

When the singing stopped, it was time to return to the tent. Lucas helped Harriet up and kept her hand in his as they walked across the camp. A series of low, rumbling growls from the camels nearby made her jump.

'What's up with them?'

'There are other caravans nearby.'

'Really?'

He squeezed her hand, bringing it to his lips. 'The camels know, and they're never wrong.'

'So you understand the language of camels?' She turned a beaming smile to him. 'It's true that you sometimes grunt like one when you're in a bad mood.'

He burst out laughing and kissed her finger tips again. 'Camels are the wisest of beasts,' he said. 'For example, it's well known that when a camel refuses to stand up in the morning, he's warning his master there's trouble ahead and it would be better to stay in his tent and drink tea than go travelling.'

'What if he's just tired or grumpy?'

'Then the man would definitely have trouble. You have no idea how awful a grumpy camel can be.'

They reached their tent. Like every night, Lucas knelt down to revive the fire. Harriet sat down and nestled against him. He wrapped his arm around her shoulders.

'The chief said the mines were lost,' Harriet mused.

'Is finding these mines so important to you?' He turned to her, his eyes piercing.

She didn't answer.

It was important once. It was her father's obsession, and at one time nothing mattered more than making her father happy and proud. Now, all she wanted was being with the man she loved. She felt a little stab of guilt when she realised she hadn't thought about her father or Archie all evening. Lucas' fingers brushed her hair aside and stroked the side of her throat.

He lowered his face towards her. Her lips parted and once again her thoughts swirled and vanished in the heat of his kiss.

In Salah appeared like a mirage on the horizon. It rose from the desert, its flat-roofed houses the same colour as the reddish gold sand dunes. Only a couple of towers and a few patches of green broke the monotony of the landscape.

'Hakim and Musa should be waiting for us,' Lucas said as he waved good bye to the Tuaregs. The caravan was carrying on towards the east, whereas they would fork west to Abalessa. 'We will leave as soon as we've found them.'

They dismounted to join the queue at the town gate. Harriet pulled the horse's bridle and Lucas dealt with the camel the Tuaregs had sold them. She was wary of the animal's temper, of the way it pulled its long neck towards her, hung its tongue out or dribbled whilst making bleating noises.

'It must be market day.' She watched the crowd around them, barefoot children, women and men clothed in long white or pale blue robes, their heads and faces covered. Some pulled donkeys and beat them with dried palm branches or sticks to urge them along. Others pulled carts or carried baskets on their backs or on their head.

'Something's up.' Lucas pointed to the gate where a group of French soldiers stood guard and stopped everyone wanting to get into the town.

'Pull your scarf over your face, keep your eyes down and let me do the talking,' he instructed sharply, adjusting his indigo blue headscarf to make sure his face was covered and the turban fell down on his forehead, shading his blue eyes. 'They're looking for someone. I'm not taking any chances.'

Her heart thumped hard and her throat was so constricted with fear she couldn't breathe as she joined the line of people queuing at the gate. Hoping the soldiers wouldn't look at her too closely, she remained a step behind Lucas and fussed with the horse's saddlebags and bridle to keep her nervous hands busy.

'*Qu'est-ce que tu viens faire à In Salah?*' a soldier asked Lucas when it was their turn.

Lucas shook his head and answered in Arabic, gesturing towards the camel and the horse.

'*Qu'est-ce que tu transportes? C'est pour le marché?*' the man asked again, laying his hand on the bags with the ransom gold Lucas had strapped onto the camel's back.

'*Marché, oui ... moi achète femme pour mon frère,*' Lucas answered in a fake broken French and pointing at her.

'A woman? But he's far too small!' The soldier peered at her with a leering smile.

'Perhaps, but he's lusty and wants a woman.'

The soldier burst out laughing and slapped Harriet on the back before waving them in.

'*Bonne chance. Allez, entrez!*'

In silence, they followed the flow of people walking up the winding alleyways to the central market square and medina, which was a maze of narrow passageways with a small channel running in the middle for waste water. Lucas knocked on a wooden door. Three knocks, followed by two then three more – a code. Where were they going?

The door creaked open onto a large, cobblestone courtyard with dirty straw and piles of horse manure. On one side was a stable block. The three remaining sides featured archways and doors hidden behind bead curtains. A man ushered them in and saluted Lucas in rapid Arabic. He helped unbuckle the bags before leading the camel and the horse away to be stabled. Lucas took Harriet's hand. He pulled a bead curtain aside and they walked into the house. It was so dark inside after the bright sunlight that she blinked a few times before being able to see the men sitting around in small groups.

Someone called from a corner of the room. A tall man stood and walked up to them. She let out a cry of alarm and gripped Lucas's arm but he only laughed.

'It's Hakim.' Lucas pulled his scarf off and grinned at his friend.

The two men clasped hands and started talking in Tamasheq.

They spent the rest of the afternoon in the tavern's dark, grimy room. They ordered food and tea and discussed the next steps of their journey to Abalessa. Or at least, that's what they appeared to be doing as they pored over Lucas' map, because she couldn't understand a word of what they were saying. Her eyelids became heavy. She yawned, rested her head against Lucas' shoulder and fell asleep.

'Harriet, wake up, darling. We have to go.' Lucas stroked her cheek, her shoulder, her arm.

She opened her eyes and smiled. 'Where are we going?'

The tavern was almost empty. Hakim had gone. It was dark outside.

'We're leaving. Hakim and Musa are waiting in the oasis for us. They have the bags, the horses and the camels.'

'What about the French soldiers? Won't they expect me to walk out with a woman tucked under my arm? You told them I was buying a wife, didn't you?'

He laughed, pecking a kiss on the tip of her nose.

'We can always say that after sampling a few, you didn't find a woman you liked enough to take home. Just walk like a man whose senses are satiated after a few hours of … ahem'—there was a twinkle in his eyes—'indulgence.'

'Easy for you to say. I wouldn't know what that feels like, I'm not a man.'

He put his hands on her shoulders and darted his eyes into hers.

'I will tell you what it's like. It's like looking at the sun rising over Mont Illamen in the Hoggar – the mountain they call "the roof of the world". It gives you the feeling you can do anything: touch the clouds, capture a star or fly like a hawk from the highest peaks.'

He paused and tapped her cheek with his finger. 'Anyway, you won't have to pretend because we're going on the roofs.'

He got up. His voice was businesslike again and his face blank. 'There have been developments I need to tell you about. In the meantime, follow me. I hope you're not afraid of heights.'

'We shall see.'

He jumped onto the roof of the tavern, held out his hand to pull her up and they ran above the streets, like shadows under the cover of darkness.

From their vantage point, they saw French soldiers patrolling the streets. The gate was closed and heavily guarded. She glanced at Lucas in alarm but he only smiled.

'Don't worry. Everything's being taken care of.'

A series of explosions outside of the town walls tore the stillness of the night. Immediately the French soldiers shouted orders to open the gates and ran out into the sand dunes, leaving only a couple of men to stand guard.

'Wait here,' Lucas ordered.

He let himself down from the roof. Silent as a cat, he walked to the guards and drew his knife out. She closed her eyes, her chest tight with fear, and heard the sickening sounds of bodies hitting the ground with a thud. When she reopened her eyes, both men lay motionless.

'Quick,' Lucas called. He caught her in his arms when she jumped and held her hand as they sneaked out of the town.

They crouched in the sand dunes until the French soldiers went back inside and closed the gates, then made their way into the oasis. They found Hakim and Musa hiding among the palm trees, their horses already saddled and the camels loaded with supplies and equipment. Nobody talked as they started on the trail to the south. They walked for most of the night, first on rocky tracks, then on sand that slipped and shifted underfoot, stopping a few times to drink and eat some dates. Only when the stars faded away and the sky became pale to the east, did Lucas decide it was time for a rest. He led them to what looked like a white hut hidden amongst sand dunes and rocks, with a lonely, bushy acacia tree and a well next to it.

'What is this?' Harriet asked as they walked inside the tiny, one-bedroom house.

'A *kouba*, the tomb of a holy man,' he answered, checking the corners of the room for snakes and scorpions. He threw a couple of blankets on the ground. 'Travellers use them to shelter, women come to pray and dream.'

'Dream? What about?'

'About what the future has in store for them, of course.' He shrugged. 'We'll stop here until dusk and travel at night. You need to sleep, but first, have a drink. I just filled my gourd at the well.'

She took a long sip of water, but the bitter liquid made her choke.

'What's wrong?' Lucas took the gourd from her and took a small taste. He spat the water out.

'It's been poisoned. With *Adenia* I think.'

Stepping towards her, he grabbed her shoulders and stared deep into her eyes. 'How much did you have?'

'Not much, only a sip. I couldn't swallow it,' she answered. The bitter taste lingered in her mouth. 'Who would do that, poison a well?'

He let go of her and walked out. 'People who don't want us to make it. Give me a minute, I'll warn the others.'

His face was sombre when he came back. 'Hakim is checking a couple other wells in the area to see if they too were poisoned.'

He paused. 'You asked who would poison a well. Mortemer would. He's done so before in his fight against the rebels. He never cared about harming villagers or nomads. He knows we're heading for Tamanrasset and is a few days ahead of us.' He hesitated. 'Hakim told me there's a reward on my head, dead or alive. Apparently the rumour is I won't get out of Abalessa alive.'

She gasped. 'So he does know about you being on the rebels' side.'

'I've been a little arrogant in thinking he'd never catch up with me.' He looked at her and added softly. 'There's something else, Harriet.

'According to Hakim, Mortemer and his soldiers are travelling with a gang of men, a dozen or so. Their leaders are Englishmen, and both wear a ring unusual enough to have been noticed.'

'A jade ring with the silver wolf?' she asked, her voice weak.

He nodded, his eyes hardening. 'Archie is with them. Hakim saw him.'

She gripped his arm. 'Archie! Did they say if he looked hurt or injured? I do hope they're treating him right.'

He sneered. 'You needn't worry about him. He is one of them.'

'I don't understand.' She shook her head.

He covered her hand with his and rubbed it gently. 'I'm not sure I do either. I've had doubts about him for a while. It looks like he went with the raiders willingly. I wonder if he wasn't the one who told them about our route, which would explain why they could find us.'

'Why would he want to steal my father's ransom when he's helping to rescue him?' She broke free and put her hands to her ears. 'I won't listen to these lies. You were against Archie from the start.'

His gaze narrowed in anger. 'Very well. I see you want to keep your illusions about the man. I'll leave you alone.'

He walked to the door. 'Get some sleep. I'll wake you when it's time to leave.' He left, slamming the wooden door behind him so hard that dried mud from the walls fell to the ground.

Harriet buried her face in her hands. She didn't understand what he'd just told her. Why would Archie pretend to be helping her father while arranging for his ransom to be stolen, therefore signing her father's death warrant? Lucas had it all wrong.

She wrapped her burnous around her and lay down. It wasn't quite dawn yet and it was still cool in the *kouba*. She closed her eyes and rocked herself to sleep.

The lion was watching over her. He was the one she'd seen before. His piercing blue eyes followed her everywhere she went, from the arid plains to the rocky canyons, from the fragrant and cool oases to the inferno of sand dunes under a burning sky. Ahar. She said his name. Ahar. It was him. It had always been him. She raised a hand, but he turned away and left her alone.

The door banging against the wall woke her with a start. Where was she? A man's silhouette stood out against the darkening sky. Her mouth, her throat were parched. Her stomach ached and pain shot through her chest. She tried to move but her legs felt like lead.

'The sun has set. Come and get something to eat before we leave,' Lucas said.

She sat up, shivery and brought a hand to her forehead. 'Have I really slept all day?'

'You have. You don't look well.' He walked into the hut and crouched in front of her. His voice softened. 'You must have drunk more water than you thought.'

His face was blurred and the room moved and spun in front of her. She brought her hand to her mouth. 'Help me.'

He scooped her into his arms and carried her outside where she was violently sick. He held her, stroked her back and murmured soothing words until it was over, then he carried her back inside and laid her gently on the blanket. She closed her eyes and drifted back to sleep.

She only had vague memories of the following night and day, of Lucas leaning over her, his eyes serious, of his hand stroking her hair and the taste of the sweet tea he patiently fed her at regular intervals.

At last the time came when her vision wasn't blurred any longer, when she didn't feel like retching as soon as she moved and when her head stopped throbbing. Men were talking outside, an enticing smell of meat roasting on a fire drifted into the hut. She got up and pushed the door open.

Lucas walked to her, cupped her chin to look into her face. 'At last. I was thinking of sending for the marabout if you didn't get any better soon.'

She managed a faint smile, pointed to the fire over which a tin pot of water boiled. 'Where did you get the water?'

'Musa found a well which hadn't been poisoned.' He put his arm around her shoulders and led her to the fire. 'Come and sit down.'

He poured some tea out for her, cut some meat and a piece of bread.

'Eat. We leave at dusk. We'll need to save water from now on. We don't know when we'll find another uncontaminated well. If all goes well, we'll be at Abalessa by the end of the week.'

She put her hands on her heart. 'Really? So I could be with my father in just a few days? It's almost the end of our journey.'

He stared into the fire in silence for a couple of minutes. 'Yes, it's almost the end,' he repeated, wistfully.

'You don't sound very happy about it.'

Then she remembered what he'd said and her smile died on her lips. How could she be so selfish? His life would be in danger the moment they stepped in Abalessa.

'You should leave, Lucas, disappear. That's your only chance. I'm sure Hakim and Musa can take me safely to Abalessa.'

'You really don't think much of me, do you Harriet?' He scowled. 'I said I would take you to your father and I will.'

'But Mortemer and his men will be waiting for you there, you said so yourself.'

He stood up and kicked some sand into the fire. 'It was only a matter of time before I confronted him and faced up to what I did five years ago.'

'What happened to your father and those innocent people wasn't your fault.' She jumped to her feet, gripping his arm.

He looked down at her. 'I might as well have lit those fires and pulled the trigger myself.' His voice was devoid of emotion, his stare blank.

'Getting yourself killed won't change the fact that they're dead,' she said softly, as a terrible pain wrung her heart, making her breathless. 'I love you so much. I want to be with you. I thought maybe once my father was free, we could …'

'You thought wrong. I never promised you anything,' he interrupted coldly. 'Apart from taking you to the south, that is.' And he walked away.

Chapter Twenty-Four

'We need to take shelter fast.' Lucas pointed to a thick orange cloud advancing towards them like a wall, obscuring the light.

'Sandstorm. Pull your veil around your face and dismount. Quick!'

Within a few seconds, the sky turned a dark yellow and the sun was no more than a white ball giving out pale, diffuse light. Gusts of wind hurled clouds of sand that whipped and stung her body despite the layers of clothing. Sand got into her eyes, her nose, down her throat. For one terrifying moment, she even feared it would fill her lungs and she'd choke on it. She dismounted and struggled to control her horse as it stomped and neighed in the storm.

A stronger gust of wind swirled around them and the horse balked so suddenly she let go of the bridle and fell back. Thankfully, Musa managed to take hold of the reins. Bending against the wind, coughing and almost blind, they made their way into a dark, narrow canyon that seemed to be made of black or dark purple stone.

Even if the canyon offered some protection, the air was thick with sand and the wind so strong she could hardly stand.

Once the horses and camels were securely tied up to thick acacia branches, Lucas got a couple of blankets out of a bag, threw one to Hakim and Musa and kept the other.

'Come here.' He gestured for her to sit, her back against the rock face, and pulled the blanket over them like a makeshift tent, securing it in place by tucking it between his back and the rock.

'There's nothing to do but wait,' he said.

She closed her eyes. Her body was weary but sleep eluded her. They'd reached the Hoggar after a gruelling trek through the desert. Lucas had been right to predict that many of the wells on their way would be poisoned, but he always made sure she didn't suffer from thirst and often passed his gourd to her without drinking.

Right now, she was acutely aware of him sitting at her side even though he was taking great care not to touch her. He had been cool, distant, almost indifferent, since their argument in the *kouba*. Her eyes filled with tears she brushed off impatiently, but she couldn't repress a sob.

'What's the matter?'

He turned to her. His hand slipped under her veil, touched her hair, her face. 'You're crying …'

His finger followed the trail of tears on her skin. She shivered under his touch.

'Don't be afraid. The storm will probably blow over by nightfall.'

His voice only just covered the tumult of the wind.

He held out his gourd and unscrewed the top. 'Here, have some water.'

She shook her head. 'No, you drink first. I've had more water than you or Hakim and Musa put together these past few days. It's not fair.'

'We're used to going without, you aren't,' he said, curtly. 'Drink.'

Her throat was so parched and raw that even the warm, slightly rank water tasted delicious. She gave him the gourd back and put her hand on his forearm.

'Thank you.'

He shrugged. She was too close. He'd managed to keep her at arms' length these past few days. It had cost him, but it was necessary. He couldn't afford being distracted, softened by her. There was no point, no future in them – in him.

'No, I really mean it,' she carried on. 'Any other man would have gone back on his word and chosen to save himself. I wouldn't think less of you if you decided to go into hiding before we meet Mortemer and his men.'

He gripped her arm and pulled her closer. 'Stop this.'

'I cannot stand the idea you are putting yourself in danger and might be—'

'Killed?' He let out a humourless laugh. 'If that happens, Hakim and Musa will get you and your father out.'

'It's not just about my father, don't you understand?' Her eyes welled up with tears again. Although he ached to take her in his arms, he didn't move. 'I told you before and I meant it. I love you, Lucas.'

His heart skipped a beat but he shook his head. 'You don't love me. You can't love a man responsible for his father's death, and the death of dozens of innocent people.'

'Why can't you forgive yourself?'

His lips curled into a cruel smile. It was time to tell her. 'You want the truth? The whole truth? You see, *darling*, the night before my father died, I was drunk. Mortemer came to find me in a tavern, spun me a tale

I would never have believed had I been sober, and I told him where to find the cave to get rid of him. All I cared about that night was winning my card game and bedding one of the dancing girls. And that's exactly what I did.'

He tightened his fists and lowered his face. 'I won the game, spent all the money on wine, and slept with a woman I can't even remember. During that time fires were being lit, people were being choked to death, burnt and shot by the French army.'

He turned to her and arched his eyebrows. 'There you have it.'

He expected to see revulsion in her eyes. All she did was shake her head and put her hand on his forearm. She stroked him gently, as one would stroke a child.

'Oh, Lucas. It must have been so hard for you to tell me. If anything, it makes me love you even more.'

'You can't love me. You don't know me. You don't know what I'm capable of.'

She slid her hand along his arm, his shoulder, and rested it against his chest. 'I know you're the bravest, the most honourable man I've ever met. That's enough.'

'Honourable?' He sneered, hardening his voice.

He had to sever all ties. It was for her own good.

'You think I conducted myself honourably with you, do you? I took advantage of you, Harriet. From the very first moment we met, all I ever wanted was the Barbarossa map and the ransom gold. I still do. Sleeping with you was a pleasant bonus.'

She gasped, withdrawing her hand. 'The ransom? What do you mean?'

'I was sure your father was dead, so I planned to claim the gold once we got to Tamanrasset. I might still do that, depending on what we find in Abalessa tomorrow.'

She recoiled as if he'd slapped her. 'You would steal Lord Callaghan's gold? For the rebels?'

'I haven't decided what I'd spend the gold on yet …'

He took a deep breath. He had to be cruel and finish it. She wouldn't love him after hearing this.

'You know I only agreed to your coming with us because of the Barbarossa map. I thought Drake was your fiancé, so I had this idea that if I seduced you, you'd feel so guilty you'd want to return to Algiers.

And you'd still owe me the map, of course.'

'It was too late to send me back when we reached the gorges of Arak, and yet you still made love to me ...'

Her eyes were alight with hope. He had to crush it.

'It was just a pleasant way of killing an hour, but the thing is that the novelty of deflowering a virgin has kind of worn off now. You're a lovely girl, but I'm used to more experienced, imaginative women.'

Her colour deepened. She put her hands to her heart, her lips moved but no sound came out.

'Please, don't say another word,' she said at last.

There was something raw in her eyes now. Despair. Disgust. Loathing. She turned away, brought her knees to her chin and wrapped her arms around them.

It hurt. He was surprised how much.

Her heart was breaking. The pain was unbearable. She sat very still and listened to the wind, hardly breathing, hardly thinking, just hurting. Hours passed before the storm weakened and then all of a sudden it stopped and there was silence.

Lucas threw the blanket off and rose to his feet. The light had turned golden on the mountains, the sky a soft blue which announced the end of the day. The two Tuaregs were already busy setting camp and gathering wood for the fire. Lucas looked at her as he took hold of the water gourds.

'There's a guelta in the next valley. Let's go and get some water. Maybe you'd like to have a swim and get changed.'

Reminded of the gorges of Arak, her cheeks became hot. She drew a quick breath but didn't reply. How could he speak to her now as if none of what he said before mattered? Did he not understand he'd crushed her, or did he not care? She was about to decline, but she changed her mind. It would feel good to wash after almost a week in the desert, to wear fresh clothes. Grabbing her bag, she followed him up a narrow passage. The climb was easy; in places, steps had even been carved in the mountain, but she wasn't prepared for what awaited at the top – a vast, smooth surface of black stone engraved with hundreds of inscriptions.

'What are they? I have never seen anything like this.'

She crouched down and traced patterns with her finger. Outlines of feet and hands, small and large, surrounded by symbols – the script her father knew as the ancient writing of the Garamantes, later adopted by the people of the desert.

'Some look new but others are so old they're almost completely worn. What do they mean?'

Lucas crouched next to her. 'This is one of the places nomads come to in order to make their betrothal official. See the woman's and the man's feet and hands, with their names around?'

'Like wedding vows.'

Wedding vows between lovers, simple and naïve, yet so powerful her throat tightened and her eyes welled up with tears. She jumped to her feet and turned away.

'Not only wedding vows,' he remarked, pointing to a series of symbols carved onto a stone. 'Vows of revenge too. See these here? That means *egha* – revenge. One of the most powerful words in Tuareg society.'

'*Egha*,' she repeated, staring at the dots and lines forming the word. 'I thought you couldn't read Tifinagh.'

'When you live with the Tuaregs for a while, *egha* is the one word you must be able to understand. It might save your life if you see it written in the sand or scratched on the rocks outside your tent … Rancour runs deep and long in the Sahara.'

'Come here.' He walked to the edge of the plateau and pointed to a distant patch of green which stood out in the reddish gold sand dunes towards the west. 'You can just about see Abalessa.'

Her throat tightened. 'What do you plan to do when we get there?'

'First we'll find out where your father is being held and make contact with the keepers. We're ahead of schedule. They won't be expecting us yet.'

He narrowed his eyes. 'Hakim and Musa will make discreet enquiries as soon as we get there tomorrow evening. Once everything's set up, I'll go and get your father.'

'What about Mortemer and the gang travelling with him?'

What about Archie? She finished silently. Lucas was wrong when he claimed Archie had betrayed her and her father. He was the gang's prisoner. She would find a way of helping him, even if Lucas wouldn't. She owed her old friend that much.

He shrugged. 'We'll have to be careful. They must have men

watching out for us. The best thing would be to split up when we approach Abalessa.'

He set off again, down a path leading to the next valley, surprisingly green with pistachio and acacia trees and tufts of coarse grass.

'I hope this water's safe, we don't have much left,' Lucas said as they walked down to a small lake, a line of worry creasing his forehead.

There was no telltale sign of the well being poisoned, no carcass of dead animals in or around the water. He cupped a little water in his hand and brought it to his mouth, then let out a sigh of relief, grabbing hold of the gourds.

'It tastes fine. Let's fill these up.'

When they'd finished, she opened her bag, pulled out her bar of soap, a new chemise, and undergarments.

He stared at her, intense, and bent down to pick the soap up.

'This scent will always remind me of you.' He handed it over to her. His fingers brushed hers, giving her a jolt.

She closed her eyes. Why couldn't she stop loving him? Despite everything he said, she still yearned for his arms, his kisses, his caresses. She needed to belong to him one more time, to forget the dangers that lay ahead. Forget the hurtful words he'd told her. She wanted that more than anything else in the world.

She opened her eyes. Slowly, she untied her braid and combed her hair with her fingers.

He cleared his throat. 'I'll wait for you up the hill while you bathe.'

'There's no need.'

She held his gaze, parted her lips. Even though he remained completely still, his pulse beat at his throat and his breathing was faster. She unfastened her tunic, pulled it open, and let it drop on the floor, then undid her breeches and kicked her boots off.

'What are you doing?' His voice was hoarse.

'What does it look like?' She smiled, throwing back at him the words he'd spoken in the Arak cave.

She discarded her trousers, pulled her drawers down and, still wearing her chemise, walked into the water. The water was so clear she could see lichens lining the stones at the bottom, and so cool it gave her goose pimples. She dived in, her eyes wide open. When she surfaced, her chemise clung to her body. She watched him, her head cocked to one side. He hadn't moved but his fists were clenched, his eyes darker, and his face seemed set in stone.

She held out her hand. 'Throw me the soap.' Her voice was husky as she repeated what he'd said word for word in the cave. 'Or better still, bring it to me.'

'What are you playing at? This won't change a thing between us,' he growled.

She dived under the water again and swam to the other end of the pond. Doubt crept into her heart. What if he didn't come after her? What if he really didn't want her any more? He said she was too naïve, not experienced or tempting enough for him.

There was a mighty splash and his arms seized her from behind, drew her against his bare chest.

'Why are you doing this? You know I can't give you what you want.' His voice was angry, his arms like steel around her. He was warm and strong and she leaned against him, wishing she could stay like this forever.

His hands roamed over her body, spreading a blazing heat through the thin, wet chemise. He buried his face in her neck, trailing kisses on her skin. He spun her around, held her arms, forcing her to tilt her face to look into his eyes.

'Is this really what you want?'

He didn't give her time to answer but leaned down and his mouth covered hers. One hand applying pressure on the nape of her neck, the other digging on the curve of her hip, he held her so close she felt his heart thunder against her as his kiss deepened. She kissed him back, matched his heat, his need, his urgency, her fingers sliding up and down his shoulders, his arms. Whatever he'd said before, he desired her. He needed her. The thought exploded in her mind like fireworks.

The sunset was setting the sky on fire and a symphony of oranges and reds and pinks mirrored in the water as he led her to the bank and kissed her again, and again.

Pleasure hit like a bolt of lightning. He reclined onto the coarse grass and pulled her down to him, and when he pushed into her a hawk let out a piercing cry high up in the sky.

The sun disappeared behind the rugged peaks of the Hoggar, leaving the surface of the lake the colour of dusk, grey and blue. They didn't talk for a long time. She lay, curled up in his arms, safe and warm.

'It will be dark soon,' he said at last, caressing her back. He lifted himself on his elbow, stroked a strand of hair away from her face and traced the outline of her lips with his finger. They were red, slightly swollen, and so inviting he couldn't resist kissing her again.

What a fool he'd been to think he could easily walk away from her. She was part of him, forever. He had hurt her, and yet she still gave herself to him. She was beautiful, generous and brave. He held her tight as if they could never be pulled apart, yet he knew that he would do the right thing. She deserved better than him, much better. However hard it may be, he had made his decision and would stick to it.

'Let's go back.' He kissed the tip of her nose and pulled himself up.

Night was falling. It was getting cold. He got dressed quickly, strapped the heavy gourds around his shoulders, and checked that they hadn't left anything behind.

Chapter Twenty-Five

They made good time after leaving the mountains at dawn and were now within reach of Abalessa. There was no sign of Mortemer's men or Drake's gang. They were probably watching the north and east approaches to the oasis. Making the long detour to the south had been the right decision.

Drake's gang … That's what he must call it now. Harriet may not believe it, but Drake was involved with the raiders. He knew it even if he didn't understand why. Yet.

Lucas looked at the woman next to him, a mixture of pride, admiration and astonishment welled in his heart. She'd made it this far despite the heat and thirst, the harshness of the terrain and all the dangers they'd encountered. As if she felt his gaze on her, she turned to him. With her Tuareg clothing and headdress, she could pass for a small, slender man, but Drake would pick her out in a crowd straight away. Lucas couldn't take the risk of taking her to Abalessa with him. He had to find somewhere safe for her to stay while he went into the village.

Musa pointed at the line of the horizon. Immediately, Lucas gripped the butt of his pistol and pulled on the reins.

'What is it?' Harriet lifted a hand to her eyes to shield them from the sun.

He narrowed his eyes to peer in the distance. 'It looks like a camp.' He let out a sigh of relief, and immediately felt a quick, deep stab of regret. A nomad camp meant safety for Harriet. It also meant they would be parting ways. Maybe forever, if Mortemer managed to get hold of him.

He ordered Hakim and Musa to ride ahead and the two men spurred on. 'Let's wait here while they warn the nomads we're coming.'

He dismounted, secured the two camels, and walked over to her to pull her from her horse. She slid straight down from the saddle into his arms. Surprise and delight lit her eyes when he pushed her headscarf aside and tilted her chin up.

Over the past few weeks, he'd learned to read her innermost feelings reflected in her eyes. From a light grey mist, they turned the colour of dull steel when she was angry, and were dark and stormy when she was in his arms. Right now they were luminous and filled with warmth. He could just lose himself in those eyes. He had already.

'What's the matter?'

He held her more closely, his throat too tight to speak, and marvelled at how perfectly she fitted against him. She was meant for him. The thought hit him, left him dizzy. He caught his breath, bent down and kissed her hard.

'Nothing. Come on, we have to go.' Letting go of her abruptly, he turned away.

It was a small camp, with only half a dozen tents – that meant half a dozen families. Children scattered and hid inside the tents as they approached and a couple of men came to greet them.

He would make sure they agreed to let Harriet stay with them tonight.

Next to her, Lucas drew rein and jumped down before exchanging traditional greetings with the two nomads.

'*Ma Toulid*?' he asked, bowing his head. *How are you?*

'*Al kher ras*,' the taller man answered with a nod. *I wish you well.* That much she understood.

From the beautiful silver Agadez Cross he wore on his chest and the intricate folding of his headscarf, she guessed he was the chief. While travelling with the caravan, she'd seen most men wear similar crosses. Lucas had explained that fathers bestowed them on their sons at their coming of age ceremony. The four branches of the cross symbolised the four cardinal points essential to nomads, because they never knew where they would die. The largest, heaviest cross belonged to the most important men in the tribe.

The men spoke then Lucas asked her to dismount. 'They say you can stay here.'

She shook her head. 'I don't want to stay here. I want to be with you when—'

His face was harsh, his voice uncompromising. 'This isn't about what you want, but about what is safe – for you, for all of us. Nobody will expect you to be here and now they've offered you hospitality, these people will protect you should—' He stopped, sighing with impatience. 'Anyway, I don't want to have to worry about you.'

Of course. He would have enough to do making contact with her father's captors and avoiding Mortemer and his men.

'Listen to me, Harriet.' Lucas stepped closer and took her hand.

'You must wait here until someone comes for you. I'm taking the ransom money. I will hide it somewhere until I find your father and negotiate with the keepers. Don't worry, one way or another you will get back to Algiers.'

What did he mean, someone would come for her, and one way or another she'd get back to Algiers? Filled with panic, she reached out for him.

He squeezed her hand briefly. His lips stretched into a smile that didn't reach his eyes. 'Everything will be all right, I promise.'

And then, she knew. 'You're not expecting to make it, are you?'

'Of course I am. If you think I'm giving up on that treasure map you owe me, you are mistaken.' He smiled again.

She watched him mount his horse and ride away in a cloud of dust with Hakim and Musa. He never looked back. As their silhouettes became smaller and disappeared in the hazy light on the line of the horizon, she did nothing to stop the tears from falling nor did she try and stifle her sobs. And when she collapsed onto her knees, she didn't even feel the sharp rocks cut through her skin.

The nomads welcomed her, fed her goat milk, dates and bread. It was a relief that she could only speak a few words of their language, because they had to leave her alone. The women and the children sometimes came to look at her as at some strange creature – their eyes huge and filled with curiosity – and touch her skin and her hair.

In the evening, she sat in front of the chief's tent along with the other members of the tribe for the ritual of tales and music. The chief pulled a few pebbles out of a pouch and settled down to tell the first story. This time, however, Lucas wasn't there to translate. All she could do was listen to the insistent, hypnotic melodies the woman playing her imzad was creating and which tore her heart apart.

She clutched her fingers in her lap, closed her eyes, red and raw from crying. When the music was over and the night had gone cool, a woman tapped her shoulder and gave her a mat and a blanket. She pointed to one of the tents, and Harriet understood this was where she was to sleep.

But sleep didn't come. As she stared at the roof of the tent and listened to the light snoring of the two elderly women sharing it with her, the calls of night birds, the bleating of the goats and the rumbling of the camels, she whispered endless prayers for Lucas.

Her thoughts drifted to her father. Did he feel she was close or had he given up any hope of being rescued? Was he even still alive? She pictured his face, tanned and weather-beaten from his many expeditions in Italy, Greece and North Africa, and his calm, intelligent blue eyes, and the way they lit up when he talked about artefacts or documents he'd discovered. In many ways more a teacher than a parent, he'd been a demanding father, braving his elder sister's disapproval to make sure she received a sound education.

Aunt Elizabeth claimed he brought her up as a boy. 'Your father forgets girls don't need to read ancient Greek, trace maps, learn how to make a fire in the woods or – God forbid – kneel in the dust to retrieve bones or pieces of old pots,' she often complained. Harriet didn't listen. She carried on studying hard to make him proud and was sometimes rewarded with a smile or a nod of approval.

Despite his frequent travels abroad and his fascinating stories, her father's life always appeared somewhat ordered, transparent, almost mundane. Yet, there were many things she didn't know about him … He'd been troubled before leaving for Algiers; he'd even argued with Archie, which had never happened before. And what was the significance of the ring she remembered seeing on his finger – the snarling silver wolf?

He'd discovered something important while studying the Hoggar rock paintings, something that made him want to break into Tin Hinan's tomb. What was there that he so wanted to find? Was it the Garamantes' emeralds, the clue to the location of the mines, or something entirely different? She sat up and held her breath. She knew what she had to do. She would go to the tomb and find out for herself.

At last the dawn sky paled and became a clear, transparent mauve. She crept out of the tent. A little apprehensive, she asked the Tuaregs for directions to Tin Hinan's tomb, putting together the few words of their language Lucas had taught her. After discussing between themselves for a long time, they pointed in a north westerly direction, gave her a gourd of water, a bag of dates, and insisted that a boy show her the way.

'Tannemert,' she said, putting her hand on her heart.

She climbed on her horse and followed the boy. He walked fast. He ran ahead at times, but there was always a wide grin on his face as if he wasn't tired or didn't feel the effects of the heat. He finally stopped and pointed to a small rocky hill standing out in the plain, next to a dried-up riverbed lined with trees, shrubs and grass where a flock of gazelles grazed.

'Tin Hinan,' he said and they started towards it.

Her heart beat fast, her throat was dry with excitement. At last, she was within reach of the sepulchre of the mysterious Tuareg queen. She spurred the horse into a gallop. The gazelles fled, jumping high above the grass and bushes, and disappeared in the hazy heat lingering over the plains.

At about fifteen feet high, and with a circular base, the tomb was both higher and larger than she'd imagined. Rubble and debris covered the ground all around, a sign that it had been broken into – maybe by her father and his men. Without waiting for the boy to catch up, she jumped down from her horse and walked slowly around the tomb, holding the reins. Many of the larger stones piled on the tomb had ancient Garamantes writing on them. Some had drawings too.

The mid-morning heat was already blistering. Sweat trickled down her forehead and along her back. She unscrewed the top of the gourd, lifted her scarf off to drink. She frowned, looked around, and held her breath. She wasn't mistaken. A faint, regular tapping sound was coming from inside the tomb.

'Hello? Is there anyone in there?' she called in English, then French.

The tapping stopped. She sighed, disappointed. She'd imagined it. But as she started walking around the tomb, she heard it again. It sounded like someone banging rocks together, or digging inside.

'*Djinouns,*' the boy said next to her, breathless and his eyes wide with fear.

'No,' she said, with a reassuring smile. 'No *djinouns.*' Someone was definitely in the tomb, but it wasn't an evil spirit. She handed the boy the reins of her horse and pointed to the top of the tomb.

'I have to go up, see who's in there.'

He shook his head, stepping back. '*Djinouns.*' And he ran away.

There was no point in going after him. He'd probably come back with men from the tribe who might force her to return to their encampment. She calculated she had about two hours to explore the tomb and find the source of the noise. She tied the horse to the branch of an acacia tree, next to a patch of coarse grass, and prayed there was no lion around. Alone and tied up, the animal wouldn't stand a chance.

Then she scrambled up the slope as fast as she could, filled with irrational hope. The banging seemed to be getting louder the higher she climbed.

She understood why when she reached the top. The tomb was open. Large, thick slabs of stone which would normally cover it were pushed aside. She stared down at the entrance of a chamber and at a rope ladder secured on metal spikes leading inside the tomb.

'Hello? Who's in there?' she called.

The banging stopped for a few seconds.

'This time I have truly lost my mind,' a man's voice said before the noise started again.

Her heart flipped. She would recognise that voice anywhere. 'My God, Father, is that you? Father, it's Harriet!' she called, leaning over the edge, trying to catch a glimpse of the man inside the tomb.

'Harriet?'

The first thing she saw was the man's mop of matted, unruly grey hair. Then he tilted his face up towards her and blinked against the sunlight. He had a wild, grey beard and smears of grime and dust on his tanned face and looked gaunt in his dirty grey shirt and ripped black breeches. She let out a cry of joy.

'Father, you're alive. I have found you at last!' She knelt down beside the hole, pulled her scarf off, held out her arms to help her father up.

'So I haven't lost my mind.' With surprising agility for a man so tall, he climbed up the rope ladder. She stood up and stepped aside to let him out, and when he was finally in front of her, she threw herself in his arms.

'There, there,' he said, as he patted her head, her back, before holding her at arms' length. 'Let me take a good look at you. You look well, a little thin maybe. How extraordinary to see you here, and in Tuareg clothes! You would give your aunt a serious shock.' He blinked a few times, then shook his head. 'I don't understand why you're here.'

'I came to rescue you.'

He let out a laugh. 'You're rescuing me? You are wonderful, I'm so proud of you.' He enclosed her in his arms and kissed the top of her head. 'But I don't need rescuing. I'm quite all right, as you can see.'

He paused, looking around. 'You didn't come here all on your own, did you?'

'Archie and I hired a guide in Algiers, and—'

'Archibald is here?' He looked around, narrowing his eyes.

'Yes … No … It's a long story.'

She took his calloused hand, almost dizzy with relief. She'd found her father and he was alive. Now they had to escape his captors, and fast.

'When we heard the news about the Tuareg attack on the expedition, we were so afraid you'd been killed too.'

He shook his head. 'It wasn't Tuaregs who attacked us. It was a gang of men who'd been following us ever since we left Algiers. We managed to lose them in the Hoggar, but they picked up our trail again. The Tuaregs tried to help but they could only save me. It was too late for the others.'

His voice shook. He swayed as if suddenly too weak to stand. In the harsh daylight, his face was thin and crisscrossed with deep lines. Her throat tightened. These last few months in the mountains and the desert had taken their toll. He looked so much older, so much frailer than she remembered.

'Why are you still in there?' She gestured towards the entrance to the tomb. 'I thought the Tin Hinan's keepers didn't want anyone inside the tomb.'

'We made a deal. They let me work here every day on the condition I give them something very precious in return – something they, and I, have been after for a long time.'

'The emerald mines?'

He nodded and surveyed the vast, empty plains around the tomb. 'Where is your guide, Harriet?'

She bowed her head, kicked a few pebbles with the tip of her boot and blinked back the tears. 'He left me at a Tuareg camp while he went into Abalessa with the ransom, searching for you.' She lifted her head.

'What ransom?' He frowned.

'Lord Callaghan generously donated a thousand pounds in gold for your release. We were supposed to give it to the Tuaregs in exchange for your safe return.'

Her father snorted. 'The cunning old devil,' he muttered.

She shook her head, surprised at the harshness of his tone.

'Oh Father, there are so many things I don't understand.' She sighed. 'I killed a man, an Englishman … he wore a ring, like the one I remember you wore, once, a long time ago.' She stared into his face. 'What is this all about? I need to know.'

His eyes became hard. He took her elbow and led her to the entrance to the tomb. 'Later, girl, I will tell you everything later. For now, let's go inside. It's far too hot to stay out in the open, not to mention the fact we make ideal targets.'

'Where are the keepers of the tomb?'

'They leave me here every morning and come for me at the end of the day.'

He went down the rope ladder and he held it straight for her to climb down.

'It's much bigger than I first thought. I almost cleared five of the twelve chambers, including the queen's.' He glanced at her over his shoulder. 'Careful what you step on, there are scorpions around.'

There was just enough light to see outlines of jars, caskets, swords, shields and spears. She coughed. The air was thick with dust and a musty, choking smell.

'Cover your face with your scarf. These chambers were sealed over fourteen hundred years ago. It'll take some time to get fresh air inside.'

He led the way down roughly carved steps into a round room filled with all sorts of objects and artefacts. In the middle was a bed with human remains wrapped in some kind of shroud. A diadem and two delicate, brittle ostrich feathers adorned the skull.

Harriet found it even harder to breathe in there. She pointed to the bed.

'Tin Hinan,' she whispered.

Her father nodded. He knelt next to the bed. Next to the body were dozens of necklaces and bracelets, flasks and jars. He gestured towards two large stone urns.

'This one is filled with coins – Roman coins.' He lifted one and handed it to her.

'Constanti …' She read the tiny writing. 'Emperor Constantine.'

'The other is filled with emeralds.' Her father plunged his hand into the tall urn and lifted the precious stones out. 'There are emeralds scattered around her body too.'

'The Garamantes' emeralds.'

Even in the semi-darkness, she could see her father's eyes shine with excitement. He took a tablet leaning against the wall.

'This is what I've been searching for all these years,' he said, tracing the symbols carved on the stone.

His finger traced the top of the tablet and he recited, solemnly. "A gift from King Igmazen of Garama to the powerful queen of the west whose eyes shine like the green stones that have made our people's fame and fortune. Her fruitful loins gave our Great King three daughters. May her name shine forever in the hearts of the people of the Veil".

He looked up and smiled. 'Well, that's more or less exact. The old writing isn't an easy script to read and is always open to interpretation. Below, here, are the instructions to find the mines.'

He pointed to a series of dots, circles and lines. 'I just finished translating it today.'

'How did you know it would be here?'

'When I found inscriptions and drawings in the mountains referring to the union of King Igmazen of the Garamantes and Tin Hinan, I knew I had to search for the queen's tomb, but we were attacked as we left the Hoggar …'

He sighed deeply. 'After they rescued me, I asked the Tuaregs about the tomb. The keepers only allowed me in here because I promised to give them the location of the mines.'

He sighed. 'They need money, a lot of money, to buy weapons to fight the French army. I also gave them my solemn promise I wouldn't disturb anything and I would respect the remains of their queen.'

'But if the tablet was here all along, why didn't they take it and find the mines for themselves? You said yourself that Tifinagh, the Tuareg alphabet, is based on the ancient Garamantes writing. They could have translated it themselves.'

'They might have, but you're forgetting something, Harriet. No Tuareg would ever break into this tomb. It is sacred. Look at these artefacts. The gold and silver, the emeralds and carnelian stones have remained buried and untouched for centuries, even though the land is so dry and barren, people hardly have enough to survive.'

She knelt beside him. It was true. The tomb contained a real treasure. The queen's body was covered with a shrivelled and dried-up sheet of leather. Her diadem was of solid gold, as were nine bracelets on her left arm. On her right arm were eight silver bracelets and around her neck snaked a necklace made of gold stars.

Harriet's father gestured to a pile of papers and sketchbooks on the ground.

'I've started to draw every single object and artefact but there's so much … I have months of work ahead of me.'

She gasped. 'You mean you're not coming back to England with me?'

He didn't answer, but combed his long, dirty grey hair with his fingers.

'Of course you're not. This is the discovery you've waited all your life for.' She took a deep breath and tilted her chin up. 'I'll stay here and help you.'

Her father smiled and stroked the side of her face gently. 'I'm not sure that's a good idea. I would be much happier if that guide of yours took you back to Algiers and you waited for me there. How good is he?'

She swallowed hard. 'Lucas is the best … But he's in danger. There's a man who swore to kill him, a French lieutenant. And there's that gang of raiders I told you about, the ones who captured Archie.'

Her father let out a harsh laugh. 'Captured? I don't think so. He's one of them, Harriet. Always has been.'

She gasped. *Lucas had been right*!

'I don't understand. Who are they, and how do you know them?'

Her father closed his eyes briefly.

'Because I, too, was one of them, once.'

Chapter Twenty-Six

He stood up and rubbed his face harshly with his hands.

'I'm not proud of it. I was a young man and got caught in … ah … a rather difficult situation.'

His voice became a raspy whisper, his breathing fast and wheezy. He closed his eyes. 'I had no other choice than do what they wanted. It was the only way for me to keep working at the museum, doing the work I loved. I tried to get out so many times over the years but they wouldn't let me.'

She stepped towards him. 'Father, you're scaring me. Who are these people? What are they involved in?'

He opened his mouth to answer but suddenly sagged against the stone wall, one hand clutched to his chest, his face grey and contorted in pain.

'Father, what's wrong?'

She rushed to him and slipped an arm around his waist to support him.

'Here, let me help you out. You need some air.'

He grimaced again. 'They're called the Brotherhood of the Silver Wolf,' he breathed out. 'I'm sorry, Harriet, so sorry I put you in any danger. You're a brave girl, you'll fight them. You still have Barbarossa's map, don't you? The treasure – you must go and find it. But before, there's something else you have to do … there are papers and files about the Brotherhood. I wrote where they are at the—'

He gasped and leaned more heavily against her. Now wasn't the time to tell him she'd pledged the map to Lucas Saintclair.

'Please don't talk,' she said.

When they reached the entrance, she looked at the rope ladder and sighed in frustration. 'I have to get help. You won't be able to climb out.' She brushed his damp hair away from his face and kissed his forehead. 'I'm leaving you my water. Here, I'll unscrew the top for you.'

She placed the water gourd next to him before climbing up the rope ladder. 'I promise I'll be quick,' she said when she reached the top.

She ran to her horse and started riding back towards the camp, but the midday sun beat down on the plains, merciless. A heat haze distorted the parched, baked landscape. She twisted the scarf on her head and made sure her face was covered. However much she wanted to ride flat out to the camp and get help, she had to pace the horse or it would collapse in the stifling heat, leaving her stranded.

Her father was ill, alone and unable to defend himself against predators – or men.

She bit back a sob of despair. Assuming she made it back to the camp, would anyone there be able to help? The horse lost its footing and slipped on loose stones as it climbed a rocky outcrop. She jumped down and patted its neck. Its eyes were sunken, its breathing fast. Too fast. If the animal didn't drink and cool down soon, it would die. She sheltered her eyes with her hand to peer into the distance but water holes and gueltas were more often than not well hidden and almost impossible to spot for the untrained eye. She pulled on the reins and uttered soothing, encouraging words for the horse to follow as she climbed up the slope in the searing heat.

Sweat trickled from her forehead, stinging her eyes. Her lips were so parched they cracked and she tasted blood inside her mouth. Her throat felt raw, her head throbbed. She stumbled on a rock, fell down on her knees and let go of the reins. Next to her the horse hung its head and panted hard. She pushed herself up, staggered a little further. At this rate she'd never make it back to the Tuareg camp.

At first she thought the sound was her heart pounding or the blood roaring in her ears. Then she saw a cloud of dust in the distance and a rider going flat out towards the tomb. His horse was black. He wore a white and blue Tuareg tunic and headscarf. Lucas!

Hope surged inside her. It was him. She had to turn round, go back to the tomb. She pulled the horse back down the slope, but the animal was so exhausted it hardly moved. She pulled harder, patted its neck and stroked the side of its mouth. It still didn't move. So she left it there and ran down the hill, her legs weak and her lungs burning. She slipped, scrambled back onto her feet and started the long walk back towards the tomb.

She was half way there when the sound of horses galloping behind her broke the burning silence of the plain. There was nowhere for her to hide, so she spun round and pulled her dagger out, waiting for them to approach.

She recognised Mortemer's red and navy blue uniform straight away. There were half a dozen French soldiers with him. The other riders were in civilian clothes, and among them was Archie. She had to send them away from the tomb, away from her father and Lucas.

'*Eh bien*, who do we have here?' Mortemer said in French when he drew rein in front of her.

She pushed her veil down and tilted her chin. Her fingers gripped the dagger more tightly. Ignoring Mortemer, she turned to Archie and plastered a fake smile on her face. He mustn't suspect that she knew he'd betrayed her and her father.

'Oh Archie, I'm so happy you're safe!' She started in a happy, excited voice. 'I've been so worried about you. You were right about Saintclair all along. He stole the ransom. He abandoned me in a Tuareg camp and went back to In Salah yesterday with the gold. You must go after him straight away.'

Mortemer and Archie burst out laughing.

'That was a convincing performance, Madame,' Mortemer said at last. 'Unfortunately for you, we've been on Saintclair's trail since last night and we happen to know where he is at this very moment.' He pointed to the tomb. 'Am I right?'

Archie rode closer, holding out his hand. 'Come with me, dear. Don't do anything silly.'

She narrowed her eyes, all pretence gone. 'Silly?' She was so angry she could hit him. 'How could you do this to my father, to his team members, to me? My father considered you like his son. Yet you betrayed him. You pretended you wanted to rescue him when you belonged to that gang all along. I hate you!'

She turned away and started walking towards the tomb but Mortemer manoeuvred his massive grey horse to block her way and she had to move back for fear of being trampled upon. Mortemer stared down at her, his eyes dark and lifeless.

'I suggest you do as you're told and get onto Drake's horse now.'

He left her no choice. She had to run. She darted towards the tomb but only covered a few yards before Archie's horse came up behind her. Archie grabbed the belt at her waist and lifted her up in the air. He shoved her across the saddle like a sack of grain before ripping her headscarf off. Then he took hold of her braid, pulled her head back and slapped her across the face.

The blow took her breath away. White stars danced in front of her eyes. She lifted a hand to her cheek and felt blood trickle down.

'That was just to give you a taste of what's to come if you resist me, my dear.' He took hold of the reins and she saw a glint of silver on his finger.

He was wearing a ring, the jade ring with the snarling silver wolf at its centre, and it had cut the skin on her cheek. He spurred his horse to join the others. Mortemer's men had already lined up at the base of Tin Hinan's tomb. One of them held the reins of Lucas' black horse. At least Lucas was inside with her father.

Mortemer pulled his pistol out. 'Give yourself up, Saintclair,' he shouted in French. 'It's over.'

There was no answer.

'Damn the man, he's hiding inside the tomb,' the French lieutenant muttered between clenched teeth. 'I'm going up there. I want to finish this, once and for all.'

'Take Harriet with you,' Archie suggested. 'I seem to remember Saintclair was rather fond of her.'

He pushed her off the horse. She landed on the rocky ground.

'Was he?' Mortemer jumped down from his horse, pulled his pistol out and held it to Harriet's head.

'Get up and do exactly as I say.'

'You can go to hell,' she riposted, wrapping her arms around her knees and curling into a ball.

He leaned forward. 'You will go to hell a long time before I do.'

He slid the cannon of his pistol along her cheek. 'Yours is a simple choice. Life or death. What do you choose?'

The cruel glint in his eyes sent a shiver of repulsion down her spine. He would shoot her there and then without hesitation. Reluctantly, she got to her feet. He wrapped his arm around her chest, holding her like a shield as they went up the monticule, the barrel of his pistol digging into the side of her head. They finally reached the top. There was nobody there.

'Saintclair!' Mortemer shouted. 'I have Harriet Montague with me. I'll shoot her if you're not out here within the next twenty seconds.'

He armed the pistol, pressed it harder and kneed her in the small of the back. She bit her lip to refrain from crying out. Next, he kicked hard at the back of her leg and this time she couldn't hold back a whimper of pain as she fell.

'Release her,' Lucas ordered from inside the tomb. 'Release her and send her back down. Then I'll come out and we'll sort this out, man to man.'

Mortemer tensed behind her. 'You're in no position to negotiate.'

'I don't mind waiting in here for the Tuareg keepers to arrive and see what they make of you and your men,' Lucas retorted calmly. 'Somehow I don't think they'll be well disposed towards a handful of French soldiers.'

Mortemer sighed. 'All right. I'll let her go. For now.'

He pushed her away from him, muttered between his teeth. 'Get down.'

'I need to check if my father is all right first,' she protested. 'He collapsed and—'

Mortemer pointed the gun to her chest. 'Get down.'

He turned away from the entrance of the tomb for only a split second, but it was enough for Lucas to run out. Darting one clear, piercing look towards Harriet as if to make sure she wasn't hurt, he lunged at Mortemer.

The two men wrestled on the ground, kicking and punching each other as they rolled over in the dust. Both were armed. Mortemer still held his pistol. The blade of Lucas' knife glinted in the sun. The fight didn't last long. Lucas straddled Mortemer, hit him on the nose, and bashed his hand onto a rock until he dropped his weapon. Mortemer yelped with pain and stopped struggling. Lucas looked at Harriet. A smile appeared on his lips.

'I knew you wouldn't do as you were told and stay at the camp,' he said. 'You never do …'

She didn't see Archie behind him until it was too late. The shot cracked, loud as thunder. Lucas let out a roar of pain, clutched at his chest and collapsed onto Mortemer.

Behind him, Archie smiled as he lowered his pistol.

Mortemer pushed Lucas off and stood up, a grin of triumph on his lean face.

'Well done, Drake,' he said. He felt the pulse at Lucas' throat and declared. 'Dead, at last. He won't make a fool of me ever again.'

It wasn't true. It couldn't be true! Harriet's heart stopped. She stared at Lucas' body, inert on the ground, at the blood stain spreading on his chest. Archie had shot him in the back and the bullet had gone right through his body.

She reached out to touch him but Archie grabbed her arm to hold her back. Mortemer kicked Lucas' body into the tomb. It fell with a thud. The lieutenant leaned over the edge, looked inside and shook his head.

'The old man's dead too.'

'Let me go to him. To them!' she wrestled against Archie.

'You can't do anything for either of them.'

'Leave me alone. I don't want to see you or be near you. Ever.'

'Too bad you feel that way, dear. We're going to see quite a lot of each other when we're married.'

He held her tighter. 'Now you're going to calm down or I'll be forced to hurt you again.'

'I don't care what you do. My father's in there, Lucas is in there.'

Desperation made her stronger. She almost managed to slip out of Archie's grip, but he held her wrists and twisted her arms in her back.

'They're dead.' He looked towards the tomb. 'I'm going down there now to see what your father found. The old man will make my fortune.'

The emeralds, the tablet with the location of the mines, the dozens of precious necklaces and bracelets and the fragile remains of Tin Hinan crowned with gold and delicate ostrich feathers. Archie would wreck it all in his greed. How could she have been so blind, so naïve when it came to him, and misjudged him so?

'Lieutenant, you need to take a look at this,' one of Mortemer's men called from the bottom of the hill. 'We have company and I don't think they're in a friendly mood.'

Tuareg warriors lined the horizon. Veiled in indigo blue and riding their tall, white mehari camels in the hazy heat, they looked more like spectres than men of flesh and blood. Were they the keepers of Tin Hinan's tomb coming to fight against the French trespassers?

'There's no time to explore the tomb, Drake. We must leave at once,' Mortemer said. 'There aren't enough of us to fight them.'

'What about Saintclair's and Montague's bodies?' Archie asked.

Mortemer shook his head and started running down the tomb. 'Let them rot in there. Come on.'

Archie pulled her along, but she dug her heels in the ground. 'Leave me here. Please leave me,' she pleaded. 'What do you care if I stay here?'

She fought him all the way down the tomb, and when he tried to lift her onto his horse, she bit him.

'Now you really asked for it,' he yelled after she sank her teeth into his forearm. He slapped her hard on the side of the head and a black curtain descended on the world all around.

Her skull throbbed. Her throat was parched and raw. She licked her cracked lips and opened her eyes onto darkness. All she could see were a few shapes – furniture probably – and a weak ray of light under a door. Men talked outside with hushed voices. Slowly, because every move hurt, she pressed down on the rough, prickly mat under her and tried to sit up. As dizziness engulfed her, she took short, shallow breaths and lifted a hand to her cheek. It was sore and swollen where Archie had hit her. The blood was dry but the cut still stung.

Who were the men talking in English outside? She squeezed her eyes shut and curled her fists into tight balls. It didn't matter. Nothing mattered any more. Lucas and her father were dead. Mortemer and Archie had won. Her breath caught in her throat. Long, deep sobs racked her body as grief took over. She wanted to howl and scream. She wanted to die.

There were footsteps outside the room, the noise of keys rattling and of the door being unlocked. Archie came in, a candle in his hand. She recoiled against the wall, felt her belt for her dagger. She would kill him.

Her scabbard was empty. Someone had removed her dagger.

'You're awake,' Archie said. He stopped in the middle of the room and looked down at her. 'We need to talk, my dear.'

'Keep away from me. I have nothing to say to you.'

He smiled, his moustache quivering lightly. How did he dare smile?

'How can you say that?' He sighed. 'You're bound to be a little … upset.' He put the candle on a low table before sitting on the couch next to her. She recoiled further, but he took hold of her leg, pulled her close and laid a hand on her stomach to pin her down.

'Don't touch me,' she hissed, rigid with disgust and pain, before turning her head to the wall.

He lowered himself towards her. 'Harriet, don't make this more difficult than it already is. There are so many things you don't know about your father. The respected Oscar Montague wasn't quite the upstanding citizen you believed him to be. He had secrets, dark secrets.'

She turned to look at him. 'My father was a good man. He lived for his work at the museum, for the expeditions, for research.' Her voice broke into a sob.

'Among other things, he liked to associate with young ladies of loose morals.'

'You're lying!'

'*Ttt … ttt …* Believe me, dear, that's the truth.'

He released the pressure on her stomach but kept his hand there, ready to pin her down again should she move away.

Doubt crept into her mind. Her father had confessed to belonging to a secret organisation. He'd looked deeply troubled, ashamed even, before he collapsed.

'Is that what the Brotherhood of the Silver Wolf is about? Cavorting with prostitutes?'

He cursed under his breath. 'What did the old fool tell you?'

'Nothing. He collapsed before he could explain.'

Archie let out a sigh of relief. 'Good. The less you know the better. If any of this comes out, not only will your father's reputation be ruined and the work he's done over the years discredited, but you and your aunt will be disgraced.'

'Do you think I care about what happens to me now?' She let out a pitiful sob.

'Surely you don't want your father's name to be sullied in a scandal,' he insisted. 'It would certainly kill your dear Aunt Elizabeth.'

'You're only thinking about yourself,' she accused. She looked at his hand and pointed to his ring. 'If my father did something wrong, so did you.'

She tried to sit up but he held her down again. 'Except you did far worse than him. You killed.'

He didn't answer. His hand slid over her stomach up to her breasts and her throat. She shuddered, tried to push him away but he placed the width of his hand across her throat and applied a light but suffocating pressure.

'Listen to me, Harriet. We are going back to Algiers with Mortemer and his men, and then to London where you will marry me.'

He squeezed harder and she couldn't breathe. 'Nobody will be surprised. We were always very close, weren't we? Then you'll give me the Barbarossa map. Your father was very foolish to think he could keep it to himself. The map and the treasure are mine.'

'And if I refuse to marry you? To give you the map?' she asked, her voice a hoarse whisper.

He chuckled. 'I don't see that you have much choice, dear. As your husband, it will belong to me anyway. If you persist in denying me, I will make sure everyone finds out about your father's dirty little secrets. I have documents incriminating him.'

He let go of her and at last she could breathe.

'What kind of man are you, Archie?' She took a few deep, long gulps of air. 'We used to be friends. No, we were more than that – we were family. My father taught you and trained you. He thought very highly of you.'

He tightened his lips in a harsh line. 'Then he shouldn't have threatened the Brotherhood. Before leaving for Algiers, he swore to expose us if we didn't cut him free. He said he had files stashed away somewhere. What happened was his fault.'

She stared into his eyes. 'It was your associates who killed my father's men in Tamanrasset, wasn't it? It had nothing to do with the Tuaregs, or the keepers of Tin Hinan's tomb.'

He nodded. 'They tried and failed before, on the way to the Hoggar. Your father was surprisingly good at eluding their ambushes. For a time, that is.'

'They killed everybody. Men you knew and esteemed, men you worked with for years.' He disgusted her. Bile rose in her throat, almost choking her.

'They were your father's friends. We thought he might have told them about us. We couldn't take the risk of letting them live.'

'The raiders who attacked us were your men too, weren't they? You told them where to find us.'

'I did. I always managed to let them know of our route, even if it was a close call in Bou Saada. Saintclair almost caught me talking to my contact in the tavern. I had to start a fight to distract him.'

'There were men following me around too.'

'You had to be kept under surveillance. I wasn't sure whether your father would try to get in touch with you or not.'

She opened her eyes wide as another truth dawned on her. 'It was you who shot Lucas' men in the Arak gorges – that's why they had no time to defend themselves.'

'Indeed.'

'You were prepared to let me die back there. You and your associates took the horses and the camels …'

'Well, you're still here, aren't you?'

'You tried to steal the ransom.'

'Let's say that it was never my intention to surrender Callaghan's gold to your father's keepers.' He stood up, walked to the door. 'Get some rest now. We're leaving tomorrow at dawn.'

His hand on the handle, he turned to her. 'What was in the tomb, Harriet? Did your father find out at last where the emerald mines are? You must tell me.'

She took a deep breath. 'Why don't you go back there and take a look for yourself?'

'I can't. Nobody can. The Tuaregs sealed the tomb and are keeping guard. They won't allow anyone near it.'

'Then Tin Hinan's secret is safe.'

Immediately her chest felt tight and she couldn't breathe. Her father and Lucas were now entombed with the Tuareg queen and her treasures, forever. This time she couldn't hold back the nausea. She leaned to the side and vomited on the floor.

Chapter Twenty-Seven

Algiers – August

There was a place beyond tears, beyond pain and despair. A place where nothing brought any joy or peace. Where it didn't matter if the sky was a deep blue and the waves rippled and shimmered under the sun. She felt neither the bracing, salty breeze from the Mediterranean nor the sirocco wind which covered the town under a layer of fine, red hot Sahara sand. She was dead inside.

Every time she closed her eyes she only saw the immense, fawn-coloured desert plains and the rugged blackened peaks of the Hoggar mountain range rising in a transparent dawn, and the clear blue of Lucas' eyes. When she tossed and turned on her mat every night, she heard his voice and the soulful melodies of the Tuareg imzad. Both Lucas and the Sahara had captured her heart and burned her soul.

They had travelled back from Abalessa in the summer heat, escorted by Mortemer and his men to Ghardaia where the lieutenant left them. He was going to Bou Saada to deal with Saintclair's rebel friends there, and with one man in particular – Ahmoud – who'd been captured and thrown in jail along with his family. Harriet dreaded to think what would happen to them.

She bit her pencil and heaved a sigh, lost in the contemplation of the arrows of light that pierced the canopy of the fig tree in front of her and fell onto the two white graves underneath. Since their return to Algiers a couple of weeks before, she came here as often as she could. The tiny cemetery of princesses N'Fissa and Fatima – the two princesses who'd died of despair after their lover disappeared in the desert – had become her refuge. She closed her eyes and a tear fell on her drawing pad, smudging the drawing of a Tuareg camp she was completing. Now she had her own cavalier to mourn. All she had left of him were a few sketches.

Their return to Algiers caused a sensation. Archie told Lord Welsford how he snatched Harriet from the clutches of their renegade guide and his rebel Tuaregs who captured and ill-treated her father, causing his fatal heart attack. To everyone around them, Archie was a dashing hero and she a tragic heroine. Having vowed to safeguard her father's reputation, there was nothing Harriet could say to set the record straight. She remained silent, indifferent, withdrawn into her own world of dreams and memories.

Lady Welsford, the consul's wife, invited her to countless tea parties and barouche rides in the newly opened Jardin d'Essai which overlooked the bay of Algiers. She also arranged for her seamstress to cut new gowns for her and was most put out to see that nothing, even an entire new wardrobe, could bring a smile to Harriet's face. In the end, the consul's wife decreed that only a return to England would soothe the young woman's sadness.

'You need to be far away from this brutal land to focus on the future. You have your wedding to look forward to,' the woman said with a broad smile. 'Archibald is such a brave, honourable man.'

If only they knew.

Harriet's throat closed. Marrying Archie was out of the question. She would run away when they reached London. She would take the Barbarossa map and go looking for the treasure, as her father wanted.

'Mademoiselle.' Aicha's agitated voice drew her back to reality. Lord Callaghan's maid pointed to the entrance to the cemetery where two armed men stood guard and stared at her, a disgruntled look on their face. 'They say it's time to go back.'

Harriet tilted her head, defiant. 'They can wait until I'm finished.'

She was under constant surveillance by Archie's associates. The two men followed her everywhere. Archie claimed it was for her protection, but he must be afraid she'd escape, although alone and without money, there was nowhere for her to go.

One of the men, a brute called Stevens, walked into the cemetery. 'Mr Drake said to make sure you're back in time for tonight's reception.'

'What reception?'

The man shook his head. 'The reception at the British consulate.'

She frowned. She'd forgotten all about it.

The man picked up her bag, a stubborn, determined look on his face, so she tidied her things and followed him out into the kasbah.

They pushed their way through the crowd gathered in the steep, narrow alleyways but all the way back to the palace, she had the uneasy sensation eyes were boring holes in her back. Yet every time she glanced over her shoulder, all she saw were blank, anonymous men's faces and veiled women.

Archie was waiting for her at the palace. He was already dressed for the reception, his shirt crisp and white, his cravat tightly gathered under his chin, his black evening suit impeccable.

'What kept you out so late?' His eyes trailed to her bag, then narrowed. 'Been drawing again, have you?' He lunged forward to snatch it from her. 'Ah! Here are your precious sketches. I bet there are a few of our friend Saintclair. Let's see.'

She swallowed hard. Begging him to give the book back was futile. It would only make him more determined. She held her head high as he flicked through the pad and started tearing pages off. Her silence as the papers fell onto the marble floor only seemed to make him more enraged. He tore out every single page of the sketchbook and looked half mad, his eyes bulging, his mouth mean and twisted when he threw what was left of the book on the table.

'There, no more drawings! Get ready now. I don't want to be late.' He turned round and walked out.

Through a blur of tears, she knelt down on the blue and gold mosaic floor to gather torn pieces of her sketchbook.

'Poor mademoiselle, all your beautiful drawings,' Aicha said as she knelt down close to help her.

Lord and Lady Welsford's summer residence was a large one-storey house in the hills overlooking the bay of Algiers. A light breeze blew from the sea, rustling palms and brightly coloured shrubs, and mixing its fresh salty scents with the deeper, sweeter aromas of the exotic vegetation.

Archie's hand gripped Harriet's elbow over her long white gloves and directed her through an elegant gathering of Royal Navy officers, personnel from the British embassy, French government officials and army officers, wealthy sea merchants and businessmen. Women were in short supply and every one of them commanded a small crowd of admirers. Music drifted into the gardens from an interior courtyard where a quartet performed. Servants walked around carrying silver trays with flutes of champagne, glasses of lemonade and canapés.

Harriet stiffened, dreading the evening of meaningless chatter and polite conversation ahead. As if sensing her reluctance, Archie held her more tightly.

'You're going to smile and look happy, dear,' he whispered in her ear. His face lit up. 'Mortemer! I didn't know you were in Algiers.'

The French lieutenant stood in front of them in his red and navy uniform. He took his hat off and bowed to Harriet.

'Madame, what a great pleasure it is to see you again.'

She barely acknowledged his presence with a flicker of her eyelids.

'I'm surprised you're not asking me for news of Bou Saada.' Mortemer arched his eyebrows and looked down at her.

She held her breath.

'Come on, tell us how you got on with Saintclair's rebel friends,' Archie urged.

Mortemer's lips stretched in a cold smile. 'Saintclair's involvement with the rebels has been proven beyond any doubt. Among other things, we now know that he organised the raid on the fort in which army cannon were stolen, that he masterminded the attack on our Blida ammunition depot and that he took great pains to destroy and relocate rebel weapons and supplies hideouts.'

He sighed, shaking his head. 'It seems he had his own motives for travelling with you to the Sahara and was intent on carrying out acts of rebellion against the French army all along.'

She still didn't say a word.

'Naturally, having been declared an enemy of France, his property has been confiscated.'

'You can't do that!' Harriet cried out. 'What about his mother and sister?'

Mortemer shrugged. 'Young Rose Saintclair let me know her thoughts in no uncertain terms but even she had to accept the inevitable in the end. I have full jurisdiction to do whatever I see fit in the interest of my country, mademoiselle. Madame Saintclair and her daughter have until the end of the month to leave their property. I will, of course, be the administrator of their estate.'

'What about Ahmoud?' she asked.

The lieutenant's lips hardened. 'Unfortunately, the man escaped, but it's only a question of time before we capture him again.'

He stared at a point behind her. 'What's going on over there?'

Archie and Harriet turned towards the garden gates. She let out a startled cry. A short, dark-haired man argued with the guards. She remembered him well. It was Rachid, the man she'd saved from Lucas' wrath outside the Seventh Star.

‘Excuse me for a moment, there’s someone I need to speak to.’ Mortemer walked over to the gate.

‘I wonder who that is,’ Archie muttered under his breath.

‘Only one of his informers,’ she replied coldly.

Archie glanced at her. ‘He seems rather agitated. Look, he’s leading Mortemer away from the gardens.’

He was right. Mortemer now stood in the alley outside the consul’s residence, a deep, unhappy frown on his face. He grabbed Rachid’s arm and shook the small man, who retaliated by yelling and waving his fist in front of him. She shrugged. They could kill each other for all she cared. She was about to turn away when she heard a strange whistling sound. Immediately Rachid collapsed, followed by the lieutenant. Someone started screaming and the British guards rushed out, shouting for help.

It was too late for the two men lying dead on the ground, a dagger between the shoulder blades. As she walked nearer, Harriet saw that both daggers had symbols carved on the hilt – Tuareg symbols.

‘*Egha*,’ she whispered as she recognised the arrangement of patterns and dots Lucas had once showed her.

‘What did you say?’ Archie snapped at her.

‘*Egha*.’ She pointed to the daggers. ‘It means “revenge” in Tamasheq.’

Archie recoiled, pale. ‘Come back here this instant. Whoever killed Mortemer and the other man might still be around.’

He didn’t need to add that it was likely he’d be the next target of a well-aimed dagger. He took her hand and dragged her away. Her heart beating hard and fast, Harriet cast a glance towards the thick vegetation all around, but saw only shadows.

Chapter Twenty-Eight

September – Aylesford, Kent

'Have some petit fours, my dear.' Lady Callaghan gestured for her maid to bring a silver tray laden with pastries. 'I had them made especially by Monsieur Philippe, Lady Portman's very own pastry chef. They are simply divine.'

She placed the dainty pastries onto a china plate which she handed over to Harriet. Harriet muttered polite thanks but left the plate untouched next to her. Lady Callaghan toyed with the tassels of the dark green silk shawl that covered her slim shoulders.

'You simply must make more of an effort, dear girl,' she entreated, a frown creasing her forehead. 'I know you're grieving for your father – we all are – but you wed soon and Archibald doesn't deserve a tearful bride. I always find that if I smile, no matter how terrible I feel, I end up feeling better.'

'I promise to do my best, Lady Callaghan.' Harriet tried not to wince at the mention of her impending wedding.

It wouldn't happen, of course. She wouldn't let it happen. She'd already started making plans to leave England and find Barbarossa's treasure on her own. As Archie and his associates had never seen the map, they had no idea where the corsair had hidden his loot and wouldn't know where to find her. With her gone, they'd have no incentive to destroy her father's reputation and Aunt Elizabeth would be spared the humiliation of a public scandal. At least, that's what she hoped. She would endure the next few days at Lord and Lady Callaghan's country manor and make her escape as soon as she was back in London.

'When I think of the terrible ordeal you've been through in that godforsaken country, how that wretched French rebel abducted you in the middle of the desert as Archibald and his men tried to rescue you …' Lady Callaghan shuddered dramatically before leaning closer to Harriet, her eyes gleaming.

'Was that man really as beastly as Archibald said?' When Harriet didn't answer, she shook her head. 'Thank God, Archibald managed to disarm him and shoot the rogue before he could kill you.'

Harriet took a deep breath, clasped her fingers tightly, unable to put up with Archie's lies any longer. 'Lucas Saintclair wasn't a rogue, but a man fighting for a just cause.' She looked straight into Lady Callaghan's eyes.

The woman pursed her lips, doubtful. 'Maybe it's preferable not to talk about him at all … Archibald might have told you already that my husband decided to give him a place on the board. This is of course a giant leap for his career, but no less than he deserves.'

Harriet gasped. So Archie had deceived everybody, including his employer. She really should warn the Callaghans about him, tell them he was involved in a criminal organisation, but would they believe her?

'Of course,' Lady Callaghan resumed, interrupting her thoughts, 'with the work still underway at Great Russell Street, he'll be extremely busy in the next few months, but don't worry, Lord Callaghan is giving him a couple of weeks' leave after your wedding so you can enjoy each other's company.'

Even if the construction of the museum's new wing was nearing completion, the disruption caused by the building work was still considerable as whole collections had to be catalogued and moved, stored in the vaults, or put on display in the new building.

'You know that in your father's absence, Lord Callaghan is only too happy to give you away,' Lady Callaghan resumed. 'He was very upset by what happened to your father. He can't help feeling responsible.'

'Oh no, he mustn't blame himself,' Harriet exclaimed. 'It was very generous of him to organise the rescue expedition and provide the ransom money. He couldn't have known that—'

She stopped just in time. What she wanted to say was that Lord Callaghan couldn't have known that Archibald Drake, the man chosen to lead the rescue, was in fact determined to make sure Oscar Montague died, and that his generous efforts to bring back her father were doomed from the start.

'My father would have a heart attack,' she finished.

'Anyhow, we're delighted to have you with us. It's such a long time since you were our guest.'

Harriet frowned. 'I don't remember ever coming here.'

'You stayed with your father once when you were a very young girl.'

Lady Callaghan flicked her silk and ivory fan open and waved it in front of her face a few times.

'Really?'

Puzzled, Harriet looked around. She'd only seen the drawing room so far, having just arrived from London with Archie less than an hour before. It was a grand room indeed. Crystal chandeliers, deep gold and dark red silk on the walls, heavy velvet drapes at the windows and colourful silk rugs on the parquet flooring gave Lord Callaghan's country home the opulence of a palace fit for a king. Lord Callaghan was a very wealthy man indeed.

'Your father thought a few days in the countryside might do you good. As it turned out, you caught a chill one evening when you stayed too long on the terrace and your father took you back to London in a hurry. You were quite ill.'

Harriet felt the blood drain from her face. This couldn't be the same house, could it? The house where her father argued with men in dark evening suits, who wore green rings with a snarling silver wolf.

She looked towards the tall windows, open to let a gentle cooling breeze in. It was unseasonably warm for September. Maybe she could plead a migraine, tell Lady Callaghan she needed fresh air and wander outside. She might recognise the terrace and the park.

Unfortunately, Lady Callaghan had other ideas. After offering her more tea and frowning at her for not eating all her petit fours, she decreed she would take her upstairs for a surprise.

'It's been very hard for Archibald and your aunt to keep the secret, but I'm sure you'll agree it was worth it,' she said in conspiratorial tones whilst leading Harriet up a majestic staircase.

'What secret?' A shiver of dread crept along her spine.

Lady Callaghan smiled. 'Follow me.'

As they went up the stairs, her eye was caught by the full-length portrait of a silver-haired gentleman in a black hunting suit. His green eyes glowed with a cruel, sinister gleam.

'Don't look at that painting, my dear, or you will have nightmares for weeks. I've begged my husband many times to hang it somewhere else but he won't hear of it. For some reason, Charles is absurdly proud of this ancestor of his.'

'Who is he?' Harriet leaned closer to the portrait.

'My husband's great-grandfather. I can never look at him without a certain *frisson*. With his wild hair and the cruel way he treated his family and staff and the peasants on the estate'—she shook her head—

'it's no wonder they called him the Silver Wolf.'

Harriet started. 'I beg your pardon?'

'He did all kinds of truly terrible things, or so the story goes. Thankfully, his children and grandchildren were nothing like him. I just can't imagine Charles riding on a black stallion, sword in hand, intent on causing mayhem in the village, can you?' She let out an unconcerned chuckle.

Harriet cast another glance at the portrait.

This was the house. Lord Callaghan himself must be involved in the brotherhood named after his ancestor. In fact, he was probably their leader. Her father never stood a chance. The whole rescue mission had been a sham from the very beginning. Far from arranging her father's rescue, Lord Callaghan commissioned his execution. When his men failed to kill him, he'd sent Archie to make sure he wouldn't come back alive from the Barbary States.

Her legs were shaking when she reached the first floor. Lady Callaghan opened a door.

'Now, this is your big surprise, Harriet,' she announced dramatically as she opened the door to a large room dominated by a four poster bed. 'Your wedding will take place this very evening.'

'What?'

The woman nodded. 'Everything is ready. Your Aunt Elizabeth took your measurements from one of your new dresses and I arranged to have this beauty made for you especially by Mademoiselle Saint-Pons, Lady Dunmore's seamstress herself,' she added, smiling smugly.

In other circumstances, Harriet might have been irritated by the way the woman continually dropped names of the Queen's ladies-in-waiting into the conversation, but in truth she hardly heard her. She stared in horror at the ivory silk and lace wedding dress spread out on the four poster bed and clutched at her chest, unable to breathe. The trap was closing in.

Lady Callaghan stared at her and patted her arm. 'You're awfully pale, dear. It's a wonderful shock, isn't it? Your fiancé clearly loves you so much he cannot bear delaying your marriage any longer.'

She carried on chattering about whirlwind romances, young brides and adoring husbands as she led her to the bed and helped her sit down.

Harriet heard that the Aylesford vicar would officiate at the wedding and a few select friends would attend the wedding supper. Her aunt would be joining them too. Lady Callaghan's voice sounded distant, yet the woman was right next to her.

'I think I need to lie down.'

'Of course, have a rest. There's plenty of time. The ceremony isn't until nine o'clock tonight.'

Harriet curled up on the silky green counterpane, squeezed her eyes shut and pretended to fall asleep until she heard the woman walk away and the door close. Immediately, she sat up. There wasn't a minute to waste. She had to leave. Her legs shaking, she walked to the case she'd packed for what Archie told her would be a few restful days at his employer's country house. It was far too heavy for her to carry on her own so she pulled a few items out – a plain dark grey dress and some undergarments, a toiletry bag, her jewellery and her money pouch. She stuffed them in her tapestry bag. She would find a way of going back to London tonight. There was something very precious she needed to retrieve from her house, something Archie desperately wanted – the Barbarossa map. She would take it and disappear.

She fastened her bag seconds before a maid came in to help her get ready. All she could think of was her escape. For now, however, she would play the part of the blushing, nervous bride-to-be.

The maid pinned the ivory lace cap on her hair, which was loose and fell in soft, shiny strands onto her shoulders.

'You look beautiful, miss,' she said, stepping back.

Harriet looked at her reflection in the full-length mirror. She tilted her head up defiantly, but her eyes filled with tears. The dress was stunning, with a heart-shaped décolleté, and a full skirt which rustled when she moved. Her Fatima's hand pendant gleamed against her skin. She touched it, lifted it to her lips, just like Lucas had done time and time again.

'What is that? It looks strange,' the maid asked, wrinkling her nose.

Harriet smiled sadly. 'It's a good luck charm from a far away country, although it failed me in the end.'

'Are you ready to go down, miss?'

Harriet glanced at the window. It was getting dark. Now was the time to take her bag downstairs and sneak out.

'I will follow you down in a minute,' she said.

When she was sure the corridor and staircase were deserted, she grabbed her bag and cloak, went down the stairs and sneaked out through a patio door.

This was definitely the house, she resolved, as she walked across the terrace. She recognised the gentle slope of the lawn, the ruined folly in the distance. As she turned to take her bag and her coat, a sound nearby startled her.

'Who's there?' she asked, alarmed. Quickly she put her bag and cloak on a bench. If anyone saw those now, they would know she was planning to escape.

'So it's true, you are marrying Drake.' It was hardly more than a whisper, but it was *his* voice.

She cried out, spun round.

No one was there. Did she imagine it?

Frantic, she peered into the gathering shadows. She must be losing her mind.

'Lucas? Is that you?' Her voice trembled as she called.

He stepped out from a dark corner at the edge of the terrace.

She lifted her hand to her mouth to stifle her cry. 'I am dreaming,' she whispered, her hand clasping the balustrade hard.

'You're not.' He walked closer.

He seemed taller, leaner than she remembered. In the blue-grey dusk, his face was sharp, severe and unsmiling.

She raised a hand to touch his cheek. He caught her wrist mid-air and gripped it tightly.

'Congratulations, Harriet. You make a beautiful bride.'

'I thought you were dead,' she whispered, her heart bursting with wonder, with love and sheer joy. Everything was going to be all right. Lucas was here, he was alive and he'd come for her.

'If only you knew how happy—'

'Save your breath,' he interrupted, releasing her. He studied her face.

'I didn't want to believe it was true until now. Somehow I didn't think you'd agree to marry the man who betrayed your father and left his dead body in Tin Hinan's tomb, the man who shot me in the back. I see I grossly misjudged you.'

The scorn in his voice cut like a knife.

He'd got it all wrong. She loved only him. He didn't know, he couldn't know that Archie was forcing her into this marriage.

'It's not what you think, I don't want to—'

'I said save it!' he growled.

She felt the heat from his body. One step and she would be in his arms. Only he didn't seem to want to take her into his arms. He looked at her like a stranger … or worse, an enemy.

'This is just so unexpected, so wonderful.' She paused to give herself time to control the trembling inside. 'How did you survive? There was blood everywhere, on your chest, on your back. Mortemer said you were dead.'

He shrugged. 'I wasn't, at least not completely. The Tuaregs rescued me, took me to their camp and healed me.'

She gasped. 'What about my father? Was he …'

He shook his head. 'I'm sorry. They couldn't do anything for him. He was still alive when I got to the tomb, though.'

The silhouette of a man stood at the patio door and threw a long shadow across the terrace.

'Harriet? Are you out there?' It was Archie.

Lucas cursed softly and retreated to the shadows. 'Get rid of him.'

She rushed back to the house, praying that Archie wouldn't spot her bag and cloak on the stone bench.

'What are you doing?' Archie asked when she reached the patio door. 'You should be inside, with us.' He looked at her, his eyes became warmer and a smile appeared on his lips.

'You look lovely, my dear. So what did you think of my surprise?' He wrapped his arms around her waist. 'I must say I can't wait until tonight.' He bent down to nuzzle her neck.

She recoiled from the unpleasant sensations caused by his wispy moustache and his greedy, wet lips on her skin.

'Not now, Archie. Please.' She pressed her hands against his chest, trying to push him away.

He laughed, drawing her closer. 'You won't be able to push me away for much longer, you know.'

She stiffened and turned away from him.

'Come back inside,' he ordered. 'We're having drinks while we wait for your aunt and the vicar. They shouldn't be long.'

She shook her head. 'I have a migraine, Archie. I need quiet and fresh air before the ceremony.'

He frowned but let her go. 'Very well. I'll send the maid out for you when we're ready.'

She made sure he'd gone back inside before returning to the far end of the terrace.

He observed the scene from a distance, his fists clenched at his side, ready to pounce on Drake. He couldn't hear what the man was saying, but the way he groped Harriet made his blood boil. It would be so easy to take him out here, walk up to him and punch the life out of him, or push his dagger through his heart.

Yet it couldn't be done. Harriet was marrying him. She must love him after all, maybe she had all along. His chest tightened and he realised he'd been holding his breath. He hadn't expected to feel this way. He should despise her, loathe her even. He couldn't. There was a vast, dark hollow in his chest.

As soon as he regained consciousness in the Tuareg healer's tent, he'd started making plans to go after her. The thought of seeing her once more had given him the strength to pull back from the deadly abyss and recover when there'd barely been a breath of life left inside him. Even if she could never be his, at least he would make sure she was safe and well-provided-for.

And now she'd chosen to marry Drake.

However much he wanted to kill the Englishman, however unworthy Drake was of her, he wouldn't interfere. He would leave. There were however a couple of things he had to do first.

'Lucas?'

She came back towards him, threw her dark cloak over her wedding dress and pulled the hood down. He narrowed his eyes, puzzled to see her carrying a bag.

'What are you doing?'

'Take me away,' she said, glancing back towards the mansion as if afraid. 'I was escaping. I must leave before Archie forces me to marry him.'

He put his hand on her arm. 'What did you just say?'

She looked up. 'I never wanted to marry him, but he said he'd destroy my father's reputation. He's after the Barbarossa map. He knows I won't be able to keep it from him once we're man and wife.'

'Drake is forcing you to marry him?'

'Of course.'

He stepped closer. All he wanted was to press her hard against him, kiss her lips and breathe in her scent: rose and woman. He'd dreamt about it often enough these past few weeks. He didn't. Instead, he hardened his heart. Harriet would remain a dream. He was a fugitive and had nothing to offer her.

She waited for his reply, holding her breath. She wanted to nestle in his arms, and beg him to take her away. She loved him, couldn't he see?

He hesitated. 'I'll take you to London,' he said, taking her bag from her. 'We need to talk, anyway.'

With the ease of a cat, he climbed over the balustrade with her bag and jumped down. Then he reached out for her and put his hands on her waist to ease her down on the gravel lane that wound its way around the bottom part of the terrace.

'We must hurry. I saw two armed guards making their rounds. I have a carriage waiting on the lane outside.'

He took her hand and they ran across the lawn. Once they reached the wall to the estate, Lucas whistled. Another whistle answered almost immediately. He threw her bag over the wall, climbed up and pulled Harriet to him. Her long skirts hampered her, but she managed to throw one leg, then the other, over the wall and find her balance as she sat on the ledge at the top. Lucas jumped, landed on his feet with only the slightest sound and extended his arms.

'Jump down, I'll catch you.'

He hardly staggered when she landed in his arms, and held her against him for a moment before putting her down.

'You may not be able to go back, you know that, don't you?' he asked, looking into her eyes.

'I will never go back.'

Chapter Twenty-Nine

The coach driver was a large, brutish-looking man who knotted his big bushy eyebrows in a frown and spat on the ground when he saw her.

'Didn't know we'd have to take a runaway bride back with us,' he grumbled, pulling his hat down.

'Let's go,' Lucas urged, opening the carriage door to help her in.

He climbed in after her and the carriage set off at speed.

It was all so strange, she thought, staring at the man opposite her. After the first, wonderful shock of seeing him again when she believed him dead, she now felt detached, almost numb. Maybe it was her way of avoiding heartbreak. She could tell by the way Lucas looked at her, cold and indifferent, that he had all but forgotten – or discarded – the weeks they'd spent together in Algeria. It was as if they'd never been lovers. As if they would never be lovers again.

She pulled her cloak down, unpinned the wedding cap from her hair and placed it on the bench next to her. Whatever happened now, she'd never marry Archie. She cleared her throat. 'Where are we going?'

'To a friend of your father's in London. His name is Theophilius Knox. He's going to help us.'

Harriet shook her head. 'I don't know him. Does he work for the museum too?'

'No, he runs a bookshop. He was kind enough to lend me his carriage and driver when I said I must get to Aylesford urgently to speak to you.'

'How did you know about him?'

He sighed and rubbed his face. 'Your father gave me his name. We had a few minutes before Mortemer and his men arrived at the tomb. He was very weak but still lucid, and there was much he wanted to tell me before … Before it was too late.'

Harriet's eyes filled with tears. Suddenly she was back on that terrible day in Abalessa. She could almost feel the savage heat of the sun on her skin, taste the dust on her lips, feel the raw despair in her heart.

'I wasn't even with him when he died,' she whispered, clutching her hands in her lap. 'I left him all alone in the tomb.'

He leaned forward, looked into her eyes and took her hands in his. They were warm and strong. 'You did what you had to do. You went to get help.'

'What did he say to you?'

He let go of her and sat back. 'He told me not to trust Drake. He said he was dangerous.' He let out a short, humourless laugh. 'He wasn't wrong there, was he?

'He also told me to stuff a handful of emeralds and gold in my pockets and give them to you. Although he wasn't happy about taking anything valuable from the tomb, he said you'd need money when the scandal about the Brotherhood broke out. And …' He paused. 'He told me how to find the Garamantes' mines.'

'He did?'

He nodded. 'He wanted me to pass it on to the Tuareg keepers, which I did when I got better. Your father had some kind of agreement with them.'

Harriet's eyes shone with excitement. 'So you know where the mines are?'

'I do. They're in the Tassili mountain range between Tamanrasset and the Tripoli territories. Maybe I'll go there myself one of these days, try and find them.'

Would he ever go back? He'd travelled to Algiers and boarded a ship bound for England under a false name. He was wanted by the French army for treason. He hadn't even been able to visit his mother and sister in Bou Saada one last time before their land and house were confiscated. If he did find the emerald mines, he might be rich enough to bribe his way into the good graces of French officials and buy the estate back. There was nothing better than money to help people forget.

As if she sensed he was thinking about his land, his family and friends, she asked. 'What happened to Ahmoud? I heard he escaped from jail.'

'That's right, and he took care of Mortemer for me in the end.'

'*Egha*,' she said. 'So it was him.'

He glanced at her. 'You remember.'

'I was there when Mortemer and Rachid were killed,' she explained. 'I saw the carvings on the daggers.'

'Shame he didn't get Drake that night,' Lucas muttered.

Neither of them spoke as the shadows thickened and the carriage bumped along country roads.

'Your father was desperate to expose this brotherhood and protect you from them,' Lucas resumed at last. 'Have you found out anything about them?'

'Not much. They are called Brotherhood of the Silver Wolf. I think Lord Callaghan is their leader. I don't understand what they stand for or how we can defeat them. They must be incredibly powerful. I don't know what we can do since there's only the two of us against them.'

'We're not alone, Harriet. Theophilius Knox can help us if we bring him the Barbarossa map.'

She glanced at him, surprised. 'The map? What does that have to do with anything?'

He darted his pale blue eyes into hers. 'Remember the letter your father sent you from Algiers?'

She frowned in concentration, trying to recall the exact wording of her father's letter.

'He mentioned that old trick you used to play on your Aunt Elizabeth.' He smiled and arched his eyebrows. 'A most formidable woman, by the way. I sincerely hope never to have to meet her again.'

'You talked to Aunt Elizabeth?'

'I went to your house this morning after meeting with Knox. I said I was a French scholar, made up some story about an ancient artefact you bought in Algiers that I wanted to study. She was the one who told me you were getting married to Drake tonight in Aylesford. She seemed very pleased about the whole thing.'

'She always liked Archie.' Harriet sighed. 'Everybody likes Archie. If only they knew what he's really like.'

'Anyway, there's a secret message at the back of the map, a message your father wrote with—'

'Lemon juice,' she finished, opening her eyes wide. 'Of course, now I understand! What's the message?'

'It's the location of a file he compiled on the Brotherhood. He said there was enough to incriminate them and that his friend Knox would know what to do with it.'

'I hid the map in the old nursery, in my house.'

'So that's where we need to go first.' He pulled the window down and shouted the address of Harriet's house to the driver, then pulled it back up again.

She was watching him. 'Why are you doing this? I mean, you could have kept the emeralds and the gold you took from the tomb and disappeared to somewhere safe. You could have even tried to find the emerald mines. Instead, you came all the way to England, risking your life for—'

'For the Barbarossa map, of course,' he cut in, coldly. 'You did say it would be mine when you returned to London, or had you forgotten?' He crossed his arms on his chest.

'I see.' She turned her face away, but not before he saw her lips quiver and tears slide down her cheek.

He clasped his arms more tightly, as if trying to strengthen his resolve. This was the only way. He'd go in search of Barbarossa's treasure, give Harriet whatever he found, and let her get on with her life. He was doing the right thing, he knew it. So why did it feel so wrong?

'There's another reason,' he added as an afterthought. 'Two reasons, actually. I promised your father I'd make sure you were safe, and I want Drake and his associates to pay for killing my men.'

She didn't appear to have heard him but kept her head resolutely turned towards the blacked-out window. Her eyes were closed. She must be tired. Maybe she was asleep.

Her chest was so tight every single breath hurt. She had hoped for another answer. She should have known better.

They didn't talk until they reached London. The horses' hooves and the wheels of the carriage echoed in the night as they drove up empty cobbled streets.

'The house will be locked at this time,' she remarked as nearby church bells chimed one.

It took another twenty minutes to reach Charlotte Street. The carriage stopped in front of the elegant four-storey house she'd lived in all her life. Lucas opened the door and stepped down first. He held out his hand. She ignored it and climbed down the footsteps on her own.

'We don't have long. I'm sure this is the first place Archie will look when he realises I've gone.'

She gathered her skirts and walked towards the side of the house. Lucas told the driver to be vigilant then followed her down a flight of stairs leading to the basement kitchen.

With luck, Nelly, the housemaid, was still out with her sweetheart. Mrs Forbes, the housekeeper, turned a blind eye since the pair was engaged to be married.

She searched through a large flower pot at the bottom of the stairs.

'There's the key.'

She unlocked the service door and let herself into the dark kitchen. 'There should be an oil lamp somewhere.' She fumbled about in the dark until she found it. Then she walked to the stove, pulled the top open, and lit a firebrand to the glowing red embers. She ignited the wick of the lamp and turned to Lucas.

'Follow me.' She held the lamp in front of her and opened the kitchen door onto a long corridor. 'The nursery is on the second floor.'

They climbed a flight of stairs to the ground floor, then two more. Harriet walked fast along the corridor and pushed the third door to the right. After placing the lamp on a table, she walked to the far corner of the room and knelt down on the parquet flooring.

Nobody came in here any longer, except a housemaid once in a while to do a bit of dusting. The floorboards were loose at one end of the room and easy to lift. Underneath was a gap big enough for the large metal box where she'd kept her treasures for as long as she could remember. Over the years, she'd filled it with colourful stones found during a walk in the park, trinkets or broken pieces of artefacts her father had brought back from an excavation, and all the letters and sketches he sent her. She'd hidden the Barbarossa map at the bottom.

She opened the lid and pulled the old, yellowed parchment out with great care.

'Is this it?' Lucas asked in earnest.

She nodded. She got up and walked to the lamp, unfolded the map and held it against the light.

'The writing is becoming visible now. Look!'

He stood behind her to look at the map over her shoulder.

'It's a series of numbers, and an address in the bottom corner, there,' Harriet remarked, dismayed. 'Theophilius Knox, Paternoster lane. My father wanted me to go and see his friend.'

'That's because Knox knows what the numbers mean.' Lucas held out his hand. 'Can I take a look at the treasure map?'

'Of course, that's why you're here, isn't it?' She tilted her chin up and handed him the map.

He glanced at the map and smiled before folding it and sliding it into his pocket.

'Barbarossa's loot is in Sardinia,' he said.

'I could have told you that.' She shrugged. 'I must go to my room to get changed.' She started walking to the door, but he caught her arm.

'There's no time.'

They reached Paternoster Row as St Paul's cathedral struck two o'clock. All the bookshops lining the small, narrow street were boarded up for the night. Theophilius Knox's was no exception but light filtered through the wooden shutters.

The driver knocked on the door which immediately opened onto a small, grey-haired man dressed in a black suit. He gestured impatiently for Harriet and Lucas to come in.

'Do you have it?' he asked Lucas as he closed and bolted the door behind them, the driver waiting with the carriage.

Lucas produced the map.

'Over here.' Knox pointed to a desk at the back of the shop where an oil lamp gave out a warm glow.

'First, my dear,' he said, taking Harriet's hand. 'I want to tell you how sorry I am your father is no longer with us.'

Harriet nodded. 'Thank you. Did you know him well?'

The small man smiled. His face creased in a thousand wrinkles, making him look positively ancient. 'He was one of my oldest friends. We studied classics together at Oxford. Oscar was always the adventurous one. He went on to travel the world and make great discoveries whereas I inherited this modest shop from my father. Still, we met often. And we talked. I knew about his troubles.'

He pulled a seat out for her and spread the map on the desk. 'Sardinia, hey? Who would have thought the old corsair would keep his secret for so long?' He winked at Lucas. 'But not for much longer, I suspect.'

Lucas smiled. 'I'll be heading over there as soon as this Brotherhood business is finished.'

'How annoying for you to have to wait for your treasure hunting until we put a stop to the activities of Archie, Lord Callaghan and their cronies,' Harriet muttered.

'Let's take a look at the back.' The old man held the map in front of the lamp. 'Get a quill and write down exactly what I tell you,' he instructed Harriet before proceeding to read out a list of numbers.

'Hmm ...' he said when he finished, stroking his chin with his index finger. 'We have fifteen lines. Each with three numerals separated with a comma. It's a code, of course.' He scratched his head as he started pacing the room.

'The numbers most probably refer to pages, lines and words or letters of a book he took with him to Algiers. Let's see … He came to see me a few weeks before leaving and asked for *Aeneid* by Virgil and *The Histories* by Heredotus. But which editions did I get for him? It could make all the difference.'

He carried on debating with himself while pulling books from the shelves and piling them on the desk.

He looked at Lucas apologetically and combed a strand of grey hair back with his fingers. 'I'm afraid it might take us a while to work this out.'

'Why don't we each try the code with a different book and see what we come up with?' Lucas suggested. He pulled a chair out, sat down, and grabbed one of the dozen or so books.

'You should go upstairs and make yourself comfortable, dear,' Theophilious told Harriet.

'I'd rather help,' she objected.

She pulled a book towards her and looked at the paper with the numbers. The book was *The Histories*. She'd read some of it before. It contained one of the few references ever made to the Garamantes and their civilisation that so fascinated her father. It was a good place to start.

The three of them worked in silence, turning pages, writing letters and words, and trying to make sense of Oscar Montague's code.

Lucas was the first to push his book back and draw a cross on his paper.

'It's not this one,' he said. He took hold of another and started the same process.

'Not this one either,' Knox said with a sigh. 'What about you, are you getting anywhere?' he asked her.

She wrote another word, but didn't lift her head from her paper. 'Hmm … I think … maybe.'

Vault twenty-six, third cabinet right after Secretum, fourth shelf, second left. Pull.

'I think I've got it,' she said as she wrote the last words and handed Knox her piece of paper. He glanced at the paper and his eyes widened with surprise.

'You most certainly have.'

'What's the Secretum?'

Knox's face became red. 'It's a … hmm … special collection, not suitable for public display. Oscar must have hidden the file as soon as the new wing was refurbished, and when he found out the organisation was trying to kill him in Algiers, sent you the map with the coded message.'

'Please, Mr Knox, tell me what you know about the Brotherhood,' Harriet asked. 'I find it hard to believe my father would ever get into anything illegal or morally reprehensible.'

Theophilius Knox shook his head, and shifted uncomfortably from one foot to the other.

'My dear, sometimes the best of us fall victim to circumstances which make refusing certain opportunities hard, if not impossible,' he stuttered.

'What kind of circumstances?' She tried to remember her father's exact words. 'My father spoke of a difficult situation.'

Knox cleared his throat, but avoided looking at her. 'You have to remember that it was a long time ago, when we were very young men. Your father became very … ahem … close to a young woman who used to do the laundry and the cleaning for our college. They … well …' Knox cleared his throat again. 'The girl went on to have a baby.'

'What?' Harriet cried out.

Knox raised his hands as if to appease her. 'Your father did his best, but he didn't have much money in those days. He rented some rooms in a little house up in the Summertown part of Oxford. For a while nobody suspected anything. Unfortunately, Charles Callaghan got wind of the affair somehow. He was a fellow student – worthless and lazy, but as he came from a wealthy family, his antics were tolerated. However, your father, unlike Callaghan, wasn't the son of an earl but the only child of a country parson who had sadly died. If the dons had found out about his unfortunate situation, they'd have thrown him out of Oxford. To keep quiet, Callaghan blackmailed your father and asked him to perform certain services for him – write his assignments and accompany him to betting shops, cockpits and houses of ill repute. Oscar was so desperate that he did Callaghan's bidding.'

'What happened to them, the woman and the child?' Harriet asked.

'Sadly, the girl and the baby – a boy – died in the cholera epidemic of '21, when both your father and I were in our final year.'

'And Callaghan carried on blackmailing my father?'

He nodded. 'After we graduated, we came back to London to seek employment. For a while it seemed things had settled down. I started working here, in my father's bookshop. Your father got a post at the museum, where Callaghan's father was a trustee. But as soon as he started courting your mother, Callaghan started calling in favours again.'

'I don't understand.' Harriet sank wearily into her chair, feeling suddenly drained and disorientated. 'Lord Callaghan's family were very wealthy and he must have had many friends from his own circle. What did he want with a man like my father?'

'You forget the thrill of having power over people,' Knox answered slowly. 'Callaghan was always a rake. He founded his own little club, gave it a fancy name, but Brotherhood of the Silver Wolf was little more than a cover for wealthy, dissolute and arrogant young men looking for thrills and indulging in debauchery – at first. Oscar was different. He was honest and hardworking. Deep down, I think Callaghan admired him, envied him even. He wanted to control him, bring him down.' Knox bent his head. 'And he did, eventually.'

For a while, the silence in the room was only broken by the tick-tock of the clock.

'What about Archie?' Harriet asked.

Lucas let out a grunt and shifted in his seat.

'Unfortunately, your father didn't see Archibald for what he really was until it was too late,' Knox answered. 'All the man was interested in was the advancement of his career. He never cared about how he got to the top, as long as he got there. No matter how often your father tried to reason with him, he believed the Brotherhood was the best way of getting a promotion.'

'There must be more to this,' Lucas remarked. He came quietly to stand behind Harriet and rested a hand on the back of her chair as if to lend her some support. Although he didn't touch her, she felt the heat and the strength from his body. She sat very straight, resisting the urge to lean back against him.

'I can't imagine Callaghan sending assassins after Montague and his team, and going to the trouble of organising a fake rescue mission with a thousand pound ransom for the sole purpose of protecting a drinking and whoring club.'

He sounded suspicious. Once again, Knox's colour deepened. He sighed.

'You are right. There is more.'

Chapter Thirty

'Would you care for a glass of port?' Knox asked.

Without waiting for an answer, he walked to a cabinet, pulled out three tumblers and a bottle, and poured some liquor out. His hand shook so much that some spilled onto the table. He immediately drained his glass and poured another.

What was the elderly scholar so afraid of? Lucas walked across the room to get his and Harriet's glass.

'Over the years, the Brotherhood forged links with the criminal underworld – prostitution, gambling, slum housing, you name it,' the old man resumed. 'To procure funds for his activities, Callaghan set up an underground art market to sell artefacts from the museum. As the chairman of the board of trustees, he had unlimited access to the building and the collections and, of course, blackmailed key employees into falsifying documents and "forgetting" to catalogue certain artefacts, thereby erasing any trace of their existence.'

'Men like my father,' Harriet whispered.

Knox sighed. 'The theft of the museum's treasures has snowballed since the building work began at Great Russell Street. I gather that by now a significant number of the museum's artefacts have been "lost" – in reality sold or given to the criminal barons Callaghan associates with in return for favours. For the past ten years, Callaghan has also been heavily involved in the floatation of railway companies – many of them fake.' He looked at Harriet. 'We are talking fraud and share scams on a grand scale here.'

Harriet sat rigid in her chair in front of him. 'My father was party to that kind of fraud?' Her voice was weak.

'He had no choice, my dear, but he hated it, especially when precious ancient artefacts were taken away and sold to private collectors. He had to carry out Callaghan's orders and forge paperwork, help ship valuable artefacts out of the museum without a trace, or secure buyers in England or abroad …'

Lucas looked at Harriet, pale and fragile in her wedding dress, her grey eyes huge and full of shadows. How she must hurt right now and feel betrayed by her father. What must it be like to learn that the man you trusted and admired wasn't as irreproachable as you believed? His most basic, primal instinct was to pull her up and enfold her into his arms, to whisper in her ear that he'd keep her safe, always. Instead, he gave her a glass of port and resumed his place behind her.

'There is something else …' Knox whispered. 'Do you remember the McNaughton trial two and a half years ago?' he asked Harriet.

'McNaughton?' She frowned and rubbed her forehead lightly with her fingers. 'Wasn't he the man who shot the prime minister's secretary? I remember there was a public outcry when he was acquitted on grounds of insanity.'

Knox nodded and took a deep breath. 'At the time, he claimed he was being coerced into carrying out the assassination by members of a secret organisation. He said the man he wanted to kill was Robert Peel himself, not his secretary.'

'No, not murder as well!' Harriet was as pale as her dress.

Knox nodded. 'McNaughton was a wealthy but fragile young man who became interested in art, science and ancient history. Needless to say, he met some people he should never have mixed with.

'Oscar found him volatile, easily suggestible, eager to impress. McNaughton told him the Brotherhood demanded he prove himself by some spectacular action as a kind of initiation rite, something which would leave its mark, like shooting a public figure. Someone suggested Robert Peel, the prime minister himself.'

'Oh my God!' Harriet's hand flew in front of her mouth. 'But why?'

'At the time, several of the criminal barons associated with the Brotherhood were feeling threatened by Peel's determination to combat crime and set up a well-organised, efficient police force. He was also trying to establish a parliamentary enquiry commission to tackle the ever-growing issue of railway fraud. Callaghan was keen to protect his investments and keep his name and the name of his associates out of any investigation.'

'So he somehow convinced McNaughton to kill Lord Peel, but the young man shot Drummond instead.' Harriet shook her head. 'My father should have told the police. No matter what the consequences for him.'

'He couldn't, my dear. He was too afraid Callaghan would try to hurt you. McNaughton wrote to your father after he was convicted. The letter is now in Oscar's secret file, along with everything else he managed to gather on Callaghan. He desperately wanted to be free, but what he wanted even more was for you to be safe. He was planning a new start with you. He told me Callaghan finally agreed to release him on the condition he gave him the file once he got back from Algiers.'

'Instead,' Harriet said, 'he sent his killers to silence him.'

Lucas whistled between his teeth. 'Now I understand why Callaghan would go to such length to silence your father. His involvement in an attempt on the prime minister's life would mean public disgrace at the very least, and more likely hanging for high treason.'

He drained his glass and put it down on the table. 'I think it's time we went to the museum to get that file.'

Theophilius Knox gasped. 'You mean to go now, in the middle of the night? But how do you propose to get into the museum?'

'I can pick locks, however large, if that's what you're worried about.' Lucas shrugged. 'All I need are the right tools and I'm sure you have something I can use.'

'You'll need me to find your way around,' Knox said.

'I'm coming too.' Harriet stood up quickly.

'That's out of the question,' Lucas said. 'I will not let you take that kind of risk.'

She narrowed her eyes. 'Don't even try and dissuade me.' She picked up her bag. 'I'm going to change out of this dress.'

'It's not a good idea, Harriet,' he carried on nonetheless. 'What if we get caught?'

'If we get caught, I shall burst into tears and make up some story about wanting to retrieve some of my father's things as a memento. I'm sure the museum guards or the police won't be harsh on a grieving daughter.'

'She is right and will be safer with us than alone here,' Knox said, showing Harriet to the room next door where she could change. He glanced around, an uneasy look in his eyes. 'Callaghan knows where I live. I wouldn't be surprised if he sent his thugs around to pay me a visit anytime soon. And the sooner this file is with the authorities the better.'

'We'll get in through there.' Lucas pointed to a small gap in the fence surrounding the building site at the top of Great Russell Street. 'The gas lights aren't working on that side of the street.'

He grabbed the satchel Knox had given him and opened the carriage door.

As soon as they'd climbed down, the driver drove away. He was to come back after half an hour. Lucas enlarged the hole in the fence and

Knox, Harriet and himself passed through. Although much of the new building was completed, the area immediately around the museum was still littered with piles of rubble, bricks, stones, wood and tools. Knox proceeded to one of the side doors leading to the basement – the one he said offered the best access to vault twenty-six.

Even though there was no guard around, they remained silent and held their breath as Lucas ran his fingers along the door to locate the lock. The couple of minutes it took him to release the mechanism with a pick from the bag, felt like an eternity. At last he pushed the door open.

'Get in,' he instructed.

She shivered as she entered the cold, dark basement. Lucas jammed a small piece of wood in the door to make sure it stayed ajar for them, and lit one of the candles he'd taken from Knox's shop earlier.

'Which way?' he asked Knox.

The elderly man looked around and gestured towards a door. 'Down here.'

The light from the candle threw huge shadows on the walls as they made their way down a corridor cluttered with crates and display cabinets.

'This one,' Knox said at last, pointing to a massive black door. Lucas handed him the candle while he once again started working on the lock.

'We have to find the Secretum,' Harriet said when they walked into the vault. 'It could be any of these.'

Lucas lifted his candle higher. The vault was lined with massive display cabinets, some with glass fronts and others with solid wood doors.

'I guess we'd better start searching then. At least we've an idea of what's in cupboard fifty-five.' He had a wide grin on his face.

Harriet turned round without answering and opened the first cabinet in front of her. How could he make a joke when they could be caught by guards any second and arrested for trespassing?

Lucas placed the candle on a crate, having formed a pool of wax in which it would stand. The three of them began their search, starting in different corners and working their way towards the centre. The second cupboard Harriet searched was a black cabinet. She opened the drop-down door and then a drawer. There was an ancient terracotta votive oil lamp. She held it in front of her … and her cheeks grew hot. There was no mistaking the shape of the handle. She put it down quickly and looked inside the cabinet again. The drawer was filled with similar lamps and amulets. She pulled out a book covered with thick black leather. She flicked through the yellowed pages, opening her eyes wide at the graphic depictions of men and women engaged in intimate activities. The book slipped from her hands and fell to the ground with a thud.

She cleared her throat. 'I think this is the Secretum,' she called, quickly picking up the book and returning it to the cupboard.

'Really? Are you sure?' Lucas came over. 'Should I check?' She couldn't see his face very well in the semi-darkness, but she thought he was smiling.

'Trust me, I know what I was looking at,' she said coldly, moving away. 'The coded message instructed we look inside the third cabinet to the right.' She stopped in front of a tall bookshelf.

'The fourth shelf.' She stood on tiptoes and extended her hand out, but it was far too high for her to reach. 'What we are looking for should be the second item on the left.'

'Let me do this.' Lucas reached out from behind her. He pulled out a thick, heavy volume, opened it, and skimmed through a few pages.

'It's some kind of history book about Rome.' He turned the book over and shook it. 'There's nothing hidden inside.'

'Maybe it's the wrong cabinet,' Knox mused. 'Unless … What's that there?' He pointed to what looked like another book right at the back of the shelf.

Lucas reached out again, and this time he dislodged a portfolio. 'I think that's it,' he said.

He put the folder on the crate next to the candle and untied the green ribbon holding it together. Harriet and Knox stood next to him as he flicked through bundles of papers and letters.

'Names, presumably with the date they joined the Brotherhood,' he told Knox. 'This looks like a catalogue of the artefacts that were sold. And this is the letter from McNaughton you told us about.'

He took a deep breath, and looked at Knox. 'We have it. Let's go.'

They made their way back down the corridor in silence, letting themselves out of the basement door. As they reached the top of the short flight of steps, the large figure of a man holding a lantern appeared in the courtyard, blocking their escape. He hadn't seen them yet.

‘Bend down,’ Lucas whispered before blowing the candle out. ‘I’ll take care of him.’

He sprang forward silently, another shadow in the night. There were muffled sounds of struggle. Lucas came back and gestured towards the fence.

‘Hurry. There might be another guard nearby, and that one won’t be out of action long.’

They sneaked out of the building site and onto Great Russell Street where the carriage was waiting.

‘Where now?’ Lucas asked.

‘Drury Lane,’ Knox answered. ‘Joseph, the driver’s brother runs a tavern. Nobody will come looking for us there.’

Harriet looked up at the sign dangling over the front door: “The Cock and Magpie”. The inn was closed, but light appeared on the first floor when Knox knocked on the door. A giant of a man with wild brown hair falling over his thick, red face appeared.

‘What is it you want? Can you not see we’re closed?’

Instinctively, Harriet moved closer to Lucas who wrapped his arm around her shoulders.

‘Benjamin, it’s Knox. We need to stay over at your place tonight. Joseph said it would be all right with you. He’s just sorting the horses and carriage.’

Immediately the innkeeper opened the door wider.

‘Sorry, Mister Knox, I didn’t recognise you with your hat pulled down your face.’ He peered at Harriet and Lucas and added, ‘Please come in.’

Knox picked a booth close to the fireplace. Pulling a few silver coins out of his waistcoat pocket, he asked the landlord if he could get a fire going, a couple of rooms ready and bring them food and drinks.

Harriet sat next to Lucas while Knox slipped onto the bench opposite and put the folder on the table. Nobody spoke as he flicked through the loose papers and documents inside. Several times he let out a little grunt, arched his eyebrows and muttered to himself.

‘So?’ Lucas asked at last. ‘Do you have enough to incriminate Callaghan, Drake and the others?’

Knox nodded. ‘I think so. Even if McNaughton’s testimony is deemed inadmissible by the courts, there are records of sales of statues and *objets d'art* to some of London's most notorious crime barons, as well as papers signed by Lord Callaghan himself regarding his fraudulent railway schemes. I fear this is too big for Bow Street's police station. I'll have to go to Scotland Yard first thing in the morning.'

'I'll come with you,' Lucas said.

There was a loud knock on the front door and Joseph entered. Once he'd joined them at the table, he started talking about a cockfight which would take place the following evening at the Phoenix, one of Drury Lane's many cockpits.

'There'll be all sorts there, including top brass,' he said, wolfing down his stew.

The men's talk turned to gambling. Harriet pushed her empty plate away, drank another sip of ale and listened to Lucas' voice. If the events of the evening had taken a strange, dream like quality, he at least was solid and real next to her. She still couldn't quite believe that Archie hadn't killed him, and that he was alive and well.

A smile floated on her lips as she leaned against his shoulder, listened to his voice. She closed her eyes and said a silent prayer of thanks. If only she could stay awake and enjoy every single moment of being with him …

He slipped his arm around her waist to support her. Her head nestled against his chest. He felt her soft, warm breath through the fabric of his shirt and held her more tightly.

'It looks like our young lady is ready for bed,' Knox remarked after a while.

'I'll take her up. Show me where her room is,' Lucas told the landlord.

She didn't wake up when he lifted her in his arms. She didn't even wake up when he climbed the stairs and walked into the small, dark bedroom and put her on the bed. The landlord lit a lamp and closed the door behind him.

He stood over the bed, watching her as she curled up on her side and her hair fell over her face. What was to become of her? She would find it hard to stay in London when the scandal over the Brotherhood broke all over the newspapers and it became known that her father had been involved. Her best bet was to use the emeralds and gold he'd brought for her and go to the country for a while.

He leaned forward and gently brushed her hair from her face. She stirred, clasping his hand in hers.

'Don't leave me,' she whispered without opening her eyes.

Against his better judgment, he sat on the bed next to her and brought her fingers to his lips briefly. He mustn't touch her. He must conclude this business in London with Callaghan and Drake, make sure Harriet was safe from them, and leave for Sardinia. And then he would go back to Algeria where he belonged, and the hell with the consequences … However much he wanted to be with her, he couldn't ask Harriet to come. He may not care about the risks to his freedom and his life, but he would never endanger hers.

'I need to give you the emeralds and the gold,' he stated, matter-of-factly. 'They're sewn in the lining of my coat. There's more than enough for you to live comfortably.'

She raised herself on her elbow and looked straight at him. Her eyes glistened with tears. Her lips quivered.

'Kiss me,' she said.

'Harriet, don't do this …'

She sat up and put her hand on his cheek. Her touch gave him a jolt. He straightened and moved back a little. He wouldn't do this. It wasn't fair to her. Or him.

She slid her hand along his face and onto his neck, caressing his skin lightly above the collar of his jacket, tangling her fingers in his hair. This time the urge to kiss her and draw her to him was so overwhelming all he could do was grab her hand and pull it away.

'Stop it,' he growled, taking in the warm, moist grey of her eyes, the smooth curve of her cheek, the dove white of her throat, and the tender swell of her breasts under her dress.

He remembered how she felt, how she tasted. His mouth went dry, his heart thudded in his chest, and his body throbbed with painful desire.

'What are you afraid of, Lucas?' she asked. 'Afraid I will make demands on you? Don't worry. I know you're leaving in the morning. I know you can't wait to go treasure hunting.'

She leaned closer, a savage glint in her eyes. 'Kiss me.'

He knew he was lost then. A groan, almost a roar, escaped from his throat as he lifted her from the bed and into his lap, wrapped his arms tightly around her waist and kissed her like a man possessed. As his mouth devoured hers, she let out small gasps and whimpers which inflamed him, body and soul. He had dreamt of her for so long. Days, weeks, months. This was no dream. He wanted her naked under him, right now. He fiddled with the fastenings at the back of her dress, managed to undo most of them before tearing the fabric apart in his haste.

'Take this off,' he said his voice hoarse.

He watched as she undressed. Then she was standing in front of him in her corset, chemise and stockings. He shrugged his jacket off, loosed his necktie and pulled her into his lap again. His hands, his mouth remembered and took ownership of her body once again. He finally accepted what he had known for a long time. She was made for him. She was his woman. Whether in a Tuareg tent in the heat of the Sahara, in the cool lushness of an oasis, or here, in a sordid tavern in the middle of London, Harriet belonged to him. Leaving her would be the hardest thing he would ever have to do.

'Saintclair, get up!' Knox called from behind the door.

Lucas was sound asleep, snuggled against her back, his arm lying heavy and possessive across her stomach, and his breath tickling her bare shoulder. She stroked his hand, his forearm, desperate to snatch a few more moments alone with him. There was a second knock and this time, Lucas stirred behind her.

'Who's that?' he mumbled before trailing kisses along her neck from her shoulder to her earlobe.

'Knox,' she said. The bristle on his cheeks rubbed deliciously against her skin and made her shiver.

'Is it morning already?'

'Hardly,' she replied, glancing at the window.

A bluish light filtered between the badly drawn curtains. She hadn't slept a wink. She wanted to savour every second in Lucas' arms. She had promised herself she wouldn't ask him to stay.

He let out a sigh and flipped her over so that she lay on top of him. 'I know you never do what you're told, but this time you must promise to stay here.' He stroked her back. 'I don't know how long we'll be with the police. I don't want you wandering around London and risk being seen by Drake, Callaghan or their men.'

She ran her hands lightly over his chest and the star-shaped scar just under his collarbone where Archie's bullet had exited. She'd gasped on first seeing it and the larger scar on his back.

His breathing quickened. He held her more tightly, so tightly he was almost crushing her. She wanted to melt in his heat again, one last time. He must have felt the same way because he caught his breath when he rolled over and covered her with his body, hard, impatient. He whispered her name and dived into her. Clasping her hands on each side of her head, he entwined their fingers and kissed her again, and again, as he drove deeper and faster.

And for a few golden minutes, nothing else but him mattered.

'Saintclair!' Behind the door, Knox sounded impatient.

Before putting his jacket on, Lucas pulled a dagger from his pocket and took out a few stitches in the silk lining. He shook the jacket over the bed counterpane. About two dozen emeralds, as well as a handful of gold coins fell out.

'I'd rather you had them with you now.' He gathered the gems and gold coins into his hands and gave them to her.

There was nothing to keep him here now she realised. He'd discharged himself of his promise to her father. This was probably the last time she would see him.

'Hide them well. You never know who hangs about in this kind of place.' He put his jacket on.

She still didn't answer. She couldn't. She sat up against the pillow, her tousled hair covering her shoulders and breasts, her hands full of precious stones and gold coins.

He looked as if he wanted to add something, but then he shrugged and opened the door. 'Well … goodbye then.'

And he was gone.

Chapter Thirty-One

'Slow down, Saintclair,' Knox protested. 'I know how eager you are to catch the afternoon train, but I can't keep up.'

Lucas grunted with impatience. He wanted to collect his travel bag from Knox's bookshop before going to the station. The day had turned cool and drizzly, and the cloudy sky reminded him of Harriet's eyes. He pulled his collar up, shoving his hands in his pockets. 'Why don't we hail a hansom cab?' he suggested.

The elderly man nodded in agreement. He gestured to a passing cab and both men climbed in with a sigh of relief. Although he'd seen very little of the town, Lucas had decided he didn't like London. The wide cobble-stoned avenue Knox called the Strand seemed perpetually congested with horse-drawn buses, carriages and carts. The pavements were crowded with street vendors, beggars and people rushing by, bumping into him. He'd yet to see anyone laugh or smile, or even look remotely happy. He missed the open spaces, the blue skies, the heat and easy pace of his country. It was just as well that his time here was coming to an end. Once in Dover, he'd board a steam packet to Ostende, then travel to the southern tip of Italy before sailing to Sardinia.

An image of Harriet as he left her that morning, sitting up in bed with her hands filled with treasures and her eyes empty and sad, flashed in his mind. He shook his head. She would be fine. She was resilient, brave and clever. She had emeralds and gold as well as her father's house at Charlotte Street, and hopefully in the not-too-distant future she'd also have whatever was left of Barbarossa's treasure, if he ever found it.

More importantly, she was now safe from Drake and Callaghan.

After several hours spent examining the file on the Brotherhood, questioning Lucas and Knox and taking their statements, Inspector Wrexham of Scotland Yard promised a full and thorough investigation. Everything seemed to be proceeding the way it should. So why did Lucas have an uneasy feeling in the pit of his stomach?

'What did you think of Wrexham?' he asked Knox as they travelled through the crowded streets.

'He seems competent enough.'

'He kept us locked in his office all morning,' Lucas muttered. 'We never saw or talked to another detective.'

Knox shrugged. 'He did go out a few times to speak to his constables, and he sent a special constable to "The Cock and Magpie" to escort Harriet back home. Don't forget he has to be discreet if he's to implicate someone as important as Lord Callaghan.'

Knox was right, of course.

'At least Wrexham said you could leave the country any time you wished,' the elderly man remarked as they pulled up at the entrance to Paternoster Row. He leaned forward and smiled. 'You'll have to let me know how you get on with that treasure.'

They started walking down the lane. Knox stopped talking and frowned. 'That's odd. The shop is still boarded up, yet James always opens up at ten o'clock on the dot. I wonder what happened.'

He pulled a key out of his waistcoat pocket and was about to insert it in the front door lock when Lucas stopped him.

'Let's go round the back.'

They knew something was wrong as soon as they saw the back door hanging on its hinges.

'Dear God. The shop's been burgled!' Knox exclaimed with alarm.

Lucas pulled out his knife. 'Wait here, I'll go in first.'

The storeroom had been trashed, shelves overturned, papers strewn around. He walked down the corridor, attentive to any noise indicating that the burglars were still there. The shop too had been turned upside down, and a young man sat, holding a bloodied handkerchief to his nose amongst the books littering the floor.

'Dear God! Poor James!' Knox said behind Lucas, as he rushed to his side.

'I couldn't stop them. I'm so sorry, Mr Knox,' the young man muttered. 'They were much stronger than me. I couldn't stop them.'

'What happened?' Lucas asked.

'I was about to open up when I heard a crashing noise at the back,' he explained. 'Two men broke in. They wanted to know where you kept your papers.'

'I think they were Welsh or had some sort of connection to Wales. I heard them mention Wrexham a few times. That's a town in Wales, isn't it?'

'What can that possibly mean?' Knox scratched his head.

'It means that the police inspector warned Callaghan, who in turn sent his thugs here.' Lucas hissed a breath between his teeth. 'Wrexham has no intention of investigating the Brotherhood. I wager the file we gave him has already been destroyed. I also bet we'll have killers on our backs before long.'

He took a deep breath … and it dawned on him. Harriet was in danger!

'Harriet … I must go to her house in Charlotte Street straight away.' He turned to Knox. 'You'll have to be very careful.'

'Don't you worry about me,' the elderly man replied. 'I've a trick up my sleeve. I spent a couple of hours last night copying the documents and lists from Oscar's file. Callaghan isn't leaving me any choice. I'm going with the whole story to a good friend of mine who happens to be a senior editor at *The Times*.'

Lucas drummed his fingers on his knees during the whole journey to Charlotte Street. When the cab got stuck behind a beer cart blocking the street while casks were being unloaded, he paid the driver and leapt out. There wasn't a minute to lose.

She put her hand in front of her mouth and yawned. It was the third time in as many minutes.

'Another cup of tea, Harriet?' Aunt Elizabeth's face was blurred.

Harriet blinked and rubbed her eyes. 'No, thank you. I feel a little strange,' she said, aware that her voice sounded slurred. Her legs, her whole body felt so heavy she couldn't move from the armchair in the drawing room.

Aunt Elizabeth tightened her lips. 'I gave you something to soothe your nerves. We don't want a repeat of what happened yesterday in Aylesford, do we?'

'What did you give me?'

'A few drops of laudanum in your tea, that's all. It will keep you calm while we wait.'

'Wait for what?' Harriet made a conscious effort to keep her eyes open and straighten in her chair.

Aunt Elizabeth stood up and walked to the window. Lifting the muslin curtains, she peered into the street. 'Archibald will be here any minute.'

Harriet's heart quickened, fear dried her throat. Had the police not arrested Archie yet? Lucas and Knox had been gone for hours.

'How could you do such a terrible thing last night?' Elizabeth complained once more. 'Do you have any idea how much you embarrassed your fiancé? Your father – God bless his soul – did you a great disservice by bringing you up so loosely. I did my best to correct your temper, your high spirits and bad habits, and show you how a young lady should behave, but …'

'Please listen to me, Aunt Elizabeth,' Harriet started, struggling to focus on the slim figure dressed in dark grey at the window. 'Archie is a bad man. He's involved in criminal activities with Lord Callaghan. In fact, Lord Callaghan was the one behind the death of Father's colleagues in the desert. He wanted Father dead all along.'

Her aunt spun round, dropped the curtain sharply and walked over to her. She grabbed her shoulders.

'How can you utter these terrible lies? Have you no shame?' Her voice shook with repressed fury.

'But it's true! Why don't you believe me?'

She didn't see her aunt raise her hand but she felt the burn of the slap across her face. For a minute, she was too shocked to react. If her aunt had been harsh in the past, she'd never once struck her.

'We need Lord Callaghan's protection now your father is no longer here and I'm not about to let you ruin everything with your spoilt, stubborn ways. You will go to your room at once and stay there until Archibald comes for you.'

There was a knock on the parlour door and Nelly came in. 'A gentleman is here to see Miss Harriet,' she announced.

'Who is he and what does he want?' Aunt Elizabeth barked at the girl.

The maid didn't have time to reply. The door opened wide and Lucas' tall silhouette appeared behind Nelly.

'Lucas, thank heavens you're here!' Harriet couldn't hide the relief in her voice. She tried to get up but collapsed on the chair straight away. Her legs felt as though they were stuffed with cotton wool.

'What's wrong?' Lucas rushed over to her. 'You look dreadfully pale.'

'Please help me get out of here,' she whispered as he pulled her up into his arms. 'Archie is coming to get me. My bag is still in the hall, with my coat.' She leaned onto his arm.

'Wait a minute.' Aunt Elizabeth stood in the doorway as if she wanted to prevent them from leaving. 'Where do you think you two are going? And who exactly *are* you, sir? Certainly not who you said you were yesterday!'

'I am a friend and intent on taking Harriet away,' he replied, tightening his grip around Harriet's waist to hold her up. 'She's taking the train to Dover with me. Please stand aside.'

Harriet looked at him, stunned. He was taking her to Dover? And then what? This, however, wasn't the time to ask. They had to make it out of the house first.

'Please stand aside, Madame,' Lucas repeated.

Was it the ice in his eyes, the grim determination on his face, or the threat in his voice? Aunt Elizabeth did as she was told.

Harriet had no idea how she managed to get out of the house and into the street and climb into the cab stationed outside. She must have dozed off while travelling to the railway station and remembered only fragments of being at the station getting tickets, coughing as a train let out a cloud of steam, and getting into the train carriage she was now in.

'How are you feeling?' Lucas asked gently from the opposite seat.

'Tired,' she mumbled. She had so many questions for him, yet her mind was fuzzy and she felt quite unable to articulate any.

'Why didn't the police arrest Archie and Lord Callaghan?' she asked at last.

'The policeman we spoke to was in Callaghan's pocket.'

'Then it was all for nothing.'

'Not quite. Knox made copies and is taking the story to *The Times*. Callaghan and Drake's days as free men are numbered.'

'I see …'

What she really wanted to ask him was what he intended to do once they were in Dover, but she was so tired. She leaned her head against the window pane and closed her eyes to the dull, rhythmical noise of the train. They were safe for now. She would think later.

The train came to a halt with a sudden jolt. She banged her head against the glass and opened her eyes, confused. It was dark.

'Lucas?' Her voice echoed in the empty compartment.

She tentatively stood up. Finding no lasting effects from her aunt's tea, she walked to the door and felt for the handle. She froze. Men shouted further up the corridor and a woman screamed. The door slid open and a tall silhouette stood in front of her.

'There you are!'

She gasped and stepped back until she stood against the window. Archie walked in and pointed a pistol towards her.

'I see Saintclair left you all alone.' He snorted. 'One of my men has probably killed him by now and thrown his body on the track.'

Harriet swallowed hard. 'It's over, Archie.' She tilted her chin up. No way would she show him she was shaking with fear. 'The truth will be all over the papers tomorrow.'

He gave out a short laugh. 'I don't think so, dear. The documents your father so painstakingly collected were destroyed this morning. The police inspector made sure of it.'

She looked into his cold, sneering eyes. They were the eyes of a stranger. 'There were copies.'

Archie came closer. 'Copies or not, nobody will ever dare challenge a man as important as Callaghan.'

'Why are you here then?' she asked.

'I want rid of Saintclair … and to collect the Barbarossa map. I know you have it. You wouldn't have left Charlotte Street without it.'

She caught her breath. It was Lucas who had the map, but she might be able to distract Archie long enough to have a chance to sneak out.

'It's in my bag,' she lied, gesturing to the luggage net above.

He took a box of fusees from his pocket, struck one to light the oil lamp dangling from the ceiling then ordered her to sit down while he retrieved her bag. She hoped he would look for the map himself but he threw the bag down next to her and asked her to open it.

'Hurry,' he said.

She took her time to look through her things, lifted a petticoat and a chemise out and folded them back again, took a small toiletry bag and pretended to look inside.

'Get on with it.'

The train jolted forward, starting again. Archie lost his footing, dropped his pistol and cursed. Now was her chance. She jumped to her feet and threw the bag with all her strength into his face before grabbing his pistol and running out towards the back of the train. The first-class corridor was empty. The second class, however, was busy. She hid the pistol in the folds of her dress to squeeze her way past people. They were all talking about an incident that forced the train to stop in the middle of the Shakespeare Cliff Tunnel.

'I heard there were men fighting in the end carriage after the Ashford stop,' one passenger said. 'That's why the guard pulled the communication cord.'

'It must have been a false alarm if the train started again,' another passenger commented whilst checking his pocket watch. 'I hope we make it in time for the steam packet. I have an important meeting in Ostende first thing tomorrow morning.'

In the third-class carriage too, people were talking about the fight that had broken out between a tall, dark-haired gentleman and two men armed with pistols.

'I was so scared. Those two men looked like thugs. The gentleman they were chasing didn't stand a chance.'

By the time she reached the end carriage, Harriet was frantic with worry. She was about to open the door that led to the observation platform when she saw a crumpled form on the floor – the guard. She knelt down next to him, saw that he was breathing, and quickly carried on to push the door. Cold air whipped her face, mixed with the smells of coal smoke from the funnel, and damp from the tunnel's wet rock face. The train's tail light gave out a feeble glow, enough to see the track at the back of the train. Where was Lucas? She walked onto the platform and leaned against the wrought iron balustrade. A noise above made her raise her head. A shadow hovered over her and she let out a frightened scream.

'Harriet!' Lucas jumped down. 'I was waiting for Drake.'

'Thank heavens you're safe! I thought Archie's men had killed you.' She hurled herself into his arms.

He held her against him and she breathed in his scent, felt his warmth around her. She wrapped her arms around his neck. He kissed the top of her head then took a step back.

'I knocked them out and threw them out onto the track sidings before we started up again. Whose is that?' He pointed to the pistol.

'Archie's.'

'Careful, it's armed,' he warned. 'You'd better give it to me.'

The door flung open and Archie ran out, dishevelled, breathless, one eye swollen and blood trickling from his nose.

'Good, I see we're all here,' he said. 'Now to finish the job.'

He looked at Harriet. 'Sorry, dear, but I'm going to have to kill you too. I wouldn't want you telling stories about me to the police.' He produced a firearm from behind his back and pointed it at Lucas.

Harriet was faster. Without a second's hesitation she raised her pistol, aimed and fired. Archie opened his eyes wide, looked down at his chest where a blood stain was growing bigger and bigger.

She dropped the pistol as if it burned her hand, and stared at him in horror as he held onto the balustrade and collapsed onto the wooden boards. A strange gurgling sound came out of his mouth, his eyes glazed over, and then he stopped moving.

'I killed him,' she whispered as Lucas took her in his arms. She started shaking and he held her closer.

'You did well, miss,' a man's voice called behind her. The guard appeared in the doorway, rubbing his forehead where a red bump was clearly visible. 'I heard what that man said. He said he was going to kill you both.'

'We'll soon be in Dover. I'll get the police on board as soon as possible,' he added. 'I take it you two are boarding the steam packet for Ostende? That's the only ship due out tonight.'

'I am,' Lucas answered shortly.

Her heart sank, but she forced a smile. There was no need to ask Lucas what his intentions were any longer. He had just answered.

'Can I go back inside?' she asked the guard. 'I think I need to sit down.'

'Of course, miss.' He offered his arm. 'I'll take you back to your carriage.' He turned to Lucas. 'Would you mind staying out here, sir, to watch over him?' He glanced at Archie's body.

When the train arrived at Dover, passengers were told to stay on board and wait for the police to arrive and take statements. A police detective interviewed Harriet in her compartment. It took her over an hour to tell him about Lord Callaghan, Archie, and their criminal associates, explain what had happened to her and her father in the Barbary States, and how Lucas had helped. From the way he shook his head as he took notes and muttered to himself, it wasn't hard to see that the man was overwhelmed by her revelations.

Finally she was allowed to step down from the train. The detective said Lucas had been interviewed earlier.

‘All the other passengers bound for Ostende have been taken to the harbour, but Mr Saintclair won’t leave until he has talked to you. He’s over there, by the hansom cab station,’ he added, pointing to the tall, dark figure standing under a gas light in the rain. He touched his hat and bowed his head before walking away.

Lucas didn’t seem bothered by the rain that ran down his hair, his face, and drenched his jacket. The gas jet threw a ghostly white light onto his face.

‘At last!’ He walked towards her. ‘Is everything settled? I tried to see you before but the constables wouldn’t let me through.’

‘The police detective seems thorough and trustworthy,’ she said, ‘even if this whole thing is out of his league. Let’s hope the police do their job properly this time.’

She raised her face towards his and forced a smile. ‘I understand you’re ready to leave.’

‘Yes, I’ve done what I came here to do. You’ll be safe now, won’t you? You can go back home to London. Drake and Callaghan are no longer threats. I’m sure your aunt will become more amenable with time, and you have your father’s gold and his emeralds.’

‘I have Tin Hinan’s emeralds and gold,’ she corrected. ‘As for my aunt, you don’t know her. If anyone can hold a grudge, it’s her. She will forever make my life a misery … but you’re right, I will be fine.’

She paused and took a shaky breath. This could be the very last time she’d see him, but she had promised herself, and him, that she wouldn’t make a scene.

‘So you see, you can go and find your treasure.’

For a moment, there was something in his eyes she didn’t understand. Was it relief, regret or longing?

‘I already found it,’ he muttered, his voice so low she wasn’t sure she heard him. ‘Goodbye, Harriet,’ he added, louder.

He took his bag and climbed into the cab.

‘To the harbour,’ he shouted to the driver.

The cab started down the main street.

Surely her heart would break now, shatter in a million pieces. Surely she would stop breathing and collapse onto the wet pavement. She didn’t have to pretend and be brave any longer. Tears started falling down her face, laced with rain water.

He glanced back before the cab turned the corner of the street. She was still standing in the rain. She might look small, lonely and vulnerable, but he knew just how strong and brave she was. Hadn't she just saved his life tonight?

Something tightened up inside him. He curled his fist and punched his thigh. What was he doing, leaving her like that? The least he could do was explain why he had to go, why they couldn't be together.

'Turn back,' he ordered.

'You'll miss the boat,' the driver warned.

'I don't care. Turn back.'

'As you wish,' the driver said with a shrug.

He caught up with her as she was walking away from the cab station.

'Harriet!' he shouted before jumping down.

She stopped and turned. 'What are you doing here?'

He put his hands on her shoulders. 'I can't stand leaving you like this,' he started. 'I must explain why …'

'You don't have to explain anything.' She wiped her cheeks with the back of her hands. 'I promised I wouldn't ask anything from you. I know you don't want me.'

He took a deep breath. It was time for the truth.

'Is that what you think, that I don't want you?' He slid his hands along her neck until they encased her face and tilted her head up towards him. 'I never wanted, never loved a woman as much as I want and love you. You are the one for me, the only one. There was never any doubt in my mind about that.'

He paused. Her eyes had lit up. A gentle smile stretched her lips.

'But we can't be together. At least not now,' he finished.

'And why is that?'

'I have nothing to offer you, Harriet. I am a nobody. No, I am worse than a nobody, I'm a fugitive, a man hunted by the French army for helping Abdelkader's rebels … Yet I must return to Algiers, to the mountains and the desert. That's where I belong. What kind of life could you possibly have with me?'

Her smile just grew wider. 'The most magical, wonderful life I could ever dream of.'

She put her hand on his cheek in a soft caress then stood on her tiptoes to kiss his lips.

He stiffened, willing himself to remain cold and unresponsive under her gentle touch, and stepped back. 'I have nothing for you,' he repeated.

'Yes, you have,' she whispered as she carried on kissing him. 'You have this.' She put her hand on his heart. 'That's all I'll ever want.'

His resolve weakened, melted away under the heat radiating from her hand, the warmth of her smile. The steam packet's foghorn echoed in the night, making them both jump.

'It's not too late, sir,' the cab driver called. 'It's only the first call.'

Could it be that he'd been wrong and they could make a life together after all? Suddenly it was as if a weight had been lifted from him. He took hold of Harriet's hand and kissed her fingers lightly. They stared at each other in silence.

'Would you like to go treasure hunting with me, Harriet Montague?' he asked at last.

'It all depends if you're any good as a guide … But yes, I think I'll give you a try.'

He enfolded her hand inside his, grabbed her travel bag and flung it inside the cab. Then he opened the door for her. 'In that case, I believe we're going to Sardinia, my darling. And then, who knows? Maybe we go to the Tassili N'Ajjer to find the Garamantes' mines. But first …'

He stopped her as she was climbing into the cab and looked into her eyes, serious once more.

'First, I have to marry you. What do you say?'

Her lips quivered slightly, her eyes filled with tears. She grew serious too.

'Yes.'

Chapter Thirty-Two

One year later, near Abalessa ...

'What exactly are we doing here?'

He turned round and winked. 'Wait and see.'

His pale blue eyes shone, a happy smile stretched his lips. He had been so carefree since coming back to the Sahara. After months of travel throughout Europe, and after finding what was left of Barbarossa's treasure in a ruined fort on a Sardinian hilltop, they decided to journey back to the Barbary States. Even if they never found the Garamantes' emerald mines, they were now rich beyond measure.

It was disconcerting to see how gold – and the promise to fund hospitals, schools and farming cooperatives, as well as railway lines and roads – had smoothed the path for Lucas' return to his native land and helped even the most belligerent French officials forget his former status as a rebel. Now he had sworn to stop fighting the French, Lucas resolved to put his newly acquired fortune to good use for his people. He had started negotiations to get his Bou Saada estate back from the French government. One thing troubled him greatly, though. In the past few months, most of the rebels had surrendered to the French army. His friend Ahmoud, however, had followed Abdelkader into hiding and nobody knew if he was dead or alive.

At least there had been good news from London. Theophilius Knox had succeeded in exposing Lord Callaghan and putting an end to his criminal activities. The scandal had been immense and the disgraced earl was now awaiting trial at the Old Bailey.

'We're here.' Lucas brought his camel to a kneeling position and jumped down.

Harriet did the same and looked around. In the transparent mauve and golden light of dawn, the rugged peaks of the Hoggar looked as mysterious as ever, dark purple, almost black. She breathed in the scents of vegetation and dust, listened to the crystalline silence surrounding them. Nowhere else was silence this clear, this vast and eerie.

She recognised this place. It was where they'd hidden from the sand storm, where they'd made love near a deserted guelta. Her heart beat faster and she smiled. She now knew why he had brought her here.

Lucas tied the camels' bridles to the branches of acacia trees.

'There's something I've been meaning to do for months,' he said, keeping hold of her hand as he led her up the hill.

They reached the plateau of black rock on top of the hill. The rising sun cast oblique shadows onto the symbols and drawings of feet and hands crudely carved into the smooth stones and their touching tokens of love. She followed Lucas to the edge of the plateau. Her throat tightened when he pointed to a smooth black stone.

'This is the place for us.' He knelt down. 'Put your hand there.'

He carved a line around her hand, repeated the process around his, then he carved their names and a series of symbols.

'I asked the Tuaregs to teach me,' he said with a smile.

'What does it say?'

He pulled her up, took her hand in his, and pressed it against his chest. As the sun appeared behind the mountains and the sky took the glorious colour of fire, he bent down and murmured against her mouth.

'*Tar Hani*. I love you.'

* The En

Thank You

Thank you so much for reading *Queen of the Desert*. I really hope that you enjoyed Harriet's and Lucas' love story and their adventures and treasure hunting in North Africa. If you did, I would be very grateful if you could take a few moments to leave a review. It is a wonderful feeling for an author to find out that readers loved the story and the characters. Reviews are invaluable, not only to raise a book's profile, but also to encourage the author to keep writing, especially when self-doubt creeps in.

Please feel free to contact me on Facebook or Twitter (details on 'About the Author' page next)

Marie

x

About the Author

Originally from Lyon in France, Marie now lives in Lancashire and writes historical and contemporary romance. Best-selling *Little Pink Taxi* was her debut contemporary romantic novel with Choc Lit. Since then, she has released numerous other books, including *Escape to the Little Chateau* which was shortlisted for the 2021 RNA Jackie Collins Romantic Suspense Award. *Queen of the Desert* is Marie's second historical romance, following on from *Angel of the Lost Treasure* which features another member of the Saintclair family.

She also writes short stories for the bestselling *Miss Moonshine* anthologies, and is a member of the Romantic Novelists Association and the Society of Authors.

For more information on Marie visit:

Twitter: www.twitter.com/MarieLaval1

Facebook: www.facebook.com/marielavalauthor

More Choc Lit from Marie Laval

Angel of the Lost Treasure
(Linked to Queen of the Desert)

An ancient secret hidden within a mother's song ...
When young widow, Marie-Ange Norton is invited to Beauregard in France by the mysterious Monsieur Malleval to collect an inheritance, she has no choice but to accept.

But when she embarks on the voyage with her fiery-tempered travelling companion Capitaine Hugo Saintclair, little does she know what waits for her across the sea in turbulent nineteenth-century France on the eve of Napoleon's return from exile. When she arrives, she is taken aback by Malleval's fascination with her family – seemingly inspired by his belief they are connected to a sacred relic he's read about in coded manuscripts by the Knights Templar.

As it becomes clear that Malleval's obsession has driven him to madness, Marie-Ange is horrified to realise she is more the man's prisoner than his guest. Not only that, but Hugo is the only person who might be able to help her, and he could represent a different kind of danger ...

Visit www.choc-lit.com for more details.

Little Pink Taxi

Take a ride with Love Taxis, the cab company with a Heart …
Rosalie Heart is a well-known face in Irlwick – well, if you drive a bright pink taxi and your signature style is a pink anorak, you're going to draw a bit of attention! But Rosalie's company Love Taxis is more than just a gimmick – for many people in the remote Scottish village, it's a lifeline.

Which is something that Marc Petersen will never understand. Marc's ruthless approach to business doesn't extend to pink taxi companies running at a loss. When he arrives in Irlwick to see to a new acquisition – Raventhorn, a rundown castle – it's apparent he poses a threat to Rosalie's entire existence; not just her business, but her childhood home too.

On the face of it Marc and Rosalie should loathe each other, but what they didn't count on was somebody playing cupid …

A Paris Fairy Tale

Is Paris the city of happily ever afters?
Workaholic art historian Aurora Black doesn't have time for fairy tales or Prince Charmings, even in the most romantic city in the world. She has recently been hired by a Parisian auction house for a job that could make or break her career. Unfortunately, daredevil journalist Cédric Castel seems intent on disrupting Aurora's routine.

As Aurora and Cédric embark on a journey across France, they get more than they bargained for as they find themselves battling rogue antiques dealers and personal demons, not to mention a growing attraction to each other.

But with the help of a fairy godmother or two, could they both find their happily ever afters?

Visit www.choc-lit.com for more details.

Bluebell's Christmas Magic

A flick of a feather duster and a sprinkle of Christmas magic …
Cassie Bell is used to mess. Her cleaning business, Bluebell Cleaning, is well known in the Cumbrian village of Red Moss. However, now it's almost Christmas and Cassie has a slightly messier situation to deal with than she's used to.

She's been hired to help Stefan Lambert, an injured army helicopter pilot who's staying at the local Belthorn Manor whilst he recovers. Stefan resents Cassie's interference and is definitely not looking for Christmas cheer. But Cassie prides herself on sparkling surfaces – so, can she bring some festive sparkle to Stefan's life too?

Visit www.choc-lit.com for more details.

Escape to the Little Chateau

Will Amy's dreams of a Provençal escape come true?
There are many reasons Amy Carter is determined to make Bellefontaine, her farmhouse hotel in the French countryside, a success. Of course, there's the time and money she's put in to making it beautiful, but she also has something to prove – particularly to people like Fabien Coste.

Fabien is the owner of the nearby château, and he might just be the most arrogant, patronising man Amy has ever met ... unfortunately, he's also the most handsome.

But as rumours circulate in the local community and secrets about the old farmhouse begin to reveal themselves, Amy quickly sees the less idyllic side of life at Bellefontaine. Could Fabien be the man to help prevent her Provençal dream from turning into a nightmare?

Visit www.choc-lit.com for more details.

Happy Dreams at Mermaid Cove

From the big city to a little yellow mobile library on the Isle of Skye ...
When Jenna Palmer agrees to the new position of mobile librarian on the tiny Arrandale peninsular of the Isle of Skye, she knows she's signing up for difficult working conditions and mediocre wages. But Jenna needs to get away, and a little yellow mobile library called Buttercup could be her escape to happier dreams ...

However, whilst Jenna can get to grips with foggy island roads, local mermaid legends and even big purple monsters, she never expected to have to contend with a boss as grumpy as Daniel McGregor, or a young book lover as enthusiastic as his niece, Katrina.
Arrandale might represent Jenna's safe port in a storm, but could she and Buttercup also become a beacon of hope to Daniel, Katrina and the entire island community?

Visit www.choc-lit.com for more details.

Printed in Great Britain
by Amazon

86685054R00155